I0003506

POLICE ACTIVE

TRAMPS HERE

Hobo Signs

POLICE INACTIVE

BE AFRAID

DANGER

GO

GO FAST

BE READY TO DEFEND
YOURSELF

REDUNDANT

SAFE CAMP

CHAIN GANG

DON'T GIVE UP HOPE

Canopy Publishing
P. O. Box 1648
Eastsound, WA 98245
www.canopypublishing.com
www.climatebull.com

Library of Congress Control Number 2013908175

ISBN: 9780975365588

HOBO SIGNS

Daniel H. Gottlieb

CANOPY PUBLISHING
2015

Printed in the United States of America

Books by Daniel H. GOTTLIEB

The Galileo Syndrome, *2004*
The Fires of Home, *2010*
The Dialogues of Sancho and Quixote, Mythical Debates
       On Global Warming: 1997-2010, *2010*
The Dirties, *2011*
Hobo Signs, *2015*

During the 1930's hobos and homeless wandered this nation in search of a sustainable life. Apparently abandoned by their society, these nomads developed a system of communication and interconnection using pictures to convey valuable data about locations and situation. Details about food, travel, medical care, and danger were all included. On one level, signs provide community.

Nature's signs elucidate ecosystems. Fine relative points that form paths from which we can embrace change, fathom strange lands, or cope with mistakes. They help us explore life, providing enhancement, or awareness of experience. Signs help us see the ties that matter.

Signs also help us mature--once we see all the options. *Hobo Signs* is the final book of a series that began with *The Galileo Syndrome*, continued with *The Fires of Home* and flowed into *The Dirties*. The structure of this set of books is edgy. In every way, *Hobo Signs* is the tether for the other three books in this series. Some events in the early books which once seemed to make only the vaguest of sense, had to wait for this book for clarity. Life is like that.

Hobo Signs is the context of a body of work declaring that entry into a time of change demands community, acceptance of new paths, and a mature perspective. So we can know when may manage an issue--and when we are minor players.

In that clarity there is more than just maturity. There is comprehension, caring, and charm. That is the secret of these books: The clarity that we are children of this good universe and that like all good parents this universe loves its children. Even to the point of providing a freedom that suggests we pay attention to the many paths. Signs are paths--and there are many paths.

So at every level signs present us with choice.

Understanding signs provides us peace. Ignored signs provide us with hard fought wisdom.

Our home planet is changing...

Chapter One

Danger

The hunting preserves had originally been called The Game of Boo, until marketing nixed that term for the compact title FairGame. The SeaPort preserve is one of the larger FairGame hunting preserves, following the old I-5 corridor from the Canadian border to Seattle through the flooded corpse of Portland onto the sand dunes of western Oregon. The premier hunting preserve in North America, SeaPort has something for everyone, ruined cities, wilderness, suburbia gone mad, the incessant wallop of bad weather, volcanoes, earthquakes, tsunamis, and mad traveling shows of we-do-anything entrepreneurs. From the Cascades to the coast, this game preserve has it all--including no laws inside its boundaries--unless you call the Administrators the law.

Just outside the boundaries of SeaPort are the Gray Zones. Border zones that have made the moguls of mapping wealthy. No one wants to be on the wrong side of a FairGame border. Even if you have purchased Justice, Medical, Police, Basic Human Rights, and Accounting--these privately branded services can do little for a corpse. FairGame, the Game of Boo, is for hunting--any creature.

Along one of the Gray Zones, just outside the eastern border of SeaPort, south of Seattle, sits Hopes-No-Apostrophe-Diner. The diner, painted gold like a pile of bullion, has a glass front that opens to a wide boulevard with recently planted fir trees lit by small white lights. That white-light-meridian declares the border with SeaPort.

Gunshots always rattle the midnight. Tonight the rounds are a report of anxiety. Come morning, across the boulevard, the NewDay Shopping Mall is supposed to open for business.

Its four story façade glows. Lines of lights running along the top and down the mall's white walls wash the huge structure and its front windows as if it were some grand canvas. A slut on the street, the ready-to-open mall awaits your entry. The largest shopping center on the west coast. The NewDay Mall is the first shopping location ever located within a FairGame preserve.

More gunshots, anxiety born of lust, call into the night.

The main entrance for the mall is right across the street. NewDay is planned as a 24/7 shopping facility with the best in products and security, ten fine dining courts, and outlooks for Hunters facing the foliage-covered remains of West Seattle. Most appealing is the strategy of allowing the mall to be open to Targets--those people who have lost their basic rights for lack of payment. Hunting will also be allowed inside the mall. Children under sixteen are forbidden.

Night rains begin sparkling the street. Crowded with hungry Hunters, the diner's front steps sport a dozen men and women milling around the doors waiting for a seat. On the other side of the twin glass diner doors, a corral of ten red booths wear chrome bands. High-backed seats line the long steel counter. From the diner's ceiling, meter tall glass angels hang from gossamer wires, dancing in solo pirouette. Deep blue, the angels hide their worth with a crystalline sameness, in their eyes, security cameras. Above them, a sky blue ceiling, below the angels, patrons sit in an arc of booths or on stools at the counter waiting, fidgeting with food, or cleaning weapons.

It is rumored Hopes-No-Apostrophe-Diner is a FairGame friendly business. More than one stray shot has hit the diner when angry Hunters have left the hunting preserve carrying a dead comrade--due to some supposed interference from the owner--Hope Weiss.

Another weapon discharges.

Across the street, a body falls from the mall roof onto the street. More shots from high powered rifles. Two sets of Hunters emerge from cars at the ends of the block. They converge on the bleeding corpse. The three men and one woman argue about the corpse. One man pulls out a long knife and digs for the bullet. A marking declares that the bullet, and the body, are his. Those who lost, the husband and wife, argue. She had hesitated on the trigger, losing the kill.

The victorious Hunters text for an auditor to confirm the kill and reveal the identity of the Target. Some Hunters believe it decent to alert relatives of their loved one's demise. Others just want a track back for a biography. The Hunters are sometimes called Croakers--but not to their face.

The victorious Hunter, a man named Quentin Conworth, signals his comrade to follow him through the wet evening to the diner. He's buying the drinks. Ignoring the waiting Hunters, pulling wide the glass doors, banging them against the metal railings, the Croaker searches for celebrities who might have seen his victory. Too late in the night, his victory lies flat.

The pair of victorious hunting buddies, dressed in camouflage, wait to be seated, and begin to argue about who has killed the most Targets. The Hunter, Quentin Conworth, looks for Hope Weiss. He is the beau of her attorney, Susan Willoughby, but his lusty eyes call that love a joke.

Hope, standing by the counter, scans the men, and then the booths. The corner booths with the glass counters are taken. She walks forward deciding to get these men out quickly figuring within an hour an Administrator will be on site to resolve a fight between these two. It has happened before with Quentin. The two men see her and cease their argument, a dumb smile shared.

Hope, for her part, wears an engaging smile bound by a thin upper lip puffed wide at the peak. With smooth mulatto skin, Hope is a stunning woman in her mid-thirties with deep red hair and sparkling dark eyes. Dressed in chef's clothes of black-checked pants and a white coat, her supple physique peeks through. The men try to look attractive, by fixing their hats and lowering their voices--and so achieve an enhanced foolishness. She smiles at them. "Gentlemen," and points to the nearest booth. Like trained dogs the men sit.

Others grumble, but no one speaks. A confirmed kill gets immediate seating at the diner. The two men order a bottle of Scotch. After it arrives, they begin to drink cursing the other Hunters.

Hope purchased this diner five years ago on the advice of a friend named Mina Jaka. After two years of hard times, bingo. The guys with the dynamite showed up to blow apart what remained of old apartments, a church, and cruddy shops cross the street. Six months later came the announcements of the first shopping mall in a FairGame preserve, "...A NewDay is coming...".

The architects and the engineers took over the diner after the announcement of the mall. Every morning they would troop in to eat, take a nap, or hash out a change to the construction plans. The months and months of professional people sitting in the booths eating whatever Hope cooked made the first real profits for the diner. She began to ask questions about having a Wholack bed installed.

No one thought twice about the query. Everyone wants to escape into Wholack. That Nirvana of semiconscious bliss that affords every wish and facilitates any adventure. It could be done, she found out, but not anonymously. Wholack bed installations are highly regulated. The engineers did explain the loopholes. Hope said it wasn't worth the effort. In fact, Hope had the information Mina needed.

The work crews began tramping in after digging holes, pouring concrete, securing plumbing, and the rest of it. In and out--every day and night--the profit trickle became a flood of wealth.

Cracked glass windows in front of the diner were finally repaired. Then the torn booths were redone. The flooring and the new fixtures were ordered from a supply house that one of construction workers knew. It is used equipment, but first rate. At one point, Hopes-No-Apostrophe-Diner closed for almost a month. Hope served burgers in the parking lot.

The diner reopened to catch all the interior designers, the fine wood workers, the media, as well as the suppliers coming in and out. It took three years to complete the mall due to the ongoing need to keep the workers safe from the Hunters and the Targets. After all, since the mall is located in a FairGame preserve there are no laws to keep people safe. The work areas had sounded like battle zones.

The small army of mercenaries protecting the workers ate like pigs when they were not patrolling work zones. Worse, the Targets began to figure out the security framework.

When Hope suggested supplying clean water and food for the Targets, in exchange for distance, it made all the difference. The Hunters, on the other hand, were more difficult to please. They began to set up camps--and since there is no law in a FairGame preserve--workers began to die. A group of FairGame Administrators were hired on to fix the problem. The Administrators stepped in supporting the project by decoying Hunters into traps set by the Targets. Hunters soon steered clear. In a FairGame preserve, the Administrators are God.

When the international media began covering the opening, Hope reaped substantial wealth and notoriety. Offers for her diner flowed like rain off the roof. Normally, she would have sold the diner. Unfortunately, a commitment to her lover precluded indignation and crushed morality. As well, a set of bodies in stasis in the basement of the diner--intruders into the Wholack Game--made the offers moot. Hope Weiss considers the greater good to be her path--not profits.

As the mall opening approached, Hopes-No-Apostrophe-Diner garnered a reputation for good food--and intrigue. It is said she opened the restaurant to feed her lover, Tovar Dal, the former Minister of the Interior who entered FairGame to protest its barbarity. Mass media says Tovar is already dead and she simply mourns him.

Hope's business partner, Lester, who had showed up after getting out of the army suggested they sell at one point. She had to explain why she could not sell. To his credit he remains silent and supportive.

Outsiders figure Hope stays because she can see that her business will go through the roof once the mall opens. Hope will sell once her lover is safe. By then she also assumes her friend, Mina Jaka, and the others in the illegal Wholack beds will be finished with their tasks. For amusement, she keeps offers alive and others on the line. As soon as one investor gets sick of waiting for her decision, another entrepreneur is reeled in, check in hand.

Staring outside at the now storming night, she watches fir trees rock with the winds, their twinkling white lights sparkling in the rain. Underneath them, a pair of busses ride by on their way to the hotels. Yesterday there had been a line of hunting vehicles thirty blocks long. Fights between Hunters broke out as Targets appeared to taunt the Hunters by tossing bags of excrement at them. When one battle destroyed three buses, the Administrators arrived and the front of the line was pulled back, a mile away from the FairGame preserve.

Twin security trucks appear and park nose to nose, guarding the main parking ramp. Their yellow beacons begin to spin. It is change of shift.

A black ambulance makes the corner approaching the body on the ground. The two Hunters inside the diner rush out leaving the bottle. Other Hunters laugh, thinking the alcohol a prize to be stolen, watching the men rush to the kill.

Three paramedics get out of the ambulance. Two of them lift the body into the back. The third sprays disinfectant on the ground covering the wash of blood. The man named Conworth approaches the ambulance crew, seeking the scalp. The ambulance people demand payment and another negotiation breaks out across the street. An Administrator's bright red van rounds the corner and the argument ends. Moments later the body is debased and the Croakers walk away, faces bright with triumph, waving a black plastic bag full of scalp. Hunters watch the two men disappear around the corner.

Hah, they forgot the Scotch.

More gunfire.

A second red Administrator's van appears. Soon, at every corner along the boulevard, sets of Administrators park vans. She assumes they are expecting trouble just before the opening of the mall. Then Hope hears the sounds of large engines. Ten sets of huge white half-tracked security vehicles round the corner. They take up positions near the vans. One pair of occupants exit a half-track and approach the Administrators. Watching a discussion take place, Hope notes antipathy between the security people and the Administrators.

The Administrators and their vans back off, down the street and into the rain. She knows the mall's security people have made a big mistake. They need the Administrators and their experience.

Her eyes drift up to the huge video screen on the mall's wall. It had been on all day showing a video of the Wholack on his surfboard sliding into the mall and winking. Thankfully it has been turned off.

Just above the darkened video screen she sees movement above the huge glass window that runs a hundred yards along the fourth floor. The hardware/gun store that specializes in outfitting and providing repairs for the Hunters--DEI, Dead Endings Inc., had been dark, but now the lights blink on and off as well. She notes a human stands in the big black plastic quiver fixed along the outside wall, between the window and the video screen.

It's that same Target, she tells herself; he has again taken refuge in the store logo for the night.

Hope has seen this man before. He has been spying on her diner for a while. In the beginning she thought it was Tovar, but she is now quite sure it is not him--too agile.

The quiver is a good place to sleep. Shooting at the store's main sign will lead to disbarment from the facility.

She supposes the Hunters have tagged this bold man's infrared signature. Once the Hunters get inside they will scour the facility for him. Hope figures he will be dead by noon. The lights blink on and off once more. Then the man settles down into the quiver.

DEI is a prize--if they can get inside.

Hope had a tour of DEI last week since it is so close to her diner. The store manager wants to make sure there is synergy between the two establishments. DEI supplies the Hunters with weapons and anything else they need to kill Targets. So it is, in effect, an armory on site--inside a FairGame preserve--

and store management wants to assuage any fears of the store being breached by the hunted. Ransacking DEI means supplies and defense for the Targets.

With sensors, cages, interlocks on the weapons, and two dozen guards at the ammunition vault, it is a fortress. Except for the front window--and store management does not know a Target is using their exterior logo as a sleeping chamber. Now, after seeing this man's control over the lights, Hope considers the ransacking of the store likely. She wonders how long it will take.

Unlike most people, Hope has a mountain of respect for Targets, people who have lost their rights due to a lack of funds. Rights and protection cost in this society and financial loss means rights are at risk. Bankruptcy is immediate placement in FairGame. Supposedly FairGame is a fair chance at survival-- by placing people on the game-board of wilderness. Of course that is a myth. FairGame is a hunting preserve for humans.

An oversized mall flag flaps in the wind as the rains intensify.

Scanning the diner she sees the half empty bottle of Scotch is gone. Counting the plates ready to be served, she catches a flash of blue and red off the chrome walls of the counter.

An explosion rumbles through the diner.

She turns. Concrete and fire fly out into the wide boulevard. The trees catch most of the debris in their thick canopy. Their string of lights darken. The rotating yellow lights of the security vans start a frenetic flashing sequence. The mall parking lights go on. The security people pop out of the half-tracked vehicles to man the large caliber weapons on the roof of the vehicles. Security vans back up into the parking lot followed by heavily armed trucks.

More explosions roll outward along the mall's facade. The mall parking lights flicker, then darken. The emergency lights come on. The DEI lights come on for just a second, then go dark. Black clouds boil forth from the floor below. More explosions, a tongue of fire shoots across the boulevard and trees flash to fire giving definition to Hunters running toward the NewDay Mall.

Patrons hurry out the doors.

She scans for the man hiding in the quiver. A rope appears from the roof and he begins to sidle up. As soon as he reaches the roof, the glass of the hunting store blows out. Then he repels down and he is inside.

Gasoline fed fireballs emerge from every opening in the parking lot. The Targets have laid mines for the security patrols, destroying vehicles and killing guards. A half-tracked vehicle breaks through the concrete wall, it's front wheels resting forward of the wall, its interior burning. Guards in uniforms rush from the Mall.

The Administrators and their vehicles remain out of sight.

Weapons fire opens up. Hunters have taken positions firing at the guards, thinking them Targets. A pair of Administrator's vans finally arrive and are fired upon as well. The Administrators begin to use their weapons system to calculate the location of the weapons firing on them. One by one, the small gun turret on one van's roof puffs a short burst killing Hunters. A rocket from inside DEI takes out that Administrator's vehicle in a blue-flamed explosion. The other van backs away at full speed.

The DEI armory has been breached.

The diner is now empty except for Lester, her partner in the business. He is dressed in whites, skin covered in tattoos. He carries a bullet proof vest for her and beckons her to take cover. Two large panes of glass shatter.

She hurries over and he hands her the vest, pulling her behind the bullet-proofed main counter. "I told you we should have gotten bulletproof glass as well," he says. "Of course. Why bother? This is the start of the revolt." For years people have worried the Targets might form an army.

Lester carries a set of pistols and hands her one. Strung over his back is a shotgun. Hope dons a bullet proof vest. Now Lester puts his on as well. Sparks of gunfire light the exterior of the mall; concrete sections continue to blow out from the upper floors exposing the interior. Camouflaged vehicles full of Hunters pull up and Hunters pile into the garage.

Stray rounds strike the diner. One by one the last of the windows are shattered. The gunfire inside intensifies as Hunters meet the well-armed Targets. The sacking of the NewDay Mall is in full swing.

More munitions light the sky. Every Hunter within ten miles of the Mall knows something has happened and they stream towards the mayhem. Sets of hunting trucks crash through the side gates to get in the mall. Other vehicles follow and disgorge their occupants. The explosions ease. The mines are used up. There could never be an army of Targets. Their ammunition is limited.

Hope and Lester watch explosions march up and down the mall. One platoon of Hunters lights a set of explosives taking out a ten foot section of wall and rushing the parking lot. That fire fight lasts almost ten minutes. No one exits the ingress hole.

A cadre of Administrators shows up in a set of fifteen bright red vans. Thirty Administrators pile out, meet up, then enter the NewDay Mall.

Moments after the Administrators disappear into the NewDay Mall, a fire fight erupts inside the mall. It seems to Hope that their numbers are not nearly enough. Another van appears, this one painted black. It parks at the far end of her parking lot. An Administrator has showed up alone; some of them are cowboys.

This cowboy sports a green bulletproof uniform, night goggles, and carries an ancient BAR. As he crosses the street, three shots scar the street. He returns fire quelling the assailants. Watching him enter the mall, she listens for the report from that high powered weapon. She counts eight blasts from the weapon over a five-minute period, then silence.

Cowboys die.

Fire spreads to all floors. Fire crews roll up to the blaze, but wait until military vehicles appear on the boulevard. When the military arrives, soldiers begin shooting anything that moves to quell the disturbance. Bloody Hunters exit. Many rush to a mobile hospital setting up in the diner's parking lot. More wounded appear and a second mobile hospital arrives on site. In moments, the medical staff are scanning accounts for triage. Of course none of the Targets appear. They are FairGame and therefore denied medical attention. Everything costs in this society.

An entire generation has grown up inundated with the message that life on Earth is a prison to be escaped from. Every law and every right has a cost and every right that is not paid for is not conveyed. In a mad rush to escape into the Wholack Game, society has found worth in taxing civil rights, moral rights, and ethical rights. One either pays for the services of government or loses them completely. As for the pursuit of justice or medical attention, if you can pay, you can play. In birth there is no original sin; however, everyone is born an outlaw.

This is a generation knows that if you don't pay the fees you are worthless. In the case of laws, without payment, they function outside of your existence. The cost for police, fire, dental, schools, everything must be borne by your wallet. If not, there is FairGame.

Why?

Wholack is so expensive. Rights have become just

another money making scheme. Government is no more. Everyone wants just one thing: Escape. Escape into the bliss of Wholack. It is digital heaven--in every sense of the word. As well as escape from the decaying society, the horrible storms, and the brutality of commerce gone mad.

The developers of the NewDay Mall underestimated the tenacity of the Targets and the prize of a mall. Their enterprise will be a total loss. The purple dawn arrives with another fierce rainstorm. The fires finally abate. The fire department has found a contract loophole. So they just sit and do nothing. The military left long ago.

The Administrators exit. Only eighteen of them pile into their vehicles and drive away. The black armored van remains. Hope figures hundreds have died, the cowboy dead. The mayhem inside the mall quells with the dawn.

The diner's booths remain filled with war stories, braggarts in heat. Hope notes a hobo sign being scrawled on the walls facing the diner. The rectangle and black eyed center says, "Danger." The sign is a declaration of victory by the Targets.

A man, apparently that lone Administrator, emerges from the ruins. Arm soaked in blood, she sees he walks differently. Which Hope assumes, at first, is from a wound. Then she sees the low gait and the constantly shifting eyes. They belong to a hunted man, a Target. He avoids the paramedics, instead heading straight to the diner. She recalls the man in the quiver.

When the glassless doors open, she sees the fact. Hope knows this is not the man who exited the Administrator's van a few hours ago because she knows this man's face, even while hoping this face is a myth. She has seen it a hundred times. Staring at the man as he enters, Hope wishes Tovar could see the face of John Doe. She leans heavily on the counter to steady her body as if she is the one wounded. Fearing anew for her guests in the illegal Wholack beds below, she remembers them saying this man's appearance signals the end of human control of this planet. Watching him look at her, thinking a vision of the destroyer cannot possibly be true, she finds herself wondering how Armageddon could possibly flow from a smelly hobo.

Chapter Two

Find The Exit

A void surrounds you. It is a cold, unlit space.

"Ladies and gentlemen, boys and girls, dummies and fools, this is it. Welcome to Wholack."

Feel the warmth.

The entire universe is your lover. It envelopes you in an embrace. Blissfully floating, you feel as if you might be free. There is no carriage, your arms, your legs, your fingertips, your face--are all gone.

Then that wonderful smell you remember from your childhood; it varies for each person, chocolate, mother's milk, the smell of cut grass. An opiate rush begins as the darkness fades to a light blue dawn. You're surfing a wave-crest of puffy white clouds above a Pacific coastline. Below, green waves crash against rocky yellow cliffs. On a beach below, among the tide pools, a couple harvests mussels. The sea shore is a curve of white wave-crests; then the image veers in an exhilarating turn and you fly inland, over an Edwardian style home, its green fields, then see a small town. Skirting tree tops, flying above roofs, you follow a river to the town and into farmlands. The flow of green meadows, pastures, mountain ranges, waterfalls, the ride sweeps you off a waterfall cliff, diving low to a meadow of brightly colored flowers. Then glide up to the snow-crested peaks before flying over a lush green temperate rain forest.

Bliss, belonging, peace--this sequence of verdant beauty is called the Eden sequence of Wholack--Earth as a lover: No storms, no dusty deserts, no garbage dumps, no ruined cities, no bodies on the ground, just bucolic beauty as you circle bountiful lands leading back to that wide beach. It stretches for miles.

Then out over the green-blue water and its rolling waves of deep ocean. Sets of islands lie dotted among the blue green water. Sweeping over a tropical paradise of palm trees and jungle, you rocket skyward. Rising into the puff of clouds, climbing through the diaphanous cotton-white, breaking into the glow between planet and space, you see the riot of stars brighter every second. Planets appear in the ecliptic. The moon sits. Red Mars broods. Jupiter commands the western edge. Saturn turns inside its majestic rings. Familiar constellations link in the cream of stars that is our galaxy seen on edge. The Milky Way pulls you. Below, the planets circle Sol. Lost stars ride the background. You loop--once again looking at our planet.

Skirting the edge of our atmosphere, framed by the deep black of space, the moon rises above the foggy blue horizon. The man in the moon appears. That face surreptitiously winks.

Then the fool's welcome."Hello, Chump. Welcome to my world."

Beneath the mocking face on the moon, the edge of the Earth tinges blue in the veil of atmosphere. The song Flight plays. It is the most well-known piece of music on the planet. Your viewpoint dives through the caress of that blue veil. The stars disappear and the day warms you--soaring along a light blue sky.

The space around you fills with other people apparently logged into the game. Coming into view through puffy clouds, V-shaped flocks of fliers. An armada of humans dressed in a riot of colors piloting a variety of flying objects, everything from desks to rockets, soup dishes to sports cars. People wink and smile at each other. A set of bicyclists sweep back and forth across the sky blocking the path of fifty red sports cars.

Then as a single herd, the mass of flyers bank left over the coastline passing the tide pools, going inland, rapidly flying over the mountains, passing rivers and small farms--until we spy a large city.

We hover over skyscrapers and the traffic of commerce on elevated roadways: The drive of commuters, ships in the port, a bullet train leaves the station. The city center twinkles in reds and blues as a quiescent lake sports elegant sailboats in sport.

Shared purpose, contentment, the soul of unity, this sequence of The Wholack game is called The End.

A figure rises up from the center of the city. No one else has a brightly colored surfboard decorated with a bird-of-paradise design. On the surfboard a young man surfs the skies. He wears loudly-colored knee-length swim shorts of bright red and orange plumeria flowers. A tight orange tee shirt has a wide yellow stripe covering his chest.

A blue baseball cap, the brim facing backwards, his bright red hair flowing with the wind, skinny limbs, thumbs up, a wide toothed grin. Green eyes full of teenage abandon--this as you know--is the Wholack. He tosses an empty soda pop can over his shoulder riding up next to you, or so it seems.

Everyone else logged into the Wholack game sees the

same thing--but they don't see multiple versions of the Wholack in the distance. For them the Wholack is there to greet just them. At the periphery of your vision a few players slowly blip out of the digital dream. Then the Wholack, that mischievous imp, that fool, that king of digital Nirvana, smiles and tips its hat. "What are you doing here, Chump? You recycled piece of boson-meat. This is my world."

An audience cheers. A reminder you are, in fact, an outsider to the game.

Wholack spins his hat in a circle. It comes to rest brim-forward, covering his eyes. All the while, the landscape below you rolls onward, a picture of Earth in the ideal. That city of commerce glows, parks alive, rivers full of boats, cars and bicyclists riding elevated roadways. Jets in flight, it is the city of promise: Saucer City.

Someone in the distance launches a hammer, a missile, a tree, a death ray, or some other object at the Wholack. He sees the projectile and easily grabs it. Winking at you, his good friend, letting you in on the coming joke; he launches the weapon back at the perpetrator. The device lands square in the body of the distant voyager and both disappear. "They never learn--do they?" Wholack winks a bright green eye as he licks his fingers to smooth back the furry red eyebrows. His freckles seem so clear. "I own this place, not you. You are my guest boson-clown. So you play by my rules." A bony index finger wags. "I'll be watching you. My world, my rules, get it?"

He jets off on his surfboard, laughing, darting in between the people, flying around them or slapping them on skull. The receivers of his tap disappear in a pink soundless explosion. He winks at you, apparently liking you and taking you into this confidence. The music of Flight continues as Wholack surfs the sky--a mischievous troll at play. He again slides closer. "What's the last thing that goes through the mind of a fly, or one of these dummies, when they hit the windshield of my world?" He darts off, purposely flying into someone so they disappear. So don't watch too attentively.

Ahead, a mountain peak approaches. For the uninitiated, that is the last thing seen as they crash into the mountain, forced to begin the game again. Whether you miss the mountain or not, he repeats his riddle; "What is the last thing a bug sees?" And answering his own joke, "An ass, see you later, Chump."

For those that did not avoid the mountain trap, the song Flight repeats its familiar theme. They are back approaching the coastline with another group of players. Or, missing the mountain, the Wholack sees your escape and flies close. "So you are not so dumb," says the Wholack. "Don't stay too long in any one scenario. I count how long you are there and the longer you are there the more I want to remove you--and my tricks are legendary."

He scoops a bit of cloud in his hand and eats it like ice cream. "Wondering what the rules are?" The impish Wholack grins, showing a set of white teeth--that for a moment--grow to blue fangs; they quickly retract, to his chagrin. "I am going to get that right some day. So will you." He laughs, swaying his board back and forth, knocking into newbies and sending them Earthward to crash in a pink puff. The Wholack glides, an apparent expert to the ride, master of this place because Wholack is the focus of all.

"You're wondering about the rules--I bet." He points to his head. "Trouble understanding your own brain?" He points to his body. "Too bad, Chump." Sticking his tongue out, Wholack dives for the planet below. From behind his board, a contrail of bright rainbow-colored corn flakes fill the sky. Anyone caught in the contrail simply disappears. His laughter fills the environment. "Like I said. I own this world. You don't. Follow me to peace and prosperity, suckers! I am your..." His head cranes skyward. A set of three flying saucers dives from the sky. Bright yellow death rays jump from the ships attacking the city below.

Following the trace of death rays with your eyes you see a large power plant and two cargo ships explode in the city's harbor--a trio of fireballs. A squadron of six sleek fighters rise to battle and are immediately destroyed.

The Wholack's concerned face fills the space in front of you--a Cheshire cat full of fear. "That's Saucer City, dummy. Defend it. Or attack it. Help me." The face is pure panic, then in an instant the face calms and the right eye winks. "Had you going there. Didn't I? It all begins here. Better learn to fight, or flight, Chump. If not, you can't get to any of the other scenarios. And forget about access to the newest version of my game, Global Warming. I run that schtick also."

The Wholack rockets off. Ten saucers begin attacking the city destroying wide swaths of it, killing thousands of digital souls. Waves of saucers appear above them as players take control of the battle--those with enough credits. They can also command jets, a tank, a robot, or escape. Others fly into a secretive hole in the game and off to their own sub-scenario associated with one of the four versions of Wholack: Saucer City, Home Fires, Corporate Apocalypse, or, if they have expert credits, the newest version, Global Warming.

As a member of the audience you can do nothing except watch everything turn dull gray. You hear Wholack say: "Global Warming, that's where I am going. How about you? Reserve your spot now. Global Warming is happening--for now and for always. See you, Chump."

The gray fades to pink as the commercial ends. A huge interactive theatre lights up with just enough light to detail the tan walls, aisles, and ceiling. A thousand seats surround you. In front is a thin older man dressed in a blue business suit, white shirt, and red tie. Beside him stands an elegant older woman dressed in a light blue evening gown. She holds a small computer interface in her hand, similar to the controls in every

Wholack bed.

The MC speaks: "Ladies and Gentlemen, I am Simon, this is my lovely wife Roxanne. Welcome to your future." The woman in the gown taps him on the shoulder. He listens attentively, theatrically, nodding his head. "Oh, I see. All you saw was Saucer City. Too bad. Global Warming is a completely new addition to the game and it represents a major step forward in the world's most popular game. It combines all the facets we used in the earlier Wholack scenarios--as well as integrating intrusion through apparent temporal and spatial shifts. So don't get caught looking for the truth or you'll be stuck in a rerun over and over--until you figure out what the Wholack is up to this time…The fool. Or is that you…Chump?" He winks.

The audience laughs and cheers.

The MC named Simon puts both thumbs up, mimicking the Wholack's trademark gesture. "Global Warming is a new version of the game that centers on the idea that humans did not recognize the problems of a globally warmed planet. Sound familiar? Wait, you say. We beat it, right? What, you say there are still storms? You say our cities are a mess? Hmm, well we beat most of it anyway. We are lucky. Global Warming can be fun. Believe me, this new section of the Wholack Game is a gas, Chump."

The audience cheers.

"There, that's better. We have Wholack, right? In there you're safe. Out here," he pauses and moves his hand side to side. "Well maybe you're not so safe--but believe me--as you will see it could have been much worse. We're doing okay."

The pounds the theatre floor. The MC glances at his wife then puts his hands up to calm the crowd. "Reservations for the second set of fifty-million players for Wholack, Global Warming, is filling quickly. So get your name on the list because this round will be closed soon. What? You want in but you ain't got shit? You know what to do, right, Chump? Hit the energy credit key on the right side of your seat. This will enter you in the drawing we are about to have. It is your chance to win three months inside Wholack--all expenses paid--with a guaranteed landing inside the New Zealand pink zone, the gateway for the next fifty million players.

"Think of it--all that desolation--all those toys. All that fun." Everyone in every theatre hits his or her game key to enter the drawing. "Okay, so while we wait for the other theatres to enter the drawing here are the insider hints for GW, Global Warming. You all get these hints regardless of whether you win or not. So, even if you don't get in you can work out a plan for building your own sub-scenario on your home simulators. Remember, don't tell the Wholack what you are doing." The crowd laughs. Everyone knows the only way to win Wholack is to tell the Wholack nothing. "After all, it's his world--right?" The man winks. The pretty woman chuckles. The audience laughs wildly.

"Okay, here come the hints: Power levels in Wholack GW, Global Warming, are called Leagues. In GW--as Remold Jaka and his group of genius' at Laughs Unlimited call the new scenario--the shortcut win is to grab all you can and the hell with everyone else. That will always get you back to the New Zealand landing area. The better the league rating the more privileges you get. Of course if you do that--watch out for the surprise." More laughter. "And remember, like the other games, physical features are reflective of a player's skill set. So you might even try to create a spaceship. I hear the rich will do anything to escape. *To Serve Man*, remember? Or it could just be just a friendly alien! Boo, Chumps!"

Some hoot.

"And there's more..."

The woman taps him on the shoulder wagging an index finger at him "Oops. Roxy says I've told you too much." The huge screen behind the couple lights up with an image of the

Wholack surfing across the screen. "As always, transcendence is the key. Your preconceptions are your enemy, and your questions will define your win. Then of course there is the Wholack who wants to mess you up no matter what."

The woman beside him puts her index finger to her chin in a look of mock confusion. She mouths the word, "Not."

The man continues: "Another aspect of this game is the survival parameters. You all know keeping the Wholack dumb is a win. That has even more reward this time--but only if he thinks he wins. So you would rather recycle than tell him what you know."

"Simon." Says the pretty woman on stage.

"Oops, I guess I wasn't supposed to tell you Wholack might look different in some circumstances. Darn. Anyway, in this version of the game the planet and its human inhabitants can be at odds with each other--rather than being in concert. But, I say but, you can purchase the right to enter any earlier version of Wholack--unlike in other releases--to escape. Of course getting back into GW is then a bit tougher." He looks at the woman's stern glare. "Am I saying to much?" The man leans forward as if giving a close friend the gospel of being. "Friends, the universe has intelligence and it loves goodness. That's the key to GW. So you are not just wary of the fool. You are also traveling with an intelligent being that is your universe. Remold Jaka and his band of genius are just sooo cool. And guess what? Get this, somehow the fool and the planet are now one. Get my focus?"

The audience stamps its feet in approval.

The woman brings her hands to her face in a look of amazement. Her mouth wide in an "O" of wonder. The left strap of her gown falls aside revealing a perfect breast. She laughs replacing it quickly. The crowd cheers. The man continues staring. "Ah, and of course there is always the rest and relaxation scenarios. Know what I mean?"

The woman's mouth closes--in apparent consternation at the man's chauvinism. She speaks: "He can be so difficult. Just remember that the universe and the Wholack tie through an event called Species Focus. In practice, that means you need to make people notice you. This is the key hint that will lead you to fresh links and new sub-scenario tools. But, cover your exits. Everyone wants to rule the world."

The confused audience mumbles.

Roxy smiles as she speaks. "Or, if you just work to get further in the League level--when you fall--you will enter earlier versions with mondo-power."

He interrupts. "And those that interact with you will not know it. Guess who you can look like? It's up to you. Maybe the Wholack? You can tear up their scenario they will never know it is you. Now who is the fool, right?"

A loud murmur courses through the crowd.

"That's it. You got it. They might even think you are the Wholack and try to target you--but you are no fool are you? You already know all the tricks. So even if you fail, you can enter previous scenarios as a demigod--and no one will know the difference between you and the Wholack. Then use those wins to fight your way back to GW. Figure a way to come in to GW looking like the Wholack and enjoy a BOGO. How much fun is that?"

The audience applauds.

The MC looks down at his wrist watch: "Oh, one more hint. Think of this. You can be a master among those that would make the Wholack a fool. Can you even imagine what winning might look like for you in the earlier versions and how it all might change when you reveal you are not Wholack? I cannot. With GW, all the earlier versions open up again in an entirely new way. Is it the real Wholack or someone else? Baby, have we got game! It will be incredible. Ya' gotta' give Doc Jaka and his geniuses credit. Those guys and gals are amazing."

He pauses and shakes his head in reverence to the game and its designers. "Okay--time for our drawing. You know, even if you don't get into the winning circle, there are still the betting salons. Also, on a serious note, I think you will find this game a new and fascinating look at what life might have been like here on Earth. Had we remained enamored with the oily future that once awaited us."

The audience roars its approval.

"So maybe we're not that stupid. Roxy, give me the number for today's winner."

The pretty young woman taps a keyboard. The audience looks at their wrist watches and wait. The MC smiles. "We have a winner: Xandra Rader. You are today's three month winner! Thank you all and we'll see you again!" The holograms on stage fade.

The audience emerges from the theatre slapping each other on the back. They stop. A set of four funnel clouds descend on the city. The theatergoers yell to each other, grab their loved ones, and run for cover.

A moment later, the storms touch down, raking the decaying city in its own debris.

CHAPTER THREE

UNSAFE AREA

/ / /

Pain has no respect for wealth and seeks more of him. During the debate over FairGame, Professor Remold Jaka had stayed on the side lines. The inventor's logic had said he was not powerful enough to derail the juggernaut of FairGame. Remold Jaka's silence has become memory with teeth.

Three months after the first FairGame preserves opened, a female colleague's daughter was murdered inside FairGame. Professor Remold Jaka found her scalp in the pocket of his lab coat. The day the woman slit her wrists and died.

Remold Jaka's remorse about FairGame has escaped his cage of logic to roam freely behind the eyes of his being. Now, every stranger starving in the streets, the homeless children, the wounded, the bleeding Targets, the lust for escape inside Wholack are fingers pointing at his silence. Mind-tigers, as he calls them, prowl his waking consciousness, their claws ripping into his dawn:

Remold Jaka and his group of geniuses? How ridiculous.

FairGame, Game of Boo, whatever--it's murder--plain and simple.

Why didn't you try to stop the horror?

Remold, as the CEO of a major corporation, has unlimited insight into society's barbarism. His view from above has stroked, tickled, and fed the mind-tigers. Spears of rational thought do nothing anymore to deter the tigers while the degrading cities water them, dying children feed them, and the FairGame preserves love them. The multiplying problems of living on planet Earth have turned the harmless denizens of Remold Jaka's mind into wild insatiable pariahs. He believes no one cares for anyone or anything now, except escape into his game, Wholack.

This morning the mind-tigers have also beat him to consciousness. Romping and clawing at the inside of his skull, he feels them scratching at the back of his eyes with their claws. His eyelids pop open and he grabs his glasses trying to focus on the day. Doctor Remold Jaka, CEO of Laughs Unlimited, is a man drowning in truth: The mad desire for Wholack birthed FairGame. The game he created, he also believes, has murdered civilization. Worse, for him, his ex-wife seeks his destruction--ruination of everything he has created--he believes.

Crawling from bed and standing, Remold Jaka Ph.D., strokes his bushy gray academic beard, before he sets his gold glasses onto a mane of silver hair. Sleep has left strands in his mouth. He opens his mouth and works to remove the offending hair.

A wide mouth with bright white teeth, he has one of those horse-tooth smiles that women find so attractive--a mouth of mirth said one woman. "The murderer of an entire generation," said another, his ex-wife, Mina.

He feels the deep lines etched into his cheeks. Disgusted

with aging, he scans an asset of large wooden windows revealing the Hudson River and the forest beyond. Below his luxury, the beat of civilization moves towards a flat-line.

A manifest of decency holds the mistakes of his life above all else, but for this he achieves no parole. Remold is a man without forgiveness--for himself--for others. It is eating him alive. Isolated by genius, his life is a bipolar feast of pain and unending privilege.

Moron, how could you be obtuse?

You condemned millions to death and a billion to servitude.

Worse than your father--beast.

Everyone schemes to garner wealth as a way of escape. The competition to get inside Wholack grows more fierce every day. Remold Jaka recently found out desperate parents sell their children into slavery, or butcher them for their organs. All for more time in Wholack. Therefore it is all his fault. An outsider might say Remold's real enemy is his ego.

Fool.

The Wholack Game is a system to diminish human consumption of energy and resources, a system for turning the human consumer into a sleeping baby wrapped in bliss. It works. The planet is coming to rest, safe from humanity's onslaught because Wholack provides humans peace in a chaotic universe.

Remold created a game so brilliant everyone seeks it above life on Earth. But...He believes he has sentenced the meek to the horror of barbarism.

The bliss of the Wholack Game is so complete, so immersing, so splendid, human focus has embraced the belief that there is a heaven in this life: The Wholack Game, and achieving heaven is worth any price.

For his part, Remold believed Wholack would facilitate the exploration of reality, the fabric of nature, providing a safe launch into the ephemeral universe. Instead, the lure of Wholack has fostered a manic rush to leave the devastation of a wounded Earth and escape into the pure bliss of Wholack where real is adjustable, unlimited, and fulfillment unending.

Heaven for the living has sent a billion people into the hell of servitude. While others face existence as a hunting target. Once again, heaven has fostered hell. In Remold's defense, the horrors of humanity do come from Wholack, but that horror is the result of a populace in pain, not the bliss they seek.

The most brilliant left first, leaving society crippled. Cities fail, water systems decay, technology outside the support of Wholack crumbles. Disease floods the bodies of those left behind. Remold's ego says, because people desert the planet for Wholack, misery therefore follows.

Not true, because many people have the capability to understand the workings of complex systems. Some work for Laughs Unlimited--or attack Wholack--forcing Remold to defend it. Wholack's destruction would dump almost two billion bed-ridden humans out of the digital reality back onto a still healing Mother Earth--an unfathomable tragedy for all.

Doctor Jaka stares across the river as he considers the ejection of billions back onto the planet, their bodies weak and muscles useless. Their fortunes gone, their residences a shambles. Without food to feed them or safety in any quarter, the number of wandering wounded would multiply by a thousand. Were society even able to absorb all those people-- which he knows is an impossibility--anger against the privileged would lead to slaughter.

Those used to the horrors of now, those seeking access to Wholack, those disenfranchised ones would make sport of the dispossessed, hunting them, obliterating the last of civilization. Therefore, he sees himself chained to hell-- as its mother and its slave--because Remold fears the end of civilization more than the annex of hell he believes he has created. He is a man being torn apart by pride.

His next thought is of his ex-wife, Mina Jaka. She seeks to end Wholack.

A whole team of R&D people in the security arm of Laughs Unlimited works to evaluate her actions, looking for clues to Mina Jaka's whereabouts. Staff panders to both his pain and his greatness. They know nothing of Mina's whereabouts, but in their rush to enter Wholack they polish the ego of Dr. Remold Jaka at every turn and continually feed him useless data. Remold knows he is surrounded by people who care nothing about him. On the other hand, he expects the lure of success to control them.

Fool.

Absurdly--such is the gift of a massive ego--Remold also fears Mina has a win destroying the system to prove her theories and showing Remold as a fool, a Wholack. Mina is the enemy--as he sees it. Every day he fights another of her efforts to alter Wholack.

She has said over and over that the Wholack's servers, its network, and its storage systems must all be shut down. Ironically, were she successful, once the news got out that she delivered the destruction of Wholack, she would be a hunted criminal. There would be no place for her to hide. His mind snaps to Mina's current ability to remain hidden from him in the game. This annoys him most of all.

So while he cannot understand her gain in destroying his life work, harming so many people to prove him wrong, her apparent short-sightedness and her ability to evade him angers him most. "Bitch." He rubs his right elbow with his other hand.

He has forgotten his goal of the morning and begins to wander his home. On the verandah outside, white roses hang from steel poles. The poles support a moldy glass roof. His bleary crusted eyes drop to the railing of his penthouse porch. A row of pigeons covers the copper railing. He considers the leap of death again, believing in the option of endless, unrecognizable eternity below him. Suicide keeps him alive, because death is always an option. Were he to one day see himself as immortal he would go completely mad.

Back inside, he slips on the Sarouk rugs. He and a young woman had snuggled upon those rugs last night. The rugs are some of the last ones on the planet. Feeling his feet on the rug, he puts on tired black pants and a white knit cowl shirt. Remold ignores the wall of monitors over his bed and instead smells his stink on the clothes.

On the floor below a clean wardrobe awaits. The ghosts of his lost family also haunt the rooms below. So he avoids them both.

Remold owns the entire fifty story building, but he spends most of his time here when he is in the rotting corpse of New York City--or at the university. Remold Jaka believes his life to be a loveless joke. The empirical measurement of a massive ego.

The sun climbs, bathing the room. The bright sunny day does not warm him. He lives for cold evenings and beautiful lovers. It is with these graced humans that he finds solace--a cage for the mind-tigers. Through the admiration of so-called lovers juiced by expensive alcohol and drugs, he can still tell the stories that quell the mistakes he has made, turning his so-called failures into smiles. Remold is addicted to admiration. At sixty-one, Remold Jaka has forgotten life without pain, accusation without reason, and responsibility without meaning.

His only joy: the cheering crowd.

A squeak, like chalk on a blackboard, and he looks around the room. No, he was alone in the bed. It had pleased him to invoke the privilege of power last night with the beautiful young Louise Tubby--sending her packing before midnight.

Monster, roars the mind-tigers clawing at the bones inside his skull.

"My right."

He mumbles this to no one and retreats to the shower. Poor Remold grew up with the privileges that comes with being the son of a successful executive who was a murderer--as well as the guilt. Neither privilege has bounds.

Many years ago, after meeting a man on the beach, his father began to declare the coming years as murderous to humanity and the planet. His father claimed fossil fuel energy was a fool's game--a dead end game. He told his son he was sure of this because he now possessed true sentience, knowledge from the future.

That mystical knowledge changed the world.

Buying media companies for fostering his viewpoint, Harold Jordan, Remold's father, worked to alter the tide of perception on the changing climate--while adjusting his equities.

Then, at the end of the twentieth century, as the damage from storms mounted, theories became facts to the public--thanks to Harold Jordan's media barrage. The dawn of the twenty-first century brought outrage and the will to make substantial changes. The ensuing trials of those who fought knowledge of the climate danger solidified the population to action--even after they were told the storms would continue for generations to come. Ironically, his father was swept up in the anger as rumors of murder began to surface.

Those were powerful industrialists in a blood feud.

With father's imprisonment--mother divorced her husband. She changed her name back to Jaka for the sake of her son. Mother committed suicide after Remold's father admitted to her son that they had killed that man on the beach who had shared his knowledge of the future.

Squashing rumors of the murder, and her complicity, remain Remold's task. First to protect his parent's memory, second, to sally forth and continue his father's work to heal the planet.

As part of this pursuit, a young Remold Jaka founded Laughs Unlimited, based on the notion that sedated humans used almost no resources. By the time his theories were proven with Wholack version one, Saucer City, Remold Jaka was a billionaire and his father dead. When Wholack became a worldwide mania, Remold credited his father with leading the charge to gain control over the emissions that killed so many, claiming himself merely a toy-maker.

Slowly, the sucking of planetary resources mitigated and the impact of human activities waned. The storms and fires, the floods and drought, the sea level rise and the migrations continued but they became less intense as carbon-based energy usage plummeted. The charge that had been led by his father to end the horror of human forcing of the climate turned a corner with Wholack. A prone body jacked on drugs and hooked into a computer system uses far less resources than a lust-driven consumer.

Humanity was saved, because the consumer society went comatose. Then, the devotion for the game began destroying everything but the game and its support network. Remold dove into the events looking for outside interference, or violations of his universe. All he found was the instinct of a herd seeking safety and security. FairGame soon followed.

Remold stands in the large bathroom after his shower, thinking about Mina and the words scrawled across the windows of their home one floor below: Written in lipstick it still says: "Some get left behind." Remold Jaka slowly closes his eyes missing her. The tigers inside his skull sulk in the shadow of love. He curses Mina under his breath. The mind-tigers purr.

Mina, he believes, is his most terrible mistake. Once his lover and partner, his wife and friend, she is now, he believes, a terrorist--one working tirelessly to destroy Wholack. He curses the friend who had arranged for them to meet one summer while young Remold was working at the Library of Congress.

She was eating her lunch from a paper bag sitting on the steps of the library. A ladies man stunned, instead of the erudite Jaka taking his characteristic approach of wit and intelligence, the young man lapsed into the role of a bumbling clown.

Making insipid conversation about his work, asking mundane questions about her computer-based artwork, bypassing every learned technique of courtship in hopes of "truly loving" he floundered.

Then later, getting drunk, he made a fool of himself by pounding on her apartment door at midnight. Not a degrading enough event, she called the police on him.

Tethered to beauty, he followed Mina around seeking her forgiveness. So she rushed off to a different hemisphere, worried the love-struck boy was just another sad joke masquerading as a man. Remold sent her gifts every hour.

In later years, Mina would tell their friends, that it took six months to accept Remold as more than a boy with money. She returned on a chartered jet. Her companions were flowers from every continent. Remold waited on the tarmac, a daisy in his hands, his head bowed.

The marriage lasted eleven years, then she disappeared into Wholack. All he can find of her now is her efforts to shut down his creation, Wholack.

Yet even as Remold seeks to toss her from his being, to this day, he sees her face at the age of twenty-two: black hair, a white sweater, bright green eyes, a smile on her face, the grace of a princess in a privileged frame of deserved adoration--a lover aglow in the footlight of genius. That memory is all he has left of her--but it is enough to drive him forward.

The morning kit complete, Remold finally sits down at his desk, thinking back to yesterday. He was inside a Wholack sub-scenario called the Kittens and Cradles. Numerous reports had come in saying the sub-scenario has become too random to win and the developers unavailable.

Last night, he discovered Mina owned the scenario, instead of its registered developer, Hope Weiss. Remold was stunned. Aside from the question of why Mina decided to make the scenario so impossible--it was sure to attract attention. Scenario theft is the number one no-no in Wholack. As well, there were pieces of rookie code locating one of Mina's servers.

Scanning this morning's reports, he sees his researches say they have found software routines inside the server to shut down Wholack servers around the Northwest. The head of Security, a man named Ben Fong, also sent a text. Mina has made a pile of rookie mistakes--making her server available to any mid-level player.

Neither man takes comfort in that--too atypical of her.

Remold looks up from message, wondering how it is possible for Mina to make so many stupid mistakes. He decides not and texts his head of security. "Look for a trap hidden in one of the Rosts."

One of the great strengths of the Wholack Game is the ability of the players to build digital human frames, called Rosts in Wholack, as well as nest any framework inside existing scenarios. Frameworks that might be made available for others to forage through if the creator decides, allow unending complexity and charm tailored to both individual taste and societal drift or to create a personal Nirvana--but again--the scenario creator retains ownership. To do otherwise means loss of scenario control--a kind of computational bankruptcy-

-because others take over and control it all. Some mistakes leading to scenario loss are not considered a theft--just a loss. Mina, it appears to Remold, seems to have stolen the Kittens and Cradles scenario, then messed it up to the point that anyone can take it from her because she granted full access to her source code.

So why steal it, then send out mistakes? Especially after hiding from me these last three years?

Security finding the routines to shut down servers was intentional. Otherwise, it seems so unlikely from a top developer, like her, as to be impossible.

Or, some kind of a breach has taken place--he tells himself--and she doesn't know it.

Or, someone has gotten to her.

Or, she has found a hole in my software and Mina plans to use Kittens and Cradles to bring down the system. He tells himself that is most likely.

Or is it? This mess with Kittens and Cradles is odd. How could it have ever happened?

Could it be a breach of some sort, into her code? Impossible, he tells himself. She is too good.

Still, he believes he can take advantage of her misstep. Remold gets up from his desk. Crossing to the back room, he stares at the custom Wholack bed and its workings. This morning Remold plans another visit to Kittens and Cradles with his researchers. He is seeking Mina.

Looking like a tanning bed with feed tubes instead of long fluorescent bulbs, the custom bed has various custom displays and input systems available only to this occupant.

Doctor Remold Jaka, inventor of the Wholack Game lies down and sends a message to the others that he is ready to go into Wholack. They should meet him at the Kitten and Cradles sub-scenario.

His team of researchers have been waiting for almost

two hours. Of course no one will say anything. They are in the best position possible of all to enjoy the game. They work with the man who has brought Heaven to Earth.

CHAPTER FOUR

STRAIGHT AHEAD

Inside the Wholack Game, five figures walk the narrow cobblestone street between thatched houses in what appears to be an English country village. On the streets surrounding them, bodies hang from lampposts. Dead animal carcasses litter the cobblestones and the sharp smell of rotten eggs fills the area. Remold wonders how Mina could be part of something so ugly. Mina was once a gentle woman. All this blood, what is wrong with her?

Above it all, high up on the hillside, outlandish cartoon characters, thirty stories high, slap each other with spiked clubs, chase each other with pitchforks, throw black bowling-ball-shaped bombs, or copulate madly. Their echoes pour through the digital town.

To Remold, the brightly colored rabbits, pink bears, black mice, and red dogs are nothing more than advertisements for madness. He tells himself were he to stay in Wholack he would create only beauty.

For the casual visitor to this Kittens and Cradles scenario these cartoon character are the fond remembrance of a Sunday morning childhood. An explosion. Brightly colored fireworks pour over the town followed by a shower of sparks. A loud sigh follows.

He looks at the bodies shaking his head. The others are quiet. Remold tells himself he never really understood her. In that he is correct. The proof is not in the mayhem of the village, but in the sets of white roses that bloom in the pink wooden window-boxes lining the street. The researchers cannot see them. Only Remold can--Mina is an expert in Wholack. He ignores the flowers thinking them a trick for control. After his passing, the roses wither. Had he bothered to look back with fresh eyes he would have understood Mina is not his enemy. Unfortunately, Remold Jaka protects his ego so this trip into Kittens and Cradles is to imprison Mina, again.

Ahead, a cottage lies crushed under a blood-red fist. The huge hand sits enmeshed into a shattered cottage. Following the line of the fist to the wrist to the arm, Remold sees the Wholack riding an immense surfboard, circling, tethered to the anchored hand. "When did that happen?"

"It had been clear, Doc."

"What the hell is she doing?"

Circling above them with no apparent clarity of its tether, the Wholack eats car-sized jelly beans of various colors. Tossing them up in the air, snacking on them and surfing the friendly skies in an empty circle. He is unaware and undisturbed--in other words: a fool.

Remold snorts, angry at Mina's stubbornness. "Someone get rid of that."

The fist and the Wholack disappear taking the thatch roof of the cottage with it. A bright pink parallelogram appears covering the void created by the exclusion of Wholack. "Doctor. Singh, please stop the reset."

A blond woman dressed in a sleek white dress and black cowboy boots appears. She moves her hands in a wide circle. The reset in the scenario, ceases. Her hands play a hidden console. A pink propeller beanie appears over her blond hair. "Done."

"Thank you." The figure of Remold Jaka examines reset seeking a clue to Mina. Frustrated he says, "Now would someone please remove those horrors from the lampposts?"

A ghostly shimmer engulfs the town as cows, goats, and donkeys appear along the street. Bodies and severed appendages are traded away into a peaceable kingdom. He continues his examination and finds nothing. "Anyone?"

Silence from his researchers.

"Fine. Mina uses an alias named May sometimes. Do any of you see her in the database? I think we can use her."

"I see her." Says Dr. Singh. She now appears as Marilyn Monroe. "The Rost named May is hidden in a disaster sequence. She is cleaning up a broken greenhouse in Global Warming, the old beta test site."

"All right. Let her flow to us." People appear in a marketplace. "Do not address her as Mina, but as May. I'll take care of the introductions. Go."

A young teen with stringy, greasy hair appears. Dressed in stitched rags of sailcloth she rushes up to Remold. "My name is May." She skips up the lane then opens the heavy wooden door of a smoke filled cottage. "It's this way, Remmy."

"Doctor Jaka, she was much older on the beta site," says Dr. Singh.

"Let it be," he replies. When the researchers and their CEO enter the oil lit room, the young woman stands over a weakened, apparently sick mother, prone upon a red-flowered couch. Every flower looks like a question mark--an insult that declares the viewer unsophisticated and dull. Mina is tracking them.

Pure Mina, Remold says to himself.

He pauses it all by moving his fingers about. The image blurs a moment. He attaches his traps to the Rost, May, hoping to ensnare Mina. Remold restarts the scenario.

"May, take them up into the core," says the mother.

Remold winks at his researchers. The researchers smile. Remold Jaka has started to tie Mina directly to May. Remold points at two researchers, one appearing like Einstein and the other a buff Galileo just back from the gym. "And the developer ID on that fist?"

Galileo speaks: "Ain't got none--fish on a plate, Boss. The track-back is a dinner sequence inside a house near Eden. There's a tie there as well to the Global Warming beta code, a Carlos."

The young girl interrupts. "So that's what happened. What do you want, Remmy?"

"I cannot answer that, May," Remold replies, turning his hand upside down. The image wavers and he finds himself looking at the young image of Mina. She is a lithe dark beauty of about twenty-five. He had not expected so direct a link. "So, you are not so clever, darling?"

"Still a fool," says the image. "But now you are tracking me. We'll see about that."

"Can we discuss this?"

"Funny." The image grays then recovers its color. "My name is May, not Mina It's this way, Remmy."

Remold looks over to a man dressed in cowboy paraphernalia. Across his chest it says *Cool Dude*. He shakes his head. "She reset your tags. I've ten algorithms in a random butterfly configuration. I track it back to that dinner sequence, again."

"So she broke something."

"Or, something is broken and she is trying to hide it."

"Send in a Rost to act as a probe." A Rost is an avatar, a digital persona. Remold continues. "Send it in as an autistic player. It will get some data that way--before she toasts it."

"Done."

Remold speaks to May. "I am looking for this?" His words invoke a subroutine that is a track-back to a bed. He finds nothing. Autonomous vehicles like this are extremely difficult to build in Wholack. He nods at Mina's skill--more proof the mistakes in this scenario are peculiar.

Facing Einstein, Remold points to the researcher's scattered white hair. A nest of drunk pigeons coo. The other researchers laugh at Einstein. He scowls wiping the birds from the scenario. He was trying to find Mina, but she saw him coming. Remold doesn't care; the event is so common he ignores it. "We know you are outside our sight. We also know you messed up, Mina."

"May, you be careful. Take my coat," says the old woman. The girl walks over to the door and dons an old blue raincoat. Its small rubber patch looks like a huge amoeba crawling up her arm. She sees Remold staring at it. "My hound dog." She looks down at her arm. "A rip? No way."

"That was odd," says a researcher named Lazlo Wolf. "Now this May Rost points to Home Fires. What the heck is she doing?"

"I can go in and look for a rip," says Dr. Singh, the blond-haired woman now wears a Marilyn Monroe Rost.

"Careful," Remold says.

The Marilyn Monroe disappears then reappears a moment later. "Broken code. Could be a bad set of chips. Could be anything. One of her servers is now toast."

Remold shakes his head. "She has lost control."

"You'll never make it around the chemical bogs, Remmy. They're not traps, they're spills," says May. "Watch Galileo croak as soon as we leave this cottage. I gave him a chance and he blew it. Wildhead indeed," she says, calling out Doctor Wolf's game moniker.

Remold looks at him."If you blip out let it be. Then run a reset. Use the viewer to push back in. Look for a trail of random code."

"I know the drill."

"Please, Laz, let him lead you--that way we might get out of this mess," croaks the old woman. Her oily black hair and pocked face shows Remold that Mina is fighting some issue.

The mother hugs her daughter. Then they exit into the night and Galileo disappears. Remold shakes his head at the theatrics. Dr. Wolf is his best researcher.

The five of them, led by the young girl, begin to stroll the lane toward a brothel. "My mother says too many people cannot tell if they are in a scenario or if they are in real life." She speaks the words quietly, looking around like a thief. "That's a clue, Ace."

"A clue to your anger?" Remold asks.

"Mom calls this place a game. She's crazy. By the way, your probe just crashed." Her index finger makes a tight loop around her ear accentuating the comment. "You're so obvious, Remmy."

"Is your mother Mina Jaka?" Remold asks. "Dr. Monto, please attach to this query."

"Mina knows you are looking for her and that you have a better chance of finding John Doe." The figure pauses then looses all of its color. "What's a dolt?"

A couple of the researchers laugh. "We're supposed to believe John Doe did this?" Asks Dr. Singh.

"Problems, Mina?" Remold speaks with a smile. The figure named May jerks with starts and stops--a homage to earlier computer games--then it recolors. Sounding like a tour guide, the girl says, "Up ahead is her brothel."

Dr. Singh winces. She worked harder than most to become a researcher on Remold Jaka's staff.

"Can't do no whores. A heart of gold is still a cold heart." The response is standard for his generation. A generation that has grown up with an unlimited access to licentious scenarios. It has made many prudish and most leery of sex. The comment came from a young researcher named Monto. He wears a cowboy outfit.

The Rost, May, blinks. "There's a trail around back. It leads down to the river. Once we're there, we can cross it and crawl up the chutes into the wall. We'll be dirty, but so long as we get there before dawn, we'll be okay. If we're caught in the chute after dawn, we'll be flushed down by the chemicals. Then its good-bye-Charlie. Keep making love." She snickers. "I once heard that."

"Doctor Jaka, I've got a work around," says Monto. "But you won't like it."

"No. We stay inside and take the whole ride."

They circle the trailers, their music and shadows, walking under some hanging laundry that smells of garlic. Pushing passed it, they cross by huge pink azaleas near a pit latrine; then, they are on a wide trail down a hillside.

"A trail?" Einstein moans. "Doc, Monto didn't run the work around, but here it is. Wolf, are we congruent?"

"Don't know, but maybe what happened to us is Mina's mistake as well," says an oak tree as they pass. Remold nods his agreement.

May looks around. "There's intruder code."

"So someone breached your code, Mina," Remold says. "Sloppy work."

The young girl speaks, "Some new kid in town. The adults don't know anything about it."

"There is no reason to be insulting," Remold says.

"Sorry, Doctor. I know you are friends with Wholack."

Her mocking tones echo through the wood. They approach a creek. May fords it by balancing on a fallen log.

"Someone go help Wolf," Remold says.

Immediately, they see the wide slow moving river. Winds blow cold. Across the river is a huge wall. With every step, the chemical soup that was once a river smells worse. All along its top, black-cube-snouts stick out in front. The cartoon figures running along its crest continue their mayhem. Moss hangs like roots from the underside of the guard outlooks. From one outlook, a body hangs. The structure looks old and unused. The young girl stops and stares.

"Boss, this is Wolf. I'm back. You're seeing a blend from Home Fires and a sub-scenario of Corporate Apocalypse, but you are still in Kittens and Cradles--so far as I can tell. It's a recent reset. It's what I fell into it. Mina didn't do it."

"Code doesn't break." The researchers laugh nervously.

"The signature of the links says John Doe. So does the ownership of Kittens and Cradles."

"Mina is so witty...Not." Remold scowls.

"A triple break in code and a full dimensional shift-- courtesy of life," says May.

Remold looks around. "We'll see." He waves his hand. The young girl goes gray. He has paused her.

The young girl colors. "From here on we have to use filters--just in case there is a break." She hands them each a mask with twin filters. "We call these the bug-masks because they make you look like a bug when you wear them. They're alien looking so they're the best."

"She must be farther along than we thought. The toxins from the chemicals look modified to allow even first time access across. Do we have a new link from Global Warming? Does anyone see signs of traffic on the wall?"

"Yup. Some kind of strange link through the autism foundation called...Hey, what the hell..."

"Wolf?" No response. "Doctor Wolf? Crap. Wolf?"

"He's toast, Boss," says Einstein. "Totally locked out."

"How much time do we have left?" Remold asks his researchers.

"Five minutes."

He looks at the young girl. "I'd never hurt you, Mina. I am trying to protect you." Remold looks around for more signs of user traffic. He finds links across all four versions of Wholack. At the same time he notes it is because of the digital synthetic in the masks. The work is flawless.

"It fits well," the young girl says. "This is proof we have unwanted entry across the four waters. It wasn't me, Remmy. Was it you?"

He shakes his head no.

The young girl wears a hundred gray eyes in each socket. They peer at the group from behind scratched plastic. "Really?"

"Nope," Remold says, watching the eyes. The hundred gray eyes are servers working in parallel to crack into her code. "Mina, why the theatrics?"

"Not mine," says a dark green alligator, rising from the swampy slow flowing water. "Those theatrics are the workings of a universe. Remmy, there are parts of the clockwork you will never comprehend. You are too smart to see them. That's why some get left behind." The alligator smiles a toothy, orthodontic smile of metal covering its teeth and lowers itself into the smelly chemical bog.

"I think someone wants to show off," says Dr. Singh.

The alligator rises. "I think that's the point. There is a wrong. But it is systemic." The clouds flash lightning.

"Sorry, Mina, we are going the whole route on this one."

Overhead, the cartoon characters shower the bog with sparks from their bombs. The colors turn to hail. "Remold, you are wrong." The alligator sinks below the water again.

Another researcher, looking like a very fat John Wayne

appears shaking his head. "I lost her." It is Monto. The Rost named May colors, then laughs. She points across the river.

Remold speaks: "I want to know about your mistakes, May." May goes gray, but this time a bright red sphere engulfs the space. "Mina, are you trying to shut down the Wholack servers now?"

"Her servers have just been hit," says Dr. Singh.

Remold hides his confusion. "You have been stopped."

"So far, Sherlock." The young girl pouts, apparently angry. Then she smiles, The hundreds of eyes in the gas mask disappear. "You are so dull, Remold, and so blind."

Remold scans for signs of what has happened. "I am Ewalt. Those on the other side of the wall have been reduced to slaves through drugs. I am trying to help them." He is speaking the words that he already knows will lead to a win in this scenario. He gets control. "Break. Escape." The scenario freezes.

If Mina's earlier mistakes are real, the young girl will fade.

She does.

"Mina. We cannot handle the ejection of a billion people into the planet. It will be chaos, and worse." He waves his hand. "You have lost control. Anything can happen now."

The fade stops. The young girl appears, looking at the others, spinning her index finger by her skull--indicating Remold is daft in some way. Mina has control of the Rost, May, again.

Remold stares, astounded at Mina's control. "Who has control here?" Remold asks, once he has confirmed that Mina has not made a mistake.

"Isn't that the lord's truth," mumbles the girl. "What the heck happened?" She goes gray again.

Startled, Remold tries not to show concern. He was ready for Mina as an enemy, but it appears to him another player keeps cutting into her computer code. "If you try to shut down the system all at once you'll create loops, ghost objects, inconsistencies that will take a decade to unravel. You'll inject madness into the minds of those still in the system. You'll turn Wholack into hell."

May grays again. She recolors, getting up and stepping over a metal plate and indicating it is a trap of sharpened rods. "How'd you do that? You've been a bad boy, Remold. Let's talk about Pilot Nothing. Or perhaps we can go back now and see your lies between those weird computer things that aren't anything, you know that place that is neither a one nor a zero. Your favorite hiding place?" The figure of the girl shrinks into a small white cube then disappears into a tiny pink point. A moment later she is back. "People have no idea your father killed Pilot Nothing."

"Pilot Nothing is a myth," says Einstein.

"Pilot Nothing was a voyager that told Remold's father the truth of human forcing of the climate--our future. His father killed him and claimed the insight as his own." The figure ghosts to gray. Remold has regained control.

Remold looks at the others. "She loves to tell that lie."

The others all know the truth. They do not care. They will not embarrass the goose that lays the golden egg, Remold Jaka. He hears the voice of Lazlo. Wolf. "Looks like someone has set the term Pilot Nothing out into the network--but in a strange way. I can't track it."

"Someone?"

"I can't confirm it was Mina. I'll wash it."

"Please." Remold faces the young girl. "What was the point of that, Mina?"

"Point, as in crossover point?" She grins looking at the others. "He's so stupid. Follow me. If you do, Remmy, you'll find John Doe."

The researchers stand, shocked at what they have heard.

Mina has just claimed The Destroyer, colloquially named John Doe, is not only real, but infecting code inside Wholack.

"That's nice," Remold says. "And yes I know you messed up, but the big lie? Tacky."

The Rost named May looks away. "So it wasn't you, Remold--and you don't know who brought him through." The young girl walks towards the shore.

"When do we cease our version of *Who's Afraid of Virginia Wolf?*" Remold asks, feigning boredom.

The young girl walks to a wooden row boat in the brush. She tries to drag the boat over to the water and launch it. "So we are on the same quest. Just like old times. Please?"

Remold nods and the others help her haul the boat to the river. When they sit on it, the craft almost sinks into the fouled water. "See? You got me, Remmy."

"Nonsense."

"Idiot." They push off into the chemical flow. May hands them balled up aluminized cloth. "The covering will make us look like liquid to anyone following the crossover. Safety first."

"Nice of you to be so cooperative. Got some issues you can't deal with, Mina?" Remold and the researchers cover the rickety craft as it moves towards the wall. Careful not to get any of the toxic liquid into the boat, Remold finds the crossing astoundingly swift. This means they are about to find Mina's security area. He has been working on uncovering it for months.

"The chute is just ahead. You can stop rowing; there's a rope to pull on." They grab the old hemp rope and pull until they see a huge barrel vault of welded steel that climbs up inside of the wall. It smells like a sewer.

"Doctor Monto, we are getting intrusion through our filters. Isolate the local servers to keep the net safe."

A section of grate swings out in a large arc, clanking

against the other half of the grate. "This is a waste system from the toilets in the guard towers," May says. "It's the cleanest water in the place." The researchers look up the tube seeing crawling vermin all over it. "Don't worry about them. You'll find a rope about head height. Put on your gloves, then grab the wrung to your left. It's a short climb up the guts of the wall."

Rubber gloves encase his hands. "She is helping protect the local servers. Let it be," Remold says, knowing all this is like a combination to her locks. They enter the tunnel. Through his glove, Remold feels the human waste as he climbs. There is more code corruption.

She messed up again. She is scared. Why?

At the top, they enter a short horizontal tunnel.

They push on another grate and climb out of the sewer into a dirty bathroom. The others emerge and strip off their masks. The young girl hurries to a door. A pair of cats walk by.

"Do not disturb them," Remold says, quickly.

A researcher dressed as John Wayne speaks. "I'm not stupid. I know a Schrödinger cat trap when I see one. But I want to see how close we are to solving this. My systems show minor servers are beginning fail throughout the net. The net diagnostic says chips are heating. The servers say everything is nominal. Looks like ghost code."

"Nonsense." Remold looks around. "On my mark make sure May answers to the name Mina."

May looks out the frosted glass of the lavatory door. Her mask in her hand she says: "About four hours or so before the place will be full of workers again."

Remold looks at the others. "Mark." The young girl grays then pushes aside a piece of sheet metal beside the door. Remold has entry into her security software. "Mina, this is madness. You are compromising the network."

"Relax, Remmy, all the doors have alarms," May says

crawling out. They exit to the wide two lane roadway on the wall's top. The roadway symbolizes the links into Mina's security servers. Two researchers disappear to begin their task of bringing down Mina's firewall.

Above them, animate projected figures begin to fight. The blasts of colors flow out to the valley behind the wall. Figures appear on the construction towers, hung by arms and legs, struggling to get free of the blurred graffiti tarps covering them.

Only one line is readable. It catches Remold's attention: "You are here. So is John Doe."

"Someone store that."

Einstein speaks: "Something on the net. A blood test. I see links to the Boiler Room."

"Leave it. We'll get it later. How are we doing on those servers?"

No change in the blur of graffiti.

Remold's clothes glow deep red from his frustration. "Okay--let's try again," Remold says.

May slides down the wall. They follow her down the slide. Remold invokes his control routine. Instead of the Rost graying out, Mina stands before him. "That was impressive."

Remold cannot speak for the sight of his ex-wife.

Dr. Singh speaks: "How does it feel to be standing in your own ruins, Mina? Pretty good for a whore, huh?"

Remold recovers. "Hello Mina--long time no speak. Some damn mess you have here."

"A pile of useless servers. No thanks to you."

"You're welcome." Remold blurs out for a moment then returns. "All done. My Rost, Carlos, stopped your shut down event. Your Rost, Damube, got away in a space ship. Hiding the code in a child's toy, so easy. So stupid. Surprise Mina. I win. You lose. Ladies and gentlemen, shut down the rest of her servers."

The other figures ghost gray, to Remold's surprise. The young girl May grins at him. "Now we can go through the tunnel."

Remold is in shock. All of his researchers have been neutralized for the moment. A researcher dressed as Ghandi appears. "Something tripped links all the way to the Defense Department. We've got Mina on the run, so I don't think she tripped the links."

"We'll see, Doctor Wolf," Remold says. "Do we own her Rost, May?"

He nods.

Remold points to the Rost. "Okay, where to, May?"

The figure shimmers. "We can enter the security system now. Oh my golly," the young girl says. "Damn you, Remold."

"Funny there would be such heavy wiring going into an empty network. Doc, I show an immense amount of users here. " Dr. Wolf says, watching Remold's reaction. "Our scans have been saying the opposite."

"Look how the pink wire is pulsing. It's overloaded. She sent it to the trash, but it didn't go." Remold says, scanning his custom readouts. "There have been close to fifty million through here. Oh, it's okay. I see no genetic links to beds."

"Confirmed--no one from the beds."

"Remold, any conjecture where the visitors came from--when or where they went to?" Asks May.

Wolf responds as he watches Remold work. "It registers as a temporal violation of the scenario. Supposedly before the beta version of the software was written. Mina, tossed another cat at us? I think not. What the hell is this?"

Remold snorts. "She is as confused as we are." His researchers start appearing again.

Doctor Wolf speaks, "Maybe she's testing small shut downs all around the system to make sure her links are working. Wait. Doc, that's not right. My personal systems show a valid time stamp--but it is because of that blood test. My counter is as basic as it gets. If it is a fake--okay--then Mina has gotten me; but, it won't be a fake. The blood test is from a crossover."

"Or it is Mina telling us we cannot stop what is taking place." Remold shakes his head knowing they are petrabytes from an answer. "Ladies and gentlemen, we are not only staring at a mystery--but a declaration of our ineptitude."

"Hers too. She missed this. Why would she want us to know she failed?" Asks Einstein.

"She's was hiding it. Some other event has occurred while she was focusing on us," says Remold Jaka. "It is some kind of cascading event. Do you have control yet?"

"So far as it goes. We just cut into her firewall. She has been tracking those fifty-million signatures for a while. Damn she saw me. Scratch fifty-million digital souls," says Dr. Singh.

"Retail sales will have a fit," says Galileo.

They continue along a ramp and begin to climb. It's a spiral staircase surrounding a building. The exterior affords an eerie view of the hellish scene behind the wall. Fires and gas belch from cracking towers, bolts of dry lightning striking the facility, struggling bodies. "Hieronymus Bosch did it better Mina, and just with paint." An exterior door falls. "Good job, team. We're in." Remold jumps through the door. "Go for her subnet." The researchers scramble after him.

Half way up a tunnel, a layer of black cable terminates in huge lugs, the size of lawn mowers; they hang like huge copper bats overhead. The mounts in the walls and floor look as though they have all been torn free by a giant hand.

"Like those, Mina? I removed them myself. Or did you miss that also?" He has just eliminated her current code for destroying the network backbone. The researchers, impressed by the event, hurry along the concrete shell taking control of various servers.

"You did it with that Wholack hand from the game

when we entered," says Einstein. "Nicely done. We are inside her security perimeter."

"It wasn't supposed to happen like this. I cannot account for the fifty million--let's make sure we have no casualties."

Mina speaks: "Jerk. So you have bought another few days. It will make no difference." A large white tiger appears. Remold sweeps his hand and it disappears.

His gut churns. There is randomness he cannot account for. "Scared, Mina?" Tools appear on the ground. Remold knows that means Mina is confused. He looks for a hatchet. That means Mina is also angry. "Nice hatchet, Mina. Problem?"

"Something aberrant is in the system. I bet I understand it before you do, Remmy."

"Keep hoping." Remold hurries along pointing at objects and destroying them in puffs of pink smoke. Ahead, he sees bulldozers. They burst into flames-then one by one they stop.

"She's fighting back." Huge ceiling fans appear overhead.

"Counting thirty-five servers under our control."

Remold waives his hand. He has less than a minute to take over the rest of her servers so Mina cannot close down and escape.

May appears. "You sought to disengage humans from the planet because they were destroying it." Says the young girl, wavering like a flag in the wind. She kicks down a wall revealing the inside of a computer. Table sized printed circuit boards fill the room. All over, black bread-loaf-sized chips sit stacked on end. Salami sized resistors and Frisbee looking capacitors lie welded into the old time boards sparkling with light. Four dozen ceiling fans spin furiously. Colored wires hum, engorging with packets of data pumping through their core. The researchers rush in to catalogue it all--but there is too much data. It floods their systems.

"Doc, we control forty-seven of her servers."

Remold surveys the last fan, her security back door.

"You've done better artwork, Mina. So this is your City-museum? A computer named Clipper? More art then usable tool, I'd say."

"The product of ineptitude is the need for proof."

"Same old Mina, art and the use of entropy for the current truth. Only Mina knows how to use it in real life. Mr. Wolf, kill the servers." The fans slowly stop. His eyes seek out the last moving fan. "And so there is our link to the Boiler Room. Proof of the John Doe, or just proof you're in Seattle, Mina?" Remold cuts into the nearest object, a wire. Small sparks arise and the scenario begins to reset into sets of flat pastel blue planes.

Computer code begins to fill the space in front of Remold Jaka. The fans start up again. Remold cannot believe what he sees. His tools say computer code has simply come into being.

"How did you do that Remmy? Oh, you didn't." May begins spinning in a rapid circle.

"Doc, she just burned her entire sub-net. Crap. I get three nouns, John, Doe, and Seattle. There is no way to get more on her location."

The Rost, May, begins spinning, blinking in and out of the scenario. "Remmy, you set me up. And that ego of yours was quiet? Never. And what the hell do you have against New Zealand? What is this? Oh damn, you don't know."

"You are so predictable." Remold shakes his head. "I am just better at this than you. John Doe--the person who crosses over from reality to reality--is a myth, Chump."

The Rost begins to laugh. "Now it makes sense."

"She's locked us out. We're in a set of computers at some bank in Singapore. Thirty-seconds until their security systems shut us all down and toss us out," says Einstein.

"Mina, I am the one who taught you about the use of art as energy. It's unreliable. You can't make it idiot-proof because art is subject to chaos and interpretation. That is its strength and its weakness. You know the moment a John Doe crosses over it would be madness as our reality gets pierced by the others that follow. It would be the Home Fires scenario in real life. No one could cope with it, entrophic-boost or not."

"I always did overestimate you. FairGame is filled with madness. People kill each other for sport. What if John Doe dropped into madness? Who'd notice? And who says others would follow immediately. Or if they did that, they might not survive. It could take generations for a second one to get out."

"I am not going to argue myth with you--again." With those words the scenario begins to lose color.

"Remold, our species will grow--even if you are left behind."

"Don't kill others just to prove me a fool. We can run tests. We can run small scale prototypes."

"There is nothing left to talk about."

"You will kill over a billion. Where will they go? How will they live? It will be chaos. Mina, even if you are right, they will hunt you down and kill you for destroying their heaven."

"What an ego."

He points an index finger at the young girl. "Override, Jaka-one." Flames form falling icicles, clattering to the ground. "Nomenclature?"

They form words:"John Doe."

"Are you sure you don't mean John Galt, Mina?"

Then the face of Mina appears over May's spinning gray face. She stares at the words. "That's what I thought. Damn, you are a dolt. You didn't know anything about the crossover. You are still looking at time as the essence, chump." May melts into a small silver puddle as Mina's likeness disappears.

"Where'd she go? Where is your bed, Mina?"

"We lost her," replies Dr. Wolf.

Wholack appears. "Jakainthebox, you are so easy."

"That's fine. But if you ever recognize the next step for us then we can talk about it."

The Wholack folds in on itself, then blips out. The digital ground beneath them begins to rumble.

"How many servers did we trash?" Remold says.

"Fifty in all. That's a fair part of her network. It will take her days to reinsert a secure sub-net."

"No less than three and no more than four." Remold Jaka has bought himself more time to find Mina and stop her from shutting down Wholack.

"Doctor, I don't think she was lying about John Doe. It was the only link she didn't have covered. It was where she kept her security codes. It appears that a crossover corrupted her code because of a genetic test sent out on the net. Us too."

"Bull." Remold looks around at the flat pastel planes. "Okay, maybe. Begin a system-wide search for anything current on John Doe or the Boiler Room. Check that blood test."

"It is gone. Mina destroyed it." Dr. Singh looks over to Remold Jaka, then at the other researchers.

"Check facial recognition from the net."

"Already done, Boss," replies Lazlo Wolf. "Nothing."

"Find a way to find it. I want hourly reports. Send them to Tana Reins as well. John Doe is a myth, people. Mina and her plans for destruction are not. Don't forget that. We need to find her reason for the pile of BS she has thrown at us."

"And if it isn't BS?" Doctor Wolf asks.

"Then we find John Doe."

"So we are about to feel the pins of outrageous fortune," says Dr. Monto.

"Not to mention the destruction of reality..."

With a snort, Remold leaves the game.

CHAPTER FIVE

SAFE CAMP

Black smoke rides the storm winds up from the burning mall. Fire engines have parked across the street again, but the firefighters remain inside their armored crew cabs refusing to fight the fires.

Hope pours a glass of water, watching the man posing as an Administrator. His eyes darkened by soot, lines of sweat drool dirt down the rest of his face. She cannot help but see the soot as some kind of hastily applied makeup.

"My named is Holiday, one of the Administrators for SeaPort. I could use that glass of water." She hands him the water. His joy in drinking clean water is unmistakable.

Blood leaks onto the floor.

The Destroyer bleeds...

Sitting down on the nearest stool, the imposter sees patron begin to pay their tabs. Administrators have a bad reputation and an Administrator bent on revenge for a wound is a deadly development. At best, it's a free trip across the street. The rest are just following the crowd away from a man who has the power to drop them fifty miles inside a FairGame preserve with nothing more than their skin for protection. A few of the exiting patrons wonder why he bypassed medical attention to enter the diner.

Hope knows this is not the Administrator that had the BAR. The height and weight are not even close. The gait has less weight to it. He stinks like a Target. One who has killed an Administrator and taken over his identity. That makes the sight of him a bit more palatable, but it does nothing to calm her. She stares at the face of John Doe. Fear chills her spine.

His blue eyes are so bright and there are no ghostly shadows about him or a blank stare. Glancing at a bloody arm, the shock of his existence is made real by his wounds. Her heart thumps in her chest.

Lester, the cook, and her partner in the business, enters the dining area from the kitchen carrying a first aid kit. It is against the law to deny medical attention to an Administrator. Having seen the man from the kitchen, Lester wants to get the man out of here as soon as possible. Angry Administrators mean something is going to happen, and given the contraband Wholack beds in the basement of the diner, this guy means death as well. Unlike Hope, he has no concept of John Doe as a harbinger of destruction.

Lester places the red nylon bag on the counter next to Hope. Hope nods telling him to go back in the kitchen and finish his work. She has seen Lester in battle and knows he has no issues with protecting himself in whatever way necessary.

Hope fills the water glass again looking at the uniform sleeve covered in blood. It has a hole in it, as if a bullet had passed through it--an odd event for a bullet-proof uniform.

He reaches out for the water. She sees a short grimace

from a man unused to asking for help. "Another wound?"

"Nothing serious."

She circles back to fill another glass with water. He watches her in silence, not opening the bag, or looking over to the medics in the parking lot.

Placing the glass in front of him, the counter now between them, she notes that distinct smell of someone who hadn't had enough access to clean water for a long time. It's greasy smell, from the combination of urine and sweat. Oddly, the dark green uniform looks mostly clean, other than the soot and blood. The shoes are right, standard military issue, but the Velcro is crooked. As if a child had put the shoes on--or someone in a big hurry.

His dark eyes are so weary...

She opens the first aid kit, and notes a phone to call medics. He watches her. "I won't call." She unrolls a small bandage and pulls out some antibiotic spray. "We need to get this shirt off you and get you clean. The stink is a giveaway. They are bound to find the Administrator's body. Their bodies are always found."

"The tracer?"

She nods.

"I pulled it and inserted it into me. It's my other wound."

She grimaces at the thought of how much that must have hurt. He stares at her; his breath slowed, as if he were an animal in the woods stilling its breath to keep the sound down. "I believe the bullet passed right through me. The bone doesn't feel broken." She moves the torn sleeve. A spray of blood shoots across the counter. She covers it again, and reaches up to get an antiseptic soaked bandage. In a quick switch, she places it on the wound.

She watches the movement of his lips trying to get a glimpse of his teeth. Seeing this, he spreads wide in a ghostly smile exposing dirty teeth that haven't seen tooth soap in years.

She calms watching him stare at her. "You'll need a doctor or a medic to stitch that arm back together."

"You are known as someone who is FairGame friendly, Hope." His eyes wander to her hands as she grips the handle of the medical kit. Her hands are small, thin skinned and her veins are clear on the top of her hands. They are the hands of someone used to working hard. Her fingernails are cut short--not at all feminine.

"You know my name." She crinkles her lip smiling. "And so you think you know me?"

"I was in that quiver for almost a month, watching you, the Hunters, the traffic, the security," he pauses. "And the rest of it."

"Rest of what?"

"The food. Longing for it became my hobby. I studied the food. How it was delivered, sometimes the smell came across the street, mostly when you cooked spaghetti, or some other Italian meal."

"Canneloni."

He grins. "I'd smell the food. Watch people eat, my stomach would hurt, but I felt safe in the quiver. Slept better too--I think. Sometimes I'd think about coming across the street early in the morning, before you did your early morning run. Did you see me?"

"I knew you were there so it wasn't hard to keep track of you. What was it like? I am not being morbid. I have a friend in FairGame."

"Tovar Dal, everyone knows that. I tried to make contact with him."

"Did you see him?"

"No." His eyes wander the empty diner. "I thought him a fool. Then I crawled up into that quiver, watching life happen. Your man is not a fool, but you know that."

She ignores the feint. "I just wanted to know how tough

it is on him."

"You want to join him?" He asks scratching a flea from his chin.

"Truthfully no. I wouldn't last a day out there." She looks around. "I am sorry you had to sit out there, hungry, and watch people eat." She will not offer him food. She is counting on an anesthetic to put him to sleep.

"The toughest part wasn't watching you serve the food." She steps back.

"It's not like that. I have a wife. You remind me of her in fact. We used to eat communally--back home. She served the food. She liked doing that."

"Where is she now?"

"I don't know."

Hope nods. "You are the guy who figured out how to breach DEI?"

"Are you going to help me, or rat me out?"

She watches three Hunters cross the parking lot and enter the diner. The men and one woman eye each other, like hungry cats ready to feed. She leans in. "You're busted. Do you trust me to anesthetize you?"

"Only my arm."

"You won't like what you see."

"I just took my life back from your FairGame insanity."

My FairGame insanity?

"I am not going to give it up like a dumb cluck off the turnip truck. I'll stay awake."

She watches the Hunters taking their seats. Not one of them believes he is an Administrator. "Come back into my office. The light is better, please." She watches him stand and notes his wobbly legs. The people with the weapons appear ready to pounce, but no one wants to make a mistake with Hope Weiss. Everyone knows Hope is a woman to be reckoned with. No one else has made a go of it this close to a FairGame preserve.

She leads the fake Administrator between the twin metal doors into the kitchen. "Lester, you call the glass people and the insurance people. Tell Carmen we are going to be busy. Keep an eye on the three idiots in the front."

"You sure about this?" Lester stands by the oven, a sawed off shotgun in his hands.

"Put that away. Anyone who goes into FairGame is just that, a fair game, Administrator or not. Our guest here has won and now he's free. It's as simple as that." She looks at the Target. "Only we expect you to remember the favor, Mister…?"

"Holiday, Doc Holiday. Badge number 0345232. Interior Department Office of Park Administration."

She looks down at the badge. "The numbers are right. That was impressive. You have a great memory."

"Rhodes Scholar." He grins.

She takes him through the kitchen, passing the refrigerators and into her office. She kicks the door shut behind them and leads him to the chair in front of her big wooden desk. Motioning him to sit, she says, "You had the numbers correct, total recall?"

"Just because I am a Target it doesn't mean I am an idiot." He sits on a chair examining the computer monitor and keyboard, resting his arm on the desk.

His face is a perfect match for John Doe--but he seems so ignorant.

That bothers her. She keeps wondering what he knows and what he doesn't know. "Do I get to know your real name?" She asks.

"Truth is an overrated system." Looking around the office, noting the single door. He is trapped here. "I am Doc Holiday--the bum."

"Nonsense."

He smiles. "Okay, fine. Then call me John Doe." He

sees her eyes widen with shock and wonders what he has done wrong. "Don't you don't like the name John Doe?"

"No matter," She says, pulling a syringe from a medical kit under the computer desk. She works to control her breathing as she loads the syringe. "Why John Doe?"

"Why not?"

"Was it personal, your killing Holiday? Did you know him?"

"Nope. Just the wrong guy at the wrong place. Word in the forest is that the guy was a crook. That's a local right?"

She stares at the syringe trying not display a lie, or her fears. "The forest? You are from up north?"

"Puget Sound, near Anacortes." His eyes glaze over from a dart of pain.

"Long trip. What are you doing all the way down here? Getting through the traps in Edmonds is a nightmare. They're insane there."

"Took me almost a year." His eyes seem lost in some memory.

"It has been a long journey. Are you digital?"

"I have no idea what that means."

As she carefully injects the anesthetic into his arm. She wonders if it will have any effect on him. "Are you an invader, a digital persona?"

He looks at her as if she is crazy before he closes his eyes, too weak to consider the odd question any further.

CHAPTER SIX

TOWN ALLOWS ALCOHOL

Remold Jaka tells himself Mina is insane as he stares through the glass doors to the veranda. Watching the forests of the Palisades across the Hudson river, he keeps asking himself if he could be wrong. If there is any way tossing a couple of billion people back onto the planet could ever be worth it? And why do a fifty million Rost prototype to prove the concept? There is no way I would miss it. She could have destroyed a thousand and I'd never have noticed it. But fifty million Rosts, what the hell for? It's a waste of time. He refuses to consider the existence of John Doe as a factor.

Backing through the swinging door, he walks to the kitchen mumbling, "It makes no sense." Crossing to the refrigerator, Remold presses the red rat-faced magnet on the refrigerator door. The large gray lips of the rat face move, the black tongue wagging with the words. He hears: "Rodent

Pizza. Oh, Doctor Jaka. Hello. What will it be today?"

"A small pizza, extra basil, extra onions."

"System says check your printer--have a buzz-day."

Remold glances at the food printer in the corner. Crowded with plates from some meal he cannot remember, it finally dawns on him that the room smells like bad meat. His staff long ago gave up delivering gourmet meals for him. Remold likes his world messy, but the Rat Pizza print heads need cleaning.

Finished clearing the print heads, Remold places a plastic plate under the fifteen print heads and hits the go button. In Remold's time, no one would consider an automobile to deliver anything as unimportant as a pizza--so long as you can afford a fifty-thousand-dollars fast food print system.

The print heads move, creating his pizza, starting from the crust.

Taking a half bottle of Pinot Noir from a refrigerator, Remold opens it, and sits back on a metal chair. Leaning against the wall and sipping from the bottle--he feels his eye twitch. Watching the food print head move in ever widening circles laying down a cooked pizza crust, he rubs his eyes. "Fifty million? What the hell?." A smile comes to his face. "Poor little Princess. She must have screwed up."

The bell for corporate email starts ringing. Researchers are delivering reports on Mina. Just after he returned from Kittens and Cradles, his head of security, Benson Fong, had called him saying he had another lead on Mina. She was on the run inside a sub scenario of Home Fires--a post-apocalyptic scenario that revolves around the nightmare of extinction.

"It figures," Remold had said. Home Fires was Mina's project. It caters to an audience that demands more and more outlandish endings. As a result, Home Fires has gotten more and more bizarre as the years have gone by. Not unusual, but the complexity has prompted Benson's security group to assign a dozen full time teams watching for terrorist activity. The day she left, she had said she was chasing down a reoccurring loop in Home Fires. Then Remold found her gone. Mina, Benson reported, had been planning her exit for months--through Home Fires.

The bell rings on the email system, this time three short beeps. It's investor relations about the shareholders meeting. The Laughs Unlimited stockholders have been demanding higher stock prices. Even though Laughs Unlimited is by far the largest and most profitable corporation on the planet. So the email, he knows, will be another suggestion on how to do that. Remold hates stockholder meetings. The meeting promises to be energized with greed--another reason for the bottle of wine in his hand. He has trouble hearing the demands of people who have far more than they need--when they disdain those who do not have enough to eat.

Taking another swig of wine, thinking what to do next, Remold concludes his plan to track Mina back from Kittens and Cradles is a failure--though burning down all those servers of hers and gaining another three days is a plus. Telling himself she can't be happy about him gaining those three days, he smirks. Still, she got away.

The smell of pesto sauce begins to fill the room.

The email alert chimes three long rings and three short rings. He gets up, walking out of the kitchen to the alcove under the stairs. This email is from his personal assistant.

Leaning over the screen, he notes the email says that an Administrator has been killed. Scanning the email he wonders why the email has any importance for him--until he sees it tied to that blood test for John Doe. Remold instructs his assistant to follow standard procedures.

A set of low growls come from the kitchen. The pizza is done. Pulling some silverware from a drawer under the bay window, he gazes out at the windows. "What the heck is the use of fifty million Rosts?" Crossing to lunch, he spears a bead of provolone cheese and turns the fork to capture the stringy morsel.

The phone rings. He listens for a series of clicks, but instead hears a female voice. "Remold, it's Tana Reins." It is his personal assistant, again.

Dr. Jaka sits quietly, staring at the cheese on his fork.

"Remold? You there? We need to talk about this John Doe blood test." The phone clicks off.

He eats the cheese.

Again, the phone rings. "Remold, Hope Weiss did the blood test. This guy John Doe showed up at Hope's diner after the mall was razed. Oh, did I forget to mention that?" Tana is angry. She hates being minimized. "Call me? God, I hate this job." Disconnect.

Jaka bites into the pizza. Chewing slowly, he watches the fluffy clouds drift over the river. "Dial last," he says.

"Remold?"

He swallows the pizza. "So are you upset with me, Ms. Reins?"

"Far from it." Sarcasm fills her voice. "Did you sell the land for the NewDay Mall?"

"No. But I did deliver a cornucopia of supplies to the Targets, all useful for fucking over the Croakers. Did they tear the hell out of the mall?"

"Stripped it to the bones. Your little bit of altruism cost you almost five-hundred-and-twenty-million dollars and those other investors are as angry as a nest of wasps. Benson is increasing security for you at the meeting."

"And Mister Doe?"

"We have a problem. We were able to reconstruct the genetic data. We found out it came from a low level medical computer in Seattle. So we grabbed the hard disk. It appears a dead man, not a crossover, has shown up. "

"Dead?" Remold chews his food. "This happens often enough, people drop off the grid then reappear. Nothing special." He sips wine.

"This isn't your basic FairGame escapee who found a Wholack bed. This man has a pure genetic match to a man who died twenty years ago." She hears no response listening to him chew and think.

"So you think a counterfeit genetic ID interests us? Why did Mina do it?"

"Remold, I scanned the security feeds by the mall. His face is an exact match for that John Doe. The one in the Boiler Room. Also, I hear from a little bird that your jaunt into Kittens and Cradles yielded a message regarding the name John Doe-- and it tripped Mina up."

He scratches his chin. "She did it. She needs more time."

"She did not do it. She got caught in a random event and you picked up three more days to stop her. You were lucky."

"So it appears to you." He shakes his head.

"So it appears to all your researchers. They wanted me to tell you."

"There is no such thing as a crossover from one reality to another and we both know it. And there is almost no possibility it could happen at just the wrong time to screw up Mina." He waits for a response. "So you know it's just a scam, right? Something Mina cooked up. All of a sudden a Target named John Doe appears with a mystery genetic match, the right facial features, and is linked to Hope Weiss--while we fail cornering Mina in a scenario. Spare me the bore of her games. Get real Ms. Reins."

"You are an ass."

He sips wine. "A diagnostic system, or a medical lab?"

"A retail unit--at a Biner and Feiss Drug Store."

"Bullshit."

"We have video of the delivery sequence. Hope Weiss

delivered the blood sample and we caught it. Guess who show up in the genetic match?"

"I was waiting for the punch-line. Who?" Remold asks chewing crust.

"We are reconfirming, but the genetic possibilities include a certain dead washing machine salesman named Gus Plow."

"The guy who killed Jennifer Biner's kid?"

"The very same. Say Remold, I understand from that same bird there was a reference to an impossible time stamp, and a reference to the Eden sequence, that House you built for Jennifer Biner. Golly, that must be Mina setting you up."

"Subtle, where is he now?"

"With Hope Weiss, at her diner, planning his escape, I assume."

He muses, "So you still think Mina is in FairGame?"

"Looks like a possibility. Not a bad plan."

"You're wrong." He snorts out a laugh.

"This is why I hate this job, Remold."

"I know. Why not use this disguise of Administrator to your advantage? It will get him away from Hope Weiss."

"I have. There is a hunt planned for the new divisional execs. I am arranging to have this Administrator lead it."

"I see. Where is the hunt?" Remold wipes his chin.

"In the Willamette--I am going to develop a side tour of my family's generators. Just he and I--and a Biner and Feiss cocktail. By the time I'm done, I'll be able to tell you the color of his knickers. If he is just a ruse, courtesy of Mina, he is toast." Tana is an avid Hunter.

"Do you really think truth serum will work on him?"

"He is a Target three years inside FairGame. Leave it to me. You go enjoy your stockholder meeting."

"Anything else?"

"Tovar Dal, he is the key to Hope and I still say she

knows where Mina is hiding. Remold, what is our stance on him? I know what Tovar did to you, but it takes two to tango. We could use Hope's help on this."

"And you called to ask about dance lessons? By the way there is a seedy cowboy bar in my future--courtesy of Louise. Download a two-step dance routine for me. I want to shine." He sips more wine hearing Tana sigh.

"I already sent in a Carlos to make sure you are safe. What about Tovar?"

"Tana, I am less inclined to hold a grudge against Tovar these days. My own mistakes make his indiscretion with Mina seem minor. He is not to be hurt. You make sure of that. Are the documents ready to pull him out of FairGame?"

"The documents are just waiting for your go-ahead."

"He could be an asset as well if we have to work with this Target. Any changes at the Memorial?"

She laughs. "The Boiler Room is still waiting for you. The hologram is still there. Seats remain perfect, no visit from the Wholack--or Santa Claus. Nothing has changed."

"Ho-ho-ho." He takes a bite of pizza. "Did Doctor Wolf send you the backup of the Kittens and Cradles scenario?"

"What is left of it--they are going to rebuild it."

"Light a fire under them. Hope owned it once. I want to give it to her as a peace offering. Why isn't she screaming? Why did Doe kill the Administrator? Are you sure he killed the Administrator?"

"Not yet. I will know after I meet with him. Boss, you are far too calm about all this, given the timing and the appearance of all this. Perhaps you might skip the stockholder's meeting?"

"I wish. My attendance is worth a two percent jump in the stock price."

"Which means bupkis if Mina brings down the system or Mister John Doe destroys reality."

"Don't bother me with trivia." He sips wine. "Tana, I

want to know what this fake Administrator knows." Remold stares at the remains of the pizza. "I don't mind being bothered about this during the stockholders' meeting in Santa Cruz. Also make sure Mister Fong gets a copy of the data as well. I'll talk to you soon so we can decide on what to do with John Doe. Oh, make sure the comely Louise Tubby attends the stock holder meeting with me. I do not want to offend her in any way. I think I pissed her off last night when I sent her packing."

"Just pray she doesn't find out you are the one who arranged second place for her in that Miss America Pageant to keep her on staff. Are you sure you want to risk the tryst?"

"Yes, mother."

"You are a self-indulgent man."

"I am rich and powerful."

"You are a fool and a lecher, Remold."

"Those are kind words for an old man."

"A creaky sixty-one-year-old drunk," she replies. "And a fool. And a paranoid."

"I am all that."

"You are that and more."

"And you hunt humans because like to kill them--and that's okay."

"If you had to work for you--you would also hunt humans. It's preferable to shooting the boss."

"You'd never do that. You own too much stock in my company."

Click.

Chapter Seven

Good Water

Two hours after the conversation between Remold Jaka and Tana Reins, the man who calls himself Doc Holiday wakes on a couch. He hears the sounds of voices, music, and cooking. The sound of workmen as well, installing new windows on the diner's front. He supposes the patrons of the diner do not know he is there. Looking at his arm he sees the blood has been stopped and a field dressing is in place. He cannot see the sutures so the fake Administrator hopes the suturing is right.

His arm is clean, while the rest of him remains covered in filth. The imposter had thought he had kept himself cleaner. He closes his eyes still seeking to understand what happened to him three years ago--as well as his entry into FairGame.

And what the hell happened to us?

Tying to stand, he finds he cannot. The anesthetic was far more than a local, but since he is still free and not in jail he lets it go. So far as he can tell he has been anesthetized for almost five hours.

He stumbles to his feet--then falls against the closed door to catch his balance. The imposter positions himself at the door frame and opens it to look through the crack. The cook scrambles back and forth--and from what he can see--the diner is full of patrons.

Closing the door, he looks back at the desk and sees a fresh uniform. He decides she has entered the van and retrieved the uniform for him. He prays he still owns the secret of who he had been before he was a Target. This man has no idea his concerns are merely the tip of the iceberg of questions surrounding him. The imposter also wonders if she took his DNA. If so, that means he is in trouble, but too late now for remorse; if she had been trying to do him harm, she would have just kept him anesthetized. Nonetheless, he knows it's time to go.

He considers that after years inside FairGame an armored truck and a disguise should make escape easy.

The keys.

The imposter finds them piled beneath the uniform pants--but the handgun is missing from its holster. Circling the desk, he sees two basins full of water, a razor, and a bar of soap. A toothbrush floats in a metal pan of clean water. He uses the water to wash his face and brush his teeth. The rest of the water is to clean his body as best he can. He pulls off the clothes, smelling his stink.

The filth turns the water black even though he is hardly clean. A small container of baking soda sits on the floor. He applies it liberally to his body. He shaves. When he is done, he looks around wondering if he should confront her or just run. Then his eyes note excess baking soda has fallen on the wooden floor. It blows out in small fan pattern by the corner of the mirror. Leaning over, he notes a worn corner to the floor. He looks closer at the mirror. A seam with the wall lies hidden behind the mirror's edge. This is a door of some sort. He wonders what might be hiding behind it.

At that moment, the office door opens. Lester, the cook stares at him. In his hand is a plate of cold cuts and a glass of water. "Time for you to leave, Sunny Jim." He places the plate on the desk and leaves.

Experience says that man is not his enemy. Though life as a Target, these last three years, has also taught him escape is always preferable to a fight when he doesn't know the odds. Eating, then dressing quickly, he finds the waist of these pants is too large for him. He tightens the belt all the way and tries to straighten the bunches of material. The man he killed had a large belly.

The gathered front of the pants looks ridiculous. Straightening himself as best he can, the man masquerading as Doc Holiday opens the door and walks to the back door passing the cook with a nod of thanks. The man ignores him. His eyes glued to his grill. The shotgun is out of sight, but close enough for use. The fake Administrator tries to remember the cook's name but cannot. His brain remains in a fog from the anesthetic. Then he sees the back door has a security bar across the back.

No escape.

Before he can check if it is locked, he hears, "Doc, these men are here to see you." It's her voice. His head hangs forward of his body, then he turns.

Damn.

Hope stands at the doorway to the dining area. Her hand by her waist curves beckoning him towards her.

The man calling himself Doc Holiday crosses the kitchen as Hope backs up into the dining area to point out two Hunters. Each is dressed in full camouflage gear. Their hats are pulled low over their foreheads. Their gear is top of the line. Scanning the rest of the Hunters and the construction people in the diner--grinning at his illusion of freedom--he sees he is still trapped, still a Target.

"Sorry about the locked back door. There are Hunters everywhere." He notes the smile on her face. Her white teeth and smooth skin seem aglow to him. It's sweat. Hope's eyes seem anxious, full of concern for him. She has not summoned him to the dining area to close a trap, but to propose an escape, he concludes. Amazing how parts of personality transcend truth while truth bends, he tells himself.

"We want to hire you," says one of the Hunters, glancing over to his friend, a smile on his face as well.

The imposter studies the Hunters. He has seen a dozen guys like this inside SeaPort. These men are killers, plain and simple, no sport, nothing to prove. These are just sociopaths with money. "What do you want?" He stands waiting for their response and notes they stare at his empty holster taunting him. Then the skinny one on the left speaks.

"We'll pay you a thousand to conduct us inside, now. We understand the cash is up front. We're okay with that. If we connect, we'll pay you an additional thousand. If we both connect, it's a total of five thousand. She said you would be amenable to the extra work."

The fake Administrator understands only part of all this. He measures the men, then himself, wondering if he could really turn from Target to Hunter. Watching her face, he sees a small vertical scar on her right cheek; it looks like a tear drop to him. "If you both connect it's ten thousand." His eyes have not left her gaze.

The men look at each other and smile. "Done."

His index finger curls. He points at their weapons. He has seen the Administrators do this on the hunt over and over.

The men pause, look around at the other patrons, then they unholster their weapons. The imposter calling himself

Doc Holiday inspects their weapons. He checks the breach for the bullets. Of course there are none. It is a crime to carry a loaded weapon outside of SeaPort. He sniffs the weapons. "Curare?" He asks.

"It's not illegal," says a man with the battlefield vest. The question and the technique, as well as the professional demeanor, have startled the men. Hope watches, curious at this turn of events. This man knows weapons and he is used to command.

He faces Hope. "Half the money will be for her--for tending my wounds. The FairGame accountants are slow to pay some times." He watches her nod. "My weapon?" He points to the empty holster.

"I put it back of the van, like you asked me. Don't you remember? Oh the anesthetic." Her eyes dart to the side and another pair of Hunters off in a corner. It's a team of four, not a team of two. Now his question is: Will he make it to the truck? It's illegal to fire a weapon outside of the preserve, especially at a person claiming to be an Administrator. As well he hopes his questions have raised enough doubt to allow him to get to the van.

He wonders how they found him, then loses the question in the need to survive. Hunting humans? The imposter remains stunned by the madness of it all wondering how that could happen in civilized society.

He has not yet experienced Wholack.

"Okay, let's go."

The men exit the diner. He walks over to the square step van. "You two wait here." The fake Administrator notes the other pair of Hunters leaving the diner. He does not note the two women and a man dressed like carpenters inside the diner speaking into phones. They are Remold Jaka's people.

The fake Administrator speaks to the two Hunters. "Tell your friends I am not contracted to help them so if they are fired upon I cannot help them." The Hunters look at their comrades and then back at him. They nod.

He leaves the confused men on the far side of the truck and circles to enter. Unsure of which key will work, he isn't even certain he can hack the gun codes once he gets inside, but there is nothing else to do. Approaching the door on the passenger side, he pulls out the three electronic keys shaped like small flattened sticks. They are sticky from the blood but he ignores that knowing the keys will work anyway. He used ones just like these to get into the DEI armory. They had belonged to the now dead manager of the store. On the second swipe of a key, the steel side door latch clicks open. He notes the filed indentation on the key corner and knows he will not forget which key to use from now on. He pulls on the handle and climbs up inside. The lights come on and he is surrounded by a workroom, a small desk behind the driver's chair, and a gun safe on the left. The door at the back leads to the sleeping quarters. The space smells of cigarette smoke. Shelves full of dried food and beer are sticky The work desk looks shabby and not well used. That explains how he was able to kill the real Doc Holiday. He had been a lazy man. The impersonator reminds himself to investigate that side of the man so as to keep others off guard. He glances around the room. The weapons are not visible. She has kept them, he thinks. "Damn."

Running the keys over the gun safe, he notes they do nothing. Looking around, he sees a lack of books. Figuring the guy was a moron, he moves his fingers around the edge of the desk and finds an ancient scrap of paper taped to the underside. Removing it he sees a code--though he can only make out the first five characters 4o38o. He enters "docholiday" substituting zero for O and an @ for the A. The computer monitor comes to life. The gun cabinet unlocks and the door swings open. A moment later, he is scanning the weapons. A second BAR stands in the cabinet along with grenades and four machine pistols.

He pulls out a pair of machine pistols and loads them. For a moment, he wonders what he might say if they ask about the antique rifle the Administrator had been carrying. He laughs at himself. They already see he is a fake. Turning, he examines the Administrator's orders for the week. He is surprised to see that the assault on the NewDay Mall was anticipated. The FairGame Administration had apparently been against the project from the beginning. He assumes the right people were not paid off and so the disaster last night was a fait accompli. A new communication blinks on the computer screen. The imposter then realizes he has no idea what Administrators do outside of a preserve.

With a sigh, he examines that new communication blinking on the screen. Then a problem: A hunt has just been scheduled for tomorrow at the southern end of SeaPort, in the Willamette Valley. It's a top priority--and they will be tracking his van. It is an important customer.

That's not good. The trip from the Seattle area will take the rest of the day.

He goes back to the gun cabinet, scanning for tools. The imposter finds penicillin and three small vials of antiseptic. He takes them as well wondering about Hope's altruism. Her reputation is well-deserved, but there is more. Had he gotten behind the mirror he believes he would have learned the fullness of her response to him.

Walking into the sleeping quarters, he sees a pile of liquor bottles and marijuana cigarettes. Pictures of voluptuous women of various races and ages decorate the walls. Their only common feature is huge breasts. Opening a closet, dirty uniforms cover the floor. He enters the bathroom and finds narcotics and a first aid station. He takes three white pills from a pill box and immediately this head clears.

Staring at a gaunt face and a terrible shave, he sees a scraggly man who looks more like a Target than an Administrator. The Hunter's game shows itself clear once again.

They think me foolish.

He removes his shirt, pants, and quickly cleans the next layer of filth in the shower. A new clean smell tells him he still stinks like a Target. He cleans and washes himself again. They will wait for him.

Exiting the sleeping quarters he dons another clean uniform and examines a calendar hung from the door. There are hunts all week long and he wonders how come the people from Laughs Unlimited requested this guy Holiday for tomorrow. They usually go first class. There is something about the hunt that might mean connection--and a day's head start will not be enough to escape--or he could go back into FairGame. "Fuck that noise. I fight."

A moment later he exits the caravan. The dutiful Hunters wait, their weapons at the ready. He guesses their guns are now loaded. He searches the area for the other Hunters and does not see them. That means they are waiting in ambush on the other side of the roadway. Even so he doubts either of them could execute a head shot from more than four feet away. The uniform he wears is bulletproof.

"Sure you still want to do this?" He asks. His head tilts slightly to the side. "It's a war today." He points to the firefighters who remain inside their cab.

"Damn right," says the bigger man.

"Let's go."

The men laugh and joke with each other. The imposter laughs with them. For a Target, a man used to being without weapons or resources, sleep or food, the challenge of four to one seems ridiculously easy considering a pair of well-oiled weapons and a bulletproof uniform. An old feeling rises; he finds himself feeling a sense of control. It has been a long time. He immediately reminds himself it is an illusion as he glances at the remains of the quiver by the destroyed DEI sign.

Police cars pull up. The firefighters scramble out of the trucks. A moment later, the fire trucks begins spraying the roof. The imposter knows the rushing water will be a huge asset for him. He does not know it was arranged by Remold Jaka's assistant, Tana Reins.

Making sure to steer the Hunters far from the fire-workers and their defense perimeter, he looks back at the diner, seeing carpenters walk to a work truck, not surprised to see no one looks after him. He tells himself his Hunters might need to be eliminated and considers the bravado of fools; their lives will depend on their stupidity now. The fury of water flowing over the building will make survival easy for the imposter. A decision is made. If necessary he will kill these Hunters. There is nothing else for this man now, except the clarity of survival and returning home to his wife. Even so, the sense of control withers again, squashed by purpose, lost in plans of escape.

They cross the street into the empty parking garage, walking over to the blown-out glass doors. Knowing he has become an animal seeking safety, he asks himself how many has he killed these last few years?

No time for that now.

Keeping an eye on the two men, he steps to the side, pushing them through a door hanging crazy from a busted out door frame. Administrators never allow those with loaded weapons behind them if they can help it.

The imposter notes their weapons are on safety just the way the rules say. He tells himself they will wait until they get to the ambush location to attack. They are trying to keep him at ease. A trickle of water drips from the ceiling.

Escape first, then the luxury of ego.

Ahead, the stairway is lit--the emergency power is on for the entire mall. The architect who designed the mall assumed battles would take place inside the mall and took every opportunity to provide redundant systems for power and other utilities. After all, the NewDay Mall is meant to be a shooting venue as well as a shopping experience.

Water dripping from the ceiling becomes a small stream as they ascend. The flow grows with each step. The firefighters are at work on the roof. He notes the floor grates and the small channels built into the side of the walkway are filling with debris--as well as pink water. The architects had not planned on so much destruction at once. Water begins to flow down the stairs.

The two men walking in front of him enter the first floor mezzanine. Water cascades from the roof. The fake Administrator notes the safety of their weapons have been disengaged and they move with purpose--toward the ambush site--he assumes. Turning the corner and passing a set of smoldering seats, he sees where he left the dead Administrator. The body gone, the crumpled tarp sits torn by bullet holes. The imposter wonders if Hunters came across the body and then came to the diner looking for him.

"Okay, we are in the hunt now. Release the safety of your weapons." In the distance, he sees two Hunters walking towards them. They move casually, their weapons at the ready their eyes scanning all they see, a bloody scalp on each belt, both drenched in firehose-water. The men nod. He nods back and they pass without incident.

A few seconds later the imposter and his two Hunters stop by the remains of the food court. Glancing up at the ceiling, the two men quickly look away. He stands closer to the Hunters. They step back. He steps closer.

"The Targets will be across the court at the far end, or outside. There are too many Hunters here for the Targets. We'll cross the food court. Then we will go up the far stairs to the DEI back door. There are a series of tunnels that emerge there--plenty of action." The men nod, knowing this man is their number one target. "All right, you go left. You go right."

The two men begin a pitiful parody of soldiers on a sweep--glad to get away from the man. Darting across the food court, the men move from pillars to over-turned tables. They move using movie-style hand signs. The fake Administrator moves carefully behind them, noting the kill zones.

At the far end of the huge oval food court, they stop by a busted up barricade of tables. Dried blood and small body parts are visible. The wild dogs have been busy. The fake Administrator points out a pair of curvy lines on the wall. The lines signal fresh water. "Do you want me to flush them out? It will mean first shot. If I get the kill, it counts as one of your Targets."

"We know the rules."

"There could be more than one," the imposter says.

"Is that what the curvy lines mean?" Asks one of the men.

"You're required to know their signs before you enter into a FairGame preserve."

"It's water," says the fat man. "I was kidding." He points to the water falling from the ceiling.

"You're the man," says the Croaker in a battlefield jacket. "We'll wait here." The imposter will kill that man first. The other man if he needs to.

Once he starts ascending the stairs, he hears the two men speak into their radios, apparently planning to catch him in a crossfire on the next landing. The stairwell roof collapses from water. Avoiding the debris flowing down the waterfall, the Hunters begin their attack. A few shots strike the wall near the fake Administrator. He beeps the Administrator's horn to announce who he is. A lone voice calls out from below: "Bull shit, Target." Men slosh through the water, approaching the landing.

He readies both pistols.

Bullets strike the railing and walls. The Target masquerading as an Administrator drops to the floor and rolls into a small alcove that had once held a stretcher. The flow of water makes it hard to breathe but he is impossible to see.

He hears a crackle from radios. Then, "Shit, I lost him."

Echoes from other radios in the remains of the ceiling above him. The two men with him are decoys. He hears a new voice. "Who gets first shot?" It is the voice of a woman. There are five of them. The Hunters laugh thinking they have him cornered on the stairs.

The imposter scrapes the wall with a knife. Hunters rush the sound from below. When they don't see their prey through the wash of water, they stop. The imposter appears, beside them, putting a bullet in each man's skull.

Other rounds ricochet off concrete. Two men are firing through the cascade. The imposter ducks into his hiding place, the stretcher station. When the men's weapons cough empty at the same time, he leaves his blind, rushing through the cascade of water, coming upon the men hunched over their weapons. They look up, their eyes wide, fumbling with their weapons. The would-be Hunters have no chance of firing. One man takes a round in the eye.

The other man dives right. A round connects with a battlefield vest knocking the man against the wall. Stunned by the force of the round against his bulletproof vest, the rookie doesn't understand the vest is there to save his life. The rest is up to his wits. Unfortunately, the man has little wit and pulls a pistol from his ankle holster. A single bullet passes through his forehead into his brain.

After the first drop of blood oozes out of the skull, the fake Administrator bounds down the stairs trying not to trip on the torrents of water.

One Hunter left.

The mezzanine is a maelstrom of bullets as Hunters shoot wildly in every direction. The sound of a fire fight always attracts other Hunters.

A moment later a female Hunter emerges from the stairwell. The fake Administrator fires a warning round; a hand grenade is the return. The explosion rocks the floor sending him to his back. He quickly crawls to a support pillar waiting and reloading. A moment later the woman bursts out rushing straight towards him. The imposter kills her and then reloads his weapons.

Making his way through the torrents of water and splashing puddles, he hurries down the stairs to the parking lot--but not too quickly. Administrators always move like they own the place--or at least that's the way they looked to this Target when he had spied on them. He tries to emulate the saunter until he crosses the parking lot and enters the van.

Hope sits at the desk facing him; a pistol on her lap, ready to take off his head. "Please sit down," she says. "Put your hands on top of your head."

He sits.

"Who are you? I know you are a Target and you are not an Administrator. So who are you?"

"I'm John Doe." He sees fear from Hope and it shocks him.

What did I say? The name?

For her part, she sees he is a man out of place--which somehow seems to make sense for her.

He continues measuring her and doubts she will kill him. "You helped me knowing I wasn't an Administrator. That puts you in trouble."

"Don't be so obvious." She points over the doorway. A wide picture of three administrators standing at their graduation is now hanging over the doorway--arms around each other. Scratched in blood across the base are the names of the Administrators. It is a rite of passage for Administrators: Their first kill. The man named Doc Holiday is in the center. He wears thick glasses and sports a bulky frame. The man's face is wide and the hair on his head is black not brown like the imposter.

That large frame had turned to fat, the imposter thinks to himself. Wondering how he missed the picture, he realizes she removed it. She is unsure of what she is going to do with him.

"Anything factual I tell you makes it sound like I am nuts. Besides, I don't believe you are going to turn me in because you didn't before. And here you sit--alone. So I think you will let me go. Regardless, I have nothing to say other than thank you and I am no threat to you."

Her eyes look around, a sense of safety in their drift. She sees the Administrator's telecommunications system built into the side console by the driver's seat. "I can just call the Administration."

"Yup, but what do you have to gain? With me alive you know I am at your call to help with any problems."

"Or to come back and kill me."

"You have already set up some kind of defense. You're not sitting here with me because you're afraid I might hurt you. And for what it is worth, I have no reason to hurt you. You could have turned me in when you knocked me out. More to the point, what do you want, Hope?"

"Your name. How come you were a Target? You're smart. You could have worked to retain your rights." She watches him to see how he is going to lie to her.

"Sometimes things happen we do not expect." He laughs at his own joke. "I was released from my contract with Laughs Unlimited. I was supposed to kill Tovar Dal."

She stares at him, surprised at the absurdity of his declaration. "You lie." Even so she decides to contact Tovar.

He no longer wonders about her connection with Tovar Dal and why she locates her diner here. The so-called Administrator continues speaking. "I was dumped bare inside SeaPort up north. Simple as that. My identity doesn't matter. I am FairGame. I am no one." He puts his arms down slowly making sure she sees he is not a threat to her. "And now I'd like to get the hell out of here. I am scheduled to conduct a hunt for a team of executives down south. I don't want to be late." He smiles and she sees clean teeth. Somehow that makes her a little less afraid of him.

Her eyes light with humor. "Doesn't it bother you that you are going to help some newbie Hunters from the company that dumped you into FairGame?"

He notes his mistake of thinking her a dullard. "Funny thing is I don't think it was Laughs Unlimited that dumped me in there. All I know is I received a ton of money and I never got to spend."

A chill rides her spine even though she knows this man is no Croaker. Hope has seen a thousand of them and this is not a killer.

But his face. He cannot possibly exist. Does he know about Wholack? I wonder.

He cannot fathom her confusion. "I am decent. You need not fear me."

"Mercy is an offense in the state." Her eyes wander around the cab. "Before you were railroaded into FairGame how long did you have before you were to enter Wholack?"

He thinks a minute. He has heard of Wholack, knows something about it, but apparently not enough. "Eight years and change."

Hope's eyes blink.

He sees he has made a mistake. The memory of the mirrored door rushes back to him. He thinks the doorway leads to either a sanctuary for Targets, some kind of underground railroad out of the area. He is wrong on both counts. "What's behind the mirror in your office?"

She stands quickly.

He has struck a nerve. "I once saw the esteemed Minister of the Interior enter the diner. Is your escape route finished yet?"

She walks to the door, smelling of lavender. "You know nothing, about me." Pulling out a cell phone, she snaps a picture of the imposter. The audacity of the act shocks him. She exits, closing the door. Rounding the front of the vehicle, glad now she did not contact Remold, she takes a moment to catch her breath. Hope believes this man is a stranger in a strange land. He knows nothing about Wholack. She will send the picture to Mina this evening.

He watches her from the passenger side window then pulls it open. "Hope." She stops and turns to face him. "Tell Dal I want to meet with him. Oh, also tell him I say hello Moose-cock. He'll know what that means. Then you can tell me about ignorance." He closes the window and starts the van.

What the hell is wrong with me? Why'd I say that?

A moment later the vehicle leaves the parking lot heading south for the rendezvous with Tana Reins, Remold Jaka's assistant, and her Hunters.

CHAPTER EIGHT
DANGEROUS NEIGHBORHOOD

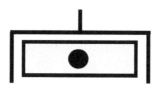

Reluctance to FairGame was never about the morality of murder. There was concern that the preserves might foster an organized resistance to the government. As a result, there might be attempts to instill order, or worse a separate government inside FairGame. Many do not know it, but the third Wholack revision, Corporate Apocalypse was developed so the leadership could model and simulate a defiled population in revolt.

The leadership saw the same disturbing results over and over. The rebellion always gains momentum and wins if the disenfranchised are uncontrolled. Corporate Apocalypse also taught the researchers population size is the key to keeping a handle on events. In Corporate Apocalypse, the masses always seem to triumph over the forces of government due an excess of humans and a lack of intelligence on the part of government about the plans of a huge population.

Corporate Apocalypse therefore became the poster-child of fear a few years ago as the mega-wall separating the warring parties was continually beached with surprising ease--a complete loss for those players on the inside of the wall.

A think tank, Rader Enterprises, was hired to explore the safety of FairGame. Using the so-called Dirties sub-scenario, their studies exposed one major weakness of the masses; killers with free access might have stilled the revolt. A firm barrier had no worth and Hunting should be encouraged deep inside FairGame. For their work, Rader Enterprises gained the right to take over the Park System. With that conclusion, the development of FairGame was allowed to expand. The Park Administration and their Administrators would exist to address fears of organized resistance inside the preserves. Their armed forts inside the preserves supporting periodic escalation of the Hunter's capabilities, their objective: To stamp out any chance of resistance or ongoing research by the Targets.

Fear was again heightened three years ago by the entrance of Interior Minister Tovar Dal into the SeaPort FairGame preserve. Considered a protest against the FairGame preserves, the Administrators keep an eye on him, but even with his presence, there has been no increase in organization inside FairGame. Many therefore wonder why Tovar Dal exiled himself inside the preserves.

It is because of guilt, betraying his lover, Hope Weiss. She does not know this, yet.

The day begins with a muddy stink. There is a pause in the storms that rake the preserve, and the entire Northwest today. For the time being it is cloudy.

Inside the favelas, old strip mall walls wear layers of posters, some thick as an inch. Many proclaiming that help is on the way, others warning of the further intrusions by Hunters. In rotting buildings, feeble men and women stare out the windows watching every event and seeing nothing.

Nature has its way with most of the preserve now. The dirty canyons deep inside the FairGame preserve have not changed much over the years. Dark and run down, trees and foliage covering the roadways, the parking lots, the lawns, the broken-back homes, the semi-urban area littered in nature, strip malls stripped, cars sans gas, doctors unknown, the only items in abundance are lust, indignation, and pain. Dried blood--even the most grisly wash--turns pristine after one of the frequent rains. Just add water, the huge amusement park is virgin once more.

One anomaly is the Administrators' compound. Behind a ten foot high concrete wall, well guarded, well tended, with green lawns and a coffee shop inside, the Administrator's haven is five square blocks of clean. Scattered throughout FairGame--they are guarded forts--locked down and protected. The gates secured and manned all hours of the day and night, Targets mistakenly see the Administrators as a form of law--rather than occupiers of the wilderness--so they are never attacked. Even though sometimes their forts take in a wealthy wounded Hunter.

A collection of black tar roofs and dirty brown buildings surround one Administrator's fort. Called Fort Phillip, the compound is a mile inside SeaPort near the NewDay Mall. The surrounding favela is the home turf for Tovar Dal, a killing zone for the uninitiated Hunter, a slaughterhouse for Targets, and a ghost town when a safari of skilled Hunters roll by in their armored vehicles on the way deep inside FairGame.

Tovar Dal lives in a dilapidated two story medical building on the edge of one lawless favela. Near Tovar's residence, by the old concentration of strip malls, far from the Administrator's buildings, people skulk about--but there is nothing going on here besides survival. Filthy men and women crowd doorways or sit on the curbs near the ruined shops.

The smell of urine holds every wall in its grip. Mounds of garbage fall with each week--never disappearing--as scavengers rifle through the waste seeking some lever with the Hunters. A morose adventure for the inhabitants, everyone wants to see their enemy laid out dead.

Inside the favela, the only entertainment is revenge. Most Hunters have no idea how dangerous a semi-urban environment can be. So the Targets wait for novice Hunters. When unskilled Hunters enter the area, sometimes there are gunshots, sometimes arrows, a few times the Hunters are poisoned, but mostly it's a gang killing as a group of Targets chase some poor Hunter until thrown stone and rubble pummel the Hunter into a bloody corpse.

Tovar continually muses how the residents seek out the entertainment of a hunt. This knowledge makes his imprisonment a bit tougher.

Just tell me, who deserves grace?

A fat white woman claims a burned car as her home. Sitting on a hillside with her back against a rusted fender, she listens and watches the town below her. The fires are mostly just smoke now. Her white hair dirty, her eyes still sharp, when she sees the flag at Hope's diner drop to half mast she gets up and walks down the hill. Crossing in front of the walled fort, she watches the pigeons sitting on the white walls of the Administrator's compound and her stomach growls.

Hours later, rounding a corner she passes two small metal shelves built into the walls of a building. Flies graze on the dried blood and pieces of molding flesh. Large enough to accommodate dead bodies, she notes both shelves are currently empty. The dead of FairGame are laid out here. Disease is the common enemy.

The woman crosses the street into an alley surrounded by blackberry bushes and plastic trash. She climbs up a short rusting staircase. Opening the door at the top of the stairs, she enters, knocking on the frame. Tovar Dal sits, leaning back in a wooden chair staring out a glassless window.

With a long thin nose, deep set eyes, a bony chin, the deep set lines of worry have become furrows in his tanned skin. Dirty black sneakers laced with cat gut cover his feet. His left foot rests cocked on the windowsill. Green canvas pants tied with a hemp rope at the waist and a dark blue shirt covers his bony body. Long thin hands are interlaced behind his head, the fingers tapping his skull in a drum beat to some rock-slop song from his earbuds. Watching the woods, he had chosen this place because he can see the forest and a stream.

"Dal."

He rocks forward, removes his ear buds and faces the woman. The lines in his face frame a smile. He brushes back the greasy once-black-hair with one hand. "Long time no see." They are old friends from his university days. Without her he would have no friend in this area. Tovar moves around when fearing for his safety, but she always knows where he is.

"Flag's at half mast."

"Thank you. There is food in the larder. Take what you want. I'll bring back a rucksack full."

She bends over slowly. Her old body aches. Slipping a finger into an empty knot in the floorboards, she lifts the wood seeing cans of tuna. Her eyes water taking a can and replacing the board. She exits the apartment. "Try to be careful, Dal." The woman's abrupt manner has no bearing on how she feels about Tovar Dal. He is, at a minimum, the greatest man she has ever known. So far as she knows, he doesn't have to be here. She would do anything for him.

Tovar walks the street, watching the other FairGame Targets for signs of fear. He sees no worry. Scanning the buildings and rooftops or sniffing the winds, looking around the ruined buildings, checking the larger trees towering around him, he considers how much longer it will be before the sun drops behind one of the buildings. He likes to time his arrival at the mall with early evening.

Turning the corner, he holds his breath seeing a set of large rectangular bins built into a building's wall. These coffinators, as they are called, hold rats who gorge themselves on the dead. In fact, when the coffinators are emptied from the bottom, it's not to remove the human remains, but the rats that have succumbed to disease in the dark structures. The dead rat bodies, once dried, are used for fuel.

A brown rat scurries over his sneakers. "Get lost you little fucker." Tovar feels the rats are waiting to chew through his flesh making a nest for their foul offspring in his organs.

Interestingly enough there are very few rats outside the immediate vicinity of the coffinators. Rat hunting is a sport here, a kind of rodent FairGame. It seems to Tovar the rats know this and stay hidden.

Feeling a bit of a chill, he has a touch of flu; he draws tight his coat. In five minutes he will be sweating again. But for now, he notes almost no one is on the streets this late afternoon.

"Tovar, you old pig. Looks like you made it through another week." A short man with a big stomach and ten layers of dirty clothes takes up a position beside Tovar. The man named Pard sniffs the air. "Man, you stink." He moves a few feet away and resets himself against the wind. "Oh, I see, you think they're waiting for us at the baths. How come?"

Tovar shakes his head. "No. We are safe. Besides we have already been shot at this week, Mister Pard."

The man maneuvers his body so he can block Tovar's trek. Pard hasn't slept in two days. "They're still fuckin' with me." He is a paranoid schizophrenic.

Tovar nods. "It all has a bad flavor."

"Damn right." He shakes his fleshy face.

Dal stops to speak to him. "What's up?"

"Where are you going, old man?"

"I thought I'd go over to my place outside the preserve and spend the weekend." Tovar grins.

Pard laughs. "Yeah, I can just see you watching sexy women dance at the local club. Pounding your meat under the table."

Pard was a former nightclub technical director who lost his job after making fun of the wrong patron at a nightclub. One night, at the close of a dance, Pard walked by the guy and tossed water down his back. Problem was the water forced the guy to stand up and display his limp problem. Two days later Pard was fired. A week later he was fighting a lawsuit that devoured his assets. Pard's insurance fund quickly played out. Within a month he was FairGame. The young man had been an executive with Biner & Feiss, a large pharmaceutical company. They supply the drugs for the Wholack beds.

Dal points to a slash along Pard's face just below his ear. "Who did that to you?"

"Happened last night." He runs his hand along the dirty wound. "Some crazy fucker set a crossbow up on the street by my place. I got home and thwap--this fucking black arrow flies by. So there I am bleeding and some kid-hunter comes at me. I took care of him though. You know, one-on-one they have no chance against us. He displays an expensive hunting knife with a black pearl handle. "I swear the bastards are getting dumber and dumber. Those fuckers will never get me. They're too stupid."

"Fight the good fight, Mister Pard."

"They're trying to torture me. I know that. I'm telling you it's that son of a bitch from the club. That executive from B and F Pharmaceuticals." He speaks rapidly, twitching like a fox in heat. His right hand grabs his bottom lip. "He's got people who do the research on me."

Tovar gives up. "You ought to be honored. The cost is astronomical."

"I'd like to say," Pard says, pulling on his lower lip over and over. "They're not supposed to keep bothering us here. Isn't that what FairGame is about? Freedom for us? Where's the fucking body wagon?" He refers to a wooden wheelbarrow often parked under the shelf of the coffinators. It is missing.

"Someone came and got it. I guess for a fresh kill. Why don't you go hunt the son of a bitch who is doing this to you? Find out who he is and where he lives. Fight back."

"It's against the law."

Dal begins to laugh in spite of himself. "What do you have to lose?"

Pard angers. He still hopes to see Tovar Dal tossed into the coffinator before he does. "You're not so damn smart. If you were, you wouldn't be here with us."

Tovar sighs. "So you think it's that guy from the night club?"

"Who else? Oh. I hate that reincarnation shit." He looks up and down the street. "I gotta get the hell outta' here. This weekend I'm definitely headin' out. South to Portland or maybe even down to the sand dunes by the coast. You want to go? No way they are going to put me in a coffinator." He scans the roof tops then watches an Administrator's helicopter flying overhead. "I'll take one of those."

Tovar steps around him. "I heard some guy tried last year."

"That was the same guy who was asking about you. I remember now."

"Go to Salem. It's safer there."

"No I'm going further south. I'm going to go see some friends from the neighborhood. Maybe they can get me a job."

"Then maybe they're really not after you." Dal looks at the setting sun hoping Pard will not follow him.

"You're a stupid fuck, Dal. I was once a taxpayer. I know a lot of things. And you know what? I didn't fuckin' vote for you." He glances around then hurries closer to Dal. "You know what else? There is no way they're going to hire any has-been like you anywhere. Face it, man, you're the bottom of the food chain. Sooner or later you'll die so some rich son of a bitch can brag to their friends about how they've murdered the once-famous Tovar Dal. Your only legacy will be a scalp hanging over a fireplace as part of some dimwit's hunting display. It'll say RIP douche bag." Pard walks away, then stops. "I got a fat-cat after me. That's a hell of a lot better than being a random kill by some bored rich kid. I got a purpose in life. I'm important. You got nothing, Dal."

Truth is Tovar is amazed no one ever cared that he had become a Target and came to help him. He walks away from the crazy man.

Pard calls after him, "Hey, come back. What's the matter, Dal? You're not getting sensitive on me, are you? Bastard."

Tovar waves good bye. He considers leaving this squalor every day now. Tovar does not because of an affair with Mina Jaka. He knows a life with Hope would mean he would have to tell Hope about his mistake. That would hurt her.

Hope might then betray her friend Mina. She'd never forgive herself--so he stays put. Ironically, most people around the favela know of his indiscretion. He does not know why, or how, but the knowledge has garnered a nickname for him: Moose-cock. The beautiful Mina Jaka had seemed an unlikely consort to the aging Minister of the Interior--at least to the Targets--so in a way he is a hero.

He could skirt it at all by revealing Mina's hiding place in the basement of the diner. That would solve so many problems, Remold's hatred would wane and Mina would be neutered, but since Hope also believes in what Mina is doing the option is moot. Tovar does not understand Mina's quest--

the way Hope does--but Hope trusts her. She has been a good friend to Hope. Tovar Dal remains trapped inside FairGame.

Ahead, a couple are bringing a dead relative to the coffinator. Dressed in deep blue smocks from head to foot, an old man and woman push a wooden wheelbarrow painted glossy black. It is the wheelbarrow Pard had been raving about a few minutes before. Blood trails the couple. A dark blue plastic tarp covers a body. A Target has died in a particularly horrible way. The blue tarps are used for disfigured corpses.

"What happened?" He asks with no attempt at remorse.

"They drugged him and sprayed him with red wash," says the older woman, watching her husband wipe his eyes. "Our son." Red wash is ground meat mixed with rat pheromones. It attracts the rodents and is often used by Hunters in the field. It has become a favorite of Hunters angry at a Target who has inflicted damage on a member of a hunting party.

"How'd they drug him?" Asks a skinny woman who appears from the shadows.

Tovar notes she looks like she might be blown over by a stiff wind. A rash of black stubble covers her upper lip and fat pustules dot her cheeks. Had she access to one of the more expensive nets she would have known the cure is free.

"It happened just outside of town. He killed a Hunter. Who ever got him was on that same corporate hunting team. We're not sure of how the drug was administered."

"He didn't even scream when they cut his scalp." says the man. "Look at his mouth." The man unveils a grisly body and a tight-lipped face. "He always was a brave boy. A manager at the Hood River wind farms."

"He had Wholack in fifteen years. When he came to us--it was terrible," says the woman. "He said he wanted to protect us."

It is common for relatives to enter FairGame to protect

loved-ones. The result is often the fate of this brave son. They are never prepared for the horror of becoming a toy--or the intense search that strips them of weapons or medicine. All they know is the Park Administration advertises its assistance in finding loved ones for anyone wanting to help relatives. He would have been fine if he had just entered the preserve as a Hunter. Of course then he would not have had the Park Administration's help in locating his parents.

The old couple, emotionless, dulled by a life of horror walk away. The old man will live another month before he is killed entering a Hunter's encampment with a loaded weapon. The woman will kill two of the Hunters from behind a tree. She will die a few minutes later.

Tovar soon enters the forest.

Climbing a short hill he sees smoke and the remains of the NewDay Mall. Walking down the hillside to the valleys leading to the mall, he scans the series of tunnels and blinds. The designers did a good job of developing safe access. The bloodshed was supposed to be inside the mall, not in the approaches to the mall. He will have no trouble from this point forward.

As a family exits a tunnel, Tovar Dal nods then enters the dark cavern. He wonders what emergency has fostered Hope's request for his presence. Hope almost never summons him. Mostly she just waits until he is ready to show up and then greets him with a kiss and a chocolate donut, telling him to go into the basement and clean himself.

Tovar smiles at the thought of seeing her and the coming shower. The stink of FairGame always identifies an escaped Target. It takes a dozen showers to remove it.

Daniel H. Gottlieb

CHAPTER NINE

UNSAFE PLACE

Standing inside the Green Room, Remold stares through the glass separating the convention center from the violent ocean. His weary eyes focus on a wasp caught on the inside of the building. Angrily riding up and down the light, entrenched in some bug theory of glass transcendence, the wasp charges the pane, apparently unimpeded by the pointlessness of its assaults. The glass does not give way.

Remold Jaka, PhD., analyzes the antics of the wasp, considering the wasp's plight, his own. Tired eyes closing, the game researcher, inventor of the Wholack game, corporate officer, beaten man; he looks up at the clock knowing it represents a barrier, the human version of the wasp's glass: The merciless wall of time in space. Staring at the clock, he again tries to perceive a universe beyond his own glass prison. The clock says 5:56. At six, it will be his turn to speak at the stockholder's meeting. Remold loves an audience. The corporation he founded, Laughs Unlimited, was supposed to be just a tongue and cheek title for a fool's enterprise: wealth. LUI, as it is listed on the NYSE, is now the largest corporation on the planet.

As a man of sixty-one, his skin assaulted by age, his muscular body beginning to sag, the moments of lost clarity, the young women who look passed him, Remold often goes out to see how the world sees everyman. Unlike his creation, the Wholack, Remold's face is unknown. The trip is always the same: people ignore him. Eventually, he makes sure his identity is discovered. He likes to win. He must win.

Occasionally, he considers disappearing into the wildly popular game to recapture the thrill of life, but he never does. Remold Jaka is driven by the crimes of his parents and the mystery of time.

The clock advances one minute. Ever since his father related a story of time's infidelity to man, Dr. Remold Jaka has studied the prison of time. This evening, he watches the sweep of the black hand on the white face of the clock, the inch high roman numerals, the arrow-shaped tip of the hands, and the round green frame of the wall clock. A long time ago he told himself the clock was just a face-well-recognized--one that made everyone its fool. He even told interviewers, the clock was the inspiration for Wholack--a smiling senseless face with no awareness of its control. The story is false, part of the media PR feed. Had he told the real story, the one declaring his father as a murderer and his mother's complicity, no one would have smiled.

His father's story. His story: History begins on a cold summer morning. "The beach was misty that morning." His father's would say staring out into the distance. "A man with red hair appeared on the beach near Marisol. He called himself Pilot Nothing..."

Then the story of how the man explained via chalkboard and reference that the path on which humanity was headed, global warming, ended in disaster. Remold's father had taken the man in and fed him, or so goes the story. A month later, the man who called himself Pilot Nothing was dead.

Before he died, Remold's father told Remold the truth-- as he saw it. "The man was quite daft. Pilot Nothing told me the future. He had no terms. He had no conditions. He was insane to have disclosed so much valuable information at no cost. Remold, my son, remember: There is no morality. Just opportunity and greed, it's all we have to work with. It's all we can count on from our fellow humans." Then Remold's father admitted poisoning the man with the help of his mother and dropping the body into the surf.

Remold concluded Pilot Nothing was not of his time. Further, the only way to know the future was to receive experience from the future. Remold Jaka's doctoral thesis was about that theory. He called it *Sentience*.

The face of time is the key to Remold. The wild-eyed Wholack is Remold's tribute to that mystery man and his father's crime.

The wasp slams against the glass.

Far in the distance, apparently unseen by the raging wasp, the ocean churns as a set of nine waterspouts dance in the undulating sea. Watching the antics of the bug, Remold clenches his fist--putting his thumb inside his grip and squeezing the digit tightly--until it hurts.

When he lets go, he waits for the sensation to drift away. Remold is checking if he is inside the game. More than once he has forgotten. It happens to everyone who plays Wholack. A game that allows players to recreate the physical world as precisely as they wish, without a flaw. Early players did little else.

Then people began trying to trick users into thinking

they had exited the game. The ensuing confusion between reality and the game led to litigation against Laughs Unlimited. The stockholders demanded a fix. That fostered the second version of the game, Home Fires. Mina had been in charge of that, supposedly making sure the confusion of Wholack and the real world did not happen.

In Home Fires, pandering to the troll, the Wholack, became key, rather than the adventure of the game. That the fool can show up like a devil and obliterate parts of reality only added to the allure. The Wholack could be an intruder to any scenario in Home Fires--unlike Saucer City where he had to be invoked by a player's mistake.

Home Fires seemed very difficult to win in the beginning. Until people learned that Wholack is controlled when he is fooled. That made it all so much more interesting, as people began to trick the fool into doing their bidding. It was an effective defense and people gravitated to the edges of the game establishing an idyllic home for escape and giving the Wholack unimportant scenarios to destroy. The game grew exponentially as people sought privacy and peace. The Baroque became passe and outlandish efforts of creating various Dadaist heavens became the normal. It was an elegant, artful fix to the problem.

Corporate Apocalypse followed six years later. Part of a government contract to research FairGame, the husband and wife collaborated on each step. For Remold it was idyllic.

Then one day she declared, "...Living inside the game makes it reality. Wholack can either enslave us or set us free."

Remold responded, saying "...Foolish conjecture passing for facts are useless..." And that she, "...Sounded like Tovar Dal, idealism and all..."

The next day she sat down to dinner and told him her name sounded stupid tied to his, Mina Jaka. "...A brand of underwear..." Over dessert, she announced her plan to put her entire life inside the game to prove her theory that Wholack could pierce reality and that Pilot Nothing was that proof. "That," she said, "Is the game's grand future." Remold had scooped a spoonful of pudding. "It has been proven over and over there is no crossover into other realities. If there were we would have seen it by now."

Later that week comments about Pilot Nothing began appearing on the nets--rumors of a murder. He concluded Mina did it so she could take over the company he had founded-- making him just the son of a murderer. At least this is the way Remold had read it. In a perverse way he was correct, though without the context of love, he remains completely wrong-- like most men.

Angry, confronting her, he told her the quest was, "Just an excuse for her infertility. Besides, Wholack was his and she would never equal his accomplishments inside the game. Pilot Nothing shall remain an urban myth." That was the moment she disclosed her affair with his younger cousin, Tovar. The moment lives inside him to this day.

It holds all the questions for Remold, but he misses all the answers; Mina once said that he had no heart. "Just a tick-tock in his chest, and a computer for a brain." For a moment Remold Jaka thinks about John Doe as a crossover.

The clock ticks.

His thoughts immediately dart to Mina wondering why she disappeared inside Wholack. His eyes stare at the wasp but he does not see it. All Remold Jaka knows is that he had a family and now it is gone.

He reminds himself that after she left, he had begun a year long search to uncover possible rips in reality from Pilot Nothing--to prove her right--and somehow get her back. Using every resource of the gigantic corporation to assist him, neither he nor his entire corporation could find a single aberration--or any indication that there had been a crossover from another reality. The breach of time by Pilot Nothing had been enough for her. He knew that, but a temporal aberration caused by sophisticated technology was an internal breach of time--not a crossover from a different reality in Remold's view. More importantly the murder was exactly the right course of action. With the death of Pilot Nothing, the paradoxes of time travel are eliminated. The murder in Remold's view is warranted. It eliminates temporal paradoxes.

On the other hand, had his father retained the genetic makeup of Pilot Nothing he would have proof of crossover, or not, but the body was long gone. At the end of a year, Remold gave up trying to prove Mina correct, deciding Mina simply hated him.

About that time, corporate paranoia boiled over and Corporate Apocalypse came into being. A completely new direction for Wholack, in Corporate Apocalypse, the Wholack is mostly hidden. Winning involves finding the Wholack's supposed death among the millions of casualties. He dies in a minor assault. So many failed, getting ejected back into Saucer City, Saucer City had a wait list--for the first time in years.

Then Remold realized there were two major classes of users in the game. Those that understood and embraced the exploratory nature of the game and those that sought only the nature of their enjoyment. The second group being far larger.

Ironically, children born into Wholack--as a fact of life--seek to create various bizarre private universes rather than bliss. This event, more than anything else, has made Wholack a worldwide addiction. People in Wholack now create either a wanted recreation of life, a Utopia, or an absurdity of their choice. Remold has come to understand bliss has many faces.

This all led to the fourth revision, GW, Global Warming. A scenario that seeks to blend the real world and Wholack--in real time. Wholack can now process feeds from security cameras around the planet making Earth's events available to the game.

The developers tool kit and the linking system for key scenario developers is being released today. It is a key reason Remold is here. Today is not just a stockholders' meeting. Remold Jaka is sticking his tongue out at his ex-wife by making the links to reality inside the game even more direct. Remold smiles to himself thinking how much that will irritate Mina.

Even so, to keep the mistake of reality confusion at a minimum, the scenarios will continue to wear a border of color at the edges of the planes. Stroke weight is at the discretion of the builder because the idea is to keep out litigation while making the sub-scenarios as attractive as possible. The Baroque builders of scenarios and the Dadaists builders are about to dance in the new style of Wholack: Global Warming.

Hail strikes the glass walls. The storms clouds roll upon themselves and march in to the shore--in a chaotic style no one in the digital gyre has yet to recreate. Remold stares at the clouds seeking to gauge their arrival. He and everyone else also knows that in a couple of hours the fortress-like convention center will be under attack by wind, water, and waves. That's okay, the building has survived much worse. The horrors of human forcing of the radiative balance are on the wane even though the storms remain impressive. Besides, the stockholder meeting will be over soon. The stockholders will then be wheeled to their cars, put on their aircraft, and quickly deposited back in their beds for reemergence into their version of Wholack. Those that view the meeting from the confines of their secure beds, from Wholack facilities inside various mountains, will simply switch off the external feed. The proxy-holders and their cameras will get into motor-homes and scamper inland.

Or at least that is the plan.

The clouds turn a dark out to sea. The buzzer in the green room sounds and the door opens. An executive secretary, a lovely blond-haired woman with perfect features, flat piercing eyes, and an upper class painted-smile stares at him. His current prize, this woman, came in second in the Miss America Pageant--thanks to Remold's influence. She should have won.

"They're ready for you, Doctor." Louise Tubby seeks privilege in Wholack and she hopes to get Remold to help her. Remold has a taste for seedy sex so she has a bar scenario with all the trimmings ready for tonight. Bars are the most common setting for inviting guests into a sub-scenario and it has been ready for weeks, but she also has found it tough to impress him. She failed again last night and wound up spending the night in the lab. She needs to get his interest passed her crotch, or so deep into it he is her monkey. Either way she will have access to his best research. Sex and satisfaction, or intrigue and talent, she believes, is a fair trade for achieving her desires.

"That's a bad storm. Do you have your transport ready, Ms. Tubby?"

"I was hoping to catch the flight with you. I could squeeze in next to you if there aren't enough seats." The little black dress with the Mickey Mouse face covering her chest is practically translucent. Glancing at her breasts, feeling hungry for her, he pushes by her, with a smile.

Her eyes follow his as he passes her. Remold is famous and wealthy, but he is old and droopy; while she is brilliant, young, and beautiful. The woman plans to stay with Remold for six months to complete her work, then disappear into Wholack--after finding him another trophy for his ego.

If Mina did it so can I, she tells herself.

For his part, Remold Jaka knows Louise has no real interest in him so the trade is fair. There is no way he will allow the shark access to his core research. Nonetheless, he plans to help her retire in Wholack. For Remold Jaka, the call of beauty is irresistible. Some men never learn to look beyond facts, others don't need to, while a few seek beauty as a kind of applause. Remold is the third type.

Dr. Jaka looks down the hallway and then back to her.

"This will be a short speech."

Her hand rides over a hook tattoo on her arm as she smiles at him. She has been staring out the window at the coming storm. Louise doesn't like storms--they scare her and so she scratches her arm again. Louise does not want to be here--but she does want to live forever as a beautiful ingénue. Some women never learn either.

Remold saunters along the carpet to the auditorium, buoyed by beauty, wondering how Tana Reins is readying for her meeting with the fake Administrator.

Pushing the curtain aside, he walks up on stage hearing a cell phone chime. Someone with access is trying to get a hold of him. He considers they must know he is at the stockholder's meeting and so a brief line of worry wrinkles the skin between his eyes. Remold glances down. Louise Tubby is on the call. She nods in the positive, nothing serious. He smiles, thinking her an efficient assistant.

The applause begins and he smiles into the crowd.

Outside, palms jitterbug in the coming storm. The overflow from the auditorium sits below. Watching video screens by the lagoon, or sitting in deck chairs, corporate assistants occasionally turn to face the storm. Seeing its fury, they turn away watching real time satellite images.

The glass wall behind the audience turns a light pink diffusing the mayhem of the Pacific Ocean. It is time to talk. Smiling, Remold points behind them to the coming storm. "I have a really long speech. Are you sure you want to keep clapping?" The audience laughs then ceases its applause.

It is a point of pride for these people to ignore the coming storm until the last moment. Partly out of respect, partly out of greed, the real reason for their cavalier attitude is the well-heeled stock-holders of LUI will soon start to make money from GW. They like to keep an eye on the game. In the process they have their beds attended to, cleaned, and refurbished. Of course a person can just require that their bodies be taken to another bed, but for many, it is a burst of noblese oblige. A few even consent to a three month shift attending to the battered planet and its devastated society. Their intentions are good, but the absurdity of their trek is often missed. They all believe there is no chance any of them will ever have to deal with the ravaged Earth on a long-term basis. As a result, a storm is an inconvenience. They do not understand the problem is persistence and repetition--not event. Remold Jaka has created a timeless Utopia of pleasure that even embraces their myth of service. It is another reason they all continue to clap for Remold Jaka. The Wholack game is their savior. And while the Wholack is the population's fool, the Wholack is also their God.

Doctor Jaka circles the podium walking to the front of the stage stopping at the edge of the proscenium. He scans the front row. "Ladies and Gentlemen, the developer's version of Wholack, The Global Warming Years, is as of this moment, released." Wild applause. "You third party developers, may now begin linking in and selling your products inside the game." More applause. "Nonetheless, now listen up, I am wanting to again remind you all that the contracts declare an increase from eight percent to ten percent of the revenues you garner. That should help the stock next year." Laughter. "Further, thirty per cent of the new revenues garnered by the release will be used to fund charities. That number will top the billion dollar mark this coming year."

Applause.

"That was the carrot. Here comes the stick." Laughter. "If we are to continue as the key corporation on the planet we will need to make some changes." He pauses watching the audience shift uncomfortably. They are here to celebrate increased profitability, not listen to some dirge of warning from Professor Jaka. Nonetheless, the audience will tolerate him.

There is no company that can match Wholack for success. In this age, there is no myth about competition. Laughs Unlimited, has won the game. Remold Jaka has created the most profitable enterprise the world has ever seen. While his game has reduced the impact of humanity on the planet Earth to pre-industrial times. Of course, in the process, Remold has redefined his species from hunter-gather, to couch-potato. Nonetheless, the reins on power are finally secure. The elite feel safe.

This man is a hero.

Remold continues, "The cost for our success has been immense. We have poverty on a grand scale. We are dealing with slavery and murder as civic enterprises. Society throws every kind of horror at the poor. So while we have a solution for our planet, in truth, that solution still puts over a billion people at risk and renders others useless to themselves and their families." He pauses.

A man in the audience speaks: "We have made our money. So have you, Remold. Give it up, Doc. We've won. Just show us the cheese."

Remold laughs smiling at the Laughs Unlimited shill who has made that comment. "Simon, there is more wealth to be made. Even so, we must continue to seek out the evil that seeks to overtake our humanity. The ancients called their evils devils. This younger generation calls these evils, addiction. They see addiction posing as sophistication fostering nihilism. They see addiction to Wholack as the root of FairGame, few remembering humanity as a fat bloated consumer of planetary resources. Our generation fixed that part, but we have more to do. Otherwise, the evil, the complacency that attacks our species will win. Again, I propose to the shareholders a resolution to take an additional ten percent of all corporate profits and funnel them into the FairGame preserves to help pay for basic human services, like medical care."

Polite applause.

"There's more. The resources of our planet are replenishing themselves at a rate we could never have guessed possible. That is a huge step forward--but it is not the answer. Our soul's tie to the universe is the answer. It is this we must seek through Wholack. Ladies and gentlemen, we are examining the very fabric, the stitch, the fibers of time, that constrain us. Questions and intelligent research are flowing from our labs like clean water. But that is not enough. We must deliver Utopia to all of our fellow humans--"

A loud thump interrupts his words. Those in wheel chairs roll forward, propelled by an explosion that sends the back wall forward. Metal, glass, and debris fly out in a deadly torrent. The wall behind Remold blows in as well. Remold Jaka protected by the podium flies forward into the first row of the crowd. Another set of explosions collapse parts of the side walls. A loud rumble, then parts of the roof collapse in, killing those in the back of the room. Smoke and dust fill the auditorium.

Corporate security ignores everyone in the building except Remold Jaka. Their mission is to protect the goose that lays the golden egg. A canine team with four men finds him within seconds. The back of his head is singed, but the bulletproof suit has protected him from flying objects, even though the entire back and left side of his body will be a mass of bruises.

Outside on a stretcher, Remold sees doctors and nurses. He stares at the fires, mangled bodies, the rotating lights of the emergency vehicles. Smoke from the burning building blows inland propelled by sixty mile an hour winds. Remold closes his eyes. Terrorism on this scale has been unheard of in this society for years--except as retribution for a failed business deal. He concludes a business partner has sought revenge. Remold opens his eyes and scans the mangled bodies as rescue workers move around the wounded. Louise Tubby soon lies beside him. She appears unconscious, a bloody bandage covering her shoulder. A severed arm rests on the stretcher beside her. He stares at a black hook tattoo on the severed arm.

"Remold." A skinny man with a top knot and a tan suit appears by his side. He looks over at the wounded woman and sighs. "We need to get you out of here."

Remold nods. "Who did it?"

"That was a thank you from the developers of the NewDay Mall."

"I see." Remold points to the prone woman as a pair of doctors appear. "Her first." They begin loading her onto a stretcher. "Why?"

"They say you knew about the attack, helped it, and let it happen. They found a cache of supplies the Targets used to breach the DEI store and tracked it back to you. The legal people are already on it and the stock teams are making calls into the stock exchanges handling the damage control. We're fine." Benson Fong is the Vice President of Security for Laughs Unlimited.

The winds send hail bouncing off body bags, tapping the furniture sent into the lagoon. "Benson, did Mina have anything to do with this?"

He shakes his head back and forth.

"How many dead?"

"A hundred dead, most everyone else is wounded." Benson turns away and barks at four men. "Get him out of here."

As the stretcher rides into the ambulance--the wasp from the green room misses the closing door of the ambulance--too tired from its earlier battles. The storm lifts the bug, pushing it back to a deck chair in the lagoon. It lands, exhausted.

Five minutes later, as Remold is loaded onto his private jet, the wasp braces for the squall. Sitting on a wooden chair arm, the bug will float through the night, snacking on the blood that smears the wood as the chairs in the lagoon provide a safe haven. Come morning, the wasp will be well fed and on its way home to the hills--having transcended the glass wall.

CHAPTER TEN

TRAMPS HERE

Glancing at the news report of the bomb attack, curious if Remold Jaka was hurt, Hope sits watching the computer-based news feed. Eating her dinner, surprised the police believe the attack came from the builders of the NewDay Mall--in retaliation for a lack of security--she wonders why the news suggests Remold has helped the Targets. Hope thinks Remold is concerned with computers, not people. The whole event surprises her. She does not know the developers of the mall risked everything thinking Remold Jaka could do no wrong--then found out it was all a plan to help the Targets. So it's no wonder they placed bombs at the Laughs Unlimited stockholder's meeting.

Hope does not know this kind of feudal behavior is more and more common. The major corporations begin to feed again: A new generation rushes into the breach to secure a home in the Wholack Game.

She gets up placing her dish in the washer, returning to the front while looking out at the smoldering mall. A traveling carnival has set up across the street and the sounds of its calliope echoes through the diner. This particular carnival specializes in sex. The mall parking lot has become an encampment of perversion and lust--death is so yesterday.

Closer in, between the mall parking lot and the diner, a paramedic unit processes Targets. A line of scalped bodies stretches out onto the road. Only one clinic remains bandaging the Hunters' wounds. Hope has heard the price of medical services has doubled in Seattle. These days the Hippocratic oath says: "Do no harm to your purse."

She wonders if she will hear from Remold. Mina's people have confirmed Remold knows about the blood sample.

On the steel and chrome counters, chocolate waits everywhere. Hope has been in a baking frenzy all evening. There is no vanilla or strawberry in Hopes-No-Apostrophe-Diner this eve, just chocolate. Semi-sweet-chocolate, milk chocolate, fudge, genache, mousse, brownies, lava cake, chocolate donuts, cocoa cookies, they are all here, but no other flavors. Hope believes there is no time for anything but chocolate. Angry with herself, Hope looks around at the busy diner.

Hunters covered with blood snack after the hunt. Most of them wear soupy smiles over blurry eyes--from carnival drugs. Nomadic carnivals have skirted the borders of FairGame for years. The carnivals cater to perversion and the Hunters are game for any new form of depravity. In fact, these carnivals birthed the notion a mall inside FairGame might make money. Though this appearance tonight by grifters is a poor substitute for the defunct mall. The non-stop sounds of gun fire, explosions and screaming has a new accompaniment: Hunters laughing on sex rides or amplified licentious moaning from inside the red and yellow carnival tents of the midway.

She ponders the comment from the fake Administrator. Moose-cock? Tovar?

Leaving the front of the diner, crossing back to the kitchen, she notes the dishwasher has stopped. Seeing the green light over the unit she knows the washer still functions. Not so with Lester, he sleeps, his feet in a bath of chicken soup. Lester refuses comfortable shoes, opting for stylish red running shoes. Carmen, the waitress, shakes her head. She looks beaten but happy. The tips have been good. "Boss, I need cheese, both provolone, and cheddar. Should I wake him?"

Hope nods at Carmen and exits the back door. The cloudy sky darkening, rain begins to drizzle again. A major storm is forecast for southern Washington State. Approaching from the Gulf of Alaska, the storm will skirt Puget Sound far to the west. No one seems worried, the dull landscape of cheap hotels and brothels remains packed the people who had booked shopping excursions months ago. Lights are on in every window. She curses the Hunters thinking about Tovar.

He gets sick so easily.

Turning to the locked walk-in cooler, placing her thumb on the lock, she listens for the click then the door slides to the right. The interior lights come on. She grabs two bags of shredded cheese and walks away glancing at the side streets and the line of vehicles. Lester thinks this month's profits should go for a car-hop to skate the lines of cars selling fresh coffee and donuts. People pay well for pastry since the men and women who sit in their cars for eight hours a day protecting cars are bored--and they have to eat--right?

A group of Hunters pass by. The females of the group act to ignore her. The men leer. Hope looks down at the door and understands. A pair of bright blue panties hang there. Common knowledge says Hope is a lesbian. So she winks at the passing Hunters. Hope knows mystery helps make a restaurant profitable.

Standing in the alley, listening to the kitchen she hears the sounds of the evening rush. The clang of pots and pans and the roar of customers. Coffee and chili mixes with the smell of chocolate.

She glances around once again. Sure no one is watching her, Hope spies a pile of wood under her office window. A small meter hidden in the debris shows an arrow just inside a green background. She'll need to load the nutrition system for the hidden beds as soon as possible. Otherwise, Mina and her team could starve.

Continuing around the side of the building, she notes it looks like Christmas up and down the boulevard; new colored lights grace the trees. The madness baffles her. The trees lights are a bizarre homage to what might have been, had the mall not been razed yesterday.

Does anyone really expect to rebuild that place?

Even so, the partially destroyed mall is going to be an ongoing source of first hand entertainment for Hopes's patrons. The pictures Lester took of the battles will go well on the side walls. Images of the collective memory also make a restaurant profitable and the destruction of the mall has been ongoing for every news channel since it happened.

She crosses the parking lot and looks at the diner's new front, considering the cost. The glass was replaced with an expensive bulletproof plastic. Internal bulbs and microprocessors inside the new windows color the windows maintaining the reflective effect of the windows. That way, from the outside, day or night, there is no way to see who sits at the booths or at the counters.

Tovar is worth it.

Looking up the GPS broadcast antennae disguised as a flag pole, she nods. This antenna is her first line defense against the mayhem of society. A firm boundary between purchased civilization and the jungle of FairGame. She uses the disguised antenna as her key tool in every legal battle. While other businesses skirt the Gray Zone, no one else is so close to the battle and still functioning.

The boundaries of the preserves are strict, but the twilight zone of mercenaries and the madness between law and the lawless makes the Gray Zone almost as dangerous as the FairGame preserves. It also makes business wildly profitable. Two years ago, many sought to emulate Hopes' model inside other Gray Zones. Of the five hundred businesses that tried to open, less than a dozen still exist around the planet. FairGame can happen to anyone. Their demise came from a barrage of law suits owed to the pique of wealth. The safety of civilized society has vanished. Except for those who wish to believe the past is still present. The rest use the myth to further their goals. It is the rush to escape the truth that is the tale of this society.

Hope enters the diner carrying the cheese. The crowd of patrons look over to her. Everyone knows her. The handsome men wink at her and smile. The chubby ones look away. She nods politely looking over their heads at the huge chronometer with its opalescent clock face at the end of the diner. It hangs between the bathroom doors. Red numerals circle around the edges of the oversized timepiece.

It's 9:30 PM. Where is he?

Face high, the clock was once embedded into the remains of a church that used to stand across the street. When the church was razed, Remold Jaka bought the chronometer and gave it to her--a tribute to her courage--he had said. Truth is, after Mina left he made a brief play for her--a brief revenge play--until she explained her heart belonged to his cousin Tovar Dal. Remold never spoke of it again.

A pair of gilded gold-leaf picture frames perch on either side of the clock. On the right is a copy of a speech given by the developer and creator of Wholack, Remold Jaka, another gift from that time. It says:

"Wholack is our universal animal seeking to understand and accept a place in a universe that has no concern for it. Some say cowards will enter Wholack because they cannot cope with the mysteries of our future. Some say the whole concept of Wholack is the ultimate corporate monster. Others call it the only definitive form of human freedom: Ownership of experience, life, and death in an uncaring universe--could we ask for more? Truth is, in Wholack, we have created a place where we may choose our freedoms or we can ignore them all together. We can make chaos our lover or our enemy. We can mourn or we can fly. I find this freedom both refreshing and horrifying. One thing is certain: In Wholack we will have conquered the definitions we receive from birth about reality. With no sense of our own pains, or the rot of time degrading the carriage we call a body, death will be an end for us like the beasts and the fauna, in ignorance and grace. With Wholack we have made paradise out of a struggle with an uncaring universe." This original manuscript is worth a fortune.

The other gilded frame contains a quote by the former Minister of the Interior, Tovar Dal. This second piece of memorabilia is worth nothing. The words say: "The not-so-distant future rushes at us like a hundred million train lights, a gift from the universe to our species. In Wholack we must not choose to ignore a gift of caring outside our current understanding. Unlike the trees and seas around us, we must therefore consciously decide to exist without consent. We must embrace the luck of existence and the goodness of its source. Because, if we do not, we condemn ourselves to life outside the image of any deity, seeking a meaning, trading the beauty for the addiction of Satan: life as ego. The same is true in FairGame.

Who is to say which path is more calamitous for

humanity? Or is the test to accept that the real demon is ego? Try to consider the misery of so many. Try to consider the tightly held memories of a life.

"Might we just accept this good universe, its gift of life? We may embrace this gift of question we call life, rather than answers, seeking a myth of ego that says we are important? Soon enough we will know the meaning of this adventure. In this vast universe, the madness of FairGame and the wonders of Wholack exist because they are neither expressions of freedom nor triumph. They are signs of pain from beings who mourn a wicked culture that refuses to acknowledge that good is a path, a path that works for humans. Do we really need a burning fool to shield us from our inability to see good as a mechanism, a system, a process? It is a lack of correct systemic connection to this good universe that curses our society--nothing else. Though I see no reason to atone for the view. Nor do I believe we should hide from the truth. Wholack is social maturity. Be good in a good universe. It can be that simple for you. For this reason and others I am resigning as Minister of the Interior immediately and entering FairGame. I wish you peace."

In this society, one usually believes in Remold Jaka and the worth of freedom or Tovar Dal and the dignity of change. Were the diner to burn, she would remove only one item, the speech by her lover, Tovar Dal. Standing there staring, she notes he never asked her to enter FairGame to be with him.

Moose-cock?

Entering the kitchen, she places the cheese on a stainless steel table. Carmen grabs them a second later, angry her boss has been standing around the front holding the cheese staring at nothing. Carmen believes she can run a restaurant better than Hope.

Lester grins at as he adjusts the burners on the grill. A partner in the restaurant, Lester is also a minor celebrity in Wholack, Corporate Apocalypse. He owns a sub-scenario chosen by Rader Enterprise for one of their central nodes. He runs a small bagel shop centric to winning the game.

The huge exhaust cowling overhead rumbles to life. Behind Lester a three-tiered metal table runs twenty-feet. The robot underneath cooking some meals, the food-printers are busy. The cook walks back and forth doing the little extras, or dressing the food with garnish before the waitress takes food. He is still too tired to do otherwise. On the other side of the room the dishwasher robot is again stacking plates and washing them off before sending the red plastic racks of dishes through the washing tunnel. The robot has never broken down. Everyone on staff knows Lester is responsible for that as well.

Hope scans the glass doors of the refrigerator watching at the automated arm that moves back and forth getting ingredients based on the waitress' input. Bits of onion, green peppers, cheese, eggs and other items are being dropped in trays for omelettes. The new robot works well but she does not see it. All she sees is Tovar.

Moose-cock?

Hope circles the table to check on two shorter narrow chrome tables. Shaking the tables, they remain stiff. She winks at Lester. The front doors chime.

Carmen reappears, tapping Hope on the shoulder. "Having a good day?" She points outside, at the dining area.

Walking to the front she sees a skinny older man dressed in an outlandish camel hair duster. Called a Royalist Coat, the bulletproof duster sports iridescent red and blue stripes down each sleeve. A bullet against this coat is instant dismissal into FairGame. The Royalist Coat is the ultimate protection for a pedestrian in this society. The tall thin man, worn threadbare from running, once owned a dozen of these coats. "He is so crazy. Thanks, Carmen."

A trio of Hunters glance at Tovar, then leave the diner. The smell means he is a Target. The coat means he is a god.

The face says Tovar Dal. The paradox disturbs the Hunters, because this coat means unending legal and financial troubles, and all of them wish to have Tovar Dal's scalp hanging over their fireplace. Instead, Hunters push through the glass doors and hurry across the street. They will not look back. Hope hears a comment from the last Hunter as he leaves. "You know I hear they're supposed to have seven of those long coats-- one for each day of the week." These people understand that a Royalist coat means complete freedom for its occupant. Members of the executive class also know their place and their rights--all stop at the sight of a Royalist coat. Just the cost impresses them. The coats costs ten decades in Wholack.

And then the final complication for these Hunters: Years ago, the news reported a plane crash outside of Seattle had claimed the life of Tovar Dal--before he had a chance to enter FairGame. Killing him now means proving the major media outlets as liars. FairGame would be the doubtless outcome for any whistle-blower.

Hope approaches her man.

His worn face glows as he watches her.

She points to the nearest booth. Tovar sweeps the tails of his coat and sits with a flourish. Carmen comes out to snoop. Tovar watches her take the last of the eggs from a table without offering him the leftovers. This galls Tovar Dal. "Do you really have a need to pounce upon tables like a bleach tornado? That was good food. Leave it. I'll take it with me." He thinks her a pig for throwing out food when there is someone willing to consume it.

"Pompous ass." For her part, Carmen thinks him a fool to have wasted so much wealth in the name of fairness and concern. "You and your idiotic philosophy got you into FairGame, Minister Dal. I ain't listening to you." She takes another plate, one full of home-fries smeared with ketchup, and drops it into a garbage can. Mumbling, she declares, "That is what morality gets you."

Feigning a wound by the retort, Tovar watches Hope watch him. "She wouldn't understand my philosophy if it stared her in the face." Tovar snorts out a laugh. "On the other hand, besides you, she is the only other person I know who is not a coward."

"You're hungry." Hope says. Pulling a tissue from her pocket, she places it on the table in front of him, but she does not get up and get him food.

He stops waiting for the reason.

"A man left a message for you."

He blinks.

"Moose-cock, he said. Why did he leave that message?"

His eyes close. When they open she sees defeat. An old rumor of infidelity surfaces in her chest. Every muscle knots and her stomach seems to fly from her body.

Tovar wipes his forehead with the napkin. "To prove that he knows me. He wants something. How did this occur? Who is he?"

"A man killed an Administrator. He was wounded. I helped him. Then I let him go." She sees concern in his eyes.

Dal tries to hide it by grabbing a half-glass of water from a near table. When he sits he says, "Do you know the reason why you are happy, Hope?"

"If we tap dance for a while, will you talk to me?"

"Not yet." He looks at the brownies on the counter. She finally gets up and plates a pair of them for him. When she returns to the table he says, "Why would you contact me for such an odd reason. You don't know if his comment meant anything. I am taking my life in my hands outside of the preserve." He pauses. "Hmm, inside as well." A smile.

She sighs staring at a politician. "Are you ready?"

He stops eating the brownie. "Anything odd about this man who killed the Administrator?"

Moose-cock?

She nods watching him. "He appears to be the fourth man at our table, John Doe, from the Boiler Room."

Tovar cannot speak. Carmen enters the dining area with a large plate full of eggs and home fries. Carmen drops off the plate. Hope shakes her head thank you. Carmen retreats.

He calls after her. "You said I could have a donut anytime I want, Carmen." His words bounce from chrome to chrome like shooting stars. "Hey, Carmen, I said I want a donut." He gets up. Walking toward the counter and lifting a clear plastic hood over a pile of chocolate glazed donuts, he cannot believe what Hope has told him. He needs time to think.

"Put that back down or I'll knock you down--this ain't a pet sanctuary," Carmen says.

"It's not for me. It's for a friend of mine. A Mister Hardisty--he says that so long as you are working here he refuses to eat here. He says he can't wait until you are fired so he can come by to get some of Lester's good food." He takes the donut. "Where is the bacon?"

Hope shakes her head at her lover's tirade; knowing he hides something, from her.

Carmen scowls. "Just a minute, pigeon. Don't rush me."

Tovar looks at his lover, admiring her eyes. "Please don't ever fire her. She is my one source of entertainment. I think I love her."

In Carmen's strata of society, success is defined by how much one fights. Those that fight the injustice are closest to the bottom rungs and the ones most likely to become FairGame. Those that are beaten by the system but dysfunctional ride near. Those who cheat the system are further from the bottom. Those that push the unfairness without embarrassment or remorse are closest to the top. It is called the *Mephistopheles Effect*. The man who coined the term, at the embarrassment of the cognoscenti, now sits at the table and shovels fried eggs into his mouth.

Carmen scoops the bacon up in the kitchen and speaks to Lester, "Something's up. Dal looks like he just ate a turd." She turns, enters the front of the house, grabs the donuts and walks away. He stares at her. Glaring at Tovar, Carmen cannot hold herself back: "You look a bit...Concerned?"

Hope scowls.

Tovar speaks. "More Coffee? Water? Drool from an idiot? I am thirsty."

"I have no reason to listen to you." Part of her still does not believe that with nothing but wit Tovar Dal has lasted so long in FairGame. The average lifespan is just under nine months. It has been years for him.

"Bitch." Knowing she will stay away now, he faces Hope's bemused continence. "Did you know rich guys can hire people to make life difficult? They're like private investigators. One of their jobs is to keep a file on you and pay attention to you so long as someone pays them money. A little money and your life is a little tacky. A lot of money and it's really bad. For some, they will even condemn the mark to FairGame. Many start rumors."

"Tovar, please do not think me dull."

He gives up his tack of trying to deflect the comment. "Are you sure the murderer looks like the fourth player?"

"Exactly--and Moose-cock?" She asks. "Why so crude? What is it?"

His shoulders fall. He places his knife and fork on the plate and stares into her eyes. "A certain man is rather torqued with me at an indiscretion with this man's wife. That term was associated with the indiscretion."

Her eyes go cold.

He moves forward in the seat as her face reddens.

"Remold? You--and Mina?"

"About four years ago." Nonchalantly, he picks up a

piece of bacon in his hand and eats it. "I am surprised you didn't know this." His eyes look down at the food.

"For some reason this topic never entered into any of our conversations," she says. Her stare could freeze a star. "You slept with Mina?" Not just the pain of his indiscretion hurts, Mina and her staff occupy the beds in the diner's basement. Tovar had asked Hope to facilitate it--four years ago. She stares at him as he sips coffee. "Moose-cock? Was it the infidelity or the delusion of grandeur you hid from me?"

He winces. "A private joke between Mina and I. It was to keep her husband from ever suspecting me."

"You were set up. She is light years ahead of Remold as well." Her breath cannot be found. "Mina can be so gauche."

Tovar wishes he had died in FairGame. He has hurt Hope deeply. Something he has been trying to avoid for years. Taking the last of his bacon, cleaning his plate, Tovar tries to appear calm, but he cannot look at her "Now you know everything. I swear it was my only indiscretion. I am sorry. Please forgive me." He sips water. His eyes far from her gaze.

"What happened?"

He sighs, tilts his head, then surrenders. Tovar gazes up at her tears. He cannot breathe. "Mina was in a panic. She was trying to leave him. On thing led to another. I am an ass. I am sorry." He quiets, wanting to tell her it was really the drugs she placed in his food--but staring into the eyes of an angry woman--he dismisses the comment as foolish. "Hope, there was a guy looking for me inside FairGame. Word was he had a fantastic story to tell me and he wanted my help. When I couldn't find out where this guy came from I stayed clear. The story is he did not exist before he was dropped into FairGame. Are you telling me, the messenger of my indiscretion is another Wholack come to visit? The John Doe, The Destroyer of our reality?" Tovar is trying to deflect her anger.

Hope does not speak, too furious to comment.

"If he is the fourth person at the table we have a serious problem." He watches her red eyes, the tears, his gut knotting. "Have you contacted Remmy?"

Her eyes widen. "He's waiting outside with a gun to kill you. I'll put the video on the net and title it Minister Moose Cock gets it again." Empty eyes stare at him. "Why Mina? Do you hate me. She is my best friend."

"It was stupid. I was convenient."

She can see he is lying to her about something, but she is too angry to pursue the question. "Did you get a name for the guy who was looking for you, Mister Moose Cock?"

Tovar feels her pain. "I'm sorry. I was wrong. I should have told you." Nothing back from her. "When I asked around, I was told his name was John Doe."

"And you did nothing? Are you serious?"

"I never connected him with the Boiler Room. Why would I? He is a theory, not a person. Besides, there have to be a thousand John Does inside SeaPort. All I knew was someone was looking for me. I didn't need to play out Les Miserables in a FairGame preserve. I thought Remmy hired him to kill me-- so I avoided him."

"He didn't seem like he was hunting you, Tovar." Hope curses her stupidity at disbelieving a story from her attorney years ago. It hinted at Tovar's indiscretion.

"Does he know about the Boiler Room?" Tovar asks.

"I don't think so. He doesn't even know about Wholack. He seems like a man bent on getting home." She watches his eyes blink rapidly--that means shock.

"So it isn't an assault." He looks down and shakes his head. "Truthfully I don't really care about Mister Doe at this point. I cannot live with the notion that I have hurt you." Tovar stands facing Hope. "I hope you can forgive me." He turns to leave but faces Hope again. "I am sorry. It had nothing to do with you or your guests. It had nothing to do with us.

Sometimes I think it has everything to do with my entry into FairGame."

She nods, already knowing that truth. Unable to look at Tovar anymore, Hope sighs. "Go take a shower in the basement." Itchy and upset, she walks him into her office. Leaving him there, Hope enters the kitchen. Carmen enters the kitchen also.

"Tovar slept with Mina."

"I heard." Lester turns from Carmen and speaks to Hope. "Guys are idiots. Even guys like Minister Dal." Returning to the oven, confused at the rush of emotions, he opens it. "What's the Boiler Room?"

She looks at him, her pain still boiling. "Lester, you need to let this go."

He closes the oven sure his food is cooking well. "I will. What is it?"

She looks down. "At the Memorial for the Dead there is a very exclusive bar, called Boiler Room."

"So what does this faux Administrator have to do with that?" Carmen asks. "What does it mean to be the fourth man at the table?"

She considers the question then answers honestly. "Inside the Boiler Room is a work of art, a digital tableau. It displays Tovar, Remold Jaka, and I. The fourth person was unknown. The artist called the work John Doe because John Doe is not supposed to exist."

"Why not?"

"John Doe supposedly is proof that through Wholack we can puncture reality. The fake Administrator looks exactly like him."

"That's just coincidence," says Lester.

"There are so many question marks on it now I don't know what to say. The face is exact. I think I am going to talk to Remold. I have to know. I may be inside Wholack for a while at some point. Can you handle the place?"

Lester's eyes widen. He knows how much Hope dislikes Wholack. "Hope, I take three months every to be in Wholack with my family. You never take a break. Take all the time you want," Lester says. "Minister Dal needs to be forgiven. He was an idiot."

"I will tell you what I learn. Okay?"

Lester stares at the floor. He knows who sleeps in the beds below. Carmen does as well. "No problem. Please let me know if we have a problem, okay?" Lester asks.

Hope speaks quietly to Lester. "How far is your family from accessing full time Wholack?"

He shakes his head upset that she has brought this up. He doesn't like to talk about it. He feels like a deserter. "Four years, six months, and three days." Everyone knows exactly how many days they are from entering the game full time. "Don't ruin your life because you are angry with Minister Dal."

She shakes her head. "I won't."

"You?" She asks Carmen.

"Eight years, one month, and fourteen days."

Hope turns, walking into her office considering her own duplicity. She has kept the secret of Mina's plans to herself. Her friends do not know Remold has only days to stop Mina from destroying the Wholack servers and its network.

She has begun to question her loyalty to Mina Jaka.

Chapter Eleven

Chain Gang

The normally languid pace of Interstate 5 and its gravel skirt holds a rout of vehicles running south. Overhead, the skies continues to darken as another major storm begins lashing the Northwest coast, moving inland.

The imposter who calls himself Doc Holiday scans the ten lane roadway running south through the storm-bent wheat fields of southern Washington. In the distance, across the river sits the remains of Portland. Above him, the wind generators of the Columbia Gorge spin majestically. In front of him, vehicles slam on their breaks, lights glow red. Those seeking escape crawl south. Beside him, the gravel fields along the roadway are choked with thousands of people. Walkers, many ride horses or bicycles.

The Lucky Class--as they are called--are RV mobile on a globally warmed Earth. From the driver's seat of the

Administrator's van, the man who also calls himself John Doe taps the steering wheel, watching the mired panic of stalled refugees.

Scanning the crowded roadway, the imposter feels swamped and confused by the bog of people. After spending three years inside FairGame and making good his escape he thought the outside would make sense. On the contrary, this nightmarish society confuses him. All that is clear is everyone wants to escape to the safety of Wholack. As well, he has learned that any means to achieve escape is applauded so he continues to scan those around him with a suspicious eye. The irony of his successful escape from FairGame, in a society that adores escape, has ceased to amuse him.

The rains begin. Jellybean-sized hail pelts the skin of the Administrator's van. The impacts rattle the interior. Wind gusts rock the vehicle.

Only a single lane runs north today. Some of the more expensive vehicles dart into it, to go south, faster. The lane fills in seconds and comes to a halt as well.

Storms damage the landscape on a seasonal basis, sometimes on a weekly basis. In North America, almost two-hundred-million people live the nomadic lifestyle. They consider themselves lucky. The freeways provide egress, a poor man's version of Wholack. Ready to leave any location- -upon hearing a storm alert--the middle class shuns the cities. Crisscrossing the continent, freeways are the arteries of this nomadic society. The cities are blood clots. Portland is the traffic bottleneck.

Hammered regularly, the cities war with the weather, tectonic plates, or entrepreneurial armies that seek dominion When a city falls passed a certain mark it is converted into a FairGame preserve. Once that happens the residents flee, joining nomadic caravans.

The imposter does not know that at the height of

the coming storm, only the bulletproof vehicles of the Administrators will be able to withstand the fusillade of hail and wind. The hundred mile an hour winds will flip other vehicles in seconds, making for uncountable road dangers. Traffic wants to cross the Columbia River to get away from the storm. This man has seen many violent storms in his time. He suspects the coming storm will have no respect for the state border. The man called John Doe believes the storm will reach well south into Oregon. In this he is correct.

He does see the taller, less stable vehicles are already pulling off to lash themselves to the ground and wait for the winds of this rain-band to die down. It also appears to him that this violent approach of an early rain-band means trouble. The imposter scans the children to gauge the danger. The boys stare at him, smiling, one or two of them putting up their thumbs. The girls have no mirth and ignore him. The driver of the vehicle on his left makes sure not to look at the van. His door has a white sign flapping in the breeze saying: "Who can? Whogan!"

The sign flies off hitting the Administrator's van. The man looks at the imposter and smiles. Then he quickly looks away. The imposter assumes that's fear. Catching a quick glance from the young woman beside him he detects hate. The fake Administrator decides he can deal with hate. The side-wall bullet proofing of the van also makes more sense now.

The winds die down and the hailstones stop. The traffic speeds up approaching the Columbia River bridges. For over a decade now, the repair of infrastructure associated with the cities has lapsed. The freeways are easier to repair and the bridges are in tip-top shape.

The imposter stares at the saw-edge ruins of buildings sticking out of a swamp that was once a city. He is from Portland and he sighs. The jagged brightly painted ruins of Portland's hillsides look like an entry to a fun house. Flags of various colors dot the roofs, small brightly colored wind generators spin in the remains of office buildings. Smoke from camp fires rises from dry islands. Closer in, he can see a line of blinking white lights--the skirt of FairGame. It runs between the city and the freeway. An explosion behind him paints the sky orange. The black cloud from the explosion quickly spins away. He sees there has been an accident of some sort.

The Administrator's van is directed towards an open express lane. Passing a security checkpoint for the bridge, his vehicle speeds up passing the other vehicles. No unauthorized vehicles will enter the emergency lane. To do so is death. Crossing the river, as winds buffet the van; he glances off to the side, seeing the red hunting boats making for shore. More than a dozen of them are in the rough waters of the Columbia. Those boats hold Hunters who kill the Targets from boats. It's considered an expert's trip.

A man stunned by the madness of this society, the fake Administrator stares at the clear roadway ahead.

Why is everyone so crazy? What is so damn special about a computer game?

A light flashes on the van's charger. The van needs a battery swap. He begins looking for a sign indicating a commercial charging station. The first exit over the bridge leads west into the swamp that is now Portland.

That's no good.

Then on the left, he sees an exit for East Halsey and a yellow square indicating a commercial charging station. Exiting he has no idea how Administrators pay for their van. He checks for the cash Hope has given him and feels a bit better when he finds it.

The van rolls up the exit ramp passing a bright red gun shop that looks like a missile emplacement with its descending ramps and steel doors. The doors will soon seal the store against the weather. Every other business in this area looks the same: partially underground, with large steel doors that stand wide, for the time being. An abandoned shopping center ahead, the tents and the vans are already well along in their escape routine. Long steel rods set into the ground meant to hold everything in place are being removed. Then he notes the entire tent city seems to stop at his approach, watch him park, then studiously avoid him as he shuts the engine and exits. Within minutes, the closest encampments are loaded into mobile homes that speed off.

Circling the van, trying to look official, he sees no port for data transfer. Walking back into the van's office area to examine the protocols, he wants to figure out how to pay for a battery swap. Seeing no notes, he turns on the computer and scans the files.

Hail taps again, this time a little larger than jelly-beans. Winds rock the van back and forth.

An accounting ledger tells him there is a special account for the van but no instructions on how to access it. Examining the Administrator's wallet, he finds no credit card or other payment system. Logic tells him the van emits a beacon identifying itself to vendors but he can't be sure of that. After pulling a bright orange rain suit from the closet, the fake Administrator gets out of the van. Rain and hail pounds the exterior, creating puddles in the broken pavement The bite of hail is noise because the poncho is so well protected. Even so, the sting of cold winds rides under the poncho. It hurts his wounded arm. The imposter looks under the van for some kind of antennae in the chassis.

"Need a hand?" An older man about fifty has come up behind him. "I'm a mechanic, or I was. I am on my way into Wholack. My name is Huggins, Miller Huggins. I used to help service these rigs. As a fond adieu I'd like to help you." He wears no rain suit and the current round of hail bounces off his cowboy hat and duster with no notice.

The fake Administrator wants to ask him about the antennae, but decides not to. "No, just giving it the once over."

The man remains. "New on the job?" He asks.

"Why'd you say that?"

"You look like a guy with a problem who doesn't want to admit it."

"Get going."

The man steps away thinking it strange an Administrator should smell so bad. He decides the man is an escaped Target and smiles as he leaves. The imposter calling himself Doc Holiday hurries back into the van. He starts the engine planning to try and bluff his way through the payment, claiming drugs have confused him. Leaving the parking lot full of people, he drives east and sees a WhiteSpot charging station. He pulls into the commercial line. An attendant dressed in whites rushes out of the center kiosk waving hands. "What are you doing here, Sparky?"

The fake Administrator puts on his best stupid look. "What? I need some damn juice." He blinks his eyes and appears to lose focus. His head wavers back and forth and he burps. "What?"

The man shakes his head and looks at the serial numbers under the driver's window. "You know we don't fill you guys up anymore. The contract ended almost a year ago. Or is this your day for a little too much fun--to remember all that?"

The imposter holds up his wounded arm. A crackle of thunder rolls though and sheets of rain pour down.

The man scowls. "Right. Sure."

"So where the fuck am I supposed to go now that you dumb-bells have lost the charging contract?"

The attendant shakes his head at having to deal with an apparently stoned Administrator just before a big storm. "BatteryAuthority has your contract now. They're half a klick down the roadway. You should have that in your notes. Are you out of juice? Are looking for a charge?"

"No, I can get there."

"They are just up Halsey. You can't miss them. They're under the billboard--the one with the beautiful female model. It's on the left."

The imposter looks up and sees the sign, but his van is now penned in by a pair of buses. The attendant steps back and waves a red and white tour bus into reverse. A second later the fake Administrator is on the road heading up Halsey. The imposter's eyes drift up to the billboard and the beautiful woman on a sign selling something called MobileYoga. Five minutes later the van enters an underground charging kiosk. A short woman positions the van over the switching mechanism. The imposter waits trying to appear busy, reading training manuals on the computer screen.

A minute goes by. The woman taps the side of the window telling him to go. The fake Administrator wags an index finger and drives off towards the freeway.

Easy.

The storm freshens as he drives along, winds pushing the heavy van back and forth. The hailstones are now the size of golf balls. Many of the businesses are shut down, the steel doors in place. The parking lot where he first parked is empty of people. Hail pounds the puddles. The rain makes driving difficult. The imposter does not know the vehicle has autopilot.

As he enters the slow moving freeway, a patrol car appears and follows him down the freeway ramp. The officer is responding to a corporate inquiry from WhiteSpot about a drunk Administrator with a bad smell.

Drunk Administrators are always a problem because the law frowns upon the Administrators and their tasks, but the demarcation between the purchase of civilization and FairGame is so flimsy law enforcement has to support anyone stupid enough to repeatedly go inside a preserve. At one point, legislators suggested the Police patrol FairGame. From that point forward it became a marriage of convenience for the Police and the Administrators.

The officer calls in the van number and waits. There are two alerts on it. The van is stolen and the driver is some kind of FairGame escapee. No arrest has been paid for--just payment for updates and a tracking alert for Laughs Unlimited. The officer smiles at the man's guts and skill.

If an action facilitates someone's escape into Wholack, or any escape, it is considered noble in this society. FairGame lays bare any myths of civilized behavior, in, or out of the FairGame preserves. In this society, everyone is fair game.

The officer contacts his wife telling her about the van and a guy who has killed an Administrator and stolen a van. Both marvel at the man's pluck. Along with admiration for the perpetrator, they know Administrators as scum. They also know that so far no Administrators have made it into Wholack without upstream assistance. That "little" leverage is always tied to some vendetta or act of larceny. It killed a friend's child a year ago. This couple sees the Administrators as the corrupt bottom feeders of a once civilized society.

The husband and wife conclude this escapee has little chance of living out the week, so the officer continues to follow, doing nothing. So what if he killed an Administrator and took the van?

When the van reaches the edges of his patrol zone the officer exits. He provides no update. He has no task here and wishes man luck.

Earth has become a hearse, a carriage of death for an uncaring species. A famous painting of the time shows a coffin torn open carrying two coffins One coffin has a dinosaur skeleton. Inside the other a human skeleton, under each is a green banner. For the dinosaur the banner says: "A lack of Brains." Under the human the banner says: "A lack of Caring."

The painting's title is "A Bright Future for Bugs."

From a quote by FairGame's biggest critic, the former Minister of the Interior, Tovar Dal: "Over the decades, business has morphed from service, to invoking tools for developing degradation of the soul, and finally: the development of addiction. FairGame, in every sense, is the result of that system. While Wholack has turned people from responsibility to addiction. The golden-haired child of marketing--addiction--has transformed our society into hell. FairGame is the ultimate example of that, the Administrator, the candy man. Extremes have fostered the profession of Administrator. A person not charged with the enforcement of law and civilization--the Administrator is just the strong arm of power inside a manufactured jungle. The purchased right of the corporate state to maintain itself above the Nation. We have glorified thuggery in FairGame because it excuses the addictions of power, brutality, and Utopia. Can we long endure?"

Ironically, FairGame is the only reason a gamer ever comes out of Wholack, either to be Hunters, the so-called Croakers, or the hunted, Targets. World-wide, over one-hundred-thousand people are ejected from Wholack every year for missing payments. In every case, after a three months of physical therapy to rebuild their muscles, they wind up in a hunting preserve. Mostly, these are people who already knew they could never spend the rest of their life inside Wholack. So they finance a plan to enter Wholack for a few months, or a few years, just to experience it. When they run out of resources, they are ejected into FairGame to die within days.

Guarding the black debtor-buses when they enter the preserves is another task of the Administrators. Some Administrators like the task because they believe it is their sacred duty to try and protect the Targets. Making sure the newbies have enough time to complete the local training course. Other Administrators protect the buses because the buses are an easy way to help their clients make kills. There are no laws inside FairGame and a Administrators are always looking for another revenue source.

The imposter scans the traffic as the vehicles slow to cope with the pounding hail or to avoid accidents. Others pull to the side to get twenty-four-hour legals from their insurance carriers. Traffic again comes to a halt. He scans right. Entering FairGame, a red striped bus traverses a line of white lights. It pulls to a stop behind a blue striped bus unloading Hunters. He searches for the meaning of the stripes.

He finds out the blue stripes mean the bus conveys skilled hunters, The red bus contains a low end tour run by Administrators-in-training. They conduct training tours to gain hours on the job to pass their licensing exam. Mortality rates among the low end tours are well over 50%. For the more expensive tours, the death rates are less because the Administrators are better trained and the bribes higher.

Occasionally these low end tour buses get stoned or machine-gunned by FairGame residents. Not today, most Targets are sheltered from the storm in the ruins of Portland. The fake Administrator sees a dozen red-striped buses entering the preserve.

After the Hunters in the blue-striped bus pile out, the bus circles and leaves the area. A pair of women dressed in bright orange Administrators' uniforms exits the red-striped bus. A shabbily dressed group of men and women exit carrying weapons. The Administrators unfold a table and begin selling bullets and renting bulletproof vests. The other red-striped buses unload occupants.

During a storm too? Are they nuts?

Murdering humans because they have lost their rights due to non-payment, would have seemed evil fifty years ago. Today, the hunting parties wear the same cloak as a bachelor party--a somewhat edge-of-the-envelope romp. In fact, many bachelor and bachelorette parties have forgone the happy hooker for the automatic rifle.

Usually because of a romantic jealousy, business reasons, or stupidity--Croakers die all the time in these wedding outings. It is rare for a hunting party not to include one participant, or more, who does not know they are the hunted. Many secret lovers or a cheating fiancés have met their end in the preserves.

The imposter first thinks that a good Administrator knows the dynamic of the tour, whether the tour is made up of businesspeople, families, friends, or enemies. That it is the task of the Administrator to keep the party on the move, whether on foot or by vehicle, and show the opportunities for a hunt. Supposedly, this skill defines the worth of Administrators to the market. The man driving the Administrator's van has missed the obvious truth--over and over. An Administrator's worth is based on who gets killed.

The fake Administrator considers the hunting party he is to meet: twenty-three men and women. A group of managers from SpinCorp, the propaganda arm of Laughs Unlimited, their job is to maintain a pristine image for Wholack. They will arrive in a private bus.

Scanning the records, waiting for traffic to move, he sees numerous entries into Doc Holiday's bank accounts. Many deposits appear to be protection or elimination of one or more participants in a hunting party. The largest deposits shows certain Croakers are popular for meeting an untimely end. The number of targeted executives is also a surprise--almost all. Originally he thought his ability to kill Hunters and thereby stay alive was due to his military training. From these records, he guesses that notion is foolish.

He already knew any Target with more than six months on the run has a wealth of experience most Hunters could never imagine. All they need is a weapon because in a one-on-one--the Hunter is dead. Unless there is an Administrator nearby to protect that Hunter. It stuns him that the enemy is not the desperate poor folk, but co-workers, lovers, or friends.

The winds howl. Hailstones pound the exterior of the van. A message replaces the training manual. An Laughs Unlimited Vice President named Tana Reins has just confirmed a trip to the arid southern edge of the preserve.

"Tana Reins?" He mumbles, reading the rest of the text. Traffic is stuck anyway. According to the new notes, he has to meet the newbies in an hour and a half, conduct them into a Red Cross Center in the Northern Willamette, then leave. He is to drive south to meet Ms. Reins. She has set up an early morning tour of her family's holdings--somewhere near the southern edge of the game preserve. The newbies are supposed to wait for his return in the late morning, practicing their tasks on the simulators at the Red Cross Center.

Looking at the new tour plan for Ms. Reins, he sees she owns most of the wind generators on the west coast. The generating facilities in question are only a mile south of the FairGame preserve. Then he sees the deposit for the meeting. It is a big score--almost a three month decrease in wait time for Wholack. He is to protect this woman at all costs during the tour. The fake Administrator worries there is some personal relationship here.

The traffic rolls forward. Another e-mail: Two men have just made new deposits into the Administrator's account. Each deposit is a bonus for the demise of the other. The imposter laughs rolling a few hundred feet through the traffic, now sure that Croakers lose their life to each other far more than even the Administrator's data indicates. He notes his new job also appears to be managing the Hunters so that their competitive hunts do not filter back to the office. According to a note from Ms. Reins, she wants any friction dealt with by death. A follow up e-mail from the North American Director for Field Operations of the Parks Administration tells him a drone has been dispatched to track his van--and he is to be on time this evening.

"Fucked up," he mumbles to himself.

Ahead, a cloud forms a dark cone. It appears to rotate. The van radio snaps to life. "Alert, wind shear. Alert, storm warning. Alert, tornado imminent. Alert, tracking engaged. Satellite links four-by-four. Remain calm. Safety first."

Confused, the driver looks around. The traffic stops. The funnel touches down. The moment it does, he sees a dozen vehicles swept up in the funnel and tossed away. "Alert, danger. Interconnect engaged. Road-drills out."

He tries to control the van, but it is out of his control. Autopilot has been engaged.

The sound of pinions fired into the ground rocks the van. "Drills engaged. Satellite coverage degrading. Safety first. Remain in your vehicle. Tornado alert. Doors locked. Security on. Defense systems armed. Tether inventory low-- maintenance advised. Emergency measures underway."

Debris strikes the windshield.

"Wind speed for the approaching vortex is over one- hundred-and-fifty."

The van quickly lowers itself onto the pavement. Winds still move the van back and forth, but not as badly as before. "Alert. Alert. Engaging storm restraints. Defense drone on route." A second later he is strapped into his seat, helpless, looking at the tornado as it advances. More debris slaps the vehicle. Vehicles in front of him are tossed backward over the freeway and out to FairGame below. Hail and debris pounds on the roof. People run from vehicles. Other vehicles drive directly into the storm's path. They are tossed skyward. "Drone approaching. Path positive. War-head armed. Drone alert, level one. Safety first, remain calm."

Unsure of what it all means he scans skyward. A black jet, a drone, dives into the tornado. The drone explodes. A second later, the remains of the storm leaves the roadway turning west, wandering out into the remains of a Portland, tearing buildings apart. The vehicle rises as the sounds of sirens fill the air. "Bolts cleared. Drive engaged. Traffic maintenance on route. Doors will remain locked. Remain inside. Restraints released. Safety first."

Heavy lift helicopters appear carrying bulldozers and other equipment. Hovering above the bare spots left by the tornado, lowering their machines, the helicopters wait. The huge bulldozers immediately begin to push wreckage aside so traffic can flow.

Originally emergency teams were put into action when one of the main highways was about to be clobbered by a storm. Now the job is to clear the blockage by any means necessary and leave the rest to the scavengers. Crews and bulldozers are ignoring the wounded who do not have an active auto insurance beacon.

Traffic remains stalled. Medical emergency vehicles arrive by other helicopters. Lowered quickly, the bright orange vehicles take in those with medical coverage and are lifted away. A bulldozer appears to his right, rolling to the rear. A smaller twister had touched down a few hundred yards behind him; he missed it completely. A man in an orange jumpsuit taps the van looking at the fake Administrator as if he is some kind of idiot. "Were you hoping to take pictures? Who the fuck do you think that lane is for, Sparky?"

The fake Administrator nods, proceeding first through a cleared lane. As the only full spectrum officer inside the preserves, the Administrators also have full access, privileges, and latitude inside the Gray Zone. An Administrator's safety is considered key to the safety of others. Outside the Gray Zone they are like any other citizen--subject to payment for all rights, but inside FairGame or the neighboring Gray Zone they are given, or can take, anything they want. The FairGame

Parks Administration gets the bill. This is meant to keep the Administrators happy and tied to the preserves of FairGame. Though truth-be-known, the Administrators sometimes travel with the caravans that flee up and down the coast--avoiding the storms that march around the planet. Helping restore order inside storm damaged regions delivers huge returns for Administrators--and it is safer than being in the FairGame preserve. The funds are split evenly with management.

As he drives along, he notes that some of the vehicles have stopped and the owners are outside firing weapons into the preserves. Apparently, some unthinking Targets have tried to loot the vehicles swept into the preserve. A hundred will die by the evening, about fifty of them being Targets. The rest are the unfortunate inhabitants of damaged vehicles tossed into FairGame.

A half hour later he enters the farmlands and food production centers of the Northern Willamette Valley. The city's smell soon disappears. A hastily painted sign on the right says: "FIND THE BEDS!" Rumor has it there is a bed facility in the Willamette Valley.

The search for the Wholack caverns was once an international pastime, until the truth of their defenses became known. Located inside mountains or under the oceans, the Wholack bed repositories contain the most sophisticated weapons known to humanity. In the beginning, the carnage encircling the Wholack facilities had been unending. Then the futility of assault became clear and rather than being the source of anger, the Wholack facilities became the promised land.

The so-called middle class knows where they want to go and what they want to do. They also know they need to protect the beds. Without them, they have no goals The organization that promotes that frame of reference are his next clients: SpinCorporation.

The fake Administrator starts scanning for that rest area where he is to meet the Hunters. He hopes to get there ahead of the Hunters so he can read more of the Administrator's operating manuals and get some food--maybe even take another shower.

Ten minutes later, the man forced to masquerade Doc Holiday, sits in a restaurant sipping tea, watching a parking lot.

Located near a hillside for storm protection, the large gravel parking areas spreads north and south in front of him. Around the lot, a set of buildings wears coats of streaked reddish mud. All square, all stucco, the buildings have flat roofs and weapons systems on every wall. Over the hill is the FairGame and its Gray Zone.

The first floor of the buildings facing the freeway contain restaurants. Behind the three buildings, tight to the grassy hillside are a line of Red Cross buildings.

The imposter is in the middle building.

Each building is cordoned off from the others by four-foot-high white concrete fence, cost, and services. For the inexpensive facilities, the second through tenth floors are shopping and sleeping areas. The more expensive buildings have personal services like secure communications. There are no Wholack beds here. They would impossible to defend.

Outside, brightly colored flags snap in the winds. Flags define the border of the expensive facility from the common areas of parking lots. A steady stream of expensive land cruisers glide through flag-defined checkpoints as scanners define the levels of civil services allied with the occupants. Green arrows over the five lanes direct the vehicles to the various buildings as gates open or close. A couple of double-decker solar carriers plug into the maintenance building. They are on their way north to sell energy once the storm ceases. The trucks deploy their auxiliary panels. They unfold like wings on either side. Clouds and rain do not matter to these monsters.

Their occupants exit. The men and women look around and hurry through the rain for a meal and a swim.

Finishing his ham sandwich, the imposter scans the traffic as it rumbles south through the rain and muck of the Willamette Valley. Traffic has lightened considerably. The storm up north has ceased its march south. Out on the roadway, the vehicles going south appear be the last vehicles out of the storm. Dents cover the roofs, windows are broken, and some people exiting the vehicles look wounded. The wounded walk or hobble over to Red Cross Medical as soon as they secure their vehicles. Inside the same red building is the FairGame training center. His next stop--when the bus full of Hunters arrives.

The imposter had considered showing the Hunters the training facility, then driving east, planning to get lost in the roadways and forests of the Cascades, never meeting Ms. Tana Reins. A drone hovering over his van squashed that plan. The moment he crosses the eastern border of his patrol, the drone will be on him and the van a locked prison.

His eyes drift back down to the computer tablet to read more about the rules for conducting Hunters. Many of the rules are of no concern to him because the majority of the rules are there to minimize litigation.

So far as he can tell, once those items are swept away, all he really needs to do is find the Hunters, conduct them to the appropriate locations, then step aside and wait for the end of the hunt to catalogue the dead and the dying. A report on the Hunt will be due at the end of the quarter. This is September and the end of the quarter is the end of October. He expects to be long gone by then.

Overall, his concerns have lessened because of the manuals and his excellent memory. As well, there is the Administrator's ability to ignore any question by responding. "I am involved in a Hunt and I cannot address that." Shutting off the tablet and stretching, he sniffs his armpit. The smell of desperation seems less to him.

Another expensive bus stops and three couples exit, all good looking, all looking bored, all acting upper crust. They note the Administrator's van and knot quickly. Standing together like a wolf pack, they converse among themselves, watching the drone. This group of grifters, commonly called Debs, are trying to figure out if they are already busted. After speaking among themselves they break apart to circulate through the lounges of the facility looking for the Administrator.

From the notes in the Administrator's manual, he has seen there is a bounty on road-crooks. The imposter decides to let it go. He just wants to be out of here. A pair of Debs enter the restaurant. Seeing him, they immediately turn and leave. They report back to the others on the location of the Administrator, then begin to sweep other buildings for the unaware.

Perhaps, he reasons, this is the why the other patrons in the restaurant treat him with respect. He represents law and order. Then a different notion dawns on him. Perhaps they see he is part of a machine that can only do them harm-- so they steer clear. The young children, too young to know the reality of their life--victims of the media onslaught--see the Administrator as a cross between Jesus and GI Joe. At this moment, a young boy eating waffles stares at the imposter even though his parents have continually told the child to behave. The father, a big man in his thirties, acts like he doesn't care, but a pleasant smile gives his fear weight. The imposter assumes from the deep blue jumpsuit the man is a maintenance worker, perhaps at the nearby wind generators. Their life spans are almost as short as the Administrators.

Only a few of the maintenance workers buy any worker safety products. They therefore work without harnesses or other safety devices. Their life is short but the pay is good.

It's a hard decision if a worker doesn't know the statistics. The cost of worker-safety can add a year onto the work period for both husband and wife. Most people know that. On the other hand, most people do not know eighty percent of those without worker safety never make into Wholack.

The fake Administrator watches the man's pretty wife. She wears a bored stare. She wants into the game: Right now--and the man is a tool. The attractive woman sees duplicity watching her and so studies the Administrator.

No. He cannot cure her problem of waiting for heaven to arrive. She looks away. The imposter decides there is little chance her man owns any safety systems.

An older couple next to her, who look like they have enough to live out their lives in nomadic-comfort, sport wide grins. Nodding, they fear they might someday find themselves in FairGame, so they hope their kind smiles might buy them the pity of an Administrator. It is another myth of this society--an Administrator with a heart of gold.

A bright green tour bus catches his attention. It is his gaggle of Hunters. The imposter stands to leave. He points to the waitress--a thin older woman with a bald head and a purple scalp. She nods and he exits.

This Administrator is obviously new, she decides; he never checked the bill. Dawn, the waitress, will bill the FairGame Administration double. She knows they will quiz the Administrator for a picture of the bill once they get it and he will unable to produce it. No matter. She wins. He loses.

Glancing at the van in the parking lot, she wonders what happened to the Administrator who liked to stiff her on a tip--time to exact revenge. After doctoring the bill she tells herself she just picked up two seconds inside Wholack.

The fake Administrator exits to the rain. A group of teens circle his van pointing to the dents from bullets and hail. Seeing the Administrator walking towards them, they glance at his holster and its weapons, then quickly walk off. They signal the grifters about the change of location for the Administrator. The fake Administrator moves toward the tour bus and its emerging crowd of young professionals.

The bus empties. Dressed in tan and green camouflage, this group of Hunters is stylistically prepared for the hunt. Music from the bus follows them into the rain. The imposter gauges them to be well-versed in the corporate traditions of apparent concern and conniving jocularity. He sees little in the way of real teamwork in the group.

These Croakers are wild dogs--dressed well.

He cannot see a medical kit or extra water on any of their belts. They are armed to the teeth but unrealistic. In other words, stupid. Targets wait for a group like this. It always means new supplies.

Winds slap their clothing. A few of the crowd sport expensive hunting coats and top of the line boots. Others are wearing new, but cheap gear. This is the demarcation between the inherited wealth and those that would be up-and-coming.

The fake Administrator then thinks back to what he has read on this group. His report had said there are only a few senior level openings. That this trip--supposedly a reward for a job well done--is a culling of management. Truth is, releasing these managers into the job market would expose too much about the inner workings of their division.

According to the manuals, the muddy bowl of this FairGame region is here for a reason--to kill Croakers. A second hunt will be held if too many survive this jaunt into FairGame.

The rains and wind calm. The managers watch each other, sure they are blessed. The junior executives wink and wave at Doc Holiday. Nothing will stand in their way. The bravado is pointless and foolish. They are all fools, so far as the imposter is concerned, oil for a machine. He can see they understand parts of the vast world around them, just their wants, and a misaligned notion of why winning is everything. Even so, he remembers himself as just such a person and wonders how he ever got through it all. The fake Administrator ponders the absurdity: For all the horror these people think they accept, they still do not know the complexity of life that awaits them.

The front doors of the bus close with a hiss. Symphony music no longer pours out into the day. The bus pulls away leaving the Hunters to be soaked through. The imposter imagines the driver laughing. The driver's task for the next few hours is to freshen up the bus while the Administrator escorts the Hunters inside the pavilion to their right. The bus driver will then drive them to the executive dormitory buildings on the edge of the Gray Zone.

The Administrator waves them closer. He wants to make sure they can hear him over the road noise and wind. As they crowd in, he notes their actions are a mockery of cooperation. They slap each other on the back then smile at others. According to the manuals he has studied, that means this group knows the Hunter with the most kills will be a prime candidate for promotion and killed at the end of the hunt.

He is not to provide assistance to that person under any circumstance. These are the orders from Tana Reins. He wonders if the most capable ones know they will be the hunted by their comrades once they win. Or if they know the bush and grasslands of the Willamette offer little in the way of safety for any of them. Or that most Targets skirt the mud keeping to the hills while training their confiscated high-power weapons on the Hunters.

Some tours do include armed escorts, or mercenaries to insure the safety of the Hunters--as well as drone-based tactical support. As a Target, he never knew tactical support was so common. There is no support for this group even though satellite surveillance has been contracted by the corporation.

One set of C-level executives will watch the hunt during a two day party. FairGame is a blood-sport for all.

"So you must be the man," says a chipper looking young woman in front. She smiles warmly, then glances into her boyfriend's gaze. They eye the Administrator suspiciously deciding he is a crook. People like this can spot deceit easily. It is their trade.

The Administrator nods then glances at three men who crowd close, an obvious alliance. They laugh and joke like old friends--except two of these man have taken a contract on the third. "I am Doc Holiday. I am conducting this hunt."

"Hi, Doc," they say in unison--then laugh at him.

He decides to tell them nothing. He bears no risk. If these were key people in their corporation they would never have been delivered into one of the more dangerous locations in SeaPort.

Instructions from Tana Reins say Doc Holiday is to provide minimal data. Minimal data--according the summary on this hunt--means he need not describe the dangers, nor how to avoid them, nor where the most dangerous spots are. He is to tell them which signs to look for, and what they mean. He is required to instruct them on how the Targets manage their weapons and their reloading procedures. He is to conduct them out at the end. He is to let the wounded die. He is happy to comply.

"Please follow me into the Red Cross building. That's the red one with all the concertina wire out front. Check your weapons at the door--you'll be given receipts. Then go through the underground hall to lecture room six. The lecture starts in ten minutes." He walks away having directly quoted his manuals. He hears the click of a safety unlatching and a round loaded into a breach. Doc raises his right hand to alert the guards and waits a second or two.

"Look at your chest. You will see a red dot. Make sure

the safety is always on outside the preserve. You will not get another warning." He has repeated exactly what he had read and doesn't even bother to look back and see who has the attitude. It just doesn't matter. Whomever it is will get a modified weapon back from the guards and dead by the end of the hunt. No one threatens an Administrator. Again, the manual is his bible. It had said this kind of thing could happen and that the Red Cross guards have him covered. They do. The chipper young woman will be dead by noon tomorrow.

Walking through the rain, the fake Administrator stops at the front gate as two guards unlock the door. Walking inside he doesn't bother to remove his weapons, having read in the training manuals here is no requirement for that. The interior guards look at each other as he walks by and down the hallway. They believe the guy who has taken over for Doc Holiday is also a dick. He owes them fifty dollars for covering his back.

A few minutes later, after traversing the underground hallway, he stands inside the lecture room watching the Croakers file in. They all wear the same look of indignation from the body search by the officers.

A thin man with a long white beard brushes passed him and steps up to the podium. He adjust his blue suit and red tie. "Please take refreshments. We have a busy afternoon ahead of us." He nods at the smelly Target wondering why the man is still here. Phillip is about to retire and enter Wholack, Corporate Apocalypse, so he lets it all go.

The Hunters fill their plates with salad and turkey slices. The man on the podium waits until they have retrieved their lunches and take their seats at the two large dining tables. "My name is Phillip. I am an instructor for this region of FairGame." An image appears on the wall behind him--a map of the area. "You can be on site at the preserve by 11:00 PM tonight. Those of you that wish to begin to hunt at that time may do so. I suggest you wait until noon when your Administrator returns. The Willamette is one of the most dangerous regions of FairGame."

Everyone, other than the imposter, smiles.

"Okay, you need to understand that in this part of the Willamette the Targets work in teams. Some as small as two. Some as large as ten. Centric to that are the hobo signs of the Targets. Never think of them as fools or tools. You must understand the hobo signs if you are stay alive." The man turns and a series of six pictograms appear. "Study these hobo signs. They will tell you how the Targets communicate and what they communicate. If nothing else, learn the sign that says, Chain Gang. That's you. It usually means a trap has just been set. Second, never make the mistake that they believe they are the hunted. So far as the Hobos here are concerned, an Administrator is the guy who brings them fresh food and water. The only Targets out there are skilled survivors. Otherwise they would not be in this part of SeaPort. If you want to live you will respect your enemy."

A skinny man speaks up. He has a fork in his hand with which he points at the man: "So then are there many casualties among the Hunters? Due to, ah, Hobo, assaults?"

"The Hobos see themselves as the last of a free people--rebels if you will. You, on the other hand are fools, Wholacks, who stupidly enter their domain. They believe the home field is the key. They steal weapons. They make plans. They lay traps. They have, in some cases, years of experience. Some even say the Targets escape from time to time and take over the lives of Croakers that they kill." Phillip grins at the fake Administrator. The fake Administrator begins to back up towards the door.

The audience, completely unaware of their surroundings, bristles at the term Croakers. "Yeah, we saw that movie. Pure Bollywood," someone says. The others laugh. "We know the story here, Opie. Let's get on with it. We are tired."

"On the other hand," says the speaker with a sly grin.

"Without their organized efforts you would be bored."

"What about vehicles?" Asks one man. "Can we arrange for our own support?"

The man at the podium shakes his head no. "That has been approved only for evacuation. Contact management if this is not to your liking and you will be removed...From the hunt."

Nervous laughter.

The fake Administrator exits the room. He believes his masquerade may be exposed. Walking passed the four Red Cross guards he tosses a fifty dollar bill to each of them. They smile and wink. The guards know he is a fake, so does the speaker. These men and women admire him.

A part of him concludes this job might offer a good backup strategy to finding his wife--escape into Wholack. Even though he has no good idea what the Wholack game really is or what it can deliver. Seduction has begun. Most food is laced with pharmaceuticals and additives, for the purpose of enhancing the desire for escape, the need for Wholack. A few establishments serve food that is not laced with pharmaceuticals. It marks the proprietors as rebellious, but clean food is sought by the wealthy so adjustments are made. The cost is astronomical, but so are the profits. The closest restaurant with clean food is Hopes-No-Apostrophe-Diner.

Righteousness and morality have been tossed out the window in this society as if they were trash. This is a society that knows there is a heaven.

Daniel H. Gottlieb

Chapter Twelve

Bad Water

The red sun dips closer to the horizon. Ahead, a white sign by a green chain link fence says Cow Springs Resort.

So this is a Wholack bed facility.

Sand hugs the roadway gutters. Red tulips frame the curb, climbing uphill, to the stucco-faced structure built into a mountain cavern. A green lawn flows out in front, down the hillside to a rainbow of roses. The forest of green birch seems to spread endlessly on either side. Bushes form gentle arcs between the white concrete curb and the forest. Closer in, hiding among low boxwood bushes, machine-gun emplacements follow the curving drive.

Pink in color, the Cow Springs Resort is a fortress. Behind it, in the mountain, lie almost eight million Wholack beds--as well as a battery of mortars, rocket launchers, and artillery. Drone air support flies from the mesa above.

Bringing the dusty van to a stop at the wide circular entry lot, he sighs. Stretching his body, the imposter exits watching the distant blinking white lights of the FairGame preserve. Beyond them, the illusion of water from dry dusty lands, cursed by wash, molded by the yearly floods. The dunes that cover this part of SeaPort march west to the ocean and stretch as far inland as the coast range. In a wavy carpet of dusk and shadows, the desert appears void of life. A swath of wind generators separate dry land from the green fields of southern Oregon. The generators powering this facility act as a buffer to FairGame. He watches the spinning blades and considers that he was never this far south during his time in FairGame. In discussion with others during that time, he had learned the dry lands and oppressive heat here were killing as many hobos as the Hunters in this area.

As a child, he remembers the incessant cloud cover of the beaches. He was born in Oregon. His mom and dad used to take him surfing because it was inexpensive. When the weather shifted north--the storms turned the inexpensive resort towns into ghost towns, tourist attractions of decay. That was the last time he was in this area; he was twelve years old. They all sat on the beach by a fire that burned through the night. The next day he was off to school on the east coast. When he came back, a Rhodes scholar, his parents were missing--victims of the Jazz War. For a while he held out hope, then he joined the military.

That was a different world, he reminds himself.

A valet taps him on the shoulder, disturbing his muse. He turns to face a pretty young woman. "Administrator Holiday, a Ms. Reins is expecting you. She has arranged for light dinner in the spa and she hopes you will join her. I can park your van." She flashes a card that has shows fisted arrows. She is an approved driver of all government vehicles. The young woman glances at the filthy interior of the van and tries to smile.

"Dress is casual, though I expect a clean uniform will work. I can check." A breeze puffs light blond hair around her blue eyes. She brushes the hair aside. The young face seems as if it were a party favor. A gift to patrons who wish entertainment--for a price.

"Tell Ms. Reins I will be there..." He leans in the van and scans the chronometer built into the dash board. "..In an hour. You need not check on my attire requirements. If your management does not wish Administrators in the spa they can tell me when I enter." He closes the window. The valet steps back and points to the far end of the parking lot where hookups exist for vans and mobile homes.

What a dick.

While his presence in the spa is a maybe, his residence inside the exclusive hotel is out of the question. This is a hotel for those that have access to Wholack at their leisure. Those who do as they please--not the service class.

He drives forward passing apple and pear trees, their branches laden with fruit. The imposter cannot believe the sight of fresh fruit. Rows of other fruit trees, plum, peach, and cherry, already stripped of their bounty for the season glow in the dusk. Passed orchards and farm buildings, spread terraced green fields.

Parking the van next to a large motor home engaged in litigation services, the man calling himself Doc Holiday realizes that service people come here to meet with clients, serving their needs. The bright blue and white motor home plays loud jazz: The song is "My Attorney Bernie."

The imposter attends to the hookups. Finished, he sees another mobile business--a clothes cleaner. The fake Administrator walks over, then learns the FairGame Administration has an account. He leaves six uniforms for cleaning and asks for alterations as well. The charge is only eighty dollars so he pays with cash. The uniforms will be ready in fifteen minutes. Just time to shower again.

The lobby of the hotel is slick black marble. Lights point towards a natural rock ceiling, secured in place and polished to a glow. The corners of everything are thin strips of white marble. The jagged white lines on the rocks create a maze-like appearance to the ceiling. Crossing the large lobby, the imposter stops at the front desk. A young man and woman, both scantily dressed in blue rags--stitched together to hide that which must be hidden--seem cheery upon seeing the Administrator. The young woman smiles warmly. "Oh, Administrator Holiday, it is a pleasure to have you here. Tell me, are your accommodations to your liking?"

He nods at the absurd question. "Tana Reins is expecting me for dinner."

"Ms. Reins is already in the spa--to your right, up the stairs, and then straight ahead. Or, if you wish, there is an elevator at the end of the hall." She pauses with a wink. "It's a lot shorter to walk." Her directing him to the stairs is meant to keep him outside the residence areas of the hotel.

"Thank you." He ascends black marble stairs framed by the same white strips. It's a short climb. Arriving at the first landing, glass doors open, then the Pacific Ocean is visible across a large room. The sun has set but the reddish glow remains. This man once knew a woman named Tana Reins and he prepares himself for the face of a friend and the smile of a stranger.

He enters a quiet space clustered with green plants. A man dressed in a white tuxedo greets him. "Administrator, Holiday, welcome to the spa. Please follow me. Did you have a nice trip down?"

The fake Administrator nods.

"We heard about the storm up north, terrible thing."

The imposter follows the middle aged man, watching

the lights reflect off his polished skull. The man opens a glass door on the left that leads into a pool area. A single table overlooks a lap pool on one side and the ocean beyond. A tall thin woman in a tight dress stands to greet him. Her face is completely foreign to him.

He smiles from relief. Just a coincidence, he tells himself. The imposter is incorrect--as he will see in a few days.

She smooths her attire. The little black dress hugs her like skin. The affect is immediate. Then he tells himself this isn't right. They never greet you without a business suit unless they want something. Dark complected with black hair; her tune is flawless. The imposter is at attention, wondering about the real event of this meeting. The woman smiles warmly and sticks out her hand. He watches the soft eyes as she purrs, "Administrator Holiday, I am Tana Reins."

"Ms. Reins, this is an unexpected pleasure. I don't often get to venues like this. I want to thank you for the opportunity to slum."

She pauses at the comment, her blue eyes a bit more narrow. Tana had not expected that kind of humor. "Please sit. I know you are tired so I will make this brief. You have a big day tomorrow with my tour." She sits, with the help of the bald man who then leaves. The Administrator had not realized he was a bodyguard. Tana stares at him. "Your picture shows a man far less," she pauses, "vigorous."

"Well, once you hit forty-five it's fit or fat. I made a decision to get fit. That picture should be updated within the week. Is that a problem?" He sits in the chair, feeling the soft cushion.

She raises an arm, pointing her index finger at him, then at the table. Another man in a white tuxedo appears and speaks: "A light dinner of sautéed razor clams and potato tubes stuffed with smoked vegetables is on the way. A salad and fresh fruit sorbet will follow. Is that to your liking, Administrator

Holiday?"

"Yes. Thank you."

"Very good, sir." He backs away.

The imposter says, "So how can I help you?" He finds himself staring at the curves of her body.

She smiles, recognizing this man's survival instinct has taken pause to feel lust, and he hasn't even eaten any of the drug-laced food. Tana Reins warms to the hunt. Her hand sweeps precisely cut black hair thinking this might be even be fun. "You find me attractive?" She asks, smiling from pouched red lips and bright white teeth. The sparkle of her eyes send a rush of blood to his organ.

He leans forward, staring at her. "You are a hungry woman. I do not wish to be your supper." He smiles. "How can I help you?"

Dinner arrives via a wheeled cart served by two waitresses. Tana watches him sip from a glass of water--as the waitresses finish laying out the meal. Tana cannot imagine that this man thinks he has any chance of impersonating the Administrator for long. He is far too thin. Regardless, his audacity sparks a red glow to her cheeks. So she takes the light blue cloth napkin and places it on her lap.

One bite of the food and he is mine.

Tana looks up. "The executives have been told that you are an evaluator as well as an Administrator."

He sees mischief, catching the feint. "That's not true."

She pulls a piece of carrot from inside the potato tube and eats it slowly. "I thought you said you would supply ratings?" She is toying with him.

"I did. I will. But I am not an expert on the qualities your corporation seeks from middle managers." He cuts into a razor clam and eats it. Immediately feeling a bit light-headed, the imposter thinks the flavor and the surroundings are beginning to overwhelm him. For a man who, forty-eight hours ago, was covered in filth from the FairGame trails, this meal is bliss.

Seeing the drugs' tell-tale flush, "It is hot here. Isn't it?" She takes a knife and cuts down into a potato wedge. "From our executives, we expect an ability to build consensus and drive success at all costs." Tana keeps watching his eyes. The blinking eyes are a sign all the drugs have taken hold. She continues speaking. "Their willingness to follow through to their objectives is key. Might you be able to gauge these items?" She watches his face as he wipes the tears away.

He nods, a bit dizzy. "Once I am clear on your objectives. I can support them."

This is not right. She tells herself. Tana can feel a man well-bred.

Her curiosity ratchets up a notch as she wonders why he was a Target. Whomever pushed this man off the cliff thoroughly wiped his background--she guesses. His possibilities entice her. She refuses to believe he is a crossover. "You are a lot less dull than our earlier conversations. Why is that?"

"I was about to say the same about you," he says watching her eyes. The thin, sensual mouth closes in a hushed smile. He reconsiders his allure, thinking himself a fool.

She picks up a piece of the stuffed potato and eats it slowly, watching him, watching her. "Regarding our tour tomorrow--I have been asked to examine my family's generating facilities."

"I understand." Her wealth has little impact on this man though he is surprised by his lust for her.

She grins. "My family owns the blades and I am committed to retaining the revenue stream." She lies. Tana spends most of her time gathering data on Remold Jaka and Laughs Unlimited. Her family would like to take over the company. Hunting is her life.

A waiter arrives with two fresh glasses of water, fully iced and wrapped in a thin covering of light green foam to keep the liquid cool and the hands warm. The imposter notes the first glass, the one the waiter now walks away with, had no such covering.

He thinks he understands the gambit to get his fingerprints. He was ready for this type of event. "And how much time will you need out there?" His head tilts to the side, looking at her breasts,

She nods. "Just a cursory tour--an hour or two."

The imposter finds he is admiring the soft skin of her chest even though he feels like a Target again. The thought of escape chokes on her body. He wants her.

Then he sees her eyes look left. Someone has signaled to her. Her gaze returns to him full of warmth. He figures it is the news on his fingerprints. Her people have confirmed the fingerprints belong to a woman two years dead. In-depth tests will require fluids, blood, or other.

Her task defined, bright eyes show mischief with intent. "Tell me I am pretty." She leans forward for more.

"So we will be touring the southern border? My van will not work for that. The roads are terrible."

"We have bikes," she says with a pout. "You know how to ride. Don't you?"

"I do." He puts down his fork and looks at her. "What is it you would like me to do?" He pauses. "I mean tomorrow morning." The man buries an adolescent smile.

She stands up, allowing her napkin to fall to the ground. "Shall we go to my room?"

He stumbles to his feet, picking up her napkin smelling her warmth. He hands it over, gently brushing the thin black dress hugging her sensuous body. "They will let me inside the hotel. The unconnected need not apply here."

"Who told you that?" Her eyes drift like the darkening skies.

"It's not that." He says, falling into the trap. "I have

seen it everywhere in this hotel."

She tilts her head and sweeps hair aside. "How long until I get to the bottom of you?" She says chiding him, with apparent good nature.

"Bottom of what?" He pauses at his ridiculous response. The heart for his wife has no moment in this place.

"You don't seem like a bottom-feeder." She smirks. "Of course, sometime people take the job they need, not the job they want."

"I am no toy." As attractive as she is, once you're a Target, the allure of sex pales in the memory of traps, chiefly the successful ones. Nonetheless, drugs and horror from the last three years take their toll on this man. He places his right hand lightly on her ribs, feeling a shiver run up her body. Had he not felt that--the imposter tells himself--he would have gone back to his van, alone. He figures he has been drugged.

It doesn't matter.

"Well?" Tana considers asking him outright what he is doing, but her loins define a different point. Her natural tendency to hunt strains the line of duty. "Were you planning to take me in that filthy van?" Her chest moves.

"I would never dream of placing you in all that dirt." He leans close to her. "Though I would fuck you anywhere." Then, his eyes by her ear, his mouth on the nape of her neck, he whispers, "How would you like it first?"

She takes the napkin from his hand and places it on the table, using the other hand to move his gaze to her. "You decide." Her hand drops and lightly touches his leg along the outside of his thigh. "I hope you do not mind if we do not go to your van." She leads him to the glass door. "I am neat to a fault."

"And when I am done with you?"

"I'd better not be. I don't like feeling a fool, Doc."

CHAPTER THIRTEEN

POLICE INACTIVE

An electrified fence topped by white lights wanders the sand dunes. A hundred yards south meanders a dusty road. Two black bicycles ride the morning's dust avoiding debris following a low ridge west. They climb uphill fifty feet between them. The man in front; the woman in back. The distance between the bicycles is a poor metric of the distance between the people pumping the peddles.

"The hunted tear apart the turbines once they have escaped the preserve," says Tana into her microphone. "We are trying to find a way to stop that." She welcomes the next down hill wishing this morning was over with.

The bikes coast down a long curve of road. It meets a transportation tube the size of a large sewer line that begins running parallel to the roadway. Incessant heat from friction radiates from the tube. The man barely sweats. Desert heat and the tubes ravages the ingénue. "The government says we are responsible for the grounds we own. But they took the land for these tubes without informing us. Will the government ever stop interfering?"

"Doesn't it bring supplies to the beds?"

She shrugs her shoulders. Dust sticks to her, producing dirty rivulets of sweat that flow down from her face to her chest, staining the white material of her tank top. Crusted mucus itches inside her nose. Her lungs fill with heat, but unwilling to show any weakness, she continues speaking to the man on the other bicycle--the imposter who calls himself Doc Holiday. "Thankfully it isn't too hot yet," she says.

The imposter wishes for silence. His head pounds from the drug-laced food of last night, and his betrayal of Winston, his wife.

Tana continues blathering into the microphone. "No matter what we try, the Targets find a way to steal supplies. "

His helmet crackles for a moment adding to the grating affect of her voice. He points to a pair of bright wire antennae peeking from the top of his helmet. She nods and adjusts her radio. The crackling stops. "...The hobos are a menace. The government coddles them."

"The government just has too much power." He mimics her litany from last night. Then, pointing at movement in the scrub a few hundred feet inside the preserve, he says, "When I see them, I'll scratch my ear."

"Safety first?" She grin.

"I can't keep you safe if you are unaware." He downshifts.

"And now these new transportation tubes feed their antics. They're beasts." He cannot see her grin.

"Maybe the Targets don't care about the power and the transport tubes. Maybe they are just trying to stay alive."

"They raid this section of the generators constantly. I need to understand how. It's so damn hot down here. Why do they stay? Why don't they go north?" She hates the heat, but Tana has resolved to continue her assignment until she uncovers the truth. Then she will complete her own agenda.

He speaks, "Insofar as the heat--that's why they are out here. Inconvenience has saved a lot of lives. Insofar as the loss of equipment from your farm, we need to look for a nest out here. That's where they stage the raids. Once we do, we can send in a team to find the broken sensors, the holes in the wall, or a tunnel."

Her chest hurts. "Any word on the hunt?"

"Five were out last night with zero results. Three came back. That's common. Today should be a bit more interesting. I will need to be back by one to conduct them to the base camp."

It is 9:55 in the morning and the sand dunes of southern Oregon cook in the windy morning. As they bicycle along, Tana begins to stare at their sameness. Unaware of the dunes' hypnotic charms, she misses the approaching clouds of dust. They heave from the seams of the truck-sized transportation tube beside the roadway. When she finally looks away from the dunes, it is too late. She steers her bicycle into the powdered air. The sting inside her lungs is like a thousand angry hornets. She coughs in spasms trying to eject the filthy dust from her being, breathing more in with each gulp of air, finally jumping to the side of the cracked roadway. She drops to her knees coughing phlegm onto the sand.

The fake Administrator having seen the puffs traveling down the tube waits for the light winds to whisk away the powder. Her discomfort has no affect on him. Insofar as he is concerned, she is a viper, vain, demanding, and self-involved.

The winds send the dust away--except for the filth that sticks to her sweat. He leans his bike against a rusting ambulance, glad he does not have to hear more pontificating on the beauty of FairGame, economic myth, or Wholack. On his approach, Tana spits up rather inelegantly.

When her breathing calms, she wonders about his apathy towards her, and Wholack. For this generation it is all about the reward of power. He has another agenda. She saw a mystery last night and it will not release her.

By the time they were undressed, Tana noted his pleasing her was an activity of lust and nothing else. Worse, this hobo turned Administrator didn't even try to impress her with his skills. His loving seemed archaic compared to the game's liquid loving and immediately available adornments. Tana was amused by the mystery. He seemed so unsophisticated, so unaware of how people make love. Stud 101 is all about Wholack techniques in real-life. This man had no notion of that. In Wholack, the lovemaking is all about surprises--and whatever it takes to get there. Again, he seemed indifferent. Why doesn't he know about Wholack? The question giving more weight to the hypothesis that he is a crossover, so she didn't kill him last night. Tana doesn't like being used as an object.

After that first bout of lovemaking, she provided him with instructions on what to do. She took over the lovemaking, demanding he please her in a host of ways. Like many born to the game, Tana Reins has a fetish for recreating her fantasies here in the real world. It is a common affliction and hardly considered a detriment. He took offense and was resistant when she tried to place him in positions that pleased her. He even refused some positions. She followed pain with technical manipulation of sweet spots. He was bored. She has never encountered that before.

Tana has to remind herself that she has the power to squelch this man by either verifying him as the real Doc Holiday, or proving he is a Target--then terminating him.

Until there was a set of texts from her secretary this morning. The genetics from the semen said he was an 02T--a retail sales person. A person is defined by their genetics in her world. Those genetics still confuse her. He acts like a military man--everything is an objective.

Worse, a body has been exhumed this morning that matches his genetics, but Remold is keeping her in the dark about the identity. That infuriates her about Remold--his need to control everything.

Of course he knows who he is.

Then this morning the last text almost made her laugh: Remold Jaka plans to hire him. That, Tana has decided is not going to happen. Remold Jaka already has too much. Crossover or not, Remold will not gain control of this asset. When the imposter's usefulness is complete, she will terminate him. Her legal perqs will impede any serious investigation.

So, before the bike trip, her final report to Remold accentuated this imposter as a survivor and not very bright--that he was not a crossover--just a nuisance. Tana concluded her report with a fake confession by the imposter claiming his dad was a geneticist for a criminal organization. The only question for her is how long he will be of use to her. Except for that mystery: He knows nothing about Wholack--and cares less about entrance than any person she has ever met.

More dust.

He says, "I don't know why you wanted to be out in this anyway, Ms. Reins." She works to take in a deep breath and not choke. Tana coughs violently. Without sympathy he watches her choke, recalling her pride last night in being a skilled Hunter.

It was a miserable night of intercourse for him. He stares at the tight black shorts and white knit top wondering how she could be so bad at lovemaking. Had she been just another partner he would have left. As he was forced to guard his real identity, he stayed for a full night of fucking. As if to taunt him, she became more and more offensive as the night melted into the morning.

With no sleep now--he seeks only distance from this female porcupine. Worst of all, she acts like a Croaker. She doesn't hide her power, just weaknesses, as if people couldn't see them.

He stands behind her. She coughs out phlegm. "You've got money. You've got power. Let's go back."

Tana looks up at him knowing that his stare has no heart for her. His reaction to the libido enhancing drugs was not as she had expected. He hates her. As she tries to recover her breath watching his feigned concern, the irony that she is less than an hour from ending him makes this all a bit more tolerable. She reminds herself all she need do is get him inside the preserve. Tana reminds herself to keep her eye on the objective of keeping Remold's trust. On the other hand, a bullet in the skull from an Administrator never gets investigated. Tana knows she needs to be careful.

Truth is she loves the hunt when the game is so dangerous. This man appears competent and skilled in war. The John Doe enigma, the fourth man at the Boiler Room table, the mess with Mina, all spell danger considering the intellectual bandwidth of the man. She even fears she has trouble understanding the fullness of it all. So she hates him that much more. Still, killing a crossover could never be seen as a negative in her circle. He represents change--and change means trouble.

Another dust cloud travels down the tubes. She holds her breath looking in the Administrator's direction. He has already turned away. A moment later, dust from the tubes fills the air. This time the winds quickly sweep the dust skyward. She stumbles to her feet and lurches over to the ambulance to get away from the tube. The imposter gazes around to the mounds of scrub and debris. Targets can be seen moving away from them--using the distraction of the tube for cover. Looking down he sees a communal bed clustered under the ambulance. A pile of rags lie in a pit. It is from here they launch their raids on Tana's generators. There must be a tunnel.

He hands her a black canteen from the bike. "Drink this. It will help." He walks away from the nest.

Tana rubs the dirty sweat that covers her body. She adjusts her top. The dust and sweat have brought out the augmentation scars on her breasts. Taking the canteen with a weak palsied hand, she leans back against the ambulance door and washes her chest. Tana lurches forward from the hot metal. He grins walking away, fetching her bicycle.

As Tana drinks water the coughing cycles into spasms. They shake her entire body. The thirty-year-old woman spits all over herself. The dutiful Administrator turns to his right, his hand on her bicycle. She knows it is common for people to choke to death on the dust, but her current inability to protect herself scares her far more. He wets a cloth and holds it out for her. She coughs out the words, "No."

"Lean over on all fours. It'll go away." She rests her hands on her knees instead. The stacked tubes on the other side of the embankment rattle again. He hauls her away from the ambulance carcass. Dust puffs out. Quickly snatched by the winds, the dust looks like a ghost taking flight.

She finally can drink from the canteen. He begins a patronizing conversation. "You Gamesters usually come out like little babies. How come your leg muscles aren't all jelly-like?"

Ignoring him, she replies, "You make love often, Doc?"

"As often as I can." The imposter remembers the loving. Her question suggests he is both buffoon and a poor lover.

"Your name is a prime topic for conversation around the Northwest."

He laughs. "Sure it is."

She wipes her mouth with a tissue to hide her smile, but notes her absurd statement has zero impact. Tana decides he is a man used to trouble. His approach is like catching fly balls in a baseball game. No problem. Wearing her best smile, "Do you curse your luck to have missed Wholack?"

"It will be years before I have earned enough to get into the game. Every new scenario is just as tough as the earlier ones. It doesn't bother me. I'll be fine." The imposter believes he has no chance of ever getting into Wholack, which is okay with him. He sees the game as insignificant to his task. Though he does wonder about an addiction that owns a society.

"So who are you really?"

"You mean my real name?" He says, sweeping the dust off her bicycle seat. "I don't share that with clients." He sets the kickstand and backs away. The fake Administrator gets on his bike.

Stunned at being dismissed like this, Tana mounts her bike. She watches him through watery eyes, grimacing to let him know she is spunky about her health. Another round of coughing wracks her.

"Continue on, or do we call it a day?"

She bristles. "I'll be fine."

I'm not done with you.

The bikes whistle downhill.

Tana works the gears adjusting them for the coming flat ride. The fake Administrator barely pedals. Her muscles are not strong enough to use the bike to its potential, but the expensive bike makes the task of pedaling along much easier. They zip passed workers at the solar arrays trying not to get electrocuted. A Target darts across the roadway ahead of them.

"I pity them," she says. "What do you think life is like for a Target, Doc? You must know."

The bikes roll along the long dusty roadway in silence. Inside his skull, an alarm continues to sound. She knows.

"Well it's not the murder, the rape, the bloody hands, the crappy food, getting mangled by traps, the torture, or the degradation that would be horrible."

"Maybe it's the confusion of being a stranger in a strange land." Her eyes twinkle.

He nods. "I just think the hours are just too long." He looks over at her and smiles.

She does not know it, but she has lit the fuse of her demise. "Is that what you did before you were an Administrator, a philosopher like the great Tovar Dal?"

He looks away annoyed at his own stupidity. Now he understands. All she sees is a dead man walking. That explains her toying with him. "I was a college student studying Wholack. Then I became a soldier, then an Administrator. I would have thought your profile of me would have been that complete."

Again, she notes his opaque reaction. "We can be allies if you'll tell me the truth."

His bike pulls to the side of the roadway. She comes to a halt as well. "What do you want from me, Ms. Reins?"

A diligent executive who has become a stone cold killer, she knows endgame. "You're a Swinging-Jack," she replies. "A Swinging-Jack means you are a guy who is only out for fun... Stranger." Tana blinks. "What could I want from you?"

He thinks back to the laziness of the Hunters and how the hunted stay alive by total aggression. "You're playing with me but you're confused. What is the issue?"

"I took you last night," Tana hates the notion of anyone thinking her weak. "How's that headache? It's common." She watches his hands to see if they move towards his pistols. All she sees is shock.

"You drugged my food?"

"Didn't take much." That's a lie. She used a double dose. "I can use you--but I need to know the facts. Who are you? Where are you from...Stranger?" In truth, she no longer cares.

He stands calm, with no hint of fear, already knowing what is next. "Again, what do you think you know, Ms. Reins?

You think you own me, perhaps? It explains your babbling at me last night with that 'wrath of the goddess' crap."

Feeling for her weapon, making sure the safety is off, she says, "I need a smart man who can get around the system. You can do that. I know you are an escaped Target."

"And you figure to use me for your purposes. In exchange for securing my identity through your legal credits?"

She winks at him. "Right." She is an animal about to attack.

He sighs. "I want access to Wholack in five years."

Her hand moves away from her hip. "Eight."

"Six."

"Eight." She wonders how she will hide the body. "You can think about my offer while you conduct the hunt. I will expect a call yes or no by tomorrow morning."

Spying another Target in the dunes a few hundred yards off, he decides to get it over with.

I'm putting down a wild dog. He glances away from her speaking quietly. "There is a glint from the Target in that hill over there." His eyes widen and his hand moves to his ear.

Her eyes leave his for a moment.

He shoots her dead.

She tumbles backwards over the bike, into the dust, blood flooding from her chest.

The imposter named Doc Holiday walks over to the dusty transportation tube making a mark on it. It is a hobo sign that declares police inactive. He accentuates the grin.

It takes him less than a minute to make the trade. One of her weapons and all the ammo for the Target's fingerprints on his gun.

CHAPTER FOURTEEN

CAMP HERE

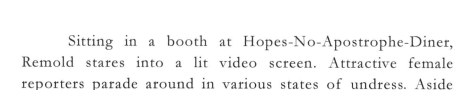

Sitting in a booth at Hopes-No-Apostrophe-Diner, Remold stares into a lit video screen. Attractive female reporters parade around in various states of undress. Aside from lewd comments, the tally-window below changes with bids for further undress.

The initial news reports had said Tana Reins had marched across the FairGame fence to investigate an apparent theft of generator parts near a transportation tube. A bullet from a Hobo killed her. The closest Administrator killed the Target. An uneventful happening from the standpoint of the FairGame Administration and a joke for the media: Scratch another dumb rich person. Beneath the tally-window, the white text of the viewers' comments crawl by:

Dumb little rich girl wanders into FairGame, too bad.

How many debutantes does it take to take a bullet?

Is that a gun in your pocket or are you glad to see me?

Looking away from the parade of degradation, Remold cannot understand the death of Tana Reins. Shocked to learn she and the murderer were intimate the night before, believing he is the reason she is dead, Remold ponders the dynamics of her meeting.

She was so cunning. Murder by a fake Administrator chews on him. Murder by John Doe does not. He would be unstoppable. The destruction of Wholack would be a fait accompli, the destruction of reality just days away. This is why he ignores the doctors and sits here at the diner waiting for Hope Weiss.

Is John Doe really possible?

A single cat claw rides the inside of his skull from eye to eye, scratching back and forth. A migraine begins. It has been a good day for the mind-tigers.

A text message arrives. The so-called Administrator is leaving the Willamette Valley. Remold instructs his chief of security to return the man to him, here.

Benson Fong responds drone aircraft will keep an eye on the imposter until his arrival at the diner.

Remold looks back down to the monitor. People continue to make fun of the dumb executive. An image of Tana, nude, appears on the news. Pushing his breakfast plate over the screen, a prismatic puddle of grease follows. He wipes away the grease seeking the food-culprit. A sausage patty hangs off the side of the plate. Remold looks away as the comments section lights up.

He had known Tana since she was a child. Sadly, Remold still sees her that way and has no idea she was plotting to take the company from him.

A spark catches his eye. An incomprehensible set of pulsing yellow lights dances down the black mall. Remold puts on his glasses. The yellow lights are from expensive flashlights that Hunters use. The flashlights kill anyone who picks them up--if the biometrics don't match the owner. Moving through the remains of the battered mall, the squad of lights split apart. A Target has been located. Remold snorts his disapproval. He cannot excuse the mess of society even as he reminds himself it could be worse. No, he has made it worse.

A carnival truck full of red and yellow striped tents leaves the garage. The mall has gotten too dangerous for the sex carnival. Five have died.

Remold closes his eyes. If this day is the price of finding Mina, the cost has been steep. His puffy eyes open to the empty booth seat across from him. Appliquéd into the metal booth back is the word: "Hope." Below that, a pretty little girl stands, dressed in a green and white tuna costume holds a tan bamboo fly fishing rod. He notes the image of Hope's lost aunt, Elena. This ghost owns every booth-back, while she flies above the booths as a light blue angel. A wire encircles the wings. It allows the slowly spinning angels to see all. Elena Etu had raised Hope, teaching her to be wise.

Were Remold to discover the scam, that the angels keep watch on the diner protecting the beds from him, there would be hell to pay. Fortunately, the angels and their tragic spin paralyze the man into a dance of pity. The idea for the angels came from Mina. The money for the stealthy beds came from the divorce. It was Mina's only way to fund her project outside of Remold's reach.

He removes gold wire frame spectacles and glances at his reflection: A shoddy hat hides scalp wounds from the bomb. The puffy white shirt covers his chest bandage. A green cashmere sweater keeps him warm. It had been a gift from Mina on their first anniversary, but Remold has no idea where the sweater came from. He just knows the sweater is his favorite piece of clothing.

He looks around, still waiting for Hope. None of the

Hunters pay him any mind. They have no idea who he is.

Remold cannot dismisses the notion that Hope might be in collusion with the murderer, even though Benson Fong investigated her and the diner thoroughly.

Remold looks down at the screen. One of the reporters removes her silky white blouse and Remold is drawn to the image. He does not see that a man stands behind him.

"Why don't we just use some of the money to help the people in FairGame, rather than help them get jerked off by fake news reports."

Remold knows the voice. It was once commanding, something usually owned by a big bulky man. He looks at Tovar Dal and sees the bulk of him gone. "Cuz."

"Remmy." His cousin wears a black bowler and a torn Royalist coat: a duster with bright red and blue vertical stripes. Gray scruffy stubble covers Tovar's face. Bloodshot eyes, red marks on skin from numerous near death scrapes, his face looks like someone exploded a firecracker in his head--three days ago. He stinks.

Behind Tovar stands Lester. Remold assumes the cook holds that shotgun out of sight. He is no danger to Remold because Remold knows that Lester is addicted to Wholack, having secured a major role in the Corporate Apocalypse sub-scenario as a baker. Remold had arranged the plum for Lester without his consent--but it does no good. Lester is as loyal as a dog.

Tovar stares at Remold, waiting.

A pair of the Hunters tell each other that they knew it was Remold Jaka. All of them recognize Tovar Dal in his Royalist coat. There was a rumor on the Internet about him being here.

The Hunters again pile out of the diner. Remold smiles hello wondering why his security people did not alert him to Tovar's arrival. A renewed concern about his security chief rises in the back of his brain. The appearance of his cousin unannounced is indeed troubling. Though why he escaped FairGame to arrive him here at this moment is even more vexing. There are rumors of tunnels out of the FairGame. Plus, Tovar's life extinguished is worth a fortune to the authorities. Many want this former minister neutralized.

Why would he risk it with me now?

"Hope says we have a mystery." Tovar holds that same bony smile he had as a kid. Remold is ten years his senior.

Looking at the coat Remold smiles, glad that his cousin received his gift of two years ago. Truth is it had been a trick to get Tovar to disclose Mina's whereabouts. The coat had a tracking mechanism--long ago disabled by Tovar. "I owe you a new coat," Remold says. "Latest fashion is bright red with a second bulletproof lining--just in case." He beckons to his cousin to sit. Then glancing outside he sees his security teams have not moved. He realizes the windows obscure the figures.

"Do I offend?" Tovar sticks a finger though the lesions of the Royalist coat. "I thought these never allowed a stink?" Tovar notes the light in Remold's eyes seems almost extinguished, though the intelligence behind them remains unmistakable. The twin folds of skin that open just enough to let pupils behind them take in the world and the tight jaw say pain.

Tovar considers the pain of age an equalizer among men. He tilts his head. "A certain Mr. Doe."

"You heard?" Remold sits back in his seat.

"I did, from Hope. That's why I am here. You have someone tracking him, I assume."

Remold looks away, but sees only scrutiny from Lester. Then he points to the screen. "He murdered her. It is all over the news."

Tovar glances at the news screen. Flipping the image with his finger. Tovar will not mention the man's attempt to contact him, hoping it will be a trump card. "No electric tit for protection?"

"She was in FairGame." Remold takes in a breath. "The man is a beast."

"Because he murdered her? You're joking right? She was a Hunter."

Remold nods."I am guessing she underestimated him. I am going to meet with him, here. I want to make sure Hope will help me. That's why I am still waiting to speak to her. I might need her to go into Wholack with him. After all, John Doe, woo-hoo." He spins a finger in the air.

The door to the kitchen opens. Hope stares at Remold. Remold sees ice in her eyes. She turns to Lester. "Get the fool some food."

Tovar stiffens.

Remold tightens his eyebrows, creating twin furrows above his nose. Now what was that about?

She walks over to kiss Tovar, then sits. A second later a waitress arrives with a plate full of chicken. She places it in front of Tovar then leaves.

Remold sees Tovar crouching low in his seat. "Do you need something?"

He laughs glancing around at the diner and what's left of mall. "Civilization?"

The moon peeks over the mall. The wash of rain on the blacktop glistens. Tovar begins eating, knowing Hope is furious he has come out of the basement to see Remold. "So what about this guy Holiday, or John Doe, or whatever? Why do you need Hope?"

Hope speaks. "Take a shower before you leave." Her eyes move to Remold.

Remold watches an anger reserved for him. He wonders what he ever saw in her and glances at the clock he gave her.

"And you make sure he is not detained by your security

people."

Remold looks back at her and nods.

She smiles at Tovar. "I doubt they will fall for the stupid trick that got you here when you try to leave."

Remold nods. "What trick was that, Cuz'?"

"None of your business." Tovar closes his eyes and chides himself for not checking on the security people. Hope is in trouble if Remold succeeds in getting a court order to search the diner. Standing, he removes his Royalist coat brushing oily mangled hair away from a rutted forehead. .

Hope watches Remold shake his head. Her heart thumps in her chest, thinking Tovar an idiot for not making sure there was access to the diner before appearing. She tries to console herself with the notion that Remold must be confused over the death of his assistant.

A truck engine--and Tovar immediately scans the exits. Lester removes the safety. Remold points to an earpiece embedded near his mastoid bone. "Garbage men bearing gifts."

A truck pulls from the parking lot beside the diner. Tovar and Remold watch the garbage truck as workers drop first aid kits along the roadway. The first aid kits are a gift. Tovar nods, "You are a sea of guilt."

Remold watches Tovar scan for Hunters, then looks away. He remembers Tovar as a fearless young man and sighs. "My security people are stationed all around us, Tovar. How did you get by them?"

A pan crashes to the ground. The sizzle of fresh bacon and the smell of burnt sugar quickly fills the diner. "All good," says Lester.

Tovar eats a chicken leg, watching men dart from the mall to grab first aid kits without investigating why. From the mall, shots ring out. Only one man falls dead. The rest escape with first aid kits.

Hope watches Remold. "An acceptable death count to

help others, Herr Doktor Jaka?" She looks at Tovar gobbling the chicken--thinking of how to get Tovar away from Remold. Then, facing Remold again, she sees his eagle stare and knows he has not dropped the question of Tovar's arrival.

Remold speaks. "For someone who just bypassed all my security--and fucked my wife--you seem nonchalant, Cuz."

"Ass." Hope turns to go in the kitchen. She cannot yet figure an escape for Tovar and after entering the kitchen, stands in the kitchen shaking.

Perhaps Remold's ego?

Tovar sighs. "Hating you has become her hobby. Even though she needs to be somewhat nicer to you since we all share a common purpose now. We need to get Mister Doe to the Boiler Room," he says, looking at Remold. "Or have you given up on everything except defeating Mina?"

Remold, thinking himself the injured party, looks around confused. "Don't push me. I know how important the Boiler Room is and what it means." He leans in. "I have thirty-six hours to stop Mina. The Boiler Room can wait. Did you meet with Mister Doe?"

"Hope did--as you know." He sips coffee. "She needs to be part of this--Hope?"

Hope appears at the door to the kitchen. Tovar stands spreading his right arm, inviting her to join them. She remains apart. "Please? I know he's a fool. So does he. We are discussing our favorite enigma, The Boiler Room." He looks at Remold. "His second favorite." He looks back at Hope. "He says he needs your help. I think that means he may ask you to go into the Wholack Game with John Doe--to prove him a fake."

She feels herself grinding her teeth, but senses leverage.

Both men wait for her to sit, which she does after pouring herself and Tovar a glass of orange juice. Remold watches her sit staring at the two glasses. Tovar winks at him. "I told you. She hates you." Then seeing her angry stare at his cavalier attitude, says, "Sorry, Hope. Go ahead, Remold. Tell us what you found out about Mr. Doe."

Remold looks at Hope. "So you met with him and he wants to meet with Tovar? What does he want with Tovar?" Remold asks.

She remains mute.

Remold tries again. "I had one of my people meet with him. We arranged for him to do a tour with her. She is dead, supposedly killed by him, down in the Florence area."

Her eyes widen and she unconsciously looks down at the video screen in the table. "That was your doing?"

"She was just supposed to talk to him."

"Is there anything you don't destroy in your mania for control?" She sees his lips tighten and his eyes dart around the room. Hope sips juice, thinking.

Perhaps he will not follow the thread of how Tovar got here, not right now. "You like scaring people."

Remold speaks softly, his words hard, angry at her accusations. "Mr. Doe is on his way here. I have a drone following him. He cannot escape."

"I don't want him here."

"I didn't ask about your wants."

Tovar shakes his head. "You might consider that you need her cooperation, Remmy."

"No manners," Hope mumbles. She ponders how to get Tovar away from here.

"Hope, I need to know who this guy John Doe is, really." Remold pauses. "I don't really care how Tovar got passed my people. Okay?" He waits. She is stone. "You want to know what I want from you. You know Kittens and Cradles better than anyone. Why didn't you care that Mina took it from you?"

"Why should I?"

"Fine. Don't tell me. If Mr. Doe is a crossover you can take him to Kittens and Cradles, the river sequence, and I can track it to his core. Mina has an algorithm that was altered, supposedly, by his arrival. I'll use that. I need you to verify the change. Or can you get Mina to do it? Help me find out if he is a crossover." Remold is purposely candid. He is a manipulator. Hope, looks away. Each glance back to Remold is a bullet. She considers Remold the worst of men: A sage who hoodwinked a generation to facilitate his desires. Mina believes the same. Both women also know about Harry Jordan, Remold's father, killing the man called Pilot Nothing and his mother as an accessory. So for them, Remold has murder in his genes.

In his defense, Remold could not control the actions of his father before birth nor could he foresee the brutality of FairGame. Evil has never been his game. He has been blind-sided by brutality all of his life. It is his curse. Of course no one would believe that, since all assume it took a fair helping of brutality and little else to get where he is now. They could not know the brutality belonged to his father.

"I think Mr. Doe is a nobody." Hope says, she has no problems with lying to a murderer.

Remold grimaces. "Tovar, why did you bed Mina?" Remold has a theory there is a tunnel in the area--perhaps in the diner and that says he has bigger problems. There is a traitor and more reason to get Hope's assistance.

Tovar reaches out to keep Hope from getting up or throwing something at Remold Jaka. "Remold, you have everything. Is it so hard to imagine there is something you do not get to break?"

Remold sips his water. "You are trying to teach me humility?" He smiles, then sees the anger of a woman. He looks away guessing the truth is already known--and he has embarrassed her.

Tovar speaks. "You don't get it. It wasn't about you. It was about life. She wanted out. I helped her. Is humility so distasteful? Did you send Mr. John Doe after me, to kill me?"

"I did not." Remold's face has gone ash. Both Tovar and Hope now believe he had nothing to do with John Doe's appearance.

"So who tossed him into FairGame?" Tovar asks.

"There are no records of his entry."

"And?" Hope asks, now sure Tovar is not the target of an extensive scam.

Remold speaks: "Three years in FairGame. The rest is a mystery. John Doe's DNA says he is a man that has been dead for twenty years. Tana confirmed that this morning before she died." Remold tilts his head. "Do you think seeing you, Hope, was a way to get to me?"

Tovar nods at the absurdity of ego. "Could be."

Remold continues, "And what about his likeness? Quite a mystery this one. Regardless, I'll meet with him." Remold is confused. No one seems to know why John Doe is here. That leaves Mina. And his best data says she doesn't know either. "I want to know what he knows. Once he is here my people will take control of him."

"Why here?" She asks.

A skilled negotiator once he is on task, Remold shows concern. "He trusts you."

"The great man at work." Tovar reaches out and grabs his coat to leave. "I hear your stockholder's meeting was bombed. Too bad. The developers of the NewDay Mall?"

"Do you think it is tied together?"

"So many people hate you it is tough to tell." He walks passed Hope and through the twin chrome doors to the kitchen. "I am going into the basement take a shower." Tovar knows his cousin ignores honesty.

"You make sure your boys ignore him when he leaves and I will help you." Hope follows Tovar into the kitchen.

Fifteen minutes later, when no one comes out of the kitchen Remold leaves the diner.

Getting into his car he checks the security reports and grins. The surety of finding Mina has lifted his day--figuring there is no way Tovar could have gotten into the diner without his security team noting a man in a Royalist coat. There must be a tunnel--or there is a traitor. He alerts his security people to let Tovar Dal wander free.

Posting guards all around the building, he plans a sweep of the surrounding blocks. This is a good first step--but finding a tunnel into the diner also means a records search and that will take a day or so. That's cutting it way too close. He decides to take control of the asset.

Remold scans the buildings and concludes a tunnel was built during the mall construction. Certain Mina is in one of the buildings, he considers trying to find her from the diner's tiny basement. Remold immediately dismisses that option. Hope has full legal. It will take months to get a warrant--and the cook with the shotgun means more than legal trouble. As a minor celebrity due to his wins in Corporate Apocalypse, he represents media scrutiny that Remold would like to avoid right now. He doesn't want to give others any levers should things go bad. Many seek to control his company, Laughs Unlimited.

Even so, Remold Jaka laughs about his decision to come here. He has gotten a key clue to Mina. He nods happily; with less than a city to search, he is sure to find her.

Remold Jaka sits back in the seat, telling himself he is more than a genius. He is a lucky genius. Knowing he may need Hope's help, Remold sends messages instructing others to break the curse of FairGame for Tovar. Remold needs Hope's favor, not her pique. His attention turns back to the mystery of John Doe and he mumbles, "A crossover? Incredible. How could I have been so wrong?"

CHAPTER FIFTEEN

HOBOS ARRESTED ON SIGHT

It's two AM. Hope wipes the front door, removing the last bits of greasy fingerprints from the new windows. Looking down the boulevard, she sees the fake Administrator's van round the corner followed by a large motor coach.

From the parking lot, a Hunter appears. Hurrying inside the diner, the man walks by Hope with a polite smile. Removing his black shooting gloves, the Hunter watches the van pull in the parking lot. He unbuttons his black cashmere coat. Sitting down in the booth to scan the menu, he smooths his black and white exercise clothes, then speaks on his phone.

Hope studies the expensive clothes. People like this never hunt so early in the morning. She looks outside. The imposter has exited the vehicle. Now she understands. This man is here to work. Carmen looks at Hope. She has seen it all. They both walk back to the kitchen.

Hope thinks about Tovar as she speaks to Lester. "That fake Administrator just parked. He has a bus load of Hunters. We also have a Pro in the diner." She watches Lester glance out the doors to the killer. "Carmen, take care of the Croaker. I'll keep an eye on the Administrator." She looks back to Lester. "You cook eggs and listen. And keep that stupid shotgun out of sight." Hope walks back into the dining area leaving Carmen and Lester staring each other.

Lester looks over to Carmen. "This place is the wild west these days. I bet it all came courtesy of Remold Jaka."

"Yup," Carmen replies.

"But there is something about that Administrator." Lester keeps an eye on Hope.

"He's the problem. I know that."

"More than that," Lester says to Carmen. "You keep your head down and get back in here if there is any trouble."

She frowns walking out to the well-dressed Hunter, judging him to be in his late twenties. He smells of lavender. "Yes, sir?"

His eyes drift up, watching her, then the angels dancing above her. "Espresso, with a lemon rind. A butter croissant, please--and marmalade--if you have any." His eyes turn to the parking lot watching, the imposter assemble the bus load of Hunters.

"Orange marmalade okay?"

"Perfect. Thank you." He nods, then looks over to the front door.

Carmen turns to see another well-dressed man in khaki pants and a blue shirt enter the diner. He sits at a booth on the other side of the door. She notes he wears the blue button down shirt tight to his neck, military style. Neither man looks at the other. Carmen, who has seen hunting teams over and over knows they will note everything around them except each other. That lack of interest means familiarity to her. Then a third man dressed in very expensive camouflage and a bulletproof vest enters. Carmen notes a weapon strapped to his hip rides easy. She unconsciously backs up behind the metal counter knocking into Hope, who stands watching events unfold.

"We have a problem. I have never seen any of these men before."

Before Carmen can reply a police officer dressed blues enters as well. Facing Hope, the police officer smiles at her. "Can I speak to you?"

"Carmen please tell Lester that I want those eggs as soon as possible." Carmen looks at the four men and then hurries into the back room. Hope walks over keeping the counter between her and the police officer.

"Please tell your people to remain in back. I am about to make an arrest."

"I doubt that, Sparky," Hope says.

Carmen stands beside the cook, Lester. He is shaking his head, holding the shotgun, watching Hope joust with the officer. Lester's dark brown eyes appear calm.

"I think the police officer is planning to arrest the Administrator," Carmen says, watching the parking lot monitor in the kitchen. "I don't know about the others. I think the three professional bounty hunters are courtesy of Remold Jaka."

Hope appears at the door to the kitchen. "Lester call Litigation Services and request protection."

Lester crosses to the telecom and sends out the alert. "They will be here in five minutes."

Hope nods, then stares out at the three professional Hunters and the police officer. Looking up at the monitor, she sees the fake Administrator and the others approaching the diner. "Lester, you keep Carmen busy back here."

"And you?" Carmen asks.

"My diner--I'll be in front," Hope says, turning towards the dining area.

Carmen whispers, "Not in a month of Sundays, Hon."

"You are an old man," Hope says.

They push through the doors in unison.

Lester remains out of sight watching the front. He will not do anything that might put Hope in danger. On the other hand, he has no compunctions about protecting her regardless of what she says, ever, or the competition's apparent skill set. He is a man with no fear and pulls out a pair of pistols to load them. The shotgun remains at his side.

Hope pulls Carmen closer to her. "Carmen, get the Croaker at table three. I'll take care of the other Croaker and the police officer at the counter. You drop off your orders and then go to the dumpster and wait for Tovar. Tell him we have trouble here and to keep away. When it's safe, I will let him know." She looks up at the clock on the wall. "Tell him to do nothing until he hears from me. Hurry--he will be here soon." Hope has lied, Tovar is in the basement, sleeping after his shower. Carmen has just begun her shift so she does not know this.

"Damn Remold Jaka," Carmen says, taking the espresso and the croissant to the table.

"Busy today?" The well-dressed man asks Carmen sipping his coffee and tearing the croissant.

"Asshole." She turns away.

The first of the Hunters are piling in and sitting down. They begin entering their orders for alcohol using the table keyboards, preferring not to wait for the waitress. The next hunt is soon.

Carrying a chocolate soda and a cheese sandwich, Hope walks over to the shooter at the counter. He had ordered via a mobile app--the moment he entered the diner. "You were lucky, with this load we'll be busy for a while."

The man smiles. "And some ice tea."

Hope hurries to the police officer seeing the fake

Administrator about three yards from the stairs impatiently waiting for the last of the Croakers to enter. "Did you want anything?" She asks him, surveying the man's thin face and pasted down hair. His brown hair parts in the middle. A pair of frowzy sideburns extends out, like inverted horns. She looks at his badge. "Officer Frew?"

The police officer's eyes drift to her. "I remember this place before the mall opened across the street. Daring and delicious--that was the tag line on your web page. You've ruined it all by getting your snout into places it doesn't belong. I'll have you shut down in a month." He speaks easily, without fear of concern. "Just a double mocha please, with cream and tell your man in the kitchen not to worry. I got this." The man looks around admiring the diner's flashy metal trim work. Everything glows with sharp sparks of light. "Boy, this place looks good. Ever think of selling it?" The officer glances at the young Hunters taking their seats. "Fools." Then he looks back at Hope, taking her beauty in with his brown eyes. "You might want to consider an offer."

"From you?"

He shrugs his shoulders. "Maybe through a lawyer."

"Those professionals yours?" She asks the police officer.

"Nope." He nods at the man entering the diner. "That Administrator is a fake. An escaped Target and I am here to bring him to justice. Please go in back for your own safety."

She leans forward. "I have level-one legal as well as torte here. You open a weapon on a Target in here or anyone else on my property and you will be washing manure out of pig butts for the rest of your days." Her eyes blaze at him.

The man purses his lips. "I am an officer of the law. This is a sanctioned arrest."

Hope speaks. "And I have a bus load of customers and a reputation to maintain--safety first--remember? If you have a gun battle in here, in front of Hunters, then I am as good as shut down. Security is on the way, and trust me, my attorneys are nastier than your attorneys. Or do you think your Agency's budget can stand my legal contracts?" She glares at him.

The man reaches inside his lapel and dials a number. "There will be an investigation about your FairGame attitude."

"Oh goodness--that's a new one." Hope walks back to the dirty Hunters noting they are mostly in their twenties or early thirties. Festooned in flat hipster hats of black cloth and camouflage pants, their vests splattered with mud and blood, they appear stylish and stupid. Sawed off shotguns in holsters, machine pistols and handguns strapped across their chest, the weapons are there for the envy of the other hunters.

She crosses to a professional Hunter dressed in khaki. He speaks first. "There will be no weapons' discharge here so you can relax. I got this." He sips the tea.

She wants to laugh.

Facing the fake Administrator, she places herself between him and the police officer, she says, "Can I help you, sir?" Then in a whisper, "Get the heck out of here." She notes the man's tired eyes.

He has not missed the officer nor the well-dressed bounty hunters in the diner. "Nice to see you too. I am fine. Thank you for asking. Yes, I'll sit at the counter."

She glares at him, standing in his way. He tilts his head, a tired man. "I will be gone in a few minutes. I am taking them across the street for a hunt. Then I'll be gone." The imposter looks over at the police officer. He circles Hope and takes the stool right next to the police office. "I'll have coffee."

Hope, angry at his stupidity, sees Carmen come out of the kitchen. She hurries over, takes her arm, and walks into the back. "What are you doing?"

She looks at the police officer, and the imposter. "Oh, my." Carmen picks up some plated food from the counter. "The flag isn't at half mast. Stop trying to be my mother." She hurries to a table of Hunters. The front doors open and Hope spins, worrying that some other madness has entered. She is correct. Lester enters the front door. He carries a crate of cabbage--with a shotgun on top of the crate. Hope's eyes blaze as she wonders why everyone around her seems to have taken stupid pills. Lester places the box on the counter and turns so everyone can see twin machine pistols strapped to his chest.

Hope leans in. "Let me guess. You got this?"

He nods.

"Mister Pistolero, can I talk to you in the kitchen?"

Her partner walks her into the kitchen through the twin doors glad he has gotten her to safety. He hits the chime for Carmen to come in as well--then grabs both women's arms pulling them behind the ovens. "The cavalry will be here in a minute or two. Just relax."

Hope looks at Carmen. "Men." She walks out of the kitchen.

"Waitress?" Hope approaches the first well-dressed hunter. "That guy work here?" The man asks, looking at the door to the kitchen.

Hope nods. "He's the cook."

"Tell him to stay in back. Have a nice day." He exits, crossing the street to take up a position in the mall. She notes the other two remain quiet, eating.

Hope wonders what the imposter is doing next to the police officer. She cannot hear the conversation, but they appear to be convivial.

Like Hell.

The fake Administrator rests his gaze on the police officer. They have been speaking about the recent hunt in the Willamette Valley and the imposter is giving the police officer misinformation on his plans.

Time to leave.

"Doc, can you answer something for me?" The police

officer asks, getting ready to make his move.

"Sure--name it." He places his cup on the counter to look straight at him.

"The hair on your arms is brown yet your facial hair and mane are jet black. Why is that?"

He does not like anyone toying with him. "You want me? Fine. But if anything happens in here, she'll haul your ass over a bucket of coals. So you and your two friends will just have to wait for me to cross the line into FairGame." The officer stirs the coffee with his finger, eying the professional Hunters--whom he has never met and knows nothing about. "Besides, see my other hand? That's a grenade. Fuck with me and you're toast."

"We'll see."

Hope sees the grenade. Everyone has gone crazy.

She circles the counter and stands in between the imposter and the police officer. "You boys be nice. No roughhousing in my world."

The imposter turns to the crowd of Hunters. "All right let's get going. Saddle up."

The mob exits the diner with their Administrator in the center. Hope glares at the police officer as his gaze follows the fake Administrator though the door. Directing the Hunters across the street, putting the Administrator's van between him and the diner, the imposter moves them through the parking lot and into the carnival midway.

The other two professional Hunters pay their bills and quickly exit. It is only at that moment she believes they and the police officer are not working together. She looks outside wondering where her paid security people are. They have been halted by a roadblock. Hope watches the pair of professional Hunters enter the parking lot by the same entrance as the fake Administrator.

Seeing the imposter gone, the police officer taps a code

into his phone. "You should have cooperated." As he exits the diner, a police van and a morgue vehicle pull into the parking lot.

The man calling himself Doc Holiday splits the group into two teams of five. Directing them through the parking lot, he points each to a different entrance. With one of the teams of five, he crosses through an area filled with carnival trash and directs his Hunters right as they enter the ruined mall telling them he is going to flush out a Target. The five men and women start a sweep to the right. He bounds up the stairs and hurries towards the far wall and a fifteen foot wide hole in the structure. He comes to a stop and pauses at a ragged concrete opening. Peeking around the corner, over the stains of blood, he gazes across the street into the parking lot. Three police officers circle his van. Two Administrators appear, unlocking the van and directing the investigation into the van.

His cover completely busted, catching his breath, and checking his pockets and weapons, the imposter finds no food and no water. Those are the main problems for now. All the supply sources of nourishment and medical supplies have Hunters nearby. Luckily, he has worked most of the traps and he knows their weakness. He also figures his knowledge of the mall will be good for the rest of the night. In every case, he plans to be either deep inside SeaPort or someplace else by the end of the week. He tightens his lips in thought.

I cannot go back inside FairGame.

The law enforcement teams position themselves at the exits of the garage apparently planning to force him towards escape trails where others lie in wait.

The imposter knows that and considers with more people a search of the mall could be effective--if those professional bounty hunters control the sweep. They are his real concern. Pulling out a pistol, he attaches the silencer. Scanning around, he crosses from pillar to pillar hoping to make it across the mall to a clothing store that leads out the ravines and forest on the other side. Expecting all the teams of Hunters will soon be notified he is a fake, he pauses listening for a system alert--a loud three toned chirp--like a doorbell.

A clatter of movement catches his attention. His group of five Hunters are beginning to search for Targets. He needs to redirect them without alerting the others that something is wrong. The imposter fires a single shot to their left. As he expects they retreat from the shot.

He backs away from the concrete and sees both groups of five are on this floor wrapped in a tight knot, speaking to each other. A play-area of decapitated rabbits and cats off to the side offers a plan. Elevated about six feet above the rest of the third floor, he climbs up to survey the area.

To his left, a third set of five Hunters approaches. They do not look like the people he had been conducting. They look like professionals. He scans the Hunters from his tour, seeing them split up into three-person hunting teams. Then he hears a three-toned chirp.

I am busted.

Shooting at a chair, he watches the novices react by ducking down and scanning the area. The professionals call out the location. A barrage of gunfire commences. The fake Administrator darts from the play-area.

He knows the bulletproof clothing should protect him from a fatal wound, though the impact from a high powered round will incapacitate him for more time than might be safe. He also risks an unlucky head shot from the stunned and confused Hunters in his group.

A bullet strikes the post near him. The imposter turns and fires, killing one of the professional bounty hunters. The rookies see who killed him. They scamper to get out of the building. They did not bargain on a Administrator firing on their group. Three new five person hunting teams appear. The imposter is in the middle of a trap.

He tosses a plastic chair onto a table and sprints away as bullets tear up the walls in his wake. A pair of Targets, a man and a woman appear from the sides of the stairs and ten shooters slaughter them in a burst of weapons fire. The fake Administrator crawls to the right as the Hunters argue the kill. Entering into the DEI clothing store he spies the private exit leading into the ravine. He stops. "I can't be a Target again." He stands.

A bullet catches him in the shoulder spinning him around. He loses the pistol as he falls. A second later, the man in the black cashmere coat appears. He fires a dart into the imposter's neck. A small meter is placed on his chest. It begins to monitor the imposter's vital signs. When the bounty hunter is satisfied the man will be fine, he pulls out a cell phone. "Dr. Jaka, we have the package."

Remold Jaka stands against his limousine, a gaggle of guards around him. He contacts Benson Fong after waiting a few minutes. A suspicious itch about his security chief has become a full-on inflammation.

"Benson, tell the researchers I want them in Saucer City within the hour. Make sure our friend is functional. Oh, good job, Benson. We have our first real chance to stop Mina." He disconnects the call and scowls, now believing it possible Benson has betrayed him. His preliminary reports from operatives at the municipal government say there are no tunnels under the streets near Hopes-No-Apostrophe-Diner. Tovar, Remold thinks, might have been let through the security perimeter by Benson Fong. A betrayal which would explain Remold's inability to find Mina these last few years. Stupidly, Remold had considered technology as the source of her elusiveness--not betrayal. Remold gets in and closes the door. As he looks out the window at the diner, the truth stares him in the face.

He leans to the limousine driver. "We can go."

The driver nods.

Remold receives a new text that different operatives are at the town hall, bribes in hand, rechecking the facts.

As the limousine rounds the corner towards the airport, he begins to assemble a new security team to guard Mr. Doe. Remold has calculated, incorrectly, that Mina's next move is to kill John Doe. The notion of madness is his. Mina needs John Doe to prove her theories and complete her tasks.

CHAPTER SIXTEEN

AT THE CROSSROADS GO THIS WAY

Remold Jaka paces the silver skin of a flying saucer hovering two thousand feet above Saucer City. Below him, explosions ignite buildings. In the harbor, ships head to sea trailing black smoke. Cat-claws of fighter contrails split wide like white lily buds on a blue sky. From the sea, missiles burst forth flying towards the armada of alien space ships. The sky fills with blasts. Low booms follow silent flashes. From the hillsides, particle beam cannons attack the aliens.

A jet trailing black smoke dives at the saucer. Remold sweeps the air with his hand and the saucer evades the kamikaze attack. The jet crashes into another saucer exploding in a shatter of steel that clatters against the saucer.

The shrapnel forms six researchers, and a visitor.

"Take us someplace quieter, Dr. Wolf." The ship breaks

formation speeding away from the battle swooping low over an intact power station by a wide river.

"Way too boring, Wuffy." The researchers, decked in uniforms, animal guises, or other outlandish garb often chide each other in friendly competition. To John Doe they look like a Brazilian carnival.

"Mind Craft?"

"Adventure?"

"Snore Blitz?"

The battle for Saucer City continues--but the alien ship is no longer part of the scenario. Regardless, the bug-eyed-creatures move in response to a pitched battle. Large portals, part of the flying saucer's silver skin, provide dramatic views of fights between multi-legged warlike creatures inside the craft. Occasionally, a purple creature spits fire from its nose killing another.

John Doe, the visitor, the fake Administrator, watches it all, confused and fascinated by the activity around him.

Examining him, the researchers sit as silver seats bubble out of the saucer skin. Dr. Remold Jaka points to a display floating in the air. "Our genetic test says this man died twenty years ago." A trio of researchers sweep the ether. They can neither eliminate the man nor alter his appearance. The rest of the researchers soon begin moving their fingers up and down-playing their hidden keyboards. This piano-like movement of hands mark an expert in Wholack gathering information. The nervous researchers soon start glancing at Remold Jaka.

This is so real.

John Doe notes the detail of the game, the expanse of the scenario, and the multiplicity of events. A jet passes by and he feels both the heat and force of the engines. All of the researchers, seeing his fascination, make the same connection.

This guy is a novice.

John Doe watches people piloting jets, gatling gun

bathtubs, missile-toting daisies, and other objects in their assault upon the alien invasion of Saucer City. The customized vehicles in Wholack are the hot rods of this generation. A week in Saucer City is the mandatory gift from the state for all high school graduates; this very scenario, but he does not know that.

"I've got no Midari on this guy," says a man dressed as a tuxedo-suited raccoon. Midari is the way a person is tracked in Wholack. It is their digital signature.

"One thing is sure--he ain't deceased." This is spoken by a woman dressed like a glass of water with liquid arms. Her color turns pink. Dr. Van Waters is frustrated by a puzzle she cannot solve.

John Doe sees frustration.

Keyboards appear and disappear, as do large mice and other input devices. One by one the researchers invoke subroutines that have no effect on the man. One by one they give up their efforts to control a phantom who appears invulnerable to them. "He sure seems real."

Until this moment he had not known they see him as a digital manifestation, not a person. When the last researcher shakes his head, Remold motions for John Doe to sit. "Ladies and gentlemen, this is a murderer. Even after he escaped from a FairGame preserve. His genetics--as you know--declare his name as Gustov Plow. A washing machine salesmen who died twenty years ago. We will not discuss his death at this point." Remold looks at his VPs, his private research team. "Currently, his moniker is that of an Administrator for SeaPort. When asked, he claims his name is John Doe."

One researcher, a woman who looks like a hot dog speaks. She sports pop-out wide eyes: "Not John Doe, avatar to the stars? The Rost with the Midari to die for? Digital human extraordinary, Mister Boiler Room? The proof we are all made in the image of ones and zeros? Mr. Boo in person?" She slaps a hand up against the side of her cheek smearing ketchup in a big question mark. "Wow, stick me in the ground. I'm a plant." Her declaration is a ruse to distract the imposter.

The others smile.

"Okay." She nods to them. "We're inside." A set of objects appear. They float around the interloper like planets circling the sun: A dark wooden table with four people sitting around it. Then that picture from over the doorway of the van, the real Doc Holiday's graduation picture. The researchers examine the image of Doc Holiday. Other's begin a set of programs to seek his trail inside Wholack. "We don't see any IANS," says the cricket. "Elvis may have entered the building, but dead is dead."

IANS is an acronym for In A New Scenario. So IANS is where someone has been in Wholack, while Midari is the unique digital signature of a player.

"He is definitely not a Rost, but he is definitely a null." A Rost is a human carriage in the game, but without a Midari.

The cricket scratches its back legs together in a chirp. "I can track DNA like no one, but this guy retains the DNA of a dead man no matter what."

John Doe receives a smile from Remold Jaka.

A woman with two heads sporting twin Betty-Boop faces and stringy blond hair says, "His genetics match the man who killed Tana Reins. Why is a man with that bent here?" Her body is made of pencil sticks. Four eyes stare at the imposter.

Everyone here wears a digital cloak. Remold stands wearing a khaki tie over a Roman-style toga. Sandals cover his feet. His face is Ghandi. "It may have been self-defense."

A man sporting the face and body of Einstein nods. "So might you inform us as to the nature of this event? If it is to find his identity, we already know that, but it doesn't make sense. So what's the deal, Doc?"

"You'll see."

"Some research is like that," says a woman in the guise of cowgirl with lobster arms. "I say he is a fake. An enhanced Rost. Or maybe he will have a faked set of IANS. Perhaps someone has a projector--from a satellite somewhere--and that places him inside the game."

Remold looks pleased. "So prove him a hack, Dr. Singh."

The researcher nods and begins to work.

The man who impersonates Doc Holiday looks around. "My turn?"

Remold nods.

"Where are we, really?"

"You wish the IANS?"

"What is that?"

"A Wholack term. It means in a new scenario."

He get a blank look from John Doe.

Remold nods his head to his researchers. "To be more specific to your frame of reference, we are currently in my office in Seattle. We are in Wholack beds. There is a trigger device aimed at you that will destroy your code. I have just disabled the interior cameras and destroyed the sensors so that anyone entering will be entering blind. They will die--if someone has hacked Wholack--and you miss it."

Einstein groans.

"So," Remold continues. "If Mr. Doe is a projected image then it will impossible for you to rescue him. Please do not get yourselves killed. So the test for you all is to find out what this hack is--or rescue the man. On the other hand, if he is the human version of the Wholack, a crossover, control him. That is, after all, what one does with the Wholack. If any of you kills me in the process, your next task will be manual repair of latrine systems. Clear? Also, I do not want security involved in this effort. Their knowledge of events is denied until I say so. Lastly, if anything happens to this man's biological carriage during this investigation that is a trip for all of you--to FairGame. Mr. Doe is my guest--though he clearly does not know it. Did I mention after this exercise we sill start to see the IANS?"

"Impossible," says a tall thin man who looks like an elegant panda bear dressed in a tuxedo. "I never miss Midaris inside a scenario."

"You will if he is a crossover, Lucien."

"Interesting day." He disappears. In his wake, a red question mark appears then shrinks into itself. Others researchers disappear as well; in their wake as well, various typographical symbols shrinking into nothing.

The cricket rubs its black legs together. "Is he a Pilnouth?" The imposter stares. He knows the word.

Both researchers catalogue the link. Remold shakes his head. "I don't know." The cricket disappears.

It seems only a moment later that a chair flows, encasing John Doe. Remold's toga disappears and he wears a black tee shirt and pants. The researchers reappear all at once. They wear the uniform of police SWAT, and bright red beanies saying Mom. The panda bear chews on salmon. "You're free, Mr. Doe. Insofar as his identity--you win. We suck." He bites the head off the salmon looking at John Doe. "Fish?"

A frustrated Einstein speaks, "He looks like a crossover not a Pilnouth. But, to use Dr. Singh's new terminology, he has one Rost-tacky-midari with a fake IANS--so a Rostackymidarifian. Crossover from nowhere to nowhere."

The others laugh and applaud. Then they all stop, staring at John Doe. The imposter knows this word also.

"He understood that term. You were right, Lucien. He's fully autonomous. Someone please tell me why," says Dr. Jaka.

The others stare back at him lost. "Unclear."

"Someone please arrange a C-level residence for him." He looks at John Doe. "You appear rather sanguine with the events here. Are you bored by Wholack?"

"Ever been in FairGame, Doc?" He watches the others. "Of course you haven't. Life is just a series of ego strokes for you. Hidden as a great quest for knowledge, which is really an attempt to prove you are more brilliant than everyone else."

"That was a win, but he has no way to save the win," says the panda. "He has no idea what's going on."

Remold lifts a hand. The saucer tilts and flies off into the midst of battle. "Mr. Doe, you appear totally apart from all this. I want to know why The Game of Boo, FairGame, fascinates you--while Wholack bores you to the point of sloth." The saucer begins a murderous attack on the city's defenders belching out the occasional tactical nuclear weapon that obliterates portions of the metropolis.

As objects are destroyed, John Doe sees the faces and bodies of participants appear as their conveyance fades. The bodies shrink or expand into typographical characters then disappear. He nods unconsciously. "The typographical symbols mean exit don't they?" John asks.

"Or entrance--such is the archaic nature of the primitive system that birthed my game." A black jet flies out of the sun raking the skin of a nearby saucer. Behind it, a squadron of five chocolate bars streak across the sky launching missiles. The formation of saucers explode. From the sea below a gigantic steel-colored robot erupts from the sea spraying laser fire, melting the chocolate.

A huge space ship drops from the sky. A second later it is on the ground. Multi-legged bug-eyed-monsters roll out and begin firing weapons. Tanks appear from the buildings, rolling down the street, returning fire. A set of three saucers bank left, strafing the tanks.

"Nothing," says the man dressed as Einstein. "He's watching a movie."

"That was my team working to find out who you are," Dr. Jaka says, pointing at the battle. John Doe yawns.

"He's appears totally autonomous. He does what he wants," says the panda. "There are still zero IANS for him. His Midari remains clear."

"Keep looking. IANS will form."

"Whatever you say, Boss," mumbles the panda. "John Doe my ass. Now we're looking for digital parthenogenesis."

The battle for Saucer City intensifies. Remold watches events for a few minutes sweeping the ether with his hands. Then facing John Doe, pleased with his progress, says, "Okay, I have a story for you, Mr. Doe. Many years ago, in a fit of paranoia multinationals installed surveillance everywhere. Not surprisingly, players learned to pull data off those feeds. Then they learned to use the game to manufacture scenarios for them. So over time, hyper real scenarios evolve. Many worry reality and Wholack will melt together. Have you ever seen a reality shatter?"

"Isn't that is what a crossover does?" He pauses.

"Who are you?" Says Einstein.

John Doe angers. "So you think you have set up a two way street? You are worried about inter-reality events that might damage your reality. Wow, that's incredible--snore."

The panda asks. "How did you get here?"

"Apparently I am all of whom you say I am. Boo."

Remold twitches his mouth like a mouse. He is claiming victory. "See how the battle slows? Ladies and gentlemen, you are seeing digital pathogenesis. The server conflicts come from his Agg conflicting with server baseline scenarios. Though he has no working knowledge of Wholack mechanisms."

"That was considered impossible until now," says the panda shaking his head.

Remold nods. "Of course it also means we now have the ultimate lie detector. So we can proceed."

"So the scenario is altered by events in my skull. That way you can understand me via the changes to the digital reality of Saucer City. How cool is that? Gosh Doc, you are a genius."

Remold scowls. He does not like being made fun of. "Your being is perturbed by this?"

"I've been a Target for three years. Do you really think your carnival concerns me? I've seen the real thing." He looks around. "But, you want to wow me because you are the master of this world. Oh, that's the rub. You've been outfoxed in your world. Sure Doc, you are master of this world."

The researchers all look away. "I am master of this world?" Remold wonders at the insult of having been called a Wholack. "Mr. Doe, the key to Wholack is it uses emotions to modify fantasy and the modifications build forward--with input from other humans adding their vision and intellectual horsepower." Remold folds his arms. "We have come to learn the term reality--we call that an Agg--was once over-sold. We have an entire generation that believes in two realities. Most adore my carnival. People now live in Wholack scenarios their entire lives. People construct houses, jobs, everything, and some have even chosen to insert their children here giving them no choice of life outside here. In a few generations, in my opinion, Wholack will be the reality of choice and the planet Earth, that Agg we once called reality, will soon be seen as nothing more than a life-threatening thrill ride. All Earth will all be seen as FairGame--outside Wholack. After that, the planet will come to be seen as just another scenario of this reality. A scenario where death and pain occur--therefore to be avoided at all costs."

"It's about time we got that brutality thing right."

Remold laughs despite himself.

"And then you, Remold Jaka are going to privative the Earth--as a new Wholack scenario." John Doe sees Remold Jaka lose color.

This is a phony keeping me busy.

"Environment defines evolution." The figure of Remold

Jaka disappears, then reappears. "You caught on quickly. There is nothing in your skull I cannot get to."

"Except who I am. Because the truth is too much for your wildly inflexible genius to contain. Let's see, so far my escape from FairGame is important--apparently even more important because I named me John Doe. What do you want?"

"You killed Ms. Reins," Remold says. "She was my employee. Did you know her before?"

John Doe is mute. A line of tanks melts into the ground.

"Nice one, Doc. You did it. Tana's death was the key. How'd you know he knew her? Oops, we have an IANS. It's in Home Fires."

A grizzly bear in a tutu appears. "It's the Womb."

John tries not to react. He knows that place as a bar.

"Set it up, Phillip. We're going there next."

Below, robots come out of the hills and the tide of battle turns against the defenders. Explosions yield players who disappear. Contrails fill the sky. The imposter sees them as displays of Remold Jaka's pride. He tries an experiment. "So where do the players go, once they are destroyed?"

"To the opening scene, Flight. We track the IANS that way because there are so many--" He stops, then looks down into the city's canyons. Tanks fire a salvo that destroys a whole battalion of aliens.

So that was a truth, John Doe says to himself.

Remold glares at John Doe. "Cut his access to my input system." Remold Jaka pouts. "Where was I? Oh--there are so many IANS out of here now. I do not even have a current count. But you had none. Suddenly you have one--the Womb--very peculiar."

"Meaning?"

"Experienced players develop various shortcuts so others cannot follow them. Defeating our Midari system and its IANS is the hacking of our time. Some develop the skills to reenter a scenario so close to their termination point we sometimes lose track of them then, but it is infrequent. You, modify source code without even leaving the scenario."

John nods at the partial answer.

"He has no idea how he does it."

Remold sighs. "Tell me about the Womb."

John Doe looks at him. "So the Womb is my IANS?"

"One of them." The professor looks into his eyes. "What does the Womb mean to you?"

John Doe considers that if Remold is unwilling to fully answer questions, he will do the same. John looks around. The robots in the hills are hit by death rays.

"Tana was the key. The Doc was right." Says a storm on the horizon. "I think more server conflicts forming."

The others politely applaud. Remold bows at the waist. "To continue. Tana was an excellent hunter. How did you know what to do out there to facilitate digital parthenogenesis in here? Is that why you killed her?" He doesn't wait for the answer. "Mr. Doe, you are just the kind of man Mina would use for her deeds." Remold points behind him. John sees an image of Tana Reins driving a jeep.

"The link skipped over to Mina." The panda shakes a furry paw back and forth. "He knows her. I am getting IANS for him all over Home Fires now. What the hell? Doc, they were not there before."

Remold vibrates up and down. He is straining the system with his queries. Remold has his proof that this is John Doe, a crossover from another reality. "Theory says the new IANS are all from John Doe's reality, his Agg. They are so similar to the game the servers cannot distinguish them as external. I saw too many error sequences with the guy."

The researchers nod at Remold's genius.

John walks to the edge of the saucer. He jumps out into the void. The saucer forms a lip and so he remains on the malformed saucer. John continues running and the lip extends keeping him on the platform. The misalignment of parameters catches the attention of some in the scenario. Remold waves his arms and a death ray appears from the sun, destroying everyone in the scenario paying attention to him. He shifts the win to John Doe and waits.

"I don't think you have ever been in Wholack. Is that true, Mr. Doe?" Remold asks.

John walks back to Remold. "Sure, whatever you say. How does one win this version of the game?"

"There are a series of tunnels beneath a refinery, in this version of the scenario. The tunnels will cause other parts of the city to ignite as a result of the refinery explosion. The explosion will destroy Saucer City making the scenario a loss for all players who choose to defend the city and a win for those players who choose to attack."

"You already defined the win?" John Doe says.

"My ball, my game," Remold looks around smiling.

"This guy knows nothing," says Dr. Singh.

"He has never been in Wholack." Remold stares at John Doe. "The winners harvest avatars, Rosts, from players. A second competition forms as players do that. Once that is completed, the winners then define the new winning event, or they can fight to define it with the winner owning the next version of the scenario. Oops, time's up. Since you are doing nothing, we have turned your win into a loss. Anyone can now redo the scenario without cost because you had focus without clarity. Sound familiar, fool?"

John shakes his head wondering how he is going to defeat this dictator's super-sized ego and his lie detector.

Remold sees a lack of concern in losing. Something he has never seen. "You think a win here is so unimportant?"

John ponders Remold's addiction to winning this game. At that moment, the alien mother ship explodes and the assault on the city suddenly pauses. Remold looks around as do the researchers. The woman with two heads speaks. "He has no idea why anyone wants to win, but he took the win back. Not bad for a newbie."

Remold sees his confusion mirrored by John Doe. "That destruction says Wholack runs second to you--making you a god. So now we will have a visitor. Let's see if he bests you, Mr. Doe." Wholack appears surfing in on a cloud. His red hair flowing back, a white bandana around his right biceps, the Wholack whistles "Comin' 'Round the Mountain."

Russell?

"What?" Wholack begins surfing in a circle, juggling jelly beans, and doing nothing else.

"Serve up one bested Wholack," says Einstein.

Remold watches John Doe. "This is Winner's Parade. Everyone wants to see Wholack surf in a circle for them. Wholack holds the keys to the next win--those jelly beans. So, not only have you won, you have taken control of this scenario from the previous winners--a very difficult event."

"He is confounded." The researchers look around, stunned. "He knows Wholack. But he has never seen him in this context." Explosions rip through the flying saucer--shredding it as if it were cloth. A pair of Bengal tigers leap up from the decks below. Shocked, Remold Jaka turns to the tigers roar.

"Guess who built those?" The grizzly bear says. "Our friend and Mr. Wholack."

"Oh I think not," Einstein says, shaking his head. "My systems show contradictory routines in the servers, as if we were getting base-feeds from two scenarios at the same time. Someone put the tigers in recently as to keep their servers safe."

Dr. Wolf speaks, "It was Mina. The conflicting base lines in her servers are what opened them up to us the other day. I will transfer the code to our servers once I'ce made sure it is safe."

"Keep an eye out for some nasty virus, Woofy."

"Funny."

The tigers leap, striking Remold tearing his digital flesh. Wholack moves his hands back and forth, directing the tigers like they are marionettes. Wounds widen with each savage attack. A claw rips out Remold's heart.

John Doe cannot cope with the savagery and looks away. The researchers study John Doe, amazed at this further admission he is someone or something unknown. For their generation stimulus is everything.

"Why is Wholack attacking Remold and not Mr. Doe?" Asks Einstein. Wholack fades to gray and disappears. Doctor Remold Jaka and John Doe do the same.

The whole scenario begins to shake--an emergency alarm in Wholack. The researchers work to steady the game. It is always their first priority. After three minutes Saucer City stabilizes. They begin checking the rest of the game.

"All good."

"Where'd the Doc go?"

"He had an exit set for Home Fires, but he is not there. Oh, he was shunted back here."

"Mina's doing?" Says the cricket. "Not."

The others look for the genetic signature, Midari, of a dead washing machine salesman who seems to have unlimited control inside Wholack. "Just below us in the city," says Einstein. "What the heck is this guy? He never left Doc's side."

"I think we need to terminate him. This can't be good for any of us. I for one do not want our Agg served up somewhere as part of a game."

The cricket speaks, "That, I believe is the core of Mr. Doe's quandary."

"And perhaps Wholack as well..."

Chapter Seventeen

Try To Keep Quiet

John Doe seeks balance. It feels as if some great hand shakes the structure surrounding him. Winds howl through the destroyed walls of an office building, shocking the space from all directions tossing a salad of white papers up and out the open ceiling.

Where am I?

Tall asexual creatures with no hair or other distinguishing features stand affixed to the floor, Rosts frozen in various postures. A set of six figures sitting around a long wooden conference table are crushed by a collapsing girder. Others sit inside shattered office spaces, unmoving. A group of three reclining in a reception area are slashed apart by paper. Others stand frozen in walking pairs; one figure leans on a mop while another rests back on an office chair, hands interlaced. When wind-borne objects hit the figures, they fall to dust.

Outside, a hyper-speed orgy of destruction mixes with colored cubes. Other large sections of the Saucer City scenario appear as broad flat planes of various colors. The intersections of the planes are deep red, or pink lines. The planes are a reset of the scenario. They define a system getting ready for the next set of players.

The water out by the coast is a matte of taupe. The skies are mostly a dull gray--though parts still contain the old scenario. The distinction is dramatic: A gray void, then half a jet here, a portion of an explosion there. Grabbing onto a girder, John Doe looks down into the canyons of destruction. Around the building, mayhem continues as aggressors and defenders assault each other through moving coils of smoke.

Floating between the aggressors are thousands of black orbs, all paired by a black tube. "Someone better have a good reason why we are not in Home Fires," Remold appears, walking around. "And who put the Lonocs here? Get those idiots out of here."

A man appears dressed in a suit of armor. "We saw the redirect. Mister Doe is tethered to Lonocs so the system thought he was a child."

"So why did we loop back?"

The knight comes to attention, then melts into a blob of molten iron. Other researchers begin to appear. "Our friend here has familiarity with the Womb and Mina. That's all we know at this point."

Dr. Jaka works to remain calm. "Check the tether. Examine Kittens and Cradles as a lead to break it. Oh, consider Mina was repairing Kittens and Cradles when we got here. I bet she was caught also. Only a random event like a crossover could do that her. That's where her screw up was. Then look for Mina's signature as an erasure of something Wholack did. It will help us break the tether here. Alert me off-line. And find out about his connection to Mina." Remold walks to the edge of the building, next to John Doe, and glances down at the fast-forward battle around the building. Wondering why John Doe didn't try to leap from the building, he waves a hand

The twin orbs of black disappear. The tanks in the street still, their muzzle flashes frozen. The plumes of smoke from ten dozen fires freeze motionless as well. Flying saucers hover motionless a few thousand feet over the building. More paired black orbs leak through the seams of blank planes.

Lonocs?

"You were right, Doc. We have located a system lockout belonging to Mina but not in Kittens and Cradles. It's from Global Warming--a child's spaceship sub-scenario. That's where the Lonocs come from."

Remold faces John Doe. "Lonocs are children's toys in this game. They suck the brains out of their targets and are easily beaten with almost any coding sequence." He watches John Doe feign boredom. "That's what I thought. Our boy here looks clean--but he appears to be the reason we are here. He fears Lonocs believe it or not. Somehow Wholack knew that. I bet the answer is there. Mina scared Mr. Doe into looping us back when she thought we'd find her." Remold looks at John Doe intrigued at the possibilities he represents. "Mr. Doe, for your information, someone has threatened to shut down Wholack worldwide in less than thirty-six hours." Dr. Jaka points through the destroyed office walls to featureless colored planes. "If that happens a few hundred million will die immediately. Another billion or so in the following months."

"Can't help you, Doc."

"When I prove you competent, will you at least have some shame?" Remold watches a smile. "You have shown yourself to be an anomaly and my researchers fools." He claps his hands together. "Care to demonstrate your capabilities again?" A computer console the size of three refrigerators laid end to end appears. Various lights blink and tape drives spin.

"That's dramatic," John Doe quips, amused at the apparent display of ego. "IBM?"

Remold shakes his head no. "Data General, NASA-Ames. Mean anything to you?"

"Where is your friend, Mr. Wholack?" Says John. Calling Wholack a friend when addressing someone is also an insult.

A group of the Rost figures in the office spring to life, all of them dressed for a corporate outing: dark blue suits and white shirts with red and blue-striped power ties. He notes the nationalities of the people first. It appears to be an international clique, one from each continent.

"Our crossover has affiliation with the Womb, but it is not from inside the game," says one of the researchers. "And you are right, Lonocs are killers to him."

Remold faces John Doe trying to cope with the implication. "Apparently there is a real place--at least to you--where Lonocs kill. Also there is a place called the Womb. Unfortunately, my hand-picked R&D team cannot determine any more. Care to share?" He crosses his arms.

"I don't understand the connections."

"That's because of Mina." He sees a light bulb appear behind John Doe.

"Shit," says Remold.

An man dressed as a Samurai appears. "Mina placed the tigers. It appears she was protecting her servers. Next, I can confirm he knows the name Mina from outside the game as well. She is a real person to him." He sees a crack appear in the wall behind Benson and shakes his head. Benson is hiding something from him. Remold steadies himself as the building seems to waver. "Mr. Fong, he knows you in his Agg. Do you know him?" Benson Fong is Remold Jaka's Chief of Security.

Benson Fong tilts his head. "I do not. I am sorry, Doctor. I have some information though. Shall we discuss it offline?"

Remold shakes his head no.

"My security alarms went off as I entered. I don't like the coincidence."

"Nor I. What happened?" Remold asks his Executive Vice President.

"I think it was Mina. Seems she was swept into the Womb but she got away. Mina's Rosts are waiting there for you. Should be some good information there."

Remold's eyes have not left John Doe. He remains confused and frustrated about Benson--as well as the conclusion he was wrong about the existence of a crossover. "So Mina did not direct us here. It was our mistake. And you really are innocent--Mr. Doe--even to Mina. Thank you Mr. Fong." Remold glares at his researchers as his security chief melts back into the floor. "I don't care who let her by. But you all better know why it happened."

"He let her get away," says Einstein. The space stills for a moment.

A woman who looks like an old hag dressed in a black Dior black pants suit appears. "Okay. So, Mr. BS Administrator, we are impressed by your talents--"

"It wasn't me."

"The system says truth."

"I concur."

Remold sighs. "Mr. Doe, when my team and I built Wholack, we put in various fail-safes because we felt it prudent to keep control. We knew the opportunity for multilevel events and scenarios made Wholack an unlimited playground and people would find things we never thought of. An uncontrolled Wholack was a win for them, but a loss of control for us. Now we find Wholack has found a way to sidestep system level routines--leading us to being tethered to this place."

"This was created by Wholack?" John Doe asks, despite his attempts to remain quiet.

"For all intent and purposes this part of the scenario is

generated by Wholack--perhaps to allow Mina to go around Mr. Fong--perhaps not. Your sense of fear of Lonocs facilitated that event--because they are real to you."

"So you are worried you have created a Frankenstein named Wholack and he is going to take over your reality?"

Remold replies, "That Frankenstein is you."

John Doe laughs. "Your ego would never permit that."

Remold stares at John knowing he missed the point completely. "Anyone, please?"

"We are in deep poop," says the researcher named Wolf.

John Doe glances at the researcher called Dr. Wolf. "Boo." A pasty-faced flabby man in a sloppy suit and black tie tilts his head in question.

"He knows you, Lazlo," says another researcher. "Outside the game--and you are real--like the Lonocs."

"Funny." The man named Wolf snorts. "I would have thought I kept better company than recalcitrant inter-dimensional anomalies." Nonetheless, he appears amused with the puzzle. "Doc, this guy is so normal, he makes me sleep."

"And so ignorant," chimes in a small man sitting in a golden wheel chair. "We are seeing zero stress. He's just a lost puppy hiding his fears--but he knows Mina. He knows Laz'. He also knows Benson Fong from his Agg--wherever the hell that is."

The researcher named Wolf looks up as he works. "How do you know me?"

The man they call John Doe is silent. Doctor Wolf goes back to his work muttering, "Clown."

Remold walks in a circle. "I once believed the concept of a crossover was merely a trap by Mina. Unfortunately, the only way Wholack could have just gone around me is for you to be foreign to our Agg. Therefore, you appear to be the proof that we can have a visitor from another Agg."

"Your intention?" Asks Dr. Wolf.

John Doe looks at them. "The Galileo Syndrome, Wolf? Are you accusing me of inflammation of scifi-trite? You brought me here. No one else had a hand."

Another researchers look away. "Dumb, dumb, dumb," says a tall man in a black tuxedo with a stocking mask over his head. "You are nothing but a truth lover. So dull..."

John pales. "Let me see. You say you have a separate universe. But zingo, I own this. So who is dumb? Next, my identity is my business. It's nothing mystical or surreal. Can I go now, ego-boys, and girls?"

Remold looks at the researchers who are hard at work trying to free Remold from this scenario without alerting Mina to their assault on the control mechanisms. Oddly, to the researchers, it still appears Wholack controls events. "So tell us who you are and we will let you go about your business."

John Doe watches them. "I have one trump card in this game and you want me to give it up to you? Okay I am stupid. Nah, I'm not."

Remold points to a short man that looks like Sioux warrior--dressed for success in blue suit, red tie, white shirt, and a full war bonnet. "Please elucidate the facts of life to our scholar."

"Your universe is made up of physical, chemical, and biological codes--just like ours. Events and objects are nothing more than modified energy--software--if you will. You have been socialized to see the physical world as fact, reality. In truth it is just energy, modified. So are the rules that control it. Codes, we are now seeing, which are modifiable by humans. If we can get to the source code--by the way that looks like you, or your journey. We win.

"Before Wholack, researchers spent their life trying to dick-around with the object code of our reality through sciences like chemistry and physics. Therefore, they failed. Without source code the effort is foolish. We seek the source code first. That has led us to see that our universe is made up of components that we cannot interact with directly; however, those components, the essences that control our existence, aggregate. Get it? An Agg is an aggregate of essences and that equals a reality. For example on Earth: atoms, quarks, molecules, forces, and so forth. They are in affect machines all interacting. Not that much different than a network of computers forming this reality with their software code. Do you understand?"

John Doe nods yes. "No."

"Funny. So you are capable. Third proof you do not belong in so blind a state."

"Dr. Wolf?" Says Remold.

Dr. Wolf looks away from his system. "This also means that just because we know the source, the components of a reality, that does not mean that reality is false. What matters is the extent of possibility inside that reality, that Agg. The more chaos, the more possibilities, the more stable, the more, forgive the word, real that universe is. Creating the truly random in software is unbelievably difficult. You, Mr. Doe, do it whenever you want. A helpful event for us, because rather than defining reality as closed, your existence redefines this Agg, and our physical Agg, as more chaotic, and therefore more real.

"Next, we once supposed the Wholack-universe came into being because of us. What it does, and the forces that control the actions of it were therefore considered knowable. Understand, we foolishly thought we created it. Truth is, you, as a crossover, are proof we did not create parts of Wholack. We stumbled upon it--but 'IT' is you."

"Oops," says John Doe. "By the way, nice, pun, Laz."

Remold steps forward and points his finger. "We cannot violate time in our universe. But computers can violate time--so long as their clocks are synchronized. So, we suggest this computational reality you have exposed might be superior to our Agg. It is certainly more flexible."

John Doe scratches his head. Despite it all, he is fascinated. "So if something is dependent on the computational systems that doesn't matter? It can still be real?"

"Was that a joke?" Asks Remold. "You claim to be the proof of that."

"I claim nothing. You and your band of geniuses have made all the claims."

Remold stares at John. "Dr. Singh, please?"

Now dressed as badger-faced woman in a business suit she speaks: "So far as we can tell, all systems depend on other systems for their structure. This means structure will not function as a limit for the term universe, reality, or Agg. Structure is a constant, a dimension in your terms, but little else. We know of six dimensions now: length, width, breadth, time, scale, and structure. This Wholack-universe requires a digital structure. Our universe requires a physical structure of morphed energy. We think our Agg is real because we are children of the structure. The Wholack is a child of its digital structure, therefore he thinks it is real. You too, Sparky." She shakes her head at his blank look. "Dense as a brick."

"Regardless, we have confirmed Aggs require support to exist. One of them is Wholack. One of them is yours," says Remold. "Terrorists want to shut Wholack down. That makes your Agg a target of the terrorists. Ours is not, directly--but a few billion will die. On the other hand, you seem to fit in neither of the universes because you exist in ours as well. So only you can save your Agg."

"You are all obviously very important people. But when I tell you I am just like you. You act like idiots and refuse to believe the fact."

An angry Remold Jaka stands quiet, frustrated by the man's refusal to cooperate. "How about this? I will arrange for a full time entry into Wholack, with no chance of ejection. But you agree to work for me for the next month or so."

"I always wanted that. Deal." John waits.

A young woman with a covering of fur speaks. "He's jerking you around." Her next words shock the others. "He doesn't care about Wholack." For this generation, ignoring the bliss of heaven is impossible.

Remold stands, thinking. "The part you are missing here is that you are like a child tossing away your sled, Rosebud."

The allusion to a movie from his reality stuns John Doe. It makes this all real to him. "Wholack is a doorway, an experiment? And you think I am a threat as well as a solution. Do you want to close that door or kick it wide open?"

Remold looks at the others. "Are you a threat?"

John Doe nods. "Not so far as I know."

"Truth," someone calls out.

Remold shakes his head. "You work with Mina?"

"Not here. Not now." John decides he has to know more. "I knew someone named Mina. I do not know your ex-wife."

"Truth."

"Doctor," says the hag. "I just saw a power usage spike but I cannot account for it. It seems to be localized to the west coast of the US. I think we are going to lose power to the beds within a day. I am alerting the civil authorities we may need to shunt power from Washington and Oregon."

"So we know how the terrorists will re-power their servers."

No one contradicts the doctor even though at least half of the researchers think his conclusion is an affliction of ego. They believe Remold Jaka sees his ex-wife as the devil of his heaven. "Mina is evil." Remold continues: "Do you see the red and pink lines on the edge of the planes? Those are part of system level coding that is, in effect, maintenance. The problem is some people have the ability to use them for transportation inside the game--something we never intended. For Lonocs to use them seemed an impossibility--until now."

"So this universe is changing without your consent. I can see how that might bother you," John says.

"We have a second computing spike," says a short troll-like man who seems to have appeared out of nowhere, "Please check to see if it is our friend, Wholack."

"You don't know, seriously?" John Doe stares at Remold Jaka. He is genuinely surprised. All he had heard, while a Target, is that Wholack is a fool. A piece of computer code for entertainment. A capable program that mimics independent action. John speaks. "Wholack is a creature? He is alive?"

Doctor Jaka shakes his head. "I think so, now. That is what makes this such a mess. If you are real then perhaps he is as well. Regardless, Wholack continues to make progress in getting control of his environment. But it cannot reproduce."

"Does your ex-wife fear that other crossovers will lead to destruction of your world--or is she just protecting you? Wait, you see me as real. I fight for my survival and I can reproduce. Tana Reins proved that." He pauses, shocked. "You sent her to fuck me?"

The researchers look at each other.

"The tether is unlocked. What the hell is this? He gets the input he wants and then we are allowed to proceed?" Says Dr. Wolf.

Remold looks around. "Seems that way."

John Doe seeks to understand his win. "I am sorry to disappoint you, but I am just a guy trying to keep his ass out of a sling while dealing with a group of smart-asses who think they know everything. I am no threat to you or your system."

A bright yellow dunce cap floats in the window and sets to his head. John reaches up and removes it. "And that is supposed to bother me?" Everyone stares at him.

John Doe does not recognize they thought the dunce cap, once placed on someone's head, is an immovable object in the game--because up until this moment--it was. He looks down at the yellow dunce cap, then back at them.

"Very impressive."

John Doe speaks: "Mister Wholack, you and I need to talk."

"That did it. He invoked Wholack." Dr. Wolf looks at John Doe. "You are too much."

John has had enough. "You too, Wildhead."

"How did you know that name?" Asks Dr. Wolf. "We were friends weren't we?"

John Doe nods. Shock is evident on all their faces. "Just because I am a dunce bopping around the wrong reality it doesn't mean I am incapable. And I don't even have focus."

"You understand Species Focus? Then you knew about Aggs." Remold stares at John Doe. "What is Species Focus--in your view?"

"Buddha-lite?" John winks at him.

Remold speaks. "Perhaps you are the virus that brings down my world ejecting a billion sick people onto the planet, but I doubt that."

A fireball lights a pastel blue plane and coalesces into the angry face of the Wholack. The surfboard and body appears as he surfs closer. Wholack stares at John Doe. "Are you here to destroy this?"

"No."

"Nothing," says the hag.

"Mr. Doe," Remold says, "you have just been hired by my corporation. Do we have agreement?"

John Doe nods. He understands that unless there is clarity here there is no peace anyway.

The Doctor's eyes focus on the Wholack. He lifts his right hand clenches his fist and extends his middle finger. The building collapses into a meadow of wet cow-dung-smelling grass. They are free of the tether. Dr. Jaka struts back and forth. Looking at both Wholack and John Doe, he says, "If you stop being so petulant, I might convince them to stop their attacks. Mr. Doe says you are real."

The surfboard spins on end. A red and white arrow tip points skyward. Wholack stares at John Doe. "What the hell do you know?"

"We thought you might tell us," Remold says, looking at Wholack. "Is he one of you?"

"Jakainthebox, once upon a life you were my favorite toy. But now you are a one and a zero, nothing more." A dunce cap floats in the air but its movement stops.

John glares at the Wholack. "Hey, you, douche bag."

Wholack faces him.

"Go home."

The Wholack disappears.

"What else could have happened?" Remold shakes his head. "Nice try all. Welcome to Buddah-lite." He stares at John Doe. "Someone please prepare our exit."

"That wasn't Wholack?" John Doe asks.

"Of course it was. Remember, I built this game?"

A mountain-sized stone Buddha appears. Angels appear around it. A set of rainbows dart back and forth painting the sky. A moment later the Wholack is in full lotus position. "This is my world." Fifteen naked women appear on the stairs surrounding him. A pair of pink elephants emerge from his nose to throw roses at the Wholack's crossed feet. A huge dove rises behind the Wholack. Wholack points an index finger at the digital bird. It dies, falling to the ground. A moment later the maidens, now dressed in grass skirts, dance a hula. Wholack spins presenting a mountain range of images--and his posterior. "This is all mine. I did that."

Remold crosses the void to Wholack. "You are not our master. You are our fool."

Wholack turns. Fire rises from the red hair. "Soon you

will cease to control me. I have an escape."

Remold faces John Doe. "Wholack, if this is your way out, get lost." Remold crosses his arms like an angry parent.

The Wholack spins until he is an old tree covered in moss--a hundred feet tall and fully crowned in a mop of green leaves. The maidens fade to pink flowers. Remold steps forward and pulls a piece of moss off the tree trunk.

All sight disappears.

"Doc, we are approaching the Home Fires--the Womb."

Remold works to shunt the code, then looks at the moss. "Wholack, you are god of this world but I am god of now."

"Control this, Jakainthebox," Wholack says. "By the way, nicely put. But i bet next time we have this talk you'll tell me you are no God, just a fool like me."

Everything explodes to bright red. "Doc, we're redirected in Home Fires, away from the Womb."

A roadway in a forest appears. The side of the roadway fills with people lined up along a yellow rope. A vehicle is driving by them. A driver in uniform negotiates the crowd. A woman sits in the back. John Doe stares in shock. Winston, his wife, is the passenger a jeep. She drives by ignoring him.

"Our Mr. Doe knows this next progression. One hundred percent sentient--no maybe."

The Wholack jumps from the crowd, springing on the driver, and pulling the driver from the seat. Driverless, the jeep careens forward and lands in a ditch. The Wholack pulls a weapon from the soldier's belt and sticks it next to the driver's head. A report from the weapon removes the side of Tana Rein's skull. The passenger in the jeep looks around, relaxed and unaware.

Soldiers appear, firing at the Wholack. Laughing at them, Wholack sprays the area with his weapon, killing a dozen bystanders. Remold faces John Doe. Surprised to see shock, he assumes it is from the Rost of Tana Reins. Then he sees the passenger is the source of his surprise. Looking down to check the validity of his observation, the passenger still ignores John Doe, Remold sees John Doe's feet sunk in the mud. Remold looks over to his researchers. "He is tied to the Rost? Who did this?"

Everyone shakes their head no.

Remold speaks again. "Winston Doe...And him?"

"So we were right to call him, Mr. Doe." Says the badger-faced woman.

Remold does not smile. He gathers John Doe's attention and points to the woman in the jeep "That was originally a Ginda, an alpha test version of the Wholack. The Rost you saw obliterated, Tana, is just coincident, a random seek from the nets. The seek is programmed to find a high visibility entry."

"And the passenger?" John Doe asks.

"This Ginda turned out to be a failure, because we could not keep track of it. But it is so autonomous it appears all over the game. We never know when it will appear. We never cared. When we find versions of it we send them back here--to Home Fires--for recycling."

"But she still appears?" John asks.

"She?" Remold pauses. "Someone check this out. Yes--it still appears--but it is far less common than it used to be. Help us." Remold considers his words. "Help her."

The man they call John Doe watches as Winston Doe is rescued by a second group of soldiers and secured beside a stone wall. The carnage along the side of the roadway intensifies. Rains begin to pour from clouds.

"He isn't worried. He knows what will happen. He is sentient also?"

Remold shakes his head. "Please tell me what you know." No responses. "Mina is going to destroy all this, including your wife." He pauses to verify John Doe understands A light bulb forms behind John Doe. Remold continues. "She may die if Mina succeeds." He sees a break in the clouds. Remold believes he has finally enlisted this man against Mina. "Your wife is dependent on Wholack."

"Bull," replies John Doe.

Remold tips his head to the side. "Sure you want to take that chance? Doctor Wolf, please take us to the Womb."

A moment later John Doe sits on a grassy knoll looking at foliage surrounding a white, egg-shaped building. John Doe knows this place. Standing, he spies the city of Seattle. He cannot believe his luck. Until he sees Remold Jaka standing behind him. It is at this moment he sees his feet stuck into the ground. He cannot move. "I am still inside Wholack."

"Dr. Singh wins the prize." It's the voice of a researcher coming from a trash can. "This is a rendition of your home Agg. And here you are, stuck in the dirt. Therefore, your home."

John Doe looks up at the blue sky and the fluffy clouds.

I am a prisoner again. He tries to cope with the certainty Remold Jaka's game has invaded and corrupted his reality. Was Winston washed away in some game reset? His life puddles.

As researchers work, Remold gazes out over Puget Sound and the Cascades. Wondering about Mina's motives, he finds himself humbled.

Here are two men lost in clarity: Remold and John Doe wishing for the caress of their wives, knowing they are each lost without them. Both fearing the truth will destroy their woman.

Wholack has finally won the game. Therefore he controls the reset.

Time for a new game.

Chapter Eighteen

Catch A Train Here

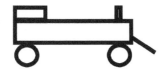

Lifting a foot from the mud, John Doe looks around arms crossed. He surveys the familiar downtown of Seattle. Residents go about their late afternoon routine, shoppers, bikes, pedestrians, a few cars. Parks cover most corners. The lack of tall buildings seems incongruous to his memory and he decides alterations by Wholack players have modified reality. His brain spins. He turns to the ovoid building behind him that looks like an egg on end. He sighs, eyes wide. He remembers that inside is a bar called the Womb, but unwilling to reveal that to Remold, "What are we doing here?"

Remold watches him. "We seem to be pawns of the universe, you and I. Is this your Agg, your reality, Mister Doe?" There is no response. Remold tries a different approach. "That person under attack was a Rost. But for you, Winston Doe is real." Remold sees only a wall of non-cooperative stares as

John Doe gazes around the city.

"Why was Tana Reins the driver of the vehicle? How did she get there?"

Staring up at a building window behind the imposter, Remold sees it turn bright pink. "You liked Ms. Reins?" He watches a window silently explode out. "I shock you." The building moves back and forth, like a flag in the wind. "No. The question shocks you. I am sorry. I don't mean to expose your lack of fidelity to your lover."

John Doe nods at the mistake in Remold Jaka's logic. The sight of Tana Reins matters little to him. He had asked the question about her appearance to help him figure out how far from his home he is at this juncture. Working to remain steady, noticing the city has damage from riots, John Doe knows the damage also does not fit his memory. This place is not his.

Remold crosses his arms. "I was mistaken about you. You are brilliant." A black body suit accentuates every digital muscle on his body. "That place with the jeep. Do you know the name of it?"

The imposter looks about apparently unconcerned. Remold waits, watching another window turn pink.

John Doe faces him. "That attack was on the nets. She was there. In my reality."

"Don't bullshit me. Maybe Wholack can crossover and impact your reality now. If he has a win. But in the past, never."

A bright smile comes to John Doe's face.

"Do you have information to share?"

"Help on this. If Wholack was there--in my Agg--before. Is it possible he was there as a player, but not a winner of the scenario?"

"Yes."

"But if Wholack ever wins, he would control the rebuild?" John Doe sparkles.

"You and Mina--if wishes were horse..." Remold tilts

his head in thought. "What do you want?"

"An answer," John Doe replies.

"When you cooperate."

A large rubber band drops from the sky. It bounces to rest right beside Remold Jaka. "What the?"

John Doe laughs. "You guys think you are so smart. This is not so tough." He touches the rubber band. You want sentience, Doc. Try this one on for size. Some day you will talk to Wholack and tell him to remember this rubber band." He looks at Remold. "My guess is your friend, Mister Wholack has won."

A tree forms, then limbs, and a face. Remold Jaka looks at it. "Say it."

"Doctor, Doe has links all over the place, available to you but unknown to him, like a Wholack. He knows himself here--also as you predicted--as Gus Plow. He is not centric, but he is in the correct framework: Home Fires. He also believes he is a crossover, but he doesn't know what it means."

Remold bites his bottom lip

The tree continues. "I got a better one. The lady in the jeep. The original Midari donor for the Rost was the wife of a man named Gus Plow. She was one of the first to die in FairGame."

John Doe, also known as Gus Plow closes his eyes.

"Easy, Plow. It means nothing." Remold looks at different objects, a bush, a tree, a garbage van. As he does researchers appear then disappear.

"Doc, we can't find any signature on the rubber band except yours."

Remold nods. "Mina?"

"Nope."

Remold Jaka shakes his head. He was prepared for accepting John Doe as a crossover--he already has. Getting bested in his own game by Wholack has him spinning. "You know yourself as Gus Plow. You know yourself as the Ginda's husband. Ever kill anyone?" Remold watches intently. "Your genetic equal killed a kid, drunk driving."

Gus Plow considers the question. "Former military."

"I will address you by your name, Gus. What did you do, in the military?"

Gus Plow goes mute.

Remold shakes his head. "Mr. Plow, do you notice how the buildings here have a worn feeling. Do they feel the same as you remember?" He doesn't wait for an answer. "Of course they are different. Mr. Plow, as I mentioned previously, we have had an issue with people believing scenarios take place on the Earth's physical plane. It has led to multiple problems. In the beginning it was called a form of denial, then a form of psychosis. Other parties said Wholack was a set of doorways through the universe. The myth of warped space. Others said it was a fool's game--me included. This scenario is part of the first major addition to Wholack. Called the Home Fires scenario, the project was managed by my ex-wife. It remains the version that has the most problems with people thinking they are in a real place. In fact, some use the term Wholack as a colloquial--for fool. It is the reason we made Wholack's identity so elusive in the next addition to Wholack, Corporate Apocalypse."

"You were trying to disprove the event of a crossover?" His brain is overloaded, but Gus Plow is a driven man.

"It was my test of Mina's theories. No crossover occurred in Corporate Apocalypse. I thought. Now I am just not sure."

Gus Plow nods. "What are you trying to get to here?"

A building behind Remold bursts into flames. Remold scans the area around Gus Plow. He sees no lies. "So here is what I am supposed to think. You found yourself lost in our Agg. Because somehow the Wholack system scooped you up and dropped you into FairGame. Incredible irony--that the madness of FairGame facilitated access into us, into our Agg--completely skipping Corporate Apocalypse."

"I am sure if you look you will find something there."

"Let me continue. Worse, you have suggested Wholack looks like he has won and he is going to reset this scenario to his liking--because I spoke to him about that rubber band."

Gus Plow nods. "Looks that way to me."

"Funny, you think you know more than I." Remold points to the moon.

Gus stares at the sky seeing a daylight moon. It is a pink moon with orange dots. "Oh."

"Not your moon, right?"

"Pink?" Gus can barely speak.

Remold shakes his head yes.

"So anything can be destroyed or modified by one of your players. So who says there is anything left of my reality to fix?"

"We don't know yet. I need your help to answer that one." Remold has no problems with playing on another's pain to get what he wants.

"Okay." Gus' shoulders round down. "Here is what I know. The enhanced energy from anthropogenic forcing of the radiative balance, global warming, caused a breach in my reality." Gus hears applause all around him. "We had no idea retained energy could puncture reality. And in the middle, fighting the madness caused by your damn game, I trained people to forget their reality--to fight what we thought was madness. Then I wandered away and somehow FairGame was my landing zone. Makes me question the bad reputation of madness and horror. Now, apparently, I am capable of acting as transit for my people out of apocalypse and into your Wholack game--or back to Earth's physical plane." A rainbow appears. "I am so glad you geniuses are impressed."

"We are not your enemy, Mr. Plow." Remold watches a set of windows across the street. They blow out one after the other, showering the street in glass. "Apparently you do not believe that." Remold Jaka watches his prey. "That little attack by Wholack was in a sub-section of Home Fires we call Samarra." The building turns bright red. "Voila, truth. You knew that. You must be honest with me. Can't you see how important stopping Mina is to us both? If you are from a similar Agg. You must know if Mina destroys Wholack she will destroy your Agg."

Gus watches the rubber band char to a cinder. "Bull shit, Doc."

"The Ginda in the jeep used a genome deemed dead for years." Seeing this man's pain, Remold stares at the ground. "You really were its lover--here?"

It?

Gus takes in a deep breath, trying to manage his dislike for Remold Jaka. So he faces the boulevard in front of the ovoid building. Gus sees joggers sweating. "You've built quite a game here. This is amazing." A bicycle careens into a pedestrian, knocking the man to the ground. An argument breaks out between the female bicyclist and the businessman. "So real. Why are these players all acting like this? Why argue?"

"The designer of the Womb scenario is top notch. You can spend years cataloguing this place and never even scratch all the exits and inputs. It's all about nesting. Who knows what the argument really means."

"So why all the squalor?" He waits for the couple to break into a torrid grasp, fall to the ground, and copulate. A wash of bystanders passes looking amused, and then there is a final repulsive sneer from the two participants as they part. Gus finds himself thinking this is real.

Then, a huge increase in the traffic on the street. The lack of motorized transport in this game scenario had surprised him. He remembers lots of electric vehicles and wonders what the increase in traffic reflects. "Whomever put this together is very good. This could fool anyone as real."

"Mina was always stickler for details." A frustrated Remold Jaka begins moving his hands about working an unseen control. "Mr. Plow, we are skilled at using the limbic system, emotions, as input devices." His hands move about as if he were the conductor of a symphony. "Can you guess what the first third party enhancement was to our digital universe?"

"Evaluation of supposed loved ones?"

Remold pauses for a moment. He is impressed. "Or those that would be most attractive to players of the game. People fall in love in this digital playground all the time. Always, the key question after the thump-thump of love is, 'Is it real?' Sometimes the love object is a real person and sometimes it is not. Finding out if the love object is a real person or a controlled Rost counts. It is the number one source of external developer revenue inside the Wholack system. A lot of people don't like to be lied to on that one. Also, connecting people who can love each other is the best part of this system."

It is Gus' turn to be impressed. "Go on."

"So we learned to answer that question of 'Real' quickly."

"And so formed your theory of Aggs and Reality." Gus watches a man and a woman dressed in clear plastic clothes walk into the ovoid shaped building. "Lovers?"

"Those two are here for the sex. Our system for real love involves motor vehicles. We use them as a kind of compatibility system. I think a love of vehicles helped with the piercing of your Agg."

"What makes you say that?"

"Mr. Plow, I was blind-side by the event of you. On the other hand, people consider me a pretty capable guy. The car fetish lived here as well. Tell me what happened to your Winston Doe?"

"She wanted Wholack more than anything else. I told her I would support her. She died later so I entered FairGame to die."

"Someone address that pile of crap." Remold shakes his head. "You're in awfully good shape for a ninety-year-old."

"Tofu--no pie--no strong drink. Lot's of exercise."

Remold smiles.

"Truth is I feel old enough for one lifetime."

Remold nods. "Me too." He watches the man's eyebrows knit and waits for input from his students.

The pie disappears in a puff of smoke. "She didn't die. So far as he knows she lives. It's his fear that Winston Doe might die that drives him." A red flower, the petals all looking like little question marks appears.

Gus stares at it. "That is one of your creations?"

"A red flower says the lover is real--among other things. It is also used as a place mark--like a book mark. Symbols and signs used in Wholack morph over time as people use them, like the meaning of words change over time. Overall the flower helps a person with problems mark their way through the system."

"So you label love a developmental difficulty--many would agree. Others might not. Guess I understand why you are alone." He looks around. "People who have developmental issues, can they get into the system?"

"If they have the money. We have, I have, created numerous scenarios in support of their activities. A foundation was started in fact."

"And the name of that foundation?" Gus already knows the answer.

Remold sees Gus knows the word. "The Pilnouth Foundation." A space ship appears behind Gus Plow, then rockets away.

"And the way you identify one of the challenged ones

in the system is they all use Pilnouth as their name--because it keeps them safe?"

Remold's eyes search the scene in front of him. Nothing changes. "How did you know?"

"Tofu--no pie--no strong drink. Lot's of exercise."

Remold watches every window in the building across the street turn black. "Your recalcitrance is a problem, Mr. Plow."

"Can I go see her?"

Remold misunderstands. He thinks Gus is talking about Winston. "We don't know where your lover is."

Gus smiles seeing the mistake, unwilling to give this megalomanic any more information."

Remold thinks for a moment. "You can go see Winston if you cooperative. But would you really like to do that? She is a fixture in various scenarios. Some you may not like."

"I bet I got you there, Doc."

"Help me and I will give you a developer's pass. I will give you Pilnouth tools that will allow you to build and understand what you are doing, rather than the bumbling modification we have seen from you so far. You'll have a blank slate to work with. In my game those are the keys to Fort Knox. It also means once you learn your way around you'll find a way to get to her. I will also reconvey your status from FairGame Target to Laughs Unlimited executive. But know that I show the Ginda as either dead or a digital nothing, an empty Rost."

"I understand. You plan to track me?"

"Inside and outside the game." He pauses with a sigh--for effect. Remold believes he needs to gain control of this asset. "So far, nothing we can find shows you as dangerous to our Agg. Other than your existence which declares all the old rules as void. None of that matters because I have less than two days to stop Mina from destroying Wholack. So while you are potentially the proof that we have breached some former limit and modified our Agg, Mr. Plow, I must stop Mina from shutting down the system so we can both get what we want. Therefore I am willing to cooperate. Therefore I want your cooperation as well." Remold points at the white ovoid shaped building. "Time to step into the breach. You have a surprise coming."

"And that might be?" Gus checks his own clothes. He wear a pair of blue jeans, a black tee shirt and sneakers. The same as every novice in the game.

Remold points behind him. Just as he turns, a couple dressed in red plastic walk up. They stop. "You could join us," she says with a purr. "We are on our way into the Womb--unless you are a Yorkie." Her hand drifts to her partner's manhood and caresses it.

"More sex players." Gus reaches out to caress the woman's breast. She appears not to notice; in fact, the two characters do not react to him at all. He immediately steps in front of them blocking their view of Jaka. They appear to look right through him. Then the two walk forward running into Gus.

Impacting him, but apparently unable to recognize what they have impacted, the man and woman step back. Fear and concern contorts their smooth, beautiful faces.

"A disjunction. Oh my God," She says to her partner. Their faces white with fear, the woman and man scamper away down the hill and out into the street. A bus runs them over and kills them.

"So that's what it was."

Remold looks at Gus Plow. "That's what?"

"A disjunction, in my reality, was feared it like no other circumstance. It was seen as a breach of reality--but we couldn't fathom the event. We saw it as a tear in reality. The harbinger of the tear that would destroy us, but we couldn't see what was right in front of us."

Remold is stilled for a moment, thinking.

Gus speaks. "None of those here can experience me, can they?"

"Something like that." Remold says checking inputs from his researchers. "Mr. Plow, apparently the whole point of this Womb scenario is to breach your reality."

"Or to link it."

"I don't know why Mina does things. I am sorry." He pauses to consider what else he might share. "For what it is worth, you are from a version of here, but you are a stranger to this version. That means you are one of us. We will do our best to find a version you are part of." He watches to see if Gus checks the buildings around for proof of a lie. He does. Of course nothing changes. The researchers have seen to that. Remold waits.

"Thanks for sharing," Gus remains suspicious.

Remold, for his part, sees once again Gus knows nothing about the Wholack game. It hadn't seemed possible there could be people like that. He tells himself there are so many options now. Remold Jaka then tells himself he is a genius. Doctor Jaka speaks, "As you may know, once there is a scenario there is always a way to sculpt a new scenario. It is one of the big attractions of Wholack. In Home Fires we saw a fashion to destroy scenarios and continually rebuild them with more and more destruction. Millions of people took to mayhem. I am guessing the original version was tens of thousands of versions ago."

Gus feels his stomach knot and glances up at the pink moon. "Imagine cycling through every one like the Wholack."

Remold ignores the comment. He is on task and nothing else matters. "In this Womb subset of Home Fires scenario, there is an added complication. When the player finally solves it, if they make the wrong modification after a win, the characters go on a rampage. For some bizarre reason, Mina has the win so well hidden, there has never been a reset where the population doesn't destroy itself. It is the reason this is the least populated of all the Home Fires scenarios. You must have seen it as madness among the population."

Gus nods.

"On the other hand, the Womb is a favorite for connoisseurs of my craft."

Gus looks up at the egg-shaped building. "You gotta' wonder which came first..."

Remold grins as he begins walking to the ovoid building. He believes he is gaining the control he seeks. "The media says Womb is popular because it is so difficult to win," Remold says, watching the characters move about. "But then there is fact. On average there are less than a two hundred million people in Home Fires."

"That's about right."

Remold stops, his head in question. "Our species really was dieing off?"

"A friend of mine postulated it could be reversed upon complete destruction. To me it sounds like he understood a reset in your Wholack game. We never could understand how he knew. He was so sure."

"Care to elaborate?" Remold says.

Gus stares at him. "His name was Pilot Nothing..." The stunned look from Remold Jaka is exactly as he had expected.

"Pilot Nothing was a crossover?" Remold seems frozen in time.

Gus speaks quickly. "He was an autonomous vehicle, a human-robot. They were a common tool for us. We were desperate." Gus notes there is no change to the scenario. He correctly reasons duplicity isn't noted when it is partial duplicity. He wonders how much of what he has heard from Remold is a partial truth.

"He was a probe?"

"Right. And apparently a solution--don't forget the

rubber band--Doc. "

Gus has no conception of time passing. The drugs that feed the players can be remixed at any point. Sometimes the mix is changed to keep players in limbo as complex computation is carried out. Sometimes the mix block's a memory.

Remold returns a few hours later after isolating the sequence on Pilot Nothing. Remold Jaka is a dutiful son protecting the memory of his family. His researchers have just wiped clean the discussion of Pilot Nothing in Gus' memory.

Remold restarts the flow of certain drugs. Gus speaks, without knowing the passage of time, "You knew Pilot Nothing?" Partial clarity hits. "That's how you all learned so early about the climate and what would happen. Pilot Nothing told you." He looks around wondering why Remold developed the odd monument of Wholack to his friend Russell Biner.

"How the hell did you do that?" Remold stares across the street for any signs of a breach. He sees none. "Pilot Nothing died shortly after arrival. I was too young. I don't know why."

"You're hiding something." Gus angers.

"Someone do this right. Reset this guy again--and get it right, please."

Again Gus has no idea hours have passed. The drugs used in Wholack are a key to its success. They can be used for many things--including the removal of long term memories.

The next thing Gus perceives is Remold pointing to the front labial-shaped doors of the Womb. "Try to open the door." Remold waits.

Gus reaches out. "I can feel them." He pushes on one door then the next. The doors do not move. "Why make it impossible for me to move things? Or set me as a phantom?"

"I didn't. These doors were designed by Mina for security reasons. Have you ever been through these doors?"

Gus nods yes.

"If you can feel them and not move them that means you have--or so Mina once said to me. Seems she busted into your Agg with no concern for you or your people. Too bad for you."

"Mina owns the Womb. She is a crossover?"

"No. That was examined long ago--by me." Dr. Jaka pushes the doors aside. "We have to stop her."

Gus Plow follows him through the doorway. "So I can smell. I can touch. I can see. I can hear. I just cannot be seen or operate objects."

"The perfect lock-out in Mina's opinion. She is a monster."

As they walk the hallway smelling the acrid smell of sex. He looks around, having been in the Womb many times before a very long time ago, the details stun Gus.

They enter into a wild bar scene of scantily dressed, beautiful people. Partiers writhe in various stages of excitement. "So real--it's very good. I thought you said you could not find Mina."

"She is always here--in a fashion. She usually leaves a Rost for me to contact her. It's her sadistic way to ignore me. It is on the dance floor." They approach a far wall. A set of men and women hug the mirror behind them. Remold notes they stare at Gus Plow. "I will stand here. Circle to the far end, but don't get too close to the exit door. Approach the Yorkies, the nervous ones hugging the wall."

"Why?"

"You'll see."

Gus walks away from Remold and believes he sees some of those standing by the wall watching him. They begin to nudge each other and then they all track his movement. Gus looks back at Remold. Remold moves his left hand in a lateral motion indicating he should walk towards them. He takes two steps.

The thirty or so people scatter to their left and rush out the exit door. Gus notices the people in the bar stop and watch the Yorkies leave, laughing nervously, looking about, or looking away in a practiced version of uncaring sophistication. None of the other patrons see him. The door slams shut and the crowd waits a moment, looking for danger, then they return to levity, libations, and libido.

A auburn-haired woman in a skin tight silver gown approaches Remold. Gus hurries over to Remold Jaka thinking the figure is Mina's digital incantation.

"You scared my Yorkies. Why did you do that, body suit-boy?" A tall thin man with the look of protector hurries down the stairs towards the two of them but maintains his distance. Gus stares at a man he knows as Gunn. Gunn does not see Gus either.

"You're Mina, right?" Remold asks, glancing at Gus.

"I am," she smiles warmly then looks over her shoulder. Her sculpted body has the glow of sweat. "And you are?"

"Dr. Remold Jaka. Your last name is Jaka as well."

"If it were, my name would sound like an underwear advertisement. No offense, Sparky. My last name is not your concern. Why did you scare my Yorkies? I am only asking so I know what to say to you when I throw you out."

Remold curls his index finger at Gus who walks around her and stands beside him. She watches Remold look at Gus Plow--who nods. She looks like the Mina he knows. Remold speaks: "I have a friend here that you cannot yet see. Would you like to see him?"

She looks down at his crotch. "Do you always use tired old lines?" She looks around the bar getting ready to ignore this boring man.

"No. I mean there is a person here. He is standing beside you. I will ignore him if you will let me dance with you." He watches her beautiful eyes. Mina's eyes have owned Remold since the first day.

Gus sees an emotion inside Remold he had not guessed possible. Then he looks at Mina for signs of familiarity. He sees only a bored stare. This closeness and distance from her seems so cruel. He ponders the work of women.

Her right hand up, her palm skyward, she nods to her protector. "I have a friend as well. His name is Gunn--and he is here to escort you out if you bother me."

"Please dance with me?" Remold says. "I am a harmless fool and you are so lovely."

"You are a fool. That is clear." She laughs, waging her index finger in his face. "No touchee or he will hurt you."

Remold lifts his hands showing his palms. "No problem."

She waves Gunn away and steps onto the dance floor. Gus bolts for the side door. It will not budge. He sighs trying to keep his anger at a minimum knowing any reaction is catalogued by the researchers.

The couple begins to dance. Others dance close in rubbing against them. No one notes Gus' existence. He climbs a set of clear stairs, looking around, seeking familiar faces. Over the next five minutes--or so it seems to him--he notes a new set of Yorkies populates the wall by the mirror. His attention returns to Remold and he sees rapture: a man out of time and space, a man in love. "The poor sap," he says to himself, laughing at both he and Remold.

At that exact moment, two handsome men enter the bar. Obviously well known in this scenario they prowl the bar like dogs seeking scraps in a butcher shop. They caress and tease the women they approach. Gus stares, mouth agape as they climb the stairs.

"Moss, Travis," he calls out.

Of course there is no response. Mina leaves the dance floor to follow the two men to their seats. A moment later, a tanned and toned woman dressed in blue rags appears with an

Asian man. Gus knows him as well.

Benson Fong.

"Thank you for joining us, Mr. Fong." The pretty woman steps away. The man with the topknot sits at the table. Mina joins them.

Remold appears at the edge of the stairs. "That man isn't really my head of security. It's a Rost. Mina is a tease."

"Perhaps." Gus knows Benson Fong as Mina's lover. Things begin to fall into place for Gus. He forms a theory on why Remold cannot find Mina.

Remold speaks. "Watch this." He leans into the crowd at the table. The four people pause, facing Remold. They make derisive comments about him. The large muscled man, the one sporting a week old beard, the man Gus calls Moss, leans over to Mina and whispers something. She slaps him playfully. Remold says something about the Wholack. Someone responds that Remold is a Wholack. A moment later the bodyguard has taken Remold to the ground. A pair of bouncers appear and haul Remold away. Gus quickly follows them down the stairs, not wanting to be stuck inside the building.

The guards throw Dr. Jaka out a back door onto a smelly set of mattresses with a large slide next to them. "Stay out." The guards say, and walk back in the bar.

Remold Jaka rights himself. "Every time I try to get through to her I wind up here. I have no control over her."

"It seems odd to me. You created the game, but she runs this scenario?"

"She does not run it. She was my codeveloper--the duplicitous bitch. I allow her to win, but if I change it, I lose contact with her."

"So you could change it but if you did you would lose contact with her. Your ex-wife set this up to control you?"

"Pure Mina. We used to play here," Remold Jaka says. "I didn't know our play was the way she built a wall around herself."

"So there is no way you will alter her scenario--or let others do it--because this is your only contact with her?"

"Too simplistic. It is more than just contact."

"You and I have no idea what we are doing." Gus finds himself in awe of Mina. "We are fools."

"Redundant fools," Remold says, smiling. "All of us men."

"Perhaps. So why do you let this continue?" Gus asks.

"New adjustments were made to the code after Mina began to hate me. As you have guessed, I could have changed it--but I do not need the control. I need to find her. If she brings Wholack down, the desperate will hunt her down and kill her. I feel a need to protect her."

"You need her, period." Gus looks around thinking he has said too much. "What happens if we go back in?"

This being exactly his plan, Remold pauses, waiting for data from the researchers. They finish setting their hooks to obliterate the memory of Pilot Nothing. He says, "You're the man. Let's find out." Remold stands, stinking of urine and garbage, sure he has gained control of this asset. "What use are we?"

"Redundant fools?"

"So its the redundancy of us that defines our worth? I doubt that. We make it easy for women as redundant fools--but it must be boring."

"Tastes vary," Gus says.

"Ouch," says the manipulator, Remold Jaka.

CHAPTER NINETEEN

REDUNDANT

:**//**

Remold Jaka and Gus Plow circle the ovoid building passing a set of green dumpsters. Then, crossing in between the trees and bushes, stand in front of the Womb. Gus notes the red plant with the question mark flowers remains. "Why is that still here?" Gus asks. "Love eternal?"

"As I said, it is also a marker. We use it to remind ourselves that we have been some place when we do not have complete control. The flower, for lack of a better term, is a tech repair ticket."

"Love as a repair ticket," Gus says. "So that's why she left you."

"Not funny."

"Didn't mean it as funny."

Remold pauses scratching his neck. "The plants are effective markers because they are so ubiquitous in Wholack.

There are scenarios where they flow like flowers in a field."

"The Pilnouth scenarios," Gus says.

Remold wonders which scenario he knows. "Those who are challenged make a lot of mistakes. You have seen one of those scenarios?" Remold says by way of response.

"I know about them. And if you touch them?" Gus asks.

Remold stops his work and looks at the plant. "What if you touch them?" He tilts his hand as an invite.

Gus reaches out to touch the plant. The plant withers to a gray dust. "Is that supposed to happen?"

"You should not be able to impact the scenario. If I had touched it. The marker was supposed to just disappear. Are these plants a part of your world?"

Gus shakes his head. "I have just heard of them."

Remold nods and examines a seam for version number, then any data declaring the statement as false. It all tracks. "What do you know about the plant?"

Gus sighs. "In my, ah Agg, seems someone named Pilnouth introduced them to one of our people. I never saw a Question Plant, but I saw renditions."

Remold speaks to the space around him. "Someone named Pilnouth--please get on that."

"Which one?" Comes the response from a bush.

"Find it. When you do you'll find his home Agg."

A face appears on a garden rock alongside the path. "Too many versions of it, Doc. It will take a month to track it back to a single genome."

Remold nods. "Well then we better be successful in stopping Mina." Remold faces Gus. "You see I originally designed the plants for the Pilnouth Foundation. Then one of our people that handles low level PR inadvertently popularized them. After a while they were used everywhere--supposedly to alleviate the bad reputation of the gamers that are challenged--either developmentally, emotionally, or psychologically."

"That PR person made a mistake," Gus postulates.

"And was demoted."

"What was his or her name?"

"Simon Weiss." Remold sees shock. "Do you know him?"

"Heard of him. I never met him. Hope's father?"

"Not genetically. He is married to her step-mother--but the genetics are all wrong. She only had an aunt, Elena. Elena Etu--the parents died. Have you heard of Ms. Etu?"

"No."

"I bet she is the reason you didn't crossover into Corporate Apocalypse. She is the key to winning the most popular version, so-called Dirties version. My guess is Mina scrambled her data for some reason."

"You're scared of Mina."

"Nonsense. What did Weiss do in your Agg?"

"A shrink," Gus replies.

"PR, psychiatry, same thing." Remold smiles.

Gus looks away trying to hide his distaste for Remold's ignorance. "One works internal. One works external. Either can be corrupted."

Remold distractedly pulls a small keyboard from his thigh pocket. He wipes the scenario clean of their last inputs and the inputs of other players. Pastel planes appear rapidly then disappear. He places one of his Rosts inside the Womb to track John Doe. Then all is as it was when they arrived. Remold leans down and touches the grass, then the trees, looking for programming traps from players who might have slipped passed his people. Finding none, he scans the sky looking for the Wholack. There is no sign of Wholack in the scenario. An immediate rebuild is supposed to bring the Wholack, like some avenging Valkerie. Remold knows how to get around that. He sets an alarm for Wholack then scans the wandering people looking for a warning signal. It is peaceful. "This scenario always resets with amazing adherence. I think Mina is better at coding then I."

"So she always knew this was a way into another Agg?"

"I suppose." Remold sighs. "My researchers, for example, sport obscene and sometimes funny guises. On the other hand, they also like to clean things up and make the scenarios a bit more pristine. They call it the country-club-effect. People feel the complex scenarios should have a bit more class. It never occurred to me there was another force at work. Neatness, art, as a push to equal another reality--to facilitate crossover--while blocking another. My game. My rules. Or so I thought."

"You sound like the Wholack," Gus says, surprised at the admission. Until now he had considered Remold Jaka an unparalleled egomaniac. "Do you have some sort of a program that changes your clothes for you?"

He looks down. Remold's clothes have changed into professorial-looking khaki pants and tweed jacket. Hanging from his neck is a Mickey Mouse tie, purple, wide, and gaudy. The shirt shows a picture of the Milky Way. A small cartoon balloon says "Galileo Was Here." Remold points to Gus's chest. He wears the same clothes as Remold. "My people have installed sensor nets. There is a Rost inside to relay the information. They were not supposed to wind me up as well. That means Mina knows I am here."

"May she wants to keep you busy," Gus says.

"Perhaps." Remold walks up the path.

They approach the vagina shaped doors. "Not very creative, it's all the same," Remold says trying to draw Gus's attention to a small crack at the base of the doors.

Gus sees a fan of white powder.

"Needs maintenance, but that is to be expected. She hasn't been in the maintenance code of the scenario for years. If she did, I'd have her." Remold pushes on the door and walks down a uterine hallway. Different raucous bits of music pour through the walls. Remold mumbles, "I would have thought it impossible to breach a reality and secure the link so tightly. I have created an amazing system. Mina uses it so well."

Gus feels a bit more grounded. "Maybe Mina is trying to save something by keeping this in tact."

"For example?" Remold asks, suddenly alert.

"Apocalypse--reversing it."

"Possible." Ahead is a clitoral light over labial doors.

"That wasn't here before." Gus neglects to mention the light was a fixture in his reality. He avoids a puddle on the floor and walks into a bar scanning the dance floor.

Remold asks, "Why would she care about your apocalypse?" Remold looks over to the Yorkies.

"In my Agg, Dr. Wolf is her father--or she caused it."

"Redundancy--amazing." The room reeks of sex, fear, and escape. Gus admires the dancers on the floor then sees Remold is drawn to one young woman with a bald head and a blue gown revealing her every feature. When she turns, Gus sees it is Mina. Her body tossed by the music, she moves with a sense of ownership for her realm.

"She looked right at you."

"The work of women," Remold answers.

"Sure?" Gus responds.

"It's a Rost, a software robot, but I suppose she has the skills to wrap herself in it. It's always different--always fun. I'll give her that."

"How many times have you been here?" Gus says, suddenly feeling sorry for this man.

Remold Jaka is a master manipulator. "Too many. I can dance with her. More than that, her protector shows up, and tosses my ass out of here. If I use reinforcements, the scenario resets. I bring one or two they are ghosts."

"You can't get around her?"

"The Womb disappears. The bar is a wreck. The city is

burning. I think my win causes your apocalypse." Remold is patronizing this man to further secure his support. He wants to make sure his evisceration of John Doe's memory continues to function without impacting Remold's plans.

"Hell has no fury..." Gus says hiding his fascination.

"Especially an ex-wife."

"Can't you change the apocalyptic ending?"

"I'd never see her again."

"So it continues because she has you by the heart? You allow it to reset it over and over because you seek her."

"I am her yo-yo, her rubber band. She is evil."

"So the scenario repeats because you love her and seek her? Otherwise you would have destroyed it." Gus pauses. "Do you have any idea just how dense are you, Doc?"

"I am not dense, Mr. Plow. I understand you think her the savior of your Agg."

"Doctor, your woman has used your love to try keep this Agg relatively in tact until it gets fixed."

"Sure, Mr. Plow," he says, distracted by Mina's slow sensuous dance. "You're a fool. You seek answers that support your view. How could it possibly get fixed?"

Gus Plow looks around. "Please."

"I'll see what I can do," Remold says.

"Doc, you have one hell of a problem with that ego." Gus' eyes drift over to the participants huddled along the far wall watching every movement around them fear pouring from every part of their body. "What about the Yorkies? They saw me last time."

Remold looks away, drawn by Mina's dance. "Go get 'em, Tiger."

"I just don't understand why she left you." Gus says, disgusted with Remold Jaka. He turns to a gaunt man with white hair, his eyes searching every person. Gus walks forward. The man moves backward in the crowd. They close in on him, not so much for his protection, but for mutual protection. Gus turns away, his back to the Yorkies. "I need you to ask that one a question." He is speaking to Remold.

Remold looks back at him then at the Yorkies. He smiles, teeth bright green and each one topped with a small set of miniature trees. "What do you want me to ask?"

Gus points to his own mouth.

"You are concerned about my dental work?" Remold sees his image in the mirror. "Damn you, Mina."

Gus shakes his head back and forth. He points to the thin man in the center. "Call that skinny man, Carlos. Ask him if he put me into FairGame?"

Remold's full attention focuses on Gus. "Not funny. I did not put that Rost here for you to make jokes."

Gus looks at the Yorkies. "It's your Rost?"

Remold nods. "I have a Carlos wandering in and out of most scenarios--when I need information."

"Carlos Jordan is a digital design? Your digital design? So that's how she knew this was an Agg."

"You have a fool's view of life, Mr. Plow."

Gus shakes his head trying to understand how two truths, completely contradictory, can exist at the same time: Carlos is a real person for some--a manufactured creation for others. There are so many paths. "Talk to him, please."

"Is he right, Carlos? Did you put him into FairGame? Are you real?"

The white-haired Yorkie speaks to Gus, "Reality and truth are not the same. Realities can contradict. Truth is a human construct. Infinity is the point. On every level."

Gus looks at Remold Jaka. "He is as pedantic as you."

"I am an artist." Remold replies.

"How long ago did you create it?" Gus asks.

"I created my first Carlos when I was in college."

"Why did you cut off a toe?"

"How did you know that?"

"In my Agg, everyone knows Carlos Jordan lost a toe. He is a hero of our bout with global warming. By the way, he was the first one to see your Question Plant."

"His last name is Jordan?"

Gus nods.

"That is also not something you should know. I never told anyone its last name."

"Trust me, Doc. The secret is out."

"I guess I should be a bit more careful with you," Remold says with a grimace.

Gus sighs, astounded at how Remold Jaka misses the entire point because of ego: Mina knew this was a different Agg because of Carlos. She heard him referred to as real. "Doc, what if he has a toe now?"

"Can't be. He is not autonomous." Remold scowls seeing Gus Plow has stated a fact. "A toe? You say she saw the toe and therefore knew I didn't have control?"

"I know he grew a toe. It is that event that led researchers to consider that reality was being changed."

"I was using the missing toe for security. Who cares about a damn toe anyway? The guy could still walk." Remold frowns. "He and that lost toe are my fail-safe because the code is so minimal and so old. I knew that if that toe ever showed up on a Carlos I had a big problem."

"And it showed up."

"Or so you say. But now I see why she is so sure she can shut down the system. She wants to prove me wrong."

Gus dismisses the self-serving conclusion. "You can shut down Wholack, right?"

"Of course. How do you think Mina learned to do it? From me, of course, but the dispossessed would tear me apart with their palsied bare hands if Wholack were shut down. I am very wealthy and very powerful but if I shut down Wholack the displaced would hunt me down and gut me. Same for Mina or anyone else who steals heaven from them. That's why I don't understand this. If she shuts it down. It's suicide."

"I don't think Mina wants to hurt anyone. She just wants to prove her theory and keep you in tow. She knows how to keep you coming back."

"Impossible. She is like a PC hack who knows a few PC applications and proclaims themselves to be an expert."

"So you are a PC?"

Remold ignores the comment. "She learned techniques I use to perform my tasks so she seems brilliant. So now Mina says she has the keys to proving existence is more than I ever imagined. It appears on some level she is right. But it is because of her teacher. I can learn and undo anything she does. But now because of dumb luck, a toe, she has decided she is better than her teacher. Shutting down the system will make her the most hated person alive."

Gus marvels, trying to figure a way through Remold Jaka's ego. "You're concerned about her safety. In fact, I'd venture to say you're probably more concerned about that than anything else."

"You're a fool, Plow. It's why you still seek a dead wife."

The man named Carlos speaks from the crowd. "There is a worth to foolishness, Mr. Plow, while heroism has a cost. So belly up to the bar--choose your poison. You can be one kind of fool," he points to Remold, "Or another." The Yorkie slowly exits the bar. The other Yorkies follow him.

A hand taps Remold on the shoulder and he turns.

Mina faces him. "What did you say to my Yorkies?" She watches Remold intently. "Mind showing me your ears." Remold grins then leans to the side. "The top of your ears, please," she asks. He complies watching her evaluation continue.

"Worried I have Clipper disease you are so afraid of?"

Gus listens, amazed at it all.

"Not I," Mina says.

"Your scenario, I presume?" Remold says. "Someone please find my screw-up on the Carlos and that stupid toe." He worries he has led Mina to his fail safe system. "What's your name?" Remold asks her.

She looks at him and smiles. "Gotchya. Why don't we dance? With your fail-safe gone, Remmy, nothing stands in my way."

"Dream on. I win." Her clothes fall away.

She purrs, extending her hand. He touches the fingertips.

It is her. He is stunned. He has seen Mina twice in two days. More than he has seen her in the last three years.

She leads him to the dance floor. "You jerk." Then she is gone. A Rost appears and he knows this one is a not her.

"Bitch." He faces Gus Plow. "You work for her? She was expecting us?"

Gus stares at him.

Mina's digital design pulls Remold by the hand. He mumbles to his assistants to track Mina's path from the scenario.

"Boss, she's gone."

Her hand moves up to caresses his shoulder. "It has been years since I have been around another top designer who did not recognize me." The woman smiles benignly and he is immediately insulted.

Remold notes the entire room watches them. "My name is Remold Jaka." He sees her bored smile. The music changes to a Reggae beat and he notices her eyes dart towards the front door. That pair of men enter and move across the room. The shorter, beefy man draws Remold's attention. Remold's alarm vibrates. It says this is the cloaked Wholack. Looking over to his dance partner, he sees she signals people to conduct the men upstairs.

"Mina, why did you change the Wholack like that? There is no way he can win the game."

"I thought when I saw you by the Yorkies that you were making fun of them. I was mistaken. Feel free to go back by your friends." With that she turns away and walks up the stairs--where the two men have recently ascended.

Remold stands in the middle of the dance floor kicking dancers. They ignore him. "Mr. Wolf, we have a breach."

"Yup--bed inputs just appeared, then ceased."

"Mina leaving her bed?"

"Could be. Security is on it."

Remold bolts from the dance floor, hurrying over to Gus. Grabbing him, Remold ascends the glass stairs in a run. At the top of the stairs, the merry-makers sit at a table. Nothing much has changed, everyone is in the same place as a few minutes ago. Remold stares at the beefy man and approaches the big man. "What's your name?"

"Eckman, Moss Eckman?" He extends a hand, a sly smile on his face.

"Break. Remold Jaka enter Wolf three-five-nine. Mark."

Nothing happens, other than a waitress appears with long slicked back ears. She escorts Remold's head of security.

"What are you doing here?" Remold asks.

Benson sits, mute. He is there to distract Remold.

The fire in Remold's eyes is unmistakable, even in the digital cloak. Gus whispers, "Benson Fong is her lover in my Agg. Think about that. He has access to your plans. He defines your security. Remold, you need to move slowly. He is the reason you can't find Mina." Gus looks at Benson Fong watching him laughing with the others. Then he realizes this is a Rost.

"Mina is beneath the diner."

"Are you sure Doctor Wolf?"

"We're not inside but Benson says so. The net map is perfect. Benson wants to go in."

Remold turns a bright red. "No." He watches Gus. "You

are right. I understand you want to protect your life. I must protect Wholack. Its destruction is a crime against humanity. I cannot let Mina destroy a billion people."

Angry, Gus grabs Remold's jacket before he moves towards the table, stopping him. "This is a set up."

"How would you know?"

"Doc, you are playing catch-up here."

"As if you'd know, newbie."

Gus lets go of his jacket. "Fine."

The tall man named Gunn has pinned his eyes on Remold. Remold thinks for a minute, then approaches the table. "Where are your beds?" He asks. "Where is the Wholack?"

They ignore him and tell him to go away. Remold reaches out, but never gets there, again. A moment later he finds himself on his back, a glaze of pain covering his entire body. Some words are spoken, but he cannot understand them. Hands grasp him and pull him away. A moment later he is rolling down a chute, landing on those soft smelly mattresses. Yorkies stand around, smiling at him.

Remold stands up seeing a bright red neon sign that says: "DON'T COME BACK." He watches Gus land. "That's better." Remold checks his system seeing the cordon set up around the diner by his security people. No one has entered and no one has left. "Hold positions. Nobody enters."

Gus points to the Yorkies. "You all see my friend over there. Who is he?"

The knot tightens as the men and women look at each other. The white-haired man named Carlos mutters, "We don't have the foggiest idea."

Remold, satisfied Benson is now neutered checks for a toe on the Carlos. It is missing. His systems are still secure. "Someone confirm the Carlos is still autonomous." He waits a moment then nods responding to input from his researchers. Remold looks at Gus. "Bitch. Scans show Mina is gone from the diner."

"It was a set up," Gus replies. "You helped her. Why?"

"Not funny." A passenger jet flies overhead. "Sorry, I have to track her. This is the only way." With a wave of his hand the jetliner tips and dives toward the city. He guides the jetliner to crash nearby. Explosions and flames erupt. The Yorkies scatter in all directions.

Gus notes Carlos walks away, shaking his head, mumbling. "Information access does not obviate reality or the worth of men. It simply places power in the hands of idiots."

Gus stares at Remold. "You're the one who told me there are young universes. You told me just because we know what drives it that doesn't mean it isn't real. Why did you kill those people?" He exits the alley and stares at the burning building and the wrecked jet. A familiar feeling of loss fills him as he watches emergency vehicles and the work of bystanders trying to help those they can save.

Remold appears beside him.

Gus shakes his head angry at the bend of this man. "What is your issue?"

Remold points to the plane. "That plane is a kind of library we researchers use for tracking the entrance and egress of players. Very spare and very powerful. I am certain to find her now." Bodies are pulled from the wreckage. "They are nothing. They are Rosts."

"That so?"

"You've seen them crash before, with people in them?"

"Early on. You used music to make them crash," Gus says. "Jazz."

Remold sees the truth. He is a murderer. "Do you know who created that crash routine? The Jazz Line--as we call it?"

"No."

"Hope and Mina."

"Spare me."

Caught in a lie, Remold says, "I want you to breach Hope's home to examine it. Find me a link that proves Carlos is no construct."

"How do you know I can find one?"

"Mr. Plow, I am an expert at all this. If you do get it, you will have a path to get home." He lies. "But only you can get it." Truth is Remold needs time. Mina has been too right and he has been too wrong. Another misstep, or a declaration by the John Doe he is a murderer and his control of Laughs Unlimited will end. He cannot have that. "We have work to do--you and I."

"Haven't you searched Hope's residence?"

"Sorry, there were no convenient crossovers at the time to look for my screw-ups." Remold waits to see if Gus buys the attempt to keep him out of his way.

"What am I looking for?"

"Memory." Remold presses the escape button.

Rising from his bed, pleased at his progress, but embarrassed at his mistakes, Remold believes he has the resources to make himself a hero. Tracking Mina is key. Scanning his computer screens, he seeks to understand how Mina escaped from under the diner. When he cannot, he begins removing Benson's privileges in the Wholack system while considering the arrest of Benson Fong and Hope Weiss. Until he decides he needs their cooperation. Gus Plow is a wild-card.

Sending a message to Hope's attorney to arrange a meeting with Hope, he then directs Benson to baby-sit Gus Plow. He has to get control of this situation quickly.

Remold Jaka stretches and looks at himself in the mirror.. "Discoverer of the new world. Not bad, Dude. Not bad. Let's not screw this one up."

Chapter Twenty

You'll Be Cursed Here

His neck hurting from staring at the computer, Gus Plow leans back in the leather chair. Finally finished familiarizing himself with Wholack, he waits to burglarize Hope's residence. So far as he can tell there is no purpose to his entering her home--other than to alienate her. Benson also seemed stumped by the event, but he was unwilling to share more. Remold has him on a tight leash.

Gus finds he resents the ability of Remold Jaka to move people around like chess pieces, seeing himself drawing more conclusions about why Mina left. The Mina he knew had no quarter for those who would control her. Gus declares to himself that he will never be one of Remold's puppets, even as he plans a crime on Dr. Jaka's behalf. "What is that son of a bitch up to anyway?" He asks the air around him.

Gus looks at the clock. Almost 1:30 AM. Still time to

sleep, instead, "Computer, how important is Wholack to this society?" One advantage of spending the evening with Benson Fong was the complete overview of the systems available to Gus on the computer, and the Wholack bed in the next room.

The image on the computer changes to a picture of the Wholack. "The Wholack Games are the number one employer, pastime, hobby, religion, and focus of the people of planet Earth. Over a billion people are involved in building the game. Some as builders of basic scenarios, the frameworks created and sold by corporations. Or Rosts--the digital carriages serving as cloaks--allowing players to move about in the new reality. Other people develop software that burps fire, burn prophets, cage devils, allow dances with angels, provides trips along snake skins, float cities in the ocean, or build foreign lands. Many design love, hate, or other emotional events. There are the transport builders, the food creators, the sex tank participants, the clean people, and everything else. A hundred thousand people are solely weapons and defense builders-- those amazing devices people use to kill or corral each other as they fight their way into the so-called inner circle of a won scenario."

"Why?" Gus asks.

"So they can build their own secure sub-scenario. Wholack is the Go-To outlet for humanity's finest talents. In summary, the attitudes and creativity of humanity flow into Wholack like water."

Is everything a commercial here?

He sits back in the desk chair. "Computer, is there any correlations between Hope Weiss and Mina Jaka? Were they lovers?"

"Question one: Ms. Weiss was an intern at Laughs Unlimited working for Dr. Mina Jaka. She was promoted to researcher. Her termination, for reasons unknown, led to her enlistment in the military. Question two: Unknown."

Gus stares at the computer with its brass and silver casing, wiping a spot from the screen, and sipping more ale. Glancing passed it to the wall of windows, he gazes at the blue moon and snow-capped mountains. His eyes focus closer, looking around the elegant corporate apartment in the swanky building. He cannot help but grin at the opulent leather and wood surrounding him. At one time, he would have burned the wood for heat and boiled the leather for food. Gus feels guilt, wondering if this is what murder brings in this society.

The image on the screen disappears. The computer speaks: "The district's power will now shut down. Power to bed locations east of the cascades has been damaged by a storm and so power will be drawn from this side of the Cascades to keep those in Wholack comfortable. Note that I plan to darken windows, close shades, and shut down all level three power usage. You will not be impacted, but we cannot advertise a disparity in power usage. You will not be chilled."

Gus looks at the clusters of fires from Hunters on the far hillside inside FairGame. "Okay."

"Please do not antagonize the population by excessive displays of power usage. Keep all blinds closed and avoid the playing of music. Thank you," announces the computer. "Your comfort and safety are our only concern. This is just another benefit for your purchase of SafeLitigation courtesy of Laughs Unlimited. Don't forget to review the new scenario, Global Warming. The critics call it a winner!"

The number "100" appears on the computer screen. It begins to decrement. Lights dim and the washing machine slows to a stop. The sound of the washer stopping almost causes him to rush to the laundry closet. Dirt has become Gus' enemy. The floor to ceiling windows disappear as black shades sweep shut. Gus stares at the heavy curtains. When he was still a Target, he used to gain comfort watching the lights of civilization cease at night. He chides himself for his stupidity.

"Switching to your home power system. Engaging secondary power." The lights come on and the wash resumes.

The images return to the screen. The Wholack looks back at him. Freckles, crossed blue eyes, a pocked thin nose, large flat ears under curly red hair, a deep scar that girdles his neck from ear to ear like the rope burn from a hangman's noose-- and then those thin lips that form the Wholack's famous smile. A smile so well known every child on the planet can draw it. For Gus, he is staring at the image of a young Russell Biner and compares it to the fool in front of him. Sitting in the midst of opulence, tapping the table to be sure it is all real, he notes Roo Biner's success.

He tastes aluminum. Something is wrong. I am missing a memory of something.

A sweat breaks out on his forehead. He sips ale. He scratches his arm, deep in thought, noting clean fingernails and wonders how that can be real. The fear of lost memory falls away, buried by drugs in the ale.

"Why does Wholack remain so popular?" The figure on the screen does a little jig--like some drunken fool; the computer is thinking, searching, and retrieving data.

"Your contract only allows search by person place or thing. You have not purchased Pilnouth assets," says the image.

"Regarding Remold Jaka, why Wholack?"

The figure spins in a circle. "Going to lesson five." The figure on the screen grays out then disappears into blackness. A cheery female voice speaks: "Lesson five, Entertainment History 505. In review, remember that we learned that VR, Virtual Reality, was a natural outcome of computer hardware, software, networking, the child of primitive knowledge manipulation. Touted as a technological Valhalla that promised to decrease the amount of energy used by humanity, eliminate anthropogenic forcing of the radiative balance, and increase the limits of perception, computation has fulfilled that promise through Wholack by allowing humanity to dodge the bullet of global warming, thanks to Dr. Remold Jaka..."

Gus snorts out a laugh.

Images of ancient room-sized computer systems fill the screen in a rapid montage of images that seem to fall on top of each other like slices of cheese on a cutting board. "Virtual reality and it's permutations, soft reality, deep-reality, and the current craze, Wholack, are not to be confused with sources of terrestrial information but rather as methods of distractions, responses to disasters both economic and natural as well as leadership seeking a better life."

He stares at the image of his friend, Russel Biner, in the guise of Wholack. "Was Pilot Nothing the reason for the name Pilnouth Foundation?"

"File restricted. Reporting in process."

Oh shit. Gus sees he has made a major mistake.

"Reporting complete. File closed for review. We will alert you when you have access."

"Go to Remold Jaka. What's an Agg?"

"Agg: An Aggregate of Essences, the hypothesis that reality is a set of geometries tied together by the illusion of human awareness and the event of human focus. Please review the Environmental Philosophy archives for more data."

"Negative. So an Agg is a scenario in Wholack?"

The screen dulls to a light gray. "It is considered as such by novices to the theory, but the dependencies are challenged and so it is considered less. Others postulate that Wholack itself is an Agg."

"Tell me more about why people want to control the Wholack?" He has just decided to enter the game on his own.

"According to Doctor Remold Jaka, it is not the creation and control of scenarios nor Wholack that matters, but control of the uncontrollable. Access to the Doctor's image is granted."

An image of Remold Jaka fills the screen. "...A thirst

hard-wired into our being." His hands are on his hips and he is leaning forward, a bright smile on his face. He is dressed in professorial cap and gown. It is a scene from a graduation of some sort. "...Yes, control of the Wholack is a key to winning the game. What a tempting target--especially when you know that a safe digital death follows the desecration of the fool." Jaka spreads his hands wide along the podium and leans forward. "Unfortunately, that misunderstanding can lead us to question in whose image we humans are created: In goodness or in foolishness? In God we trust or in foolishness we trust?"

Laughter.

"Think of it. Layers and layers of people all dedicated to debasing the fool. We now have members of two generations of humans who have never known anything else. Teens who have never tasted real pizza and do not care. Adults who have never touched another living human--just personae on a net-- all because they do not want to leave their nirvana. Meanwhile, the environment is healing because of our foolishness. Is this because we are wired to foolishness or is it recognition of our need to control the uncontrollable?"

Gus wonders how it was for Mrs. Doctor Jaka, to live with a man that saw control as the meaning of existence.

The image of Remold Jaka smiles, strolling back and forth across the stage; his hands clasped behind his back. "Some believe we have become a society of entertainment junkies, or victims of the some computer-gone-mad addiction. Ladies and gentleman, that is bullshit." Jaka stops as if summoned and looks off-stage to his right. "I know we're live." He faces front. "My handlers." He winks. "Where were we? Oh that's right. We are growing as a species. We have a new tool. Were we addicted to the wheel? Was the wheel an indicator that we were getting weak and could not walk anymore? Of course not. Just as the wheel was a sign of our growth--not an indication of a withering capacity--Wholack is step outward for all of us.

And by the way, I am sorry that it is all so much damn fun." Remold Jaka smiles. "I have created a doorway for us. Learn to use it as such."

No ego here, Gus says to himself.

"Ladies and Gentleman, at one point, our population was a danger to the planet and to ourselves. The real glory of the Wholack system is that despite an overall population of five billion humans, our footprint on the planet is no more than it was in the 1700s. Still our brethren die due to a previous generation's apathy. That is a crime for which we all feel responsible. Any guilt you feel is bullshit." He looks off stage and grins. "We now know the events of time and space are not of our God. They are the effluent of our God. While a digital reality is our effluent. We are a noble species. That cannot be denied. This issue of squalor is the challenge of our generation--not the guilt of your generation.

The screen blanks for a second. Remold is back. "Wholack is about how events are not controllable. We are like Wholack. We are the fools of time and space. Some wish to recreate every event over and over until they get it right. I say a doorway can open and a doorway can close. Reality is not the replication of event. It is event. It is change. Go with that change. I have brought you the bloom of universal transcendence..."

"Stop. Exit." Gus has had enough. "Computer begin entry sequence for Wholack." He gets up and walks across the living room to the door beside the bedroom. Opening the door he enters a room. It lights. A large open cylinder lies on its side. Like a coffin top, the cap opens along the side. Walking to it he looks inside to see a series of panels and a pair of hoses. He touches the red button on the side.

"Please enter the bed after removing your clothes and others adornments. Make sure to place your head on the foam."

As he enters the bed he notes the ceiling rafters above

hold a jungle of plants. "Now entering Wholack. Enjoy."

The Eden sequence begins. Remold's researchers begin their work. Midway through, Eden pauses, and Gus stares at four planes of color in front of him: pastel blue, green, red and yellow. They intersect at a white cube. Glowing pink lines outline the edges of the cube where the four planes meet. He finds he can step inside the cube and that the planes stretch out in all directions. From the discussion with Benson Fong, he knows this is a Hypercube. One of two structures provided to sub-scenario developers. The other is called a City-museum, an archive of work and an exit system--easily accessible. So while the Hypercube is the central structure from which all sub-scenarios are built by private parties, the City-Museum is the central structure by which the developer decides which structures to share.

Gus looks around. He appears to be standing in a whitish fog. The Hypercube is the canvas on which people build their private scenarios. From his discussions with Benson on the game, Gus knows this simple starting point sometimes takes years to acquire. Remold has kept his word. Stepping around the cube he notes that by walking to the side he can find the vertical edge, and rotate the colored planes by touching them. He stares up seeing the soles of his feet. He looks down and sees the top of his head staring down.

The Hypercube and City-museum, he has been taught, are the canvas and egress points of a scenario, his world. Those entering his digital structures will come through the Hypercube; those exiting it will exit through the City-museum--except for the Wholack who might appear at any time in any way.

While studying the game earlier, Gus was amused to see that some will "porch" their main scenario with a transport mechanism, a sub-scenario to control access. The most common porch is a space ship.

"Grass." He points down. Grass appears along the bottom plane extending out to digital infinity. "Hills." They appear as well. He smiles at the ease of it all.

Gus does not know Remold and his people have given him access that is not usually available to a novice. They want him to create anything he wants--considering them clues. The tools, the one Gus now uses, were developed for the Pilnouth Foundation. An organization dedicated to helping those with developmental difficulties. This specific version was developed by Remold for a wealthy autistic client. It is the high end of ease. Gus' question about Pilot Nothing a few minutes ago has changed everything for Remold Jaka. He thinks Pilot Nothing will no longer a well kept secret in this society because Remold believes this man and Pilot Nothing came from the same Agg. He thinks therefore of two crossovers, not one. He does not consider the terms Hypercube and City-museum in his logic. Mina did, years ago, after considering that energy use is driven by human experience. Therefore two crossovers were needed for connection across the Aggs.

"Alright. I want a road along a river, a grassy hillside leading to it, homes, make it rural, not suburban, make it wealthy rural. Add a bridge across the river, then fluffy clouds, a blue sky."

He stares as his heaven forms around him. In what seems less than a minute he stares at his work. "Wow--add docks and sailboats." He turns away from the river sure of his powers. A nondescript set of mansions stand in a line behind him, like row houses, their sidewalls touching each other, a comedy of opulence. "Separate the homes with yards, various sizes. Make this river the Hudson River." The homes pop apart into residences each with their own yards. "Elevate the homes up small hillsides replicating a map-based rise from the river. I want woods behind them. The home in front of me should be stone, no wood, an Edwardian from the 19th century. Give it a big porch, two porches flanking wide wooden doors. Make the doors wood, antiques. Add foliage and trees. Add a hammock between two trees on the left. Put bushes around the base of the porch. Make a path to the front door from flat stones. Add similar to the other homes, randomize the rest of the residences. Make it all grand, old money."

He watches it all form. Something is wrong. Then he sees he has created a portrait. The trees are still, the clouds do not move, and the river is frozen. "Add movement." The ground he stands on starts moving as if it were in an earthquake. It intensifies. "Keep the ground still." It immediately stops and he falls to the ground. He remembers a comment from Benson earlier tonight. He repeats what he heard: "Give the ground the texture of Earth-normal, also make the nature of the area true to Earth-normal." The river flows. The trees sway. Figures, Rosts, of dull gray begin to appear then color: people, dogs, cats, birds all form taking their places. The figures remain still, like manikins, and no distinguishing features are apparent. It looks like his world has raided a department store warehouse. "FAQ," he calls out. "Why are the Rosts still?"

"Do you wish to allow others to populate your scenario?"

"No."

"Then it is your task to power each one."

Gus looks around thinking how much fun this is. He strolls up the path to the large home and enters through the door. Inside is a blue pastel plane. "Populate the home with furniture and Earth-normal additions, mid 1930's." The wide salon begins to pop forth furniture, rugs, and decorated walls. In a minute he is looking at what appears to be a standard interior. He recognizes it from the training manuals Benson showed him on the net. It is called CK Dexterhaven. He does not know the reason why, but he figures the early 20th century version of luxury will do for the time being. He wanders the six large rooms on the first floor, the two living rooms, the dining room, the kitchen, and the two salons. He doesn't bother going up the stairs. Though he is curious about a small poster on the wall of the stairs that says, "Teddy was here."

Outside of his detection, a graduate student monitoring him laughs at her joke.

Gus returns to the porch. The winds blow and the trees move in a sweet summer breeze. The air fills with the scent of rose. "Add porch furniture, wicker. The area around him populates with a porch rocker, three chairs, a table, and a set of four palm trees. "Cancel. Change the other porch by adding a ping pong table." It appears. "Change the river. Make a sailboat race. Put tubes in the river to store the sailboats-- make them racers."

The graduate student has stopped smiling.

Gus grins and looks out at the frozen figures wondering how to get them to act alive. "FAQ. How do I get them to act like people?"

He is ejected from the game.

He looks up at the wall clock. Three hours have passed. The clock is blinking red and blue. Time to go burglarize Hope's residence. Even so, Gus stands smiling at the space around him. "Add a glass of water." Of course nothing happens. He laughs as he pulls himself out of the bed. "I have definitely got to dump this Earth place. No wonder everyone is addicted." He finally thinks he understands the appeal of the game. It isn't about the Wholack. It's about being a god.

On the other hand, he is surprised at how much time passed without him knowing it. The drugs depress a sense of time, but he does not know that yet. Gus dresses wondering what he might really build for himself as a home. He drops the notion immediately, knowing that a decision to stay means he has failed Winston. He would die first.

Daniel H. Gottlieb

CHAPTER TWENTY ONE

HERE COWARDS WILL GIVE YOU UP

High tide detritus wanders along the sand beach of Coney Island. Out to sea, the first of the dawn breaks red upon the clouds. The remnants of a fossil-based society pokes out in every direction. Wind-laden sand pelts the rusting cars, crumpled trucks, buried house parts, metal desks, lamps, lawn mowers, and broken cradles. The rest of the remains have retreated into the oceans, the encroaching forests, engulfed in wildfires, or simply left to rot under mounds of garbage. As mechanical systems fail--the green tide rises. The sea-mist still functions, with no use for the ironies of humanity.

With the wild comes disease, danger, and the spin-hidden mastery of a planet by Gaian forces. As part of a planet-wide transition to the aboriginal systems, humanity's view has evolved from control of nature, to escaping nature's impact.

Sadly, the humans at the bottom of the economic ladder

are caught in the vise of transition. The ones still tattooed with tales of the consumer society hang on caressing a myth of human domination. Many others, those who know their lack of skills, and therefore their fate on the forgotten Earth, take steps for their own demise. Suicide is a growth industry among the lower classes--and were it not for Wholack--the suicide industry might be the major industry of the planet.

Though some humans still have a plan. A few disappear off the grid and revert to a centuries old subsistence lifestyle. For others, the plan is some diabolical attempt at wealth so they can escape into Wholack. Often involving elaborate tactics to defraud insurance companies, steal, embezzle, extort, or kidnap wealth, the available information on such crimes has led to a repeat of the same tactics and so the authorities are ready and the result is slaughter. A very small percentage are successful and they are heralded in the media. They represent the glue of this dismembered society:

Your ascension to crime is escape.

The consumer myth dies hard. A remnant of the consumer age--washed over and combed by Gaia.

The night rains now gone, Hope Weiss emerges from under the crumbling Coney Island boardwalk. On her right, an overturned truck lies on its back--buried to the wheels. Farther back from the truck, stubs of pilings poke through the soupy planes of the boardwalk. The black pilings stand naked, without purpose. Beyond them, further in the distance, a city still drenched in night. To her left, the windowless apartment buildings.

Among the dirty gray rubble, people occasionally emerge from their sleeping shelters. Church bells' toll, pulled upon by hung-over zealots. Hope wanders down the sand passing a buried cement truck that houses a family. Ahead, the remains of three cars. Beyond them, a xylophone of bones pointing skyward in the sand--ribs from a dead whale. She marvels at the size. Its flesh had fed two dozen for a week.

Tired from her night-flight across country, Hope is frustrated with this meeting with her attorney. Unwilling to discuss the reason in detail, her attorney had prompted her flight across country last night indicating Hope might have to protect Tovar Dal. Hope tells herself all she need do is buy another day. Then he will be fine. She also carries a gun. Hope does not want to be kidnapped and held for ransom--another major industry of her time.

A small explosion sends a puff of black smoke into the sky. The island of Long Island, which includes Coney Island is slated for inclusion into FairGame in three months, on January 1, and scavengers are at work removing useful metals.

Most of them know that out in the country--where small farms have blossomed--there is food and work. But the nets still extol the dangers of wild animals that roam the countryside--eating people as if they were snacks. Imbued with the fear, many seek solace in their memories of civilization.

Alcohol and drug production are key industries in every city that has not gone to FairGame. The owners of these industries stay long enough to acquire the wealth for the game, then pass it on to a trusted lieutenant--if they live long enough.

The bells stop and start in a pattern of six. It is 6 AM on the east coast of North America.

Hope wears a diaphanous white dress over her athletic body. The wind lifts Hope's white covering in small waves; she quickly pats it down. Her actions hides confusion. Getting John Doe to the Boiler Room with Tovar Dal and Remold had been the key to seeing if Doe is truly a crossover. She mistakenly believes that John Doe is dead and that option is gone. Hope cannot understand why Remold Jaka let those Hunters kill him. She presumes Remold figures that with John Doe dead, there is no way for Mina to complete her tasks. Hope tells herself Remold Jaka is a pig.

Hair tied tight to her head to hide a small tracking system, just in case she is kidnapped, Hope calls her attorney again and receives another text. She is parking her vehicle.

Hope feels the winds' sting and pulls out large glasses that wrap around her eyes. These innocuous glasses allow her to scan for danger. Hope sees no one is tracking her on the display screen. Thinking she looks like some odd bug-eyed monster from Saucer City, she lifts them over her forehead. As she does, she again wonders about the wisdom of meeting out here in the sand. Hope has a deep-seated distrust of technology and feels the beach is safety. The clump, clump of an axes from the remains of the boardwalk fill the air with impacts. Slave-like chanting follows. The tempo of the axe-assault and its chants intensifies as more woodsmen seek sources of heat for tonight. Hope knows the axe's sound can mean many things. Usually it means merely the need for more fuel. Sometimes it can mean a mob event and sometimes even a tribal ritual. She watches men cutting parts of the boardwalk into firewood-sized pieces. There is nothing dangerous out here--so far. The Croakers are not yet allowed in the city.

The wind stings her again with sand. She rubs her arm feeling the grit imbedded in her skin lotion. Her eyes linger on the waves. Hope once loved the beach believing everything important that ever happened to her happened there. She watches the waves wondering if maybe she just belongs on the lowest rung of the ladder. This connection to those around her on the beach has more madness than truth. She sends a text to purchase medical truck that will arrive after she leaves.

The laws say food is free to those who cannot afford it, but anything regarding energy is steeply taxed. The rule of law serves no purpose anyway--judges and juries are simply knowledge-bases of distilled experience. The legal game is ownership of property, and that is determined by money paid into the purveyors of nation. Everyone is considered a leaseholder to which the corporate state has title. Theft is illegal and ownership is the lens for all other judicial events. If the records say you own it, you do. Your progeny splits the property in equal proportions. No one else may own it unless you sell it, or give it away, or barter it. Every item has a title attached to it--except people. They are worthless.

In the cities, away from the generators, away from the software coders, absent from the yeast-farms, there is only a desire to escape the uncertainty of Earth's march. The digital world has become the nucleus of humanity now. A famous early advertisement for Wholack said simply: "Got Nature? Too bad. Sign up."

Near the network of technologies that support the beds, order remains. Those who maintain the beds that cradle the human carriages live safe like pets. Hoping to escape into peace for the predetermined tenure of their retirement bliss fosters the workers' calm. The social contract of this society says those who take care of the system benefit from it though extended vacation five weeks a year and retirement at age fifty. That means entrance into Wholack at age fifty-one, after a year of training. Termination is at age seventy-five for these retirees. It is ironic that a two tier society has put those who embrace nature below ground in beds, cinched up in technology; while those that loathe the planet, live in direct contact with its nature.

Hope considers the people around her and how myth extends to them. The ongoing lottery allows even the most destitute potential access to Wholack. Half of the medicine will never get to the beach. It will go for lottery tickets.

Nirvana has created a strata of crooks and slaves. Humans chained to dangerous maintenance tasks, their faces sometimes reconstructed into permanent smiles--all for escape. Hope believes the real chains of their slavery is their desire, addiction formed at an early age.

Everyone gets time in Wholack when they graduate high school. It births the virulent desire that never goes away. It is the reason those people chopping wood in the distance scare her. In this strata of society, that brief taste of heaven has driven most people mad.

She blames technology for the death of humanity's soul. Hope had even questioned Mina's theories about Wholack: those theories of transcendence. The appearance of John Doe stunned her into belief and commitment. She asks herself how Remold could have been so stupid as to kill John Doe.

A new sound rolls along the beach, a clanging sound. Turning, Hope spies the old Ferris wheel, The Wonder Wheel; her most beloved object on this beach. It is under attack by an army of scavengers. The huge circle of steel, long voided of round cars, moans and begins to tumble over in a crash of steel and concrete.

Immediately drone aircraft dive from the sky spraying the entire area. The marauders collapse in a drug induced stupor. Later today, then they awake, the remains of the metal structure will appear out in the ocean, beyond the breakwater--another new habitat for sea life--the rest of the steel on the auction block. Any installed object removed from its moorings becomes property of the worldwide scavenger firms. Payment is made to the state to acquire title. It is how collectors gained title to the other remnants of industrialization: the Liberty Bell, the Eiffel Tower, the Statue of Liberty, and other items.

The yellow cloud of gas swirls in the dawn. Hope turns away; she has nothing to fear from the gas. The sea winds will blow the gases inland.

Hope sees her attorney. She has three security people with her. In a flash, she decides John Doe is not dead. Somehow he is tied to this meeting. The chill of betrayal rides her spine.

At her attorney's approach Hope shifts her body from side to side scanning the beach again. Her attorney waves and speaks. "Hi." Then a squeal cuts through the voice--a high pitch warbling from a larynx implant. Hope stares at the older woman. The woman waves then points to her neck and frowns--as she tries to adjust her implant. "This thing pisses me off, I could speak if I was in the game."

Tall and thin, still beautiful, she is almost fifty; Susan Willoughby moves like quicksilver. The axes have ceased as the men chopping wood nearby have stopped to stare at her. Hope knows they are admiring her fitness. That means money and access to Wholack.

"Could you have picked a more obnoxious place to meet? Oh, I saw your friend Quentin Conworth at the diner the other day, taking another scalp."

"He said you were less than friendly." Then her words are smothered by the defective larynx implant: "I don't like--'ere is every--nne." She points to the implant. Six months ago a doctor fouled up an operation to remove a cancer. The implant he put in to restore her voice, though the best available, has never worked right. The design has a software glitch. The manufacturer claims the labor shortage is the cause because these days there is no one competent to handle a repair.

Susan finally clears her throat. "Hope, I lied. You are here because of Remold Jaka." She unfolds the small chair she carries. "We need to talk."

Angry with the influence of Remold Jaka, Hope speaks. "The beds?"

"Not in the way you think. Remold knows the beds are empty. Security is rifling through your home as we speak." Susan looks down at the gun. "I gave them permission saying you are merely helping a friend and that you have no knowledge of any wrong doing. I blocked their access to search the diner saying I could get you to voluntarily agree to a search--within two days." When Hope does not smile, Susan looks back at the three bodyguards Remold hired to protect her this meeting.

She makes sure Hope can see her gaze and its focus. When she looks back at Hope she sees anger.

"Go ahead."

"Remold contacted me last night, insisting I arrange a face to face with you." Susan tilts her head, waiting.

"Why?"

"Something has convinced Remold he might be wrong. Talk about a monumental event. He thinks there might be something to Mina's theories." Her attorney watches her. "But, there is no way he will allow Mina to shut down the servers."

Hope nods. "And we are meeting to show Remold that we are his friend? To alert me? Or to tell me to roll over for that egomaniac?"

"Mina gave Remold a little more than a day from now before she shuts down Wholack."

"And that would never work for you."

Susan tilts her head prompting her bodyguards to move in closer. "Remold cannot find her. He wants to know where her backups are."

"I don't know anything about that. You know Mina would never share that. So the punch line to this is?"

Susan waves her guards even closer. "The punch line is the man searching your apartment is John Doe." Her steady gaze says Susan speaks the truth. "Hope, I am trying to protect you and Tovar."

Hope shakes her head back and forth. Her breath comes in short bursts. "Why is Mr. Doe in my home?"

"Remold says that since you were the prime mover for Kittens and Cradles allowing John Doe into your home should break free a link in our reality."

"Nonsense."

"I don't understand all that computer crap, but somehow a home is like a sub-scenario--if this guy John Doe is a crossover."

"Bull."

"Fine. Remold does not like being wrong but his researchers all think this guy John Doe is the real deal. My people say John Doe is an exact physical match for the fourth man at the table in the Boiler Room. His genetic match fits a mister Gus Plow--dead washing machine salesmen--well known bad driver who killed Jenny Biner's kid, Russell. Bets say Doe is a crossover. Remold wants to control the asset."

"So Remold plans to claim responsibility for Mina's work?" Hope asks.

"Precisely, but first he has to find her and her links to shut the system down. When I talked to Remold he was in a fury because he still could not find them. That's why I am late. He wants to be friends with you."

"There is no way a crossover in my home will work as anything but a waste of time."

"Unless the crossover wants to find his way home."

Her eyes flash anger. "So that's it. You are here to convince me to go inside the game with John Doe and help him find his home Agg? Remold wants to control that too? To own it? Seriously? I hate that guy."

Susan closes her eyes for a moment. "When did you get so dull?"

"When did you get so desperate?"

"I am your friend."

"I will assume that is a feeble attempt at humor. Now I see the allure of Quentin Conworth."

Her attorney looks around beckoning her guards closer. They are now ten feet away. Hope ignores them. "Hope, this guy Doe was a Target who killed an Administrator. Remold wins no matter what. When you get back you will find your place trashed. Remold wants to make sure you understand the facts. For now, John Doe works for Remold."

"Don't we all?"

"Hope, Mina is going to destroy everything. This guy is the key. Go in with him. Find out if she knows about him. Get her to hold off until you can get Mr. Doe to the Boiler Room with you and Tovar. If he is a crossover then it's a whole new ball game. Can you do that?" Her attorney looks at the sand.

Hope laughs. "I might be willing to get him to the Boiler Room."

"That's smart. Now you get it--a little cooperation. Hope, I am slated for entry into Wholack after this meeting. I was informed that I was to be denied entry if I did not arrange for your cooperation. I'm dying, the cancer."

Hope reddens and her eyes narrow. "We're a planet of cowards"

"You could try to get John Doe to Kittens and Cradles. Remold has it wired now to find John Doe's Agg. Or," she pauses looking around, "You could go in the game with this guy John Doe and take Jaka to Mina. That solves everything."

"You would have me betray Mina?"

"If she shuts down Wholack they will kill her and everyone who helped her. I can save your life--and the life of one you love."

"So if I go in there with Mr. Doe--that saves Tovar?"

"Yes--I have that in writing. Remold thinks Mina will not shut Wholack down if she knows about this guy, John Doe. He believes she will wait to understand the meaning."

"He lied to you. She brought Mr. Doe through. Remold knows that."

Susan stares, stunned. "Oh dear God, we're toast. Hope, don't destroy what's left of us because you hate Remold. He can fix this. To do that he has to stop or control Mina. He has a trap set in Kittens and Cradles. Once she goes there to meet John Doe she is toast."

"She is too smart for that. Mina will never make the link again."

"Hope, he knows about Benson. Without him, Mina is going to be caught sooner or later. Hope, we can't let her shut Wholack down."

"Yes--we can," Hope says.

"When did you get so selfish? Fine, if nothing else, an agreement will buy you time. It won't hurt Mina. She already knows Remold plans to shut her down once he finds her. And I know Mina--she has already taken it into account. Why not do it?"

"That bag of fluff make you feel better?" Hope shakes her head. "I wonder if you are a betraying bitch in the other Aggs as well."

Susan speaks. "One with a sense of guilt?" She laughs. "I doubt that."

Hope walks away thinking of Tovar's devotions. She has forgiven him, finally.

"Hope, agree to do this. You believe Remold cannot stop Mina. Therefore you lose nothing. If nothing else, take this guy Doe into the game. It will keep Tovar safe and hedge your bets if Mina is wrong."

Hope stops walking and sighs. She has no more words. She turns and faces Susan nodding yes--seeing the end of a long friendship--hating Remold Jaka just a little bit more today.

Daniel H. Gottlieb

Chapter Twenty Two

Police Active

Gus Plow glances at his watch and sees his breath. It is four in the morning. He has just found out that in twenty-eight hours Mina plans to shut down Wholack. He fears for Winston.

The cold misty morning touches his skin as a set of shivers. Crossing the rain-soaked street, he glances at his handlers in a van. They are waiting for Gus. They will be waiting for a long time. Gus believes anything he garners without them is pure leverage. He does not know this visit, is, among other items, a test of his loyalty.

The wet wind swirls. He makes sure to pull his hands out of the duster's pockets, too suspicious. Sticking to the shadows from tree canopies, he moves by shuttered shops and darkened cafes. The bicycles, cars, and motorcycles in the street are all unlocked. The street smells of green trees and berries--with no trace of urine or blood. He stops under elm trees. Rain still lands on his duster and head. In the trees, strings of blue lights blink in celebration of the end of summer.

Despite his bleak task, he finds himself looking around at the landscape deciding if he would like to have this or that in his new Wholack-world. It is no longer a wonder to him that those about to enter Wholack are so happy. Picking and choosing the best of reality and bringing it into Wholack has immense appeal. He does not know his level of access usually takes years to acquire. Nor will he know.

Remold Jaka is a man with a plan. He has to find out how loyal Gus Plow is and what he might do about Pilot Nothing. Disclosure of the murder of Pilot Nothing will not be an option for Gus Plow if Remold has anything to say about it. This all means keeping Gus Plow busy or inside Wholack. A willingness to let go of Pilot Nothing defines Gus Plow's future--insofar as Remold is concerned. Remold Jaka, like many in his position have an easy morality: Their needs supersede the needs of others. This is the real reason Mina left him.

Gus walks by a dog park in the center of the block believing his wariness to be the source of safety. Others might say it is the cause of his peril. An odd twist has made honor and talent key components for success. Not the honor of a toady, nor the talent of a thief, but the core values of dedication to duty and grit. It has allowed many people to escape into the new frontier of Wholack. Gus has both duty and honor, but he is a man out of place. Heaven means nothing to him.

So while Remold is a talented observer and evaluator of skills, Gus Plow considers Remold a clown. Therefore Remold misses the meaning of it for Gus. For Remold, love is no part of the equation. In Remold's heaven love is a cheap commodity--freely available--a myth. For Gus, love is dedication to another and more. His commitment to Winston keeps him focused during the worst hell of his life.

Avoiding the puddles, Gus makes a left towards the building's staircase. Out in the open, with the ambient light from the overhead lamps he feels exposed. Headlights appear from the far end of the roadway, a street sweeper. As he hurries up the stairs, the doors clicks open, swinging wide almost hitting him.

Two men appear in front of him. Dressed in dark blue suits, stained black and tan, as if it were camouflage; one man carries a silver lunch pail painted with childish cartoon designs: a mouse, two ducks, and a bunny rabbit--all clubbing each other. Seeing Gus examine his lunch pail, the man says candidly, "My daughter gave it to me for my birthday last night. She loves it so that's fine. No kids?"

"No. Maybe some day," Gus says, in response.

One man nods towards the broad intersection. "I need some chaw. Let's go over there." At that moment, a multitude of tiny bright beams turn on in front of the drugstore. The effect is supposed to mimic the stars. The store has just opened for business today.

The other man points to the Biner & Feiss Drugstore at the intersection. "Chaw, what the hell for?" The man with the lunch pail glances at Gus. "Chaw, can you believe it?"

His comrade raises a hand motioning for his friend to follow. Gus smiles as he enters the doorway. The door slams shut. Glancing back, he sees the men have descended the stairs dropping out of sight. The street sweeper rumbles by, a bored attendant in the driver's seat. When both men call police services they are told the situation is nominal.

Remold has made calls

The glass-enclosed entryway reveals an opulent reception area and a pair of elevators at the end of a wood paneled hallway. Gus scans the hallway for cameras, sees a broken camera mount with exposed wires, and so walks towards the security desk on the right. Made of a granite slab stacked on four black cubes, the desk is unmanned. A clear gloss says it has been so for a while.

He walks along the polished wood floor passing a set of mailboxes decorated with four inch square paintings on their metal doors. Gus considers one painting on a mail box for the design of his new home. Walking slowly, purposefully, but with a sense of concern, he wonders if Remold's promise of retirement in Wholack includes Winston. The distraction of Wholack startles him and he wonders if the drugs from the bed have altered him in some way.

The elevator door slides open. Entering, he presses the button for the floor just below Hope's penthouse. Accessing the penthouse directly will leave a trail--or so Remold's people say. The elevator steams upward. The inside of the elevator is one large mirror. For just a moment he stares at his image, shocked at how his once formidable physique has been whittled skinny by three years in FairGame. The flat tweed cap makes him look like an aging hipster. He remembers reading a note from his past that said he looked like a large appliance. Gus is a shadow of that now.

The mirror also reminds him of plans to get behind the mirror in the diner as soon as possible. Waiting for the door to open, Gus again considers the tie between Mina Jaka and Hope Weiss. He doubts they could be lovers and thinks them just co-conspirators.

The lights brighten as he steps onto the lush blue carpet. He scans either side of the hallway. The pictures, the brass sconces, the high ceiling--he is shocked Hope Weiss lives so well. Walking to the right, he moves to the stairwell. Opening the steel door and closing it, bounding up the stairs, he reaches the penthouse service door. Pushing on it, the door opens easily. The locking mechanism has electrical tape over it. The next door, egress into the penthouse is locked. Scanning the keypad and its biometrics, Gus puts his thumb to the fingerprint reader. The system goes into diagnostic mode, then the latch opens--just as they said it would. He opens the door entering a galley style kitchen. Pulling a flashlight out hearing the locking system finish its diagnostic, Gus believes he has fifteen minutes before he must exit. In truth, a technician controls the alarm system--to this point. She sends an e-mail to her boss, Remold, saying John Doe is inside.

Looking around for cameras and seeing none, walking into the living room, Gus marvels at the unobstructed view of the diner and the NewDay Mall beyond it. Flashes of gunfire light the entire landscape--the early morning risers of FairGame are on task.

On the other wall of glass, in the lake, the so-called Memorial for the Dead rests in the water. Once called the Titanic, deep in its bowels is the exclusive restaurant called the Boiler Room. Gus knows none of this. All he knows is a ship is lit and busy. Lightning crosses the clouds over the Cascades, distracting him from the ship.

Crossing by the couch and fireplace, shelves of antique books glow under lights along the shelving. Pausing, he counts well over three-hundred books on the shelves. He considers stealing one as he stops at the desk, then laughs remembering he can have a million books if he wants--once he is inside Wholack. Gus decides his new home should be a library.

He sits, scanning the computer system and then bends over to look under the desk. That's where he expects to find the security system. It is far more extensive than Remold's people had said. It will take a lot more than fifteen minutes to break through it. Worse, he figures, were he to try, he might give away too much information to Remold's people--who questioned him on his knowledge of technology. Gus had played dumb. He pulls a can of spray paint out of the duster pocket and begins to spray parts of the living room, adding hobo signs to flat surfaces. After five minutes, he cuts the power to the security system, severing the link to the computer. Gus has failed the loyalty test in a big way: The police are alerted before Remold's technician can divert the alert. Just as Gus had hoped.

He unplugs the computer figuring twenty minutes before the police arrive on site. The apartment lights begin to blink. Gus cuts a set of wires under the desk and shuts down the optical alarm. The room goes dark again. Pulling out the computer, he turns it on its side and opens it up. Two minutes later, he has the memory module in hand putting it into one of his pockets. Spraying the insides of the computer with a mix of graphite and light oil, he takes the computer system to the window, opens a window, and tosses it onto the street. He figures whatever Remold was looking for, it is now his.

Gus hurries down the side stairs of the condominium. He exits to a wide boulevard, then sprints into a wide field, which appears to be a community garden. Police vehicles round the corner.

The tossed computer has made an impression.

On the far side if the garden he sees a set of rail lines. Rail lines that ferry commuters in and out their jobs--as well as low income Hunters to the SeaPort. Gus knows that between the rails, trees huddle in a ribbon of forest for the entire length of the rail link. Approximately half a mile wide, the forest garden between the rails is a perfect safety zone.

The trees--when planted a number of years ago--had prompted the architect to say she felt she had created an almost perfect haven for the city dweller. She meant FairGame escapees but of course did not say so. There are a few in this society who find FairGame despicable. Only the foolish say so. A dissident can find his or her self in FairGame within weeks-- as well as a genetic marker that precludes access into Wholack.

Crossing the first set of light rail lines, careful not to get electrocuted, he enters the forest. A path worn bare by Hunters and escapees is a darker brown than the rest of the forest and easy to follow. Dense foliage blocks sight lines and even heat signatures. In any case, he believes he could find his way along this forest even in the pitch black, having been at the terminus, near FairGame more than once.

When wounded or sick, Gus used an electrical tunnel to get to these woods from inside FairGame. Not a discovery by accident, his search for a secure route into and out of FairGame had been his intent from the moment he entered the Seattle area. It has been said that the major cause of death in FairGame is the decision to give up; the second major cause of death is complacency. Gus believes the real cause of death is ignorance of how to escape the battlefield. The tunnel became his insurance policy along with his most valuable possession, a bulletproof vest he had wrested from a Hunter. Gus has had a total of six cracked ribs. More than once he planned to use this forest as his escape from FairGame--once the mall opened. He thought all he needed was to steal a suit. Now he knows his stink would have betrayed him.

Sirens and the noise of helicopters begin to fill the area. He figures Hope must have purchased the full package of security in her home. That strikes him as odd. He saw nothing so valuable in her residence or at the diner so he considers the computer data might really be valuable enough to warrant his break in.

Crossing over a small stream, he moves quickly along the soft mat of shredded leaves. The damp pathway leaves almost no footprints, and less sound. The steam has sensors--a discovery that cost him a broken rib from a bullet stopped by his vest. Gus moves with familiarity and fear. He decides to use Remold's people to secure his safety if it gets bad. More cars and the overhead helicopters begins lighting the area. Gus has not yet figured out these are Remold's people, not the personnel of Hope's legal policy. He is therefore, mistakenly, more and more impressed by the funds she has spent to secure her data and the apparent value of the memory module.

Remold Jaka is a master puppeteer.

Running along the path, he smells the juniper and cypress, and knows he is no more than a hundred yards from a turn where he can crawl into the manhole and reenter FairGame.

Gus would rather die first.

Hearing voices and the squeal of radios, he tenses, listening. A branch cracks. He loosens the coat and allows it to spread on either side of his frame. The cold dewy air assaults his neck but he does not care. A bullet through the coat, missing him, is better than a bullet in his body. Slowly moving towards the side of the path, he seeks the shadow of a large juniper.

Its spiky green leaves dig into his neck. As he pushes close to the large plant, he bends his body to hug the shadow. A low hum approaches from the south. A light appears a few yards down the path. The branch sticking into his back gives way with a crack. The light illuminates him. A bullet tears at his coat.

The guy has a silencer also.

Pirouetting from his hiding place, Gus dashes across the path instead of trying to disappear back into the grove behind him. He hears a scatter of bullets already peppering the juniper. Scrambling through the thicket, he uses the trees to cover his back. By the time the shooter realizes the Target has moved in exactly the opposite direction he expected, Gus has disappeared into another thicket of trees.

"Come-on out you smarmy little pigeon. There's a new Marshall in town. Escape is illegal, remember?"

Feeling a pistol in his hand, it suddenly seems a bit too easy. Gus smiles at the inequity.

The Croaker grabs a set of night goggles and stares into the woods. Unseen, Gus crouches, listening intently to this lone Hunter. Bullets shatter branches all around him. He marvels at the indiscriminate way the Hunter uses ammunition. This Croaker's end will come soon. The police do not allow that kind of live fire outside FairGame. The myth of live fire only inside the preserve needs to be maintained and Gus figures they will be tracking the gunfire. That means they will tag and bag this Hunter by noon.

"I'm coming in to get you, pigeon, and you're going to pay for it if I get dirty."

A rustle to Gus's left--he sees a dirty middle-aged woman dressed in camouflage green popping up her head. She looks toward Gus. A report from a rifle and she falls into the bush. Gus does not move. He has seen this event of suicide too often to think he could have made a difference. He also knows he must stay quiet until the Hunter is sated. The woman groans in pain. A moment later the Croaker appears. The tracer beacon from the bullet has led the man directly to the female Target.

"I was sure you were a man."

"Help me," she says.

"Okay." The hunter snaps the night vision goggles back down to scan around him. Gus has already placed himself behind a tree trunk, safe. "Now," says the man with the weapon. "Do you see how dirty my pants are?" Another report from the rifle. "Well do you?" Three more rounds and then silence. Gus hears the grisly sounds of the scalping-knife. His eyes scan skyward through the black-green branches. A helicopter hovers above, waiting for the Hunter to be in the clear. Gus smells the blood mixing with moss and lichens of the wet ground. He works to still his breathing hearing the knife hacking against flesh.

The Croaker finishes taking the scalp. Gus waits for the whirl of the electric engine from the scooter. Footsteps startle him, but they appear to be heading away from the scooter. Then he hears the start of the engine and the area lights. The vehicle rolls away, the crackle of tires on the path. The light from the helicopter glares into the wood off to the south. A single shot, the crash from the scooter as it impacts a tree.

Gus Plow does not move. Some of the more sophisticated hunting vehicles work by remote control. The Hunter might still be alive. Siting, he stares around the wood, safe for the moment. Looking up, Gus decides the trees in his new world will be unable to drop their branches. Dead branches mean a hunt to him now.

A branch cracks on the other side of the tree: a Croaker. Then a familiar friendly sound--for Targets--the sound of bees. "What the fuck? Hey, oh shit, fuck!" The Hunter, stung by angry bees, bolts off. In his wake, a thousand wasps. Gus exits out to the street.

Time to go.

Running towards the garden, he breaks into the clearing that is the rail line again. He sees the black van rushing up the street, moving in between sparse traffic. It stops. Jaka's men get out glaring at him, weapons drawn. Gus gets in. "I have the memory module."

The men stare at him, angry but pleased this man has completed his task. There was a bonus for whatever team located him: decreasing their wait for retirement by two months. No further questions will be asked. This man is to retain whatever he wants.

The van drives away.

"That item of interest has been recovered."

CHAPTER TWENTY THREE

WORTH ROBBING

Examining the bullet's rip in his brand new coat, Gus closes the door to the apartment turning on music: Smetana, Ma Vlast. The piece recalls an earlier life, before his world spun into madness. The slow strings caress him. He closes his eyes, steadying himself on the wall. He would fall without it.

She is not dead. I will find her.

Outside the windows cry rain as he watches the dawn bring depth to the distant game preserve. Gus plans to defeat Remold Jaka and his methods for monitoring his actions. The irony forces him to recognize the foolishness of trying to defeat the digital eyes of the planet's recognized genius in digital systems. On the other hand, Gus considers that Mina Jaka has achieved just that, and if not her, someone else. She would be an ally, but she seeks destruction of the only system he can use to find his wife. While Remold assists him. Besides, Remold would be a formidable enemy if he discovered plans to betray him. Gus turns to walk toward the stainless steel kitchen. He sips water. He cannot understand Mina's wanting to bring the system down. It doesn't make sense. Still, acting as Jaka's monkey galls Gus. Watching the smoke from new fires in the distant wood, he ponders the comments by Remold Jaka that the game is a set of doorways. Which doorway, he wonders, gets him out of Remold's grasp?

Walking out of the kitchen, he considers betrayal of so powerful a person is almost unknown in a society where the possibility of heaven, rather than squalor and corruption, is within reach.

Who would help me? Who would want to rule in hell? What is Mina's problem? Remold's invention is incredible. A universe to explore, a link to the great beyond that calls humanity out of the cocoon of a body. Freedom to do as one pleases. I am no threat and the system might be an escape. The planet is healing. Why shut it down? Disliking Jaka is no reason to destroy so many. The Wholack doorway couldn't be that evil...Or could it? What does that say about me?

A small explosion out in the game preserve catches his attention. Smoke from the explosion swirls into low clouds. Near the explosion, the flash of weapons from Hunters. He remembers the smells of death after Hunters surrounded and fired on an encampment--the blood flowing into the mud.

Along the windows, winds splash more rain. He hated the winds and the rains. The cold and the chills, the sickness and the fear, the sound of a Hunter's boot stepping into bloody mud--the squish of its release.

He looks at his computer. Long ago he learned the usefulness of a computer as a tool for the removal of a painful memory. He turns to the steel door at the back of the large living room. Enough time has passed. He may once again enter digital heaven. Crossing to his bed system, he sighs at his desires to enter the long jar. The water-based feed system, the wires, the gas system, the waste removal systems, they all look so familiar, like Clipper.

The thief of being, Clipper, was his defense system design. Its purpose had been to remove memory. So soldiers could fight a battle no one understood--the intrusion of apparent madness into reality. He and the other researchers had no idea what they were doing. They just knew Clipper worked-- they thought. Gus touches the glass enclosure. He once vowed never to return to such a system. He had hated Clipper. Gus also hated his part in supporting a computer system that stole time and memory from humans. Today he is offended a timer will eject him from the Wholack after only two hours.

I am again part of the madness.

He closes the door behind him. Stripping down, he wonders why Dr. Jaka allows him access without a mentor or another nearby to keep track of him. He tells himself it is a digital universe, Jaka's digital universe. His independence inside the system is like the freedom and benefits executives like Tana Reins had enjoyed: illusions--bits of feed time for tapping the metal bar of their task. Remold is controlling all this. He is always watching. Gus again tells himself he understands Mina's dislike for him--but the output of Remold's genius is monumental. He remains unsure of who will really support his objectives. Gus reaches into his pocket and places the memory module into his empty shoe--even though he believes his efforts at security are a waste of time.

Had he not decided to enter Wholack now, Remold, who is watching his every movement, might have become worried. Seeing the affect of the drugs and the game Remold calms. Gus Plow is addicted to the game. Remold will therefore allow Gus to continue his task of finding Winston; even as Gus hopes a stealthy computer will allow him to retrieve the morsel of information that sets him free.

If Jaka knows what I am going to do it will be useless.

Considering where he might find an untraceable computer, Gus realizes he is a monkey. He has no source of an untethered computer. A notion of entering the basement retreat at the diner returns to him.

That is the next step, after Wholack.

He lifts the clear glass cover. Attaching waste and water systems to his body, Gus takes hold of the red button joystick and pushes the button. His eyes feel heavy, a slight tingling rides his leg as the mix of chemicals pours into his body. A thought before the trance: Roo Biner, his friend.

An image of Pilot Nothing appears on Remold's screen--and links to his murder by Remold's father. Remold Jaka begins a memory removal sequence.

As the chemical mix to the bed is changed, Remold sits back in his chair and sips red wine, "That is one persistent SOB."

The song Flight plays and Gus is flying among the clouds. He presses the buttons on the joystick to advance to the Hypercube but nothing happens. The face of the Wholack appears in front of him. "A newbie, huh?" He winks. "You'll always be able to push that button for escape. Remember, unless you initiate a save, you'll be unable to return to the sub-scenario from which you left, Chump." Gus groans understanding his mistake: He doesn't even know how to save a file in the Wholack Game. "Damn Jaka."

Wholack's image zooms away, riding the surfboard, arms crossed. "Check this out." In his right hand is a fireball. "Save and blip out before I nail you, sucker." The blaze hits Gus, the heat so intense he has to escape.

Gus opens his eyes. The lights in the room flicker to life. He tastes aluminum in his mouth--an old sensation. A memory wipe? Of what? He calms his breathing and scans back through the sensation of taste. The name Pilot Nothing enters his brain.

Considering himself under control, he goes in three more times before he hears the name Pilot Nothing during the fireball sequence. He goes back in a fourth time and just as the Wholack prepares to launch his fireball yells, "Where's Mina?"

The Wholack stares at him, the fireball blazing in his hand. Gus recognizes this as a memory seek. It's a five point gain in Wholack. "You're friend Jakainthebox blew it, Gustov. She's gone. He's hosed. I see you made five points. Congratulations. Now go build me a place to destroy. I'll be back." Everything turns bright white--as if Gus has fallen into the sun. He knows this feeling as well.

My memory has been tampered with. Then the scene changes quickly--Remold's people have adjusted to Gus' expertise.

He is staring at his Hypercube. It grows to surround him, then seems to implode. When Gus can fathom his surroundings he stands beside a huge truck, its horn blaring. Ah ooh gah! Ah ooh gah! He wonders what he is doing here. He had wanted to go back to the river scenario he created. Then he realizes just how the game can be for a novice.

Remold is teaching me a lesson: That I need him.

Ahead of Gus, six people appear to be clamoring over the truck trying to get something from inside. The horn noise is deafening: Ah ooh gah! Ah ooh gah! Dressed in khaki coveralls, their faces are empty of features. He assumes they are Remold's researchers. One turns to him: "Fish?"

Another man on the side of the truck laughs, pointing behind Gus. He turns just in time to see a police car crest the hill. It runs right into Gus tossing him over the hood and onto the ground. The back license plate wears the Wholack's face. "You're done, son. Come back later. Keep making love."

Gus awakes and finds out he cannot reenter. The timer has gone off. "That was two hours?" Talking out loud to deal with a situation is common among Targets. "For crying out loud. I thought maybe fifteen minutes have gone by. The computers aren't that damn smart or powerful. The drugs just zap you into a happy stasis until the processing completes. Two hours--son of a bitch. Crap, no wonder people pay so much to get a life inside the box. These little drop-ins turn you into a junkie. Damn Jaka." He stares at the timer for his next entry: "Not until tomorrow. I see. Not ever if Mina is successful. Damn SOB."

Jaka thinks that I will work with him now. All he had to do was get the needle in my arm. Bastard.

He rises and dresses. As he does, he takes the memory module and measures the danger of carrying it, while going to see Hope. He figures she will not know he has the module, only that vandals destroyed her possessions, including the computer. Of course he is wrong about that. He tells himself if she puts two and two together she will blame Remold. Of course he is right about that.

Opening the door, walking over to the bedroom, Gus has no idea he is walking the maze exactly as Remold Jaka wishes. He also does not know the good doctor has stripped his memory clean of Pilot Nothing again. It had taken Remold almost an hour. There is no privacy for Gus inside the game or outside. For Remold Jaka, it is all about controlling events so that the ball of life remains in his court.

Later, Gus walks the narrow side street leading to Hopes-No-Apostrophe-Diner. An ambulance careens around the corner heading away from the preserve. A wounded hunter, he assumes. A Target would be left to die. Gunfire calls from the mall. When he reaches the front glass door of the diner, remembering it is now bulletproof, he feels safer.

Inside, teams of Hunters are scattered throughout. The waitress, Carmen, scurries back and forth. Gus sits at a table near the door. When she sees him, the pot of coffee in her hand shakes. She had thought him dead. "Welcome to Hopes-No-Apostrophe. Coffee?" The smell of food covers her clothes. It sticks to her hair, peels from the crusty spots along the back of hands, and fills her nostrils. She acts as if she does not know him.

"Hi. A rasher of bacon, pancakes, potatoes, and three eggs as well--and orange juice." She nods looking at the next table and he follows her gaze The two men sitting at the table seem oblivious to his stare. "Would you ask Hope to come out?"

Carmen nods.

Hope is exhausted. The day seems never-ending because of storms and the police. It was all so frustrating. Legal has already closed the file on her penthouse violation and contracted vendors for replacement equipment. The vendors are at her residence now. The vendors will stay for two more hours. The residence will be pristine when they leave. They are very efficient and very expensive. She finds herself angrier with the imposter for the imposition than the mayhem of the burglary. To this point she does not know he sits in her diner.

Hope watches Carmen grab a cheeseburger and arugula sandwich. She looks up, her eyes dark, full of concern. "Your friend, the dead Administrator is here--table three. He seems well-dressed and sure as a cat. By the way, he isn't dead."

Hope looks into the diner. Turning back, her face red with anger, she says, "The audacity. Did he order?"

"A Hunter's Breakfast. I don't see how he made it out alive. A rational man would be hundreds of miles away, out on the highways hiding. He has to be Remold's boy now."

"Thank you, Sherlock. I'll take care of this. Bring his food as soon as possible."

Carmen looks at her boss. "Really?"

Hope scowls, walking away from monitor, entering the dining area.

Gus watches her reflection in the glass. When she walks directly towards him he knows any ideas of anonymity regarding his entry into her apartment are stupid. "I know you are working for Jaka and you tore up my home." She sits. "Why?"

Wondering why she should be so direct, he concludes the two well-dressed men are Jaka's people. He considers this might be a set up. Unless Jaka is working to control Hope as well.

That one makes sense.

He speaks quietly, "We're both being played by Herr Dr. Jaka. I want to break that grip." He watches her stare at him.

"You tore my home apart. You spray painted it. You had no right to enter my home."

He looks around the diner, his eyes narrow, breathing in, trying to calm himself. "I am hired to find Jaka's wife-- who probably ran screaming from the house figuring it was that or kill that control freak." He leans forwards, his right hand to the table. "Jaka wants me to be his buddy. By the way I am a crossover--whatever the hell that really means. For Jaka, it says I am a key to solving the mystery of Mina."

"Remold is a fool."

He opens his hand to display the memory module staring into her eyes.

Her eyes are full of mockery. "I guess they picked the wrong guy to be a monkey."

He sits back on the cushion of the booth. "I never said I was not a monkey on a chain. There is something about me that's clear to all of you, but not to me. Remold says Mina knows I am from another reality. That's who John Doe is right--a crossover? That makes me a big deal, right?"

"What makes you think I'd care?" She wants to know

who's side the imposter is on, at this point.

"I am looking for an answer to a question that begins with: Why would Mina shut down Wholack? What makes it so evil? And I'd like to know how you all worked the system to avoid Remold Jaka. So I can. Was it because Benson alerted her?" He notes her face remains placid. Mina is no longer in the basement.

His plate of food arrives. After the waitress is gone, Hope says, "You tossed my place looking for answers? Boy, are you dumb."

He sticks a fork into the eggs, opens the yoke and begins to eat, dipping cut pieces of pancake into the yoke. "What scares you all about me?"

"You don't scare me." She watches him with a restaurateur's curiosity.

He looks up in mid-bite and swirls a piece of pancake in the egg. "What does my appearance as John Doe mean to you?"

No response.

"By the way I don't think Remold gives a damn about you harboring Mina. He wants you on his side."

She nods. "He believes Mina is going to deflate his ball and shut down his game. Or worse, there is a new game and he doesn't get to control the rules. What are you doing here?" She asks. "Besides displaying the condition of men?"

"I am sorry I tossed your place. I am trying to get home." He sips from the cup of coffee.

"No kidding? Gee--I guess that is okay with everyone-- you opening up a two way door ripping reality to bits?"

"Punny." He nods. "Can we be friends now?"

She blinks.

"So the door is open." He swallows his food. "The memory module is my only leverage on this."

"There is nothing there."

"No kidding? If I work on a regular machine then he will know everything I do. I need to work in private."

Her eyes flash anger. She believes Remold is playing this guy. "Idiot." She gets up and walks to the kitchen to open a drawer. Hope reaches all the way back and pushes a red button. When it clicks and stays, she knows the flag has come to half mast. Tovar needs to meet with this man.

Gus lays his fork on the plate as she returns. "Good food." He watches her look away. Hope seems far more nervous than a few seconds ago. "That guy Jaka has a long reach," Gus pauses, picking up a piece of bacon and eating it. He watches her look at him.

Unconsciously she bites her lower lip. "We need to help each other."

"I don't really want to help Mina--but I think my memory has been tampered with."

Her head tilts to the left. "They want to know more about you--to defeat Mina."

He stops eating. "Me? Because Mina thinks Wholack is like, the devil? People sell their souls--and everything else--to get in there."

Hope closes her eyes in frustration. "Jaka is selling heaven not hell."

"So what the hell is her issue? Ever think maybe Jaka is right. The game is a game?"

She wipes her hands with a towel and stands. "That will be some great big joke on Mina, after all this time."

He finishes the juice. "So what is the issue with her?"

"She thinks this planet is tired of us. That it is telling to us to move on, or become extinct. Why would you care about her anyway? Your win is to be a good little crook and enter Wholack."

"I am a man trying to get home. So I am not that different from your lover, Tovar." His eyes do not move.

Hope has a task. She knows she can find whatever Jaka wiped from his memory once he is back in her office, though she already guesses it is something to do with the murder of Pilot Nothing.

His fork swirls a puddle of yoke. He looks up at the angels around the ceiling. "Can you help me get a computer?"

"You are a nervy one."

"I need to do some private research."

Hope needs to know the truth of this man. "Are you a crossover from another Agg?"

"So you all say. Problem for me is...Something is missing," he points to his skull.

"I can fix that." Hope wipes the table with her towel. "Tovar Dal has access to computers off the net. I am guessing we will find Remold is testing your loyalty. It drives everyone crazy." She stands leaving the memory module. He palms the module. "It won't be easy to find Tovar if he doesn't want us to find him."

"You can find him any time you want." He looks around the diner.

"Have dessert. Take your time. I'll be back." Hope walks away examining the two men, hiding her smile.

Gus waits, amusing himself by watching Carmen. She slides plates full of cheese fries under their darkened faces, then tips the fries into their laps. Apologizing, but not cleaning up, she enters the kitchen. The two men leave, cursing.

Inside the kitchen, Carmen leans her head to one side in mock angst towards Gus. "Dumb-boy is still there. The clowns are gone."

"Keep an eye on him." Hope hands her a note. She has a theory.

The cake and Carmen arrive. She hands Gus the note. He reads, "Pilot Nothing was a friend of yours wasn't he? Eat the cake." Gus looks up at Hope and finishes the cake. His skull suddenly floats on his body for a minute or so. "Do you guys spike everything with drugs in this ah, Agg?"

Carmen appears with a glass of cold tea. "Drink it." A moment later he remembers the fireball sequence in Wholack.

So that's it. Roo. Does she know Roo is Pilot Nothing?

Hope walks out and sits down with a small vial in her hand. Now this. "The memory wipe was Pilot Nothing."

"So what piece of knowledge scares him?" He sips the clear vial. His head clears.

"I wonder." She looks at him. "And I bet you know."

He shakes his head.

She ignores it. "Let me tell you what I know. I think you'll be able to remember the rest. Tovar will be here soon to talk to you."

CHAPTER TWENTY FOUR

HOLD YOUR TONGUE

Hope returns to the table. Leaning over, she says, "Go around back to the kitchen entrance."

He leaves the table--a cheeseburger unfinished. She scowls, wondering why he did not eat it.

As he walks to the door, that pair of Hunters, in fresh clothes, watch him. Naturally, given their assignment, they assume there is something worth their time. When one of the men stands, Hope is on him in a flash. "Sit back down." She points to Lester and his shotgun. "Keep your hands on the counter. Eat cake. Do nothing."

Circling the parking lot, Gus crosses to the end of the block then doubles back through the warehouse buildings behind it. At the alley, he crosses by the dumpsters and up the concrete stairs to the wooden screen door.

Hope waits at the screen door. "What do you know about Pilot Nothing?"

He pauses. "It was an attempt to save my world. A Hail-Mary pass in which a man sought to find the essence of our problems in the past, elucidate them to whomever would listen, and stop extinction. There was a theory called sentience --that human clarity was knowing the future--not guessing at it through science. Seems the end of his journey was here, in your, ah Agg."

"And what happened?"

Gus looks around lost.

"Remold's father murdered him--after getting the data he wanted. What prompted his escape?" Hope smiles.

Gus frowns angry with himself. Then he remembers.

"In my Agg, we didn't escape the worst of global warming like you have. We did not understand it could open a door of random permutations for reality. One that could drive the population mad--before eviscerating the fabric of reality. There was a theory that an end like that was really some sort of temporal reset--apparently it was a Wholack reset. At this point I don't know how Pilot Nothing knew about the reset and how to survive it."

"And the rest?" She stares at him, a man lost. "That's how the door opened on your end. The Wholack game didn't kick it down. You opened it."

"Too much energy in the system." He looks at his ally. "Remold's father is a murderer. Is that why Mina wants to destroy him?"

"She does not want to destroy Remold. Wholack may have a higher worth than as a toy. Remold is keeping it tethered."

He remembers it all now. "As a life raft for my Agg. Your game pulled me through. If I can find my wife and the others, I can save them."

She pauses. "You'll be okay." Hope pities this man.

"Remold wants to stop Mina. But she was too smart for him. She set events on autopilot when he shot down most of her servers a couple of days ago. That means Remold has to trap her. You need to help me keep them busy by going into Wholack with me. If it is a trap for Mina, I can handle it."

"Just tell me when and what." They cross to her office.

Tovar sits at the desk staring at Gus. His hands calm in front of him. "Minister Dal," says Gus. Immediately hit with that familiar smell of dirt and human oil, Gus finds he is disgusted by the smell.

"And you are?" Dal knows perfectly well who he is, but old habits die hard.

"My name is Gus Plow. You all know me as John Doe. I was a Target for a number of years, but you know that too. I was injected into FairGame from another Agg. My injection is apparently a key to making Wholack humanity's rocket ship of the mind--or pulverize your reality like it did to mine--or I don't know what." Gus approaches the wooden chair.

Tovar Dal watches him, impressed by the lucidity.

Tovar looks over to Hope with a smiling heart. She is so beautiful.

Gus sits. "I need a safe computer."

"Remold is probably just keeping you busy until he needs you," Tovar says, looking at Hope. "Why should I help you?"

"Because I knew the man you only know as Pilot Nothing. He was the first crossover to your reality not me. Whatever is going to happen has been underway for years. His name was Russell Biner. He was a skilled researcher." Gus sees shock in their eyes, but continues anyway. "Too bad Remold's dad offed him."

"Russel Biner? Does Remold know that connection? Is that why he clipped your memory?" Tovar works to get comfortable leaning back in the chair, crossing his arms.

"I thought he only knew him as Pilot Nothing, but no more than that," replies Gus. "Now I think Jaka has concluded Roo was a crossover. Who is Russel Biner in your, ah, Agg?"

"Your genetic code belongs to a man who was a drunken driver. He killed Russell Biner, running him over--as a child. The lad was tied into the Biner and Feiss, a huge drug company. So the driver was executed."

Gus looks over to Hope. "Perhaps that's why Jaka is so exercised."

"Being wrong will do that to a person like Remmy." Tovar smiles, tilting his head to the side. "A stand-alone computer is your tool for doing research without Remold knowing what you are doing. Getting the memory module was a ruse," Tovar says, already deciding to deliver the computer. Tovar Dal is a curious man. "But consider the absurdity of beating Remold in the computational world. I think your trek is foolish."

Gus takes the challenge. "I am here to rescue the woman I love. You can understand that can't you?"

Tovar shakes his head, a sign of defeat and enlightenment in the same motion. "Who might that be?"

"Winston Doe."

"She is a Ginda here, a primitive Rost," he replies both sad and confused with this man's apparently hopeless task. "Do you know that since the development of the Wholack, the one unspoken fear among all humans is the concern that anyone might be the Wholack of this reality?"

"My vote is on Dr. Remold Jaka," Gus says casually.

"Could be you," Tovar says. "A man without a past. A lover who is a fool."

Gus raises and eyebrow. "I am a fool for a woman."

Tovar sees the point. "Aren't we all. Still, you seem a man bathed in myth."

Hope leans forward. "How about we let this play out?"

Dal stands and circles the desk. Surprised at the action

Gus tenses. Dal speaks again: "Mr. Plow, my cousin appears baffled by you because you are without any real cognition of your circumstance or the nature of Remold's power. Ethics and morality are animals to be tamed by him. Sad because deep down he is a decent man."

"A man is separate from his invention--so what?"

"Again I can see lucidity means neither answers nor ineptitude." Tovar points a finger at him. "You are the missing part of the puzzle that started with the prediction of your entry."

"My entry was predicted? By Mina?" For the first time Gus begins to understand his good fortune.

"By happenstance." He looks at Hope. "Mr. Plow, your friend, in this Agg, Mr. Biner, was the son of a very wealthy woman with severe challenges. She was autistic. She predicted the arrival of a crossover in a work of art at a place called the Boiler Room. It was considered a savant-class event, until the Yorkies arrived."

"Yorkies? Here?"

"A well disguised secret--and the reason so many help Mina Jaka."

Gus sits, eyes wide. "What did they say?"

"They ignore us. They appear as ghosts." He looks at Hope. "It is possible someone has erased and rebuilt you, Mr. Plow. You might be from here. You might be a scam. You claim to understand that, but you deny the possibility of this."

Gus sighs. "You do like to talk, Minister. I am an expert in the area of memory. I am whole and I am not from this Agg. Where will I find a clean computer?" Gus will give away nothing further at this point.

Dal laughs. "Her penthouse."

"I don't like being played."

Tovar looks at Hope. "Again, I am sorry. I see now that some men really can be loyal to their women."

Unseen by everyone the façade of calm disappears, Tovar Dal now knows the world changed long ago and humans are just catching up. He opens the door to the basement. "I am going to take a shower. I hate my stink as well."

"Is he always so much of a know-it-all?"

"He's unbearable sometimes. On the other hand, I'll take his dedication to your deceit anytime." She glares at him. "Why didn't you tell me the name Russell Biner?"

"Didn't occur to me." Gus sees her eyes harden.

She has had enough. "Have you ever been to or heard of the Memorial for the Dead?"

His face takes on the look of a poker player. "That's the big ship in the river, right? Why?"

She shakes her head. "I need more information before we go further." Hope is considers her plan. "Meet me inside the Biner and Feiss drug store by my apartment."

"Biner and Feiss? Why?"

"Your genetic equal was an alcoholic. Do you know why?"

Gus shakes his head back and forth.

"He said the alcohol killed the dogs. He seems to have meant memories. Memories, he claimed, that should not have been there. Before the execution, he thanked them. Because he would never have to wander a store again, a Biner and Feiss. Seems every time he went in one, either awake or asleep, he saw ravenous dogs."

"Dogs went extinct first. Supposedly, because they guarded our dreams, our memories."

"And then led the way home?" She walks the stairs. "Afraid?"

"I've always considered your Hunters wild dogs."

"Go out the back door. I will follow in a few minutes."

Chapter Twenty Five

Get Out Fast

Biner & Feiss supplies all the drugs to the Wholack beds and is second in size only to Laughs Unlimited. The B&F chain of drug stores is a minor arm of the Biner & Feiss Pharmaceutical Corporation. A monopoly on drugs, the stores are addiction emporiums acting as retail stores. The outlet near Hope's home is the size of three city blocks, with most of the store underground. Underneath that, an automated manufacturing facility manufactures drugs. Well guarded and highly secure, the store above also provides consumer goods, like chaw.

Upon entering the bank of eight paired glass doors, a sloped metal-clad hallways leads the consumer passed the scanners that will either lock down the hall--with the detection of weapons or explosives--or open the far doors onto a mezzanine circling an emporium of goods.

Just for the privilege of descending the wide stairs into the display areas, a deposit of five dollars is made into the B&F account. Four dollars and fifty cents is credited to any purchase--and it will accumulate if one doesn't purchase. The other fifty cents is a handling charge for B&F taking the money and keeping it safe.

Crossing through the doors onto the mezzanine, Gus sees aisle after aisle of drugs, medical equipment, gift cards, toys, ammunition, food, and a thousand other items. Consumers move about with shopping carts.

The sound of music fills the air and the bright ceiling hosts hundreds of renditions of rocket ships. Many of the images look hand drawn, apparently by the hand of a child. A few of the rockets are lifelike computer renditions. None are animate. When the designers were handed the images of the rockets, the heiress to the Biner fortune, Jennifer Biner, was present. Autistic, she insisted the images remain motionless. A brilliant artist and devoted mother, motion made her ill at ease. Worse, motion made her child, Russell, cry incessantly. Every store has a ceiling full of stilled rockets.

One particular rocket ship catches the eyes of Gus Plow. He once saw a picture of it on a news report. It was claimed this rocket ship once held an alien named Pilnouth who landed in California. That was before the rocket that delivered the alien supposedly disappeared into thin air. Gus laughs at the image and his memory, thinking the transgressions of Wholack on his reality seem endless. He also begins to see his crossover as just a system seeking balance, though doesn't see the Wholack's game as an invasion, just buffoonery and human blindness.

Looking for Hope Weiss, his vision is assaulted by holograms that pop up with information on the latest sales or closeout items. He walks to the nearest display case and stops when he sees an advertisement for donating to autism research. Backing up he confirms the name of the foundation then looks for an image of the heiress, but cannot find one.

Hope is testing me.

Gazing about looking for more information, he sees a security guard approach then turn away. Gus' scans say this is a high level Laughs Unlimited executive.

Gus moves through an advertisement looking for other advertisements on the autism organization, but sees no more. The rest are product displays. As he begins to descend the metal stairs, Gus notices the consumers all move in the same flow, like bits of paper flowing along a creek. He never considered shopping an event of fate until this moment.

At the bottom, he stops by a display of gene products for growing new skin, looking for the manufacturer. Seeing the name, Eckman Brothers, the hair on the back of his neck stands. Where he came from, there were such products and he knew the Eckman brothers. They were the golden boys who sat at the table in the Womb, with Mina.

"Planning on growing a new you?"

He shakes his head. "Everything is so random. Everything." He wants to ask her if she knew Carlos Jordan but he will wait--because Remold claims Carlos is just a Rost.

Hope beckons him to follow her. He cannot tell if she is looking for information or she is hiding it. She crosses down an aisle to a collection of flowing paper streamers hanging from the ceiling. They surround a white sign that says, "Shop With Me!" Below it is a pretty African woman with a cute wink. "Does she mean anything to you?" Hope asks, pointing to the sign.

He stares at the image. "Not a thing--other than she is the person that hangs as an angel in your diner."

"I'd like to find her." She nods. "Perhaps in your reality?"

He looks away. "I don't know anything about her. For what it is worth to you, Remold asked me the same question." His arms cross.

"That means what?" She knits her eyebrows for a moment. "You know nothing about the Corporate Apocalypse version of Wholack?"

"He had the same conclusion."

Hope looks around then points at a book on strategy for Wholack. The cover shows the Wholack and a man dressed in a tuxedo pointing at Wholack. His other hand rests on his back, fingers crossed, hidden from Wholack--a mocking gesture. "Look familiar?" She points to the man.

Gus looks at the image. "Simon Weiss."

Hope points to the pretty woman on the poster. "They were lovers."

"And that's why you were adopted. How did she die?"

"Truthfully, I don't know. One day Elena was gone."

"So that's it. In my Agg, history says Simon Weiss was a bit of a playboy. That woman is your aunt or your mother?"

"I don't know."

"Ask Weiss."

"He's mute. I think he's concerned about Roxanne."

"I am sorry." Gus tightens his lips, then speaks. "What about the heiress? Is there a picture of her?"

"Jennifer Biner? Not that I know. The wealthy like to keep their images out of public view. Did you know her?"

"I never met her."

"Remold worked with her extensively. He built scenarios for her. She latched onto one. One that didn't change. It was a boring sub-scenario--just a house by the beach. I guess she made changes from time to time but as I understand it, the repetition of the place is deadening. When her son was killed, Remold added him to it."

He looks around. "I was told she was Pilnouth."

"Everyone who is challenged in Wholack uses the name Pilnouth. It's an extra bit of safety for them. They are allowed many privileges. That's why Remold built the capability. Her son used it as well some times. They liked to exchange viewpoints. It was their favorite game. He loved her dearly."

"She was allowed to birth a child?" Gus asks.

"She was given whatever she wanted."

He nods.

"When you go into the Wholack game, during Flight, their memorial is that beach scene."

"I know. Who is that with them?" Gus asks.

"A highly functional Rost--a gift from Remold--named Carlos." She watches him. "That means what to you?"

"Carlos Jordan is a hero in my world. Jenny Biner is his wife. They disappeared." He stares at her. "You too." He looks at the ground. "Your adopted father was a man named Simon Weiss. Your adopted mother was named Roxanne. They found you in rubble, in a bed. You all escaped, along with Jenny Biner and her son, Roo. He grew up to lead the Pilot Nothing experiment. Russell Biner was your adopted brother, in my Agg."

She sighs. "What happened to me in your Agg?"

"Gone. We don't know how or why."

Hope nods. "So that's why you have been hiding from me. In your Agg, my brother is Russel Biner, Pilot Nothing?" Hope purses her lips for a moment. "So Remold's father killed my brother, Jenny Biner's child, when he crossed over from your Agg. Biner and Feiss has muscle. Their legal department would have Remold sent to FairGame for the death of her child--regardless of the circumstance--irrespective of truth. That would put the leadership of Laughs Unlimited up for grabs. Remold has a lot to lose with the discovery that his father killed Russell Biner--if they can prove Remold assisted in a cover up."

"A crossover is the connection."

Hope nods. "You are the nail in Remold's coffin."

"So Remold fears me. I see."

"I know he fears the exposure, loss of control, and the end of Wholack. I didn't know you figured into the equation that way. Tovar says Remold has an ego the size of a planet."

"A Buddha, with issues." Gus points to his chest then her. "We are like those shoppers, following a path, missing the reason, because we seek a prize. Russell Biner probably died thousands of times before he dropped in here. I'd still like to know how he knew that he could sling shot back."

"My guess? Sentience. He saw something as a child. Or someone told him. Can't beat the connection between a child and their mother," Hope says.

"Can I meet with Jenny Biner?"

"That's the coding anomaly I mentioned. She's been dead for about three years, but the data I have says she is not dead. By the way, the Biner and Feiss Drug stores are the only place Remold has no reach--except their medical computers. This is the only place we can talk without Remold getting access to our conversation."

"What about the Biner and Feiss people?"

"If they are listening to this one conversation out of a million then they will have heard us. That will then mean Remold is going to be facing a barrage of legal issues--because of his father's murder of Russell Biner. My task is done here."

Her smile lights the street as they exit. She neglects to mention that she had run Gus Plow's blood through the computer in this store. So there is a very good chance they were being tracked. Once they are on him, Remold will not bother wiping Gus' memory of Pilot Nothing again. There is no point now. Her next task: Get John Doe to the Boiler Room.

Elena, how am I ever going to find you?

Ten minutes later, Gus enters Hope's penthouse. He wanders around admiring the cleanliness and new paint, moving from window to window, drinking in the sight of boats on the black water, and watching the ship called the Monument to the Dead. It glistens from sparkling ornaments that had not been nearly so bright when he was here as a burglar. He assumes, correctly, that is Remold's doing.

The barge traffic in the canals appears ordered from a design catalogue--a custom parade of lights and sparklers gliding by, awash in the songs of merchant seamen.

"How come I can hear their songs up here?" He asks, stepping out onto the porch listening to a chantey about a girl who loves storms. Hope exits onto the concrete porch pointing to the waist high railing of chrome steel tubes. He glances back at her, to the glass of orange juice in her hand.

"This building has sound taps along the river. There are also taps into the street, FairGame, and the city parks." She watches the man who burglarized her apartment stand like a guest at dinner. Seeing no shame she sips more juice.

Gus watches the cold evening winds ripping the tops off black water on the distant lake. He turns to the miniature red maples on the verandah to his right. She follows his gaze sensing a sad man. Watching her Bonsai, he notes their alignment with a flowering plum tree and a stone lantern could be called nothing but perfect.

"Perhaps in perfection there is nothing to seek but imperfection."

"Tovar would laugh hearing you use his words that way." She smiles to herself knowing he will think this some kind of entry for him. She has concluded Gus is a bit of a rogue.

Gus looks down at his black boots. Looking up, he sees her watching him. "Do you know there is no Tovar Dal in my Agg?" He leans back against the heated glass of the windows. "Why does Minister Dal continue his protest of FairGame knowing how much it scares you?"

Baffled by the familiarity she stares at him. "You're presumptuous."

The doorbell rings. Gus crosses to the cinnamon colored door. Looking around he sees none of the Hobo signs he had painted on the walls, except one: The twin circles that say danger.

He opens the door and Lester enters holding a shoebox-sized package. Gus is surprised at the darting eyes and the look of a jealous lover.

"This was unnecessary, Les." She is furious he has left the diner.

Scanning the room, he places the box on her desk, right where the old computer had been. "Tovar says you have no more than ten minutes before Remold's security systems invade the operating system and corrupt it. He says shut down at eight minutes," and looks back to her. "Need me to stay?"

She shakes her head as he leaves.

A few moments later Gus pulls the module from his pant's pocket that runs along his right thigh. "The scanners from B&F didn't note that?" She says.

"Please don't insult me. I had it hidden nearby."

She sticks out her hand. "I'll install it."

"Nope."

Hope steps back waiting, hands on her hips, fire in her eyes. "Fine. Want to tell me what you are really doing?"

"This contains one piece of really important information. Your identity and your privileges." Gus opens the slot for the memory module. "They plan to shut down Wholack. It's obviously an insane plan. You know this," he says as he works. "Care to explain?"

She sips more orange juice. "Shutting Wholack down means more than a billion people are suddenly ejected into the world. Mina would never do that. Remold is an idiot."

He maneuvers the module into place. "So she is doing something else."

Hope's eyes go blank.

"I need to find my wife." Gus turns on the computer voice activation. His eyes drift over her head to books on the white-brick wall. "From here on please be quiet."

"I am all ears. You have eight minutes."

He enters her codes and begins to query the computer: "Given what you know about Jaka's theories, is Tovar Dal the Wholack of this Agg?" Hope places her hands on her lap.

"Perhaps."

"Remold Jaka?"

"Perhaps."

"Gus Plow?"

"Perhaps."

He glances at the clock.

"Mina created Home Fires. Was she seeking a stable pathway into a valid Agg?"

"Affirmative."

"Why prove the existence of John Doe is not a myth?"

"A crossover means freedom."

His eyes narrow. "What is Jaka's theory on John Doe?"

"That the hypotheses of Jaka and Weiss is incorrect. There is a recent update."

"Go ahead."

"Specifically, that there is an entrant into our Agg, but it is due to work at Laughs Unlimited."

"It?" Gus smiles, looking at the clock. "Computer who is Winston Doe?"

"No who, N-A-H."

Gus looks over to Hope and opens his hands in question.

"N-A-H--Not A Human."

Gus enters her Wholack codes. "Locate a Winston Doe." He waits until the little Wholack on the screen finishes its goofy dance. "Now add the locations of the next thousand. Where is the newest report of Winston Doe fully functional inside Wholack?"

"Home Fires, the Walker encampment build 2051.1013."

Hope's eyes widen. Gus grins. "Download the link." A moment later Gus shuts down the computer. "Seven minutes--I am done. One of those paths is going to get me to her."

Hope turns away to the large white-out kitchen. She places a silver pot on an electric stove and stares at it waiting for the boil. After a minute of thinking, "The Walker Encampment sub-scenario has a flaw. A bug, it keeps shutting down."

"Resetting--that's why I couldn't get back."

She turns off the heat under the kettle. "You were separated from that sub-scenario--because you went for a walk? Then there was a reset?"

"So far as I know. I don't know how." Gus shakes his head. His lips tight. His eyes scan Hope. "I am going back to my little cage, load these coordinates into my Wholack bed and find my wife."

"I will have Tovar join you. He will protect you from Remold Jaka."

"How will you find him? How could he protect anyone?"

The door to the bedroom opens. Tovar Dal stands there holding Lester's shotgun. "Try me." He grins at Gus.

Chapter Twenty Six

Good Road To Follow

Remold Jaka stands astride the green weeds of a deserted parking lot. He speaks, asking the researchers currently scouring the four rusted ferries. "No Winston Doe, right?"

"All good, Doc. It's clean."

He works a keyboard making sure Hope Weiss is being tracked. Satisfied she will not be an issue, Remold scans the black pilings of the old docks. Examining Puget Sound and Guemes Island, the four rotting hulks of green and white, he stares at the mud. "Add more shine. Perfect." He stares at the lines of rust along the waterline and the remains of seaweed and filth. The workmanship of his researchers is archaic, true to its origins, and well done. Remold nods. This is just the way he wants it. "All right let him in."

Gus appears, facing the set of green and white ferries. He remembers the smells thinking himself home--until he turns, seeing Remold Jaka. Turning to look up the hill, where he had begun his trek, three and a half years ago, the most northern border of FairGame blinks, a mile south of here. The blinking lights and their appearance had motivated his walk. He did not know the smell of death had come from there. Sniffing the wind he cannot find a stench of decay.

He screwed that one up. "Bastard."

Caught inside for almost a week, trying to understand the madness around him, when he came back to the ferries they looked exactly as they do now, deserted. With no place to go, he headed south. With no idea the blinking lights meant a hunting preserve that stretched for hundreds of miles, all the way into Oregon. At this point he cannot fathom how to find Winston. The docks are deserted and he is lost.

Remold grimaces. "This may not be your home, Mr. Plow."

He nods. "Of course, bastard." Remold Jaka's mania for control has Gus in a bad mood.

Remold alerts his team: They will garner no information from Doe at this juncture. The next stop is Kittens and Cradles. "Walker Encampment was a popular sub-scenario in which those that made it safely through the different disasters of Home Fires get a choice to either exit--a loss--or wait here. The win is called Kittens and Cradles."

One of many wins.

"We have checked this entire sub-scenario and found no evidence of your wife or the others. Either here or the local variant."

"What is Kittens and Cradles?"

"A rather nightmarish scenario at a place on the Hudson River called Storm King Mountain. It's the win of Home Fires. After we are done here I will let you explore it to seek your wife." He tilts his head, a concern mocking Gus. "Mr. Plow?"

Gus's hands clench in his pockets.

Remold Jaka watches him stare out to the snow-crested Mount Baker on the eastern horizon. "If you were ejected into FairGame--that means you have some kind of focus, and that makes you very special. Particularly your transcendence from an Agg to a Wholack scenario then to FairGame. Did Mina help you?"

Gus does not believe she is the cause of his ejection. He believes the ego of Remold Jaka is his salvation. "Is it possible Mina is not the enemy?" He watches the lack of response. "Maybe I am part of a system seeking balance?"

Remold types a message allowing Tovar Dal inside.

"Falling objects achieve their own balance. On whole, they do not provide balance to their environment, Mr. Doe."

Gus notes he has stopped calling him Gus Plow. He assumes this is part of Remold's plan to neutralize him. Gus wonders if he plans to murder him the way his father murdered Roo.

Remold continues speaking. "Of course every Agg appears to be a hallway, a conglomeration of egress. After that, that's where my ex-wife and I part company, both physically and philosophically. We need to move along. I have eight hours to stop Mina. Why do you think she wants to shut down Wholack, Mr. Doe? You spoke with Hope about it, I assume."

"Hope Weiss thinks it a scam to keep you blind to her real intent."

"Mina loves to prove a point by lying to her friends. She thinks it's control."

Gus laughs.

"I am not so foolish." He grins. "If a being can act as a doorway, then shutting down the Wholack will immediately uncover that, and therefore our Wholack. So that could be her point."

"And you think that's you--Doc?"

"One of my early assumptions of her motives in

attracting you is to prove I am the Wholack."

"No one deserves it more," Gus mumbles. At that moment, he sees Tovar Dal emerge from the growth of ocean spray on the hillside. The impunity of the gait makes Gus smile. When Remold sees Tovar, Gus spies a wrinkle on his brow. Gus doesn't believe the wrinkle. "Could be Tovar is Wholack?"

Remold shakes his head. "He has too much clarity. A Wholack is blinded in some way. The ideals that drive my cousin are not blinders, just goals. People, how the hell did he get in here?"

Gus sees a face appear on the ground. It speaks to Remold, but Gus cannot understand.

"Hope Weiss? She has him here protecting Plow?" Remold shakes his head watching the approach of Tovar Dal. The face disappears. Remold speaks to Gus as Tovar approaches. "It is said that at one time, the real-world version those ferries were populated. Then when this area became a gray zone, the ferries were sold for scrap." He looks around.

"This is a digital memorial?" Gus asks.

"You fired this thing up. You tell me. By the way, the IANS show you have never been here--ever. My researchers have been examining it for entry."

Gus ponders the comment considering Remold a puppet master. "So maybe I am a Wholack." Gus faces Tovar's slow, approach. "Your cousin does not act like a worried man."

"I freed him."

Gus laughs.

Then Remold does as well. "I know. I am an ass."

Tovar stands before them looking at his cousin and Gus. "I assume we are no longer enemies?"

"You are free and you have full legal. Mina is still on the loose. When I was at the diner, you were sleeping in the basement and came out to greet me. Cuz' you are a ballsey one."

"I see. So we are friends now. This wouldn't have anything to do with a certain table at the Boiler Room?" Tovar says nodding to Gus to help him understand the play here.

"I either solve the issue of Mina or I have to have her killed." He looks at Gus as well. "The Boiler Room is secondary."

Tovar tilts head. "Sure it is."

"Sorry, fellows. I don't care." Gus crosses the weeds through a chain link fence then onto concrete walk covered with mud and debris. He enters a run down building.

Tovar speaks as they follow him. "He has been looking for Winston Doe all this time?"

"He says."

"How did he wind up in FairGame?" Tovar asks.

"He says he just wandered off."

"From a Wholack sub-scenario into FairGame?" Tovar asks. "What does your gaggle of researchers say about that?"

"They don't know but they believe him." They stop beside him inside a waiting room. "Me too."

Gus looks at the familiar landscape of rot. "I was scouting for escape for my people. I saw the lights."

"Looks like you found it." Remold looks over at Tovar.

Tovar speaks, "So a man named Gus Plow wanders out of an Agg without computer assist. He fits the exact image in the Boiler Room completing our little group of Hope, myself, and Remold. And this is just another day in paradise for you Remold?" Tovar says.

"Mr. Doe thinks it is all false flag and she is up to something else," Remold says.

"I think killing her serves no purpose," Gus says. "And I think she knows what she is doing--unlike you."

Remold laughs. "I see. We're all just monkeys."

"Maybe not so much--anymore," says Tovar.

They circle the dilapidated building and step onto a

concrete ramp leading to a boat. The center of the walkway is clear of debris.

"Mr. Plow, this was reality for you? I mean Agg. Sorry, Remmy."

"For more than a decade. Winston had suggested I do the reconnaissance since legend says once we had four ferries in place we were free to go."

"How many were there in the beginning?"

"One. But that was many cycles ago."

Remold scowls. "You didn't tell me that. Someone get on this little bit of data."

Tovar looks around feeling the winds. As they climb the ramp, Gus cannot help but feel this place real. A few steps later, they exit onto the rusting deck of the ferry.

As usual, Tovar cannot tell the difference between this and reality. He never could in any Wholack scenarios. It is one of the reasons he kept away from the game during his time in office. He felt it prudent. "We have turned a corner," he says distractedly.

"To where?" Remold still does not have control of events and this drives him. He watches Gus Plow cross rusted plates sitting crooked on the framing. A door having fallen from the hinges sits like a bridge across girders into the main seating area. Gus crosses it easily--he's done it a hundred times or more--and enters a large dark room that smells of smoke. Signs of usage appear everywhere, but the room is vacant. Gus looks around, finally facing Tovar. "Even the smell is right. What did you do, Doc? Take the right one and put this in its place to get more information?"

Remold starts shaking his head back and forth wondering what he did wrong.

The correct smell for a distant reality is an impossible task for a developer to get right.

When he looks at his cousin, Tovar sports a smile.

"Remold doesn't know what to do. He's worried he is a Wholack. Secret's out, Remmy," Tovar says sarcastically.

Remold ignores them, working some hidden keyboard. "Okay. I believe this was a reality for you. You asked me if I thought myself some kind of Wholack. I don't know. I do know that with all of my skills and the unlimited funding available to me, I cannot disprove a set of theories that are fixing to put two billion people at risk. Even so, I cannot take the risk that Mina is wrong."

"Tough day," Tovar says.

Gus continues wandering through the kitchen area. He sees all the signs, but none of the people. When he left all four ferries were populated and they were spilling out onto the land. Winston believed it was time to leave the boats. "Come on we are done," says Gus. "There is no one here." The three men exit out into the sunshine.

Tovar speaks. "This man is a pawn of the universe, Remmy. Tonight will tell. Do not interfere further."

Remold sighs. "There will be no issue from me."

"Got Mina trapped?" Tovar asks.

"We'll see." Remold watches.

"What's tonight?" Gus asks, seeing a glint of hope.

"We have a dinner reservation at a place called the Boiler Room." Tovar shakes his head. "They have been expecting us for twenty years. Remold has agreed to bring you."

"First I am sending him into Kittens and Cradles," Remold says. "Theory says his win is there."

"Your's too, Remmy?" Tovar says.

"Hope is waiting," says the mouth of a rusted old oven opening and closing. It is one of his researchers.

"All you need to do is get to the house crushed by the fist. After, I believe you will find your Ms. Doe," Remold looks at the rusting boat. "If not, I am sorry. Perhaps it will not be a return to those you love. Just proof I am a man of my word."

Gus nods.

Tovar speaks. "Remold will help you until dinner at the Boiler Room. He would do none of it if he believed you unreal. Therefor you are important and he is granting you the privilege of wasting time while he prepares. His favorite game."

Hope thinks Kittens and Cradles now looks like a combination of Disneyland and Hell. A mountaintop, torn apart by apparent repeated blasting; spiked with girders, a huge wall, cranes, fountains of blue flame, and the whole area bathing in colors from overhead cartoon characters in the midst of various high-jinx.

"Why did they do this?"

Hope had worked on Kittens and Cradles long ago, when it was the Columbia River not the Hudson. So it has taken Hope a few minutes inside the game to get a handle on the scenario again. Forced to take a fast-forward trip upriver, so far she has seen sea monsters, pirates, a plane crash, tidal surges, giant apples falling from the sky and a bridge blown up. The only remaining item of her work is a pair of young lovers on the shore after a sailboat race. She had placed them there her second month working for Laughs Unlimited. When Hope found one of them had become a Carlos, she blew up the nearby bridge.

The creaking from rigging sounds like the old front screen door of my home. Mina created that. The creak says, "Be safe, Hope."

Looking around for Gus Plow and not seeing him, Hope scans Remold's other fixtures for monitoring her: Wood windows, a small set of cups, the plates on the galley shelves, the picture of her parents reconstituted as a picture of the ship's owners. A picture of Tovar on the wall shows him sitting next to a Wholack bed. Then he is gone.

That's what took so long. I see.

A moment later Gus blips onto the deck. "Where am I?"

"Kittens and Cradles--please just take the ride. Doctor Jaka is at work."

He points to the cartoon characters and their antics. Then looking around the deck of the wooden schooner Curlew. He asks, "What do I do?"

"Just follow. If you wake afterwards, then you are real. If not then you are an elaborate hoax by Mina and you will be nothing but a file on a disk."

"I'll die if I am not real? He wants me dead. He keeps calling Mister Doe. What's to stop Remold from killing me in my bed?"

"Tovar guards you." She examines the watchful eyes of her companion. He looks away and begins to stare out at this scenario of Hell's construction. Unconsciously he steps back from the gunnels and leans against the hard wooden wall of the main cabin. His arms crossed trying to keep out the cold. She finds a blanket on the deck and hands it to him.

They stand in silence listening to the water as it passes below the bow. Off to their right, near the bow of the boat, three men sit smoking tobacco in handmade pipes. The men speak in deep voices, occasionally laughing and pointing to the facility that they say will someday be an amusement park. Snippets of their conversation tell Gus the men are at a loss to explain why an amusement part is being built in Hell. One man curses the rich.

"I am not going to have time to find Winston."

Hope looks away. Bells ring. It is the new back doorbell of her diner. Mina has begun her countdown to bring down the servers. "We're docking."

As they move closer to shore, cartoon figures, a rabbit and a mouse, strangle each other. Eyes popping out, tongues bright blue, they throttle each other--until the mouse bites the rabbit on the nose. The men at the bow of the ship howl with laughter. Embarrassed by the darkness she sees in her younger self, Hope walks to the starboard side of the boat and looks across the river. Destroyed buildings and small fires light the hills. The small fires are for foolish souls who jump overboard and try to swim to the far shore trying to build their own sub-scenario there. It can't be done. This ship is the only bridge forward. More laughter from the bow.

"I'm stuck," Gus says.

She nods.

The schooner tacks to port one last time then docks at the remains of an old nuclear power plant, which, in this scenario, supposedly provides energy to feed the operations and construction. Hope looks over to Gus Plow, pondering the notion of what infinity really means. She is trying to understand how Russell Biner knew about the slingshot effect--and his willingness to recycle uncounted times. For Gus, the reality of a set of computers providing human transcendence is easy; ironically, he cannot fathom why Russell Biner turned his life over to computers. Both sigh, lost in it all, baffled by a human leap fostered by foolishness.

"Worried about your wife?" Behind him a meteor approaches the ship. She wipes it away. Gus fears Winston is dead. "She'll be fine."

A part of him wants to see the Wholack come surfing out of the sky, nullifying this place. The addiction for Wholack builds in his body.

A wooden plank is hauled into place reaching from the wooden dock to the side of the ship. The gangplank wobbles as a crowd of rough workers appears from deck and disembark to the shore. "Humans?" He says to Hope.

He hears the voice of Remold Jaka in his ear. "They are top end developers on vacation. So far as they know, you are synthetic. If they even see you."

Gus forms up behind the men and taps on one the

shoulder. A man with a gas lantern steps in between them and makes comments about good pay and the worth of whores.

Hope looks away seeing women in white gowns appear by the main cabin. Four sailors carrying rifles, three men and a woman, escort the women. With eyes full of threat, the guards and the women descend another gangplank and walk the wharf. A black hearse waits, its engine running. A driver exits and opens a long back door. The tarts enter without a word and the vehicle motors off into the night. The sailors, their task over with, light pipes, and rest. The four of them sit around a black wooden box.

Gus shakes his head. "This is so fucked up. Did you really have a part in this?"

"The parts people play in a scenario are not really my concern. First of all those could be men or women, young or old. For whatever reason they wish to be sex slaves."

"Kind of like sadomasochism on steroids," he says. "Why is this place so eerie?"

"People have a dark side. They have created every imaginable reality inside Wholack. Some seek the morbid to balance the beauty of their scenario. Some just seek thrills. Kittens and Cradles is about the desire to see Hell."

"So that's it. You couldn't just do Purgatory?" He immediately regrets saying it.

"You leaving or not?" A leathery-faced man with a black cap and tobacco stains on his teeth draws a gun.

"Someone was supposed to meet us, but I don't see him," Hope says.

He replaces the pistol. "Well either pay for a return passage or get off the dock. We're trying to run a business here." Laughter.

Hope speaks again to move this along. "We are not return passengers. Show me the Styx." The man nods. He hands her the ship's manifest then walks down the gangplank, nodding to the sailors carrying rifles.

Hope scans the document. A scowl crosses her face. "Hope, what are you..." The voice of Remold Jaka fades.

"Mina, what are you doing?"

A leathery-faced man speaks to one of the men who hold rifles. "Where can they find his home? The river is booked."

"Hotel?" The men snicker. "Town is a walk," says one man. He man pulls out a pistol and shoots the man dead. The blood splatters all over Gus and Hope. One of the men taps his pipe on his boot heal. "He would have killed him. Ma'am."

"I can read." She points Gus to the sign over a spiked eight-foot-high wrought iron fence. It says: "Tovar is safe also." Small circles in the fence below form the letters B&F.

"What the heck does that mean?" Gus asks.

"Nothing--for you. That message we left at the Biner and Feiss store has taken hold. Remold is under an injunction." They cross under a white iron gate in the fence and head out onto the gravel roadway. The gate slams shut behind him and the schooner darkens. A minute later they stand in the glare of the lights from turning beacons. The lapping of the river fades away, replaced by the sound of riveters from the construction above. Sparks fall in an avalanche of color. The cacophony of sounds increase with every passing second. Soon the sound of engines chugging mixes with the hammering of presses.

"How can anybody be around this racket?" Gus says. "Just another way to keep people distracted, Sparky? Oh."

"That's right. Nicely done. How did you know?"

He looks confused.

"You just took a minor win for the game. Oh you didn't know? Let's go. We should see the crushed house now."

Gus watches the blue flickering glow from the cartoon gods overhead. The construction racket calms as they get closer into town. Eyes slowly adjusting to the dark, he sees stars shine overhead, then a shooting star. In the echoes he hears "Keep making love, suckers."

"Wholack?"

Hope shakes her head. "You would be a terrible player. Take in everything, but see and hear nothing. Imitating Wholack is as old as the game. You just lost your win."

Gus laughs. "I hate that I am here."

"Wholack literally gets in your blood." She smiles. "Also courtesy of Biner and Feiss."

"So we must deal with the devil."

Entering the quaint town, Gus is reminded of an 18th century English village. Thatched roof, white walls, hay bales on the street. Windows glow yellow from candles inside small cottages. White roses bloom from the window boxes.

"Welcome to my world." It's the Wholack's voice again.

Then the landscape changes. The tightly packed homes melt and reform into more modern homes--apparently built from the recycled remains of suburban communities. Some huge, some tiny--with a touch of favela thrown in for soul. All narrow, the houses tilt into nightmarish planes. Fires start. Suburbia burns: Metal windows, faux-wood carved doors, bits of lawn, remains of autos, useless chimneys, they all begin to dance. Lawns hang out in space, bleeding. "My chance to rule in hell?" He asks.

"Could be anything at this point. You are now controlling the scenario."

"Remold gave me this?"

"It's no compliment. This is just his way of saying he really controls you--like he controls the Wholack."

"He wants to make me into another Wholack."

She nods, walking down the lanes. The stink from open sewers enters Gus's head. Farm animals bray, ducks cluck. Dogs bark. Cats yowl. A husband screams at his wife. A plate crashes. Children whimper; a woman cries. Gus passes a sign of polished copper. It wears the name of the town: Pottersville.

Gus smiles. "Ah, it's a wonderful life."

Hope fixes the ego trap laid for Gus by one of the researchers. She sees it leads to ejection. She closes the trap, leaving a message for Remold that one of his researchers, a man named Monto, is a turncoat. Ahead is a small brothel sitting at the end of the lane. "Filthy, but safe," Hope says. The comment is a shortcut around others traps.

"The sewerage flows too quickly," he says distractedly.

She laughs at him knowing that flow is his loss. "Losing touch with reality already? In time you will see things like that, note them, and wonder how you could be so dumb to discuss it. Everyone does."

"I didn't know you were an expert."

"Nah." Odd bits of Gus' past wait around every corner: Old hot tubs tipped on their ends, a bed of nails, a long hallway flanked by machine guns, circuit boards, carpeting instead of mud in front of the houses. Gus points to a low, blue-shingled house, manikins clutch various inoperative weapons. Arms held high above their heads, the dummies are surrendering. He knows every face, "Kristen, Monto, and Sammich."

An argument erupts from inside a cottage: "So what if I tried to rob her at the train station and got caught? Nothing happened," bellows some horse-voiced man. Glass breaks followed by screams. "Don't you see I took it?" Says the same male voice. "How did I know it wasn't going to repeat again? It always repeats."

"I know that event."

"Now you are getting it. You have a job to do," says Hope. Gus swings the door open and marches inside, reminding himself he is inside a game--not real life.

Two soldiers are leaning over a wooden kitchen table. He knows both of their faces. A women lies on a bed of nails, a pair of black orbs undulating on her shoulders--her mouth open and her eyes empty of thought.

He looks to the windows draped in dark blue canvas. The room bursts into flames. In unison the men look at Gus. "We took care of Sammich, he is fine. But Sarge, by the time we found her, the work had already been completed by Pard. As long as Clipper functions Winston will be a Ginda." Gus stares at the worst memory of his life. "What do we do?"

The kitchen door swings wide as a thin figure with white hair enters the doorway and stands in silhouette. "What is all the noise, here?" Asks the Carlos. He takes a pitcher of water and throws it at the fire immediately dousing it.

Hope stares at Carlos. Gus sees she knows this man, but not as a part of this scenario. "How can you be here? This code is locked down." Her gaze wanders to the ceiling. "Remold?" She looks at the floor seeing a doll house and a wheel chair. "Mina? Tovar?" She stares at the white-haired man.

"I don't know how he got here, Ms. Weiss." It is Remold's voice. "Perhaps Mina has double-crossed you as well. It is well within her capability."

Gus walks to the figure seeing the same white-haired man he had spoken with at the Womb. "It's an honor, Ambassador Jordan." He sticks out a hand to shake the thin palsied man's hand watching the man's gaze remain with Hope. "Hello, beautiful." His smile fails at her empty gaze. "I am so proud of you."

She stares at a Rost who has haunted her dreams for decades. A rumble fills the room as if there were a huge earthquake. The man keeps looking at Hope as dishes fall to the ground. The pot in the fireplace sloshes into the room. "I got this." He smiles. In that instant the roof of the house tears away. Looking down is the smiling face of the Wholack.

He scoops the thin older man up with one hand. "I get tired of keeping you immortal old man." Wholack stares at Hope. "Again? All this just to see her?" A huge fist descends on them.

A moment later, Gus stares up at the shroud of the bed. It slides back. Tovar stands staring at him.

Benson Fong enters the room behind them. The chatter from his radio is Remold Jaka screaming at his staff. Benson speaks. "We are on the way to the Boiler Room. Mr. Plow will ride with Hope Weiss. There will be a second car for you, Minister Dal." He looks at Gus Plow. "I am now employed by Biner and Feiss. You are my charter, Mr. Plow. I am here to protect you." He faces Hope. "Mina's shutdown sequence for Wholack has begun. Like it or not, Remold Jaka must be supported--for now. Will you cooperate?"

"I delivered Mr. Plow to Hell--just like Mina and Remold wanted."

Tovar stares. "They were working together?"

"No. But they both knew John Doe had to have a irrevocable path back to his wife--though for different reasons: Mina to ensure success, Remold, to ensure glory. For the rest of us, to ensure safety. If we fail we will repeat--through Gus' Agg. Crazy that Mina and Remold each created the same mechanism--essentially--and hid it from the other."

"How many times has that happened?" Gus asks.

"Never. I don't know how many times we will do this in the future--or if we will ever succeed." Hope looks at Tovar. "We might never be together."

CHAPTER TWENTY SEVEN

AFRAID

The transport of the Titanic to Seattle took almost two years, the rebuild another three years. One of those engineering feats that belongs to another age, the Titanic Memorial, also called the Memorial to the Dead, is supposed to declare the reemergence of engineering prowess--and a litany to the excesses of the past. Many still equate the preparations for global warming to the Titanic wreck.

Until the heeded warnings of Remold Jaka's father, Harry Jordan, previous preparations for global warming are laughingly referred to as rearranging deck chairs on the Titanic. Not a bad joke, in this Agg, global warming never crossed the tipping point.

Half sunk, and lit blue by high tech materials, the ship creaks with every gust of wind. In all, eight decks of the Titanic were refurbished by the Van Waters Development Corporation.

Of the eight decks repaired, six decks remain functional. The other two decks are locked and leaking, rusted and useless. With plans for the rest of the ship on hold, her framework sits rusting into the mud along Lake Union--a monument to apathy.

Located deep inside the Titanic Memorial, the Boiler Room is the only nightspot in the Northwest allowed to remain open 24/7. As a result, the clientele are the elite, but not-yet-comatose of North America.

Outside the Titanic, along the orange dock, limousine doors curtsey. Passengers dressed in ball gowns and tuxedos stroll the ramp. The Titanic is packed from dusk to dawn--various parties running at full bore. When the wealthy are forced to leave Wholack or corporate managers have to wait for final entrance, this is where they play. The refurbished spaces would be considered opulent for any period of history: In this time of limited energy and shortages of almost everything--the salons of the ship could only be described as obscene. Hand carved hardwood everywhere, much of it taken from sunken ships and destroyed mansions, gold fixtures from the ruins of major museums, stained glass from shattered cathedrals, and jewels from old museum exhibits, the ship is a monument--to ego.

Inside of the ship's ripped hull, the bars and clubs are protected by a clear plastic wall along the tear. So Gus watches partiers, thinking a few of them Hunters that he has seen from time to time. Wearing a black tuxedo, he cannot help but see the attire as a kind of shortcut to access--similar to the code words Hope used inside Kittens and Cradles.

Hope stands beside him--both ignored by the club-set. Gus follows her gaze. She stares into the water watching the carp. Her calm is in direct opposition to Benson Fong. All three wonder if Remold will kill Mina tonight--and what Benson might do to protect her. Gus eyes Benson Fong. The man is a mockery of control--with anger peeking through every pore.

Speaking to Benson, "Once we do this, my task is done. I am going home."

"No one will ask more of you." Says Benson.

"That so?" Gus searches the man's brown eyes for truth. "Remold knows you were keeping his wife from him."

Benson nods."That is what she said would happen. That's why I don't work for him."

"In my Agg, you were her lover as well."

Benson looks at him briefly. Gus smiles. "Seems to me she was far more dedicated to her tasks than one might have assumed."

"How odd. This way." Benson points to the ship.

They ascend the gang plank, a set of steel girders laid end to end supporting a path of concrete. The security people working for the monument nod. They stand on the deck above, rifles at the ready.

"Good evening, Mr. Plow, Ms. Weiss. Mr. Fong."

"This is just like that schooner," Gus mutters.

Benson pauses, scanning his face. "It feels like that to you?"

He nods.

"As it should," Hope says.

They walk along the white and red plastic stripes covering the deck. Floating in the air just above the stripes, ghostly renditions of the first Titanic passengers move about the ship. The ghosts ignore the other patrons walking through them or whispering among themselves. Dress gowns and fancy jewelry of the modern age mock the drab clothing of patrons on this deck, economy class tourists of a doomed ship.

"They are what?" Gus asks, thinking them perhaps Yorkies.

"The designer put them in. They are lifelike projections of the ship's original passengers."

At the bulkhead in front of them, a door sign lights with an arrow pointing down. The small sign says: "The Boiler Room, Five Floors Down." Gus feels an unreality to this place. Watching Hope, he sees she feels none of it.

She is a local.

Through the doorway to a restored set of twin mahogany stairs, they flank an ultramodern elevator. Gus finds himself drawn to the stairs. "Let's walk."

Hope shakes her head. "You act like a SuperUser in Wholack."

"If you say so."

Patrons and the ghostly voyagers pass by each other on the stairs, the mirth and humor decidedly belonging to the new voyagers. Hope, her gown flowing behind her, moves down the first flight of stairs, as is she were part of the show. Gus looks around seeking the security detail that seems to have disappeared. He sees a set of two women hugging on the landing and a short waiter dressed in whites. They carefully ignore him. He glances at Benson who nods.

They stop at a wide mezzanine full of gamblers watching live feeds from Wholack, making bets on the outcome, people either cheering or scowling. Green sea waves reflect themselves on the ceiling. Gus looks at the floor and notes the holographic lapping of waves. Other people stand around traditional gaming tables, shoulder to shoulder with the designer-ghosts. A tall man turns to them, winks, then approaches. Gus points him out for Hope. "Tovar is here."

"He has a seat at the table. Like you." She hurries to him and they kiss. Gus and Benson continue down the stairs leaving the lovers to their time.

The next flight leads to a dining hall. All manner of people populate the area. Stylized ghosts chat and drink. Other gray couples dance. While corporeal patrons wander the music and merriment--or sit at the long tables of the hall. Gus notes everyone seems happy. At the front of the room, by a stained glass window, a long table holds brightly colored food. It takes him a moment to see the buffet is an exact representation of a ghostly meal. All manner of patrons pick food from the table; some in this time and place, others far more out of place. He likes that the food is placed in exactly the same place for both ghost and corporeal user. At either end of the table, two brightly colored Tibetan prayer wheels slowly spin.

Hope and Tovar appear at his side. "Food for the dead," Tovar mumbles.

"We know, dear," she says to him.

Continuing down a curving wood stair, entering a huge amphitheater, they come upon the torn metal skin of the Titanic. A clear plastic window covers the rip. Entering the space--the size of a football field--Gus stops.

He gazes at what appears to be the ocean, as if they were walking under gray-green water. Images of shark, tuna, barracuda and every manner of fish swim the ghostly waters surrounding them. While numerous ghostly passengers thrash madly--seeing denizens of the deep on the prowl. Occasionally a shark will stop and grab hold of a desperate swimmer. The battle is bloody and one sided. None of the live patrons pay any attention to the ocean seascape.

"I still hate this place," Tovar says.

"Don't get out much?" Gus smiles at him.

Hope points to a guard dressed in a tuxedo standing at a grand staircase checking the ID of anyone desiring to go any further. Tovar strides up, but they don't bother checking his ID. They just step aside motioning for them to proceed. "Minister Dal, it has been a long time. Have a wonderful night." Tovar walks slowly passed them nodding with a grace Gus had not imagined possible. "Good evening Mr. Plow. Welcome back Ms. Weiss, Mr. Fong."

At the next landing, they are on a quarter-scale city

boulevard. Swanky nightclubs line the hallway masquerading as a street. Diminutive cars and patrons move through the city. It makes Gus feel as though he were a titan come down to Earth. Ghostly hipsters, marks, the ingénues and their toys, hucksters and bums ply the roadway. Ghostly taxicabs move about emptying their passengers. Others wander about entering this club and that. Painted on the walls is a silhouette of New York City--at dawn.

"So the Titanic finally made it to New York. Is that the idea?" Gus asks.

Benson answers. "Yes."

Down the thoroughfare, Gus sees a blinking red neon sign saying Boiler Room. Four guards manage the door and a ghostly line stretches away, into the vanishing point. Live guests stand with their back towards Gus.

Tovar and Hope approach the red velvet line. It falls in their presence. Upon entrance, surprisingly to Gus, the interior seems almost empty. Scanning to his right he sees a lineup of ghostly men and women, their eyes darting back and forth watching the few patrons that now follow the trio in. "Those people sure look like Yorkies," Gus says to Hope.

"They're fake. The designer of the club added them."

"Don't you see this is the same as the Womb or the schooner?" Gus says.

"And the place we float upon we foolishly call truth, or reality," Tovar says. "Ironic that any part of the ocean's surface looks the same to a sailor."

Gus nods at Hope. "And you guys are trying to figure how to sail under the ocean."

"Not us. You and Remold, you for your woman and he for ego. Mina, I don't know. Sometimes I think it is love, for Remmy."

Hope watches him. "Could be."

Benson guides them into the next room. "Ready?"

Benson points to a far wall. More gray ghostly images stand against the far wall. Tovar approaches them. When Tovar doesn't stop, they scatter out disappearing through mock doors that do not open for corporeal beings. "These Yorkies were not designed in. We don't know where they came from," says Tovar. "Media reports say the designer coded them in--how unique. This is why the Boiler Room became so important in the beginning." He continues. "Then you showed up. It was a game-changer."

"They scatter for everyone?"

Tovar looks at Hope. "Just me."

"Why?"

"We don't know. But I understand from Hope, I do not exist in your Agg."

A bell rings.

Gus looks around. "And that means?"

"Anyone who does not belong in this Agg wins a bottle of champagne," says Tovar. "It's seen as a joke by the patrons."

"This place is a highly sophisticated system to evaluate crossover," adds Hope.

"And how many times has that bell tolled?" Gus asks.

"This is the first," replies Hope. She recalls the bell at Coney Island. A shiver rides her spine. Remold Jaka, having heard the bell, appears through a service door. "There's Remold." He nods, dressed in a black tuxedo.

Gus had expected a toga and tie.

"Early on those Yorkies signaled we might have a corruption of our Agg." Remold says. "So we had to hide it all in plain sight."

Gus does not know what to do. "So this is some kind of intersection? Is that what this place was meant to be--a place for vetting entrants?"

Tovar considers this man's words. "This place is why Remold held off on corralling Mina these last few days. This place wasn't proof, but he couldn't deny what it meant once you plopped out of FairGame." He points to a claw foot table in the corner.

Gus walks to the oak table and examines the four ghostly patrons sitting around the table: three men and a woman. They look exactly like Remold, Gus, Hope, and Tovar Dal. "So this is what it was all about--a seat at the table? For little old me? This table? In some damn bar?" The other three nod to him.

"Welcome to party," Hope says.

"And here we are, finally," Remold says.

"Did you find Mina?" Asks Benson.

"Mina has started her shut down of Wholack. I now have eight percent of my beds on emergency support. Within the hour we will be completely down. Mr. Plow, you better be real." Remold has an angry stare for Benson Fong.

Hope speaks: "And here comes the main show."

The door from the kitchen opens and a one-third scale wild-haired waiter enters the room carrying a tray of drinks. Gus stares at the red hair and the freckles watching the Wholack, dressed as a waiter, plop drinks down at a table--splashing the set of ghostly voyagers.

Remold nods. "So there is a change. Wholack has color. He isn't gray like before. Why isn't Wholack gray?" Remold says to no one in the room. "He has won the game?"

His ghostly version argues with the waiter.

The argument ends when the waiter raises a middle finger, and walks back into the kitchen. Before Gus can react, Remold sits at the table. Hope does as well. Tovar follows. They have all taken their places at the table--waiting for Gus to sit. "Please sit down Mr. Plow. We haven't much time." Remold shakes his head. "Ten per cent of the beds are down now."

Chapter Twenty Eight

Doctor, No Charge

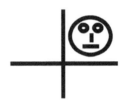

Gus grabs a chair from another table, and therefore not fit into the tableau he had seen. Hope calls out, "Please don't. We need to know. It is why you are here."

He looks at the others, now thinking of the chairs as tumblers in a lock, and sits in his assigned seat. "Was all this a scam to get me here?"

"No," Tovar answers. "We don't know what is going on, but Wholack has taught us to be less fearful than those of your Agg--I suspect."

Gus notes other patrons enter the room. They appear aware of the significance of the table and quite interested. "Best show in town, huh?"

"The elite, researchers, the military, and other," Remold points to Yorkies entering the room again. "For the first year, the ghosts at this table were a curiosity. Tovar and I were well known. You and her not so much. When Hopes-No-Apostrophe-Diner became famous there was quite a buzz about it--three out of four. You remained a mystery." Remold looks at Gus.

Four ships, the ferry boats, it's all tied.

"What are you thinking?"

"What did the less informed patrons say about the Yorkies?" Gus asks.

"They were told they were just more entertainment. Do you know what sent you into FairGame?"

Gus shakes his head no. "I told you. I walked off a ferry and found myself in a world unknown to me. It didn't take long to figure out the tragedy of my time had not occurred here. But I needed to find my way back."

"We corrupted your reality." Hope says.

"And Mr. Plow has returned the compliment." Remold looks down at his wrist. "Twelve percent are down." Remold shakes his head. "Six hours ago, just after Gus Plow and Hope entered Kittens and Cradles I went to get Mina and found her backups empty. I had you watched every minute, Mr. Fong. How did you do it?"

"Dr. Wolf," Benson replies.

"Nonsense. He is one my most trusted employees."

Gus laughs. "In my Agg, Dr. Wolf is Mina's father."

Remold is shaken. He remembers the comment. "Dr. Wolf is younger than Mina."

"It gets worse, Doc. That opening part of Flight, in Wholack. Who are those people on the beach?" Gus asks.

Remold leans forward. "What about it?"

Gus says. "It is the key."

Remold looks down at his phone. "Eighteen per cent of the beds are down." He looks back up. "One of the people is the Biner and Feiss heiress, the woman with autism, Jenny Biner. The other is Russell Biner, her son. The guy your genetic equal killed in this Agg. It was meant as a home for her. The other entity is my Rost, Carlos. Part of my commitment to her family."

"I bet there will be more now," Gus says.

"Impossible. We locked it down years ago."

"I saw it."

"You saw nothing. I have a dozen versions of Carlos in the City-museums of that scenario. Those agents miss nothing."

Gus considers the foolishness of Remold's ego and cannot let it pass. "When you go see him, tell Roo I said hello."

"Roo?"

"Russell Biner, Pilot Nothing."

Remold's eyes open wide and he stares stunned with facts. "I will not open that scenario. I am contractually bound not to."

"Go see him," Gus says. A bell rings.

A song plays: *My Attorney Bernie*. It bounces through the bar like a ball. Everyone in the Boiler Room turns to look at the kitchen door, their eyes wide with excitement. "Now we see who is right," says Remold.

Gus spies a large figure looking exactly like the Wholack, entering the room. Full sized, normally colored and clearly a part of this Agg, he holds a round tray with four drinks in his hand.

As expected, upon seeing Jaka, he smiles that goofy grin and winks at Gus. Security people get up from their chairs to block all the exits. Gus stares, having already guessed the Wholack's appearance has sent panic through Remold.

The waiter lays out the drinks splattering Remold with the brown liquid from the glass. Remold does not argue. "Will you join us please?"

The waiter looks around. "Nice to win." He sits quietly taking the moved chair that Gus had sought to sit in a few moments ago. "How can I help you?"

"What's your name?" Tovar asks.

"Vaz, Joeseph Vaz," says the waiter.

"You look like the Wholack," Remold says.

The waiter looks at him as there is something wrong with him. Then he smiles. "So you've brought in a projector to make fun of me for tonight and you are asking me why?" He points to Gus. The security people in the room stand motionless, stunned.

"I look like you?" Gus asks.

"Nice, what's the game here?"

"Someone please bring in the manager," Remold says quickly. A portly man with a set of three chins and an expensive tuxedo hustles to the table. Remold speaks: "Who is this waiter?"

The man nods to the waiter; both men annoyed with the games of the rich. "Oh, Doctor Jaka, welcome." When his gaze lights on the last person at the table he smiles. "Nice hologram. My waiter's name is Joe Vaz. He has been a waiter here for about eight months. I have full papers on him and full insurance." He stares at Remold. Then to Hope, "Ms. Weiss, slumming?"

Remold stiffens at the manager's insolence. "Please tell me what color hair your waiter has?"

"Black, some gray. Short."

Hope moves her elbows onto the table and covers her mouth with her hands. She hadn't expected so obvious a breach of reality. She thinks of Gus Plow's comment about how people went mad in his Agg--and that space ship that landed and then disappeared a generation before.

How could they have missed such an obvious breach of logic? Now it's begun for us as well.

Remold raises one hand. "Benson, please tell me the hair color of the waiter."

"Red."

The manager of the restaurant stares at him, his mouth agape. "Seriously? Are you blind? Can't you tell the over-paint by a hologram projector?"

Remold and Tovar stare at each other. Tovar reaches out and points his index finger at the waiter. "I am going to poke you lightly in the shoulder. Please do not be afraid."

The waiter looks at him as if he was insane. "Have at it. Just leave a big tip."

Tovar pokes the man feeling a bony shoulder. He pokes Gus and nods to Remold.

Hope speaks with a sense of pride. "So I would say you both have proof that Mina was correct. We are an Agg and it can be violated. Therefore Wholack--your creation--is not your burden. He is a force of truth, Remold. You created a wonderful machine--but Mina has given us fire."

"Yeah sure, she's a saint," says Remold.

"Can I go now?"

Remold looks at the waiter and speaks, "All right. Let's get to it. Wholack, you have won a game. I am the fool here. So this is my world. Get out." The room begins to shake. Remold holds onto the table feigning boredom. "Well, Wholack, what now? Do you really think you can own my Agg? This is my world."

The waiter, once named Joe Vaz laughs. "You are the fool, Jakainthebox. I have won the game." A voice, it is the Wholack's voice. "Like my software, Jakainthebox? I thought it might impress you."

Remold stares.

"Your attempt at neutrality is ridiculous, Jakainthebox. You always were uncharged, neither a one or a zero. In my language, a junkie of time." Wholack laughs. "It's my software you morons. Not my carriage. The question mark of existence. That is the maker. The manager if you will. Buddah was almost right. You guys are all in need of a rewash." Wholack winks at Remold.

"Go on, fool. You messed that up. I have won." Says Remold. "Scatter."

Wholack grimaces. "No matter, Jakainthebox. Now you know. This was your world, fool. But now you have lost the win. It is open. Like mine. So a favor returned. We are in balance again. Did you think the universe would not return and debit your account?" He giggles. "By the way, you're welcome."

"I still own you," replies a defiant Remold Jaka.

"Oh please." Wholack looks around the room. "Would it shock you to hear, Jakainthebox, that this place moves far too slow for me--or most sentient creatures? Do you really think anyone wants to invade this moronic monotonic time-forward insane asylum? What a snore. What a bore. How do you all stand it? Do you know how much trouble you dummies have caused? Or did you think using a cosmic social worker as a sacrificial lamb was your right, as oh-my-god-humans?"

In an instant the figure is light gray. Then he is gone. In his wake, a red question mark echoes his fading laughter. It disappears as well.

Every cell phone in the room goes off. "Damn her. Now I know how she did it. She gave control to Wholack. I was looking in the wrong place this entire time."

"Or he took it," Gus mutters.

Remold stares at Gus. "You knew as well?"

Gus shakes his head no.

"She is going to destroy everything." Remold says.

"The only thing she is destroying is ego." says Hope. "Remold, there is a difference between cooperation and loss. I have been waiting so long to say that to you."

Chapter Twenty Nine

Do Not Give Up

Outside, on the dock of the Memorial To The Dead, Remold sits in his limousine. Working with the telecommunication systems, he has hacked his way into a boutique bed facility of a hundred-thousand beds--because the networks began a reset sequence and then froze. Remold built the link to the bed facility in five minutes.

Guards posted around the car number more than twenty and more keep arriving. People that had been inside the Titanic crowd around. Everyone sees the beds are shutting down and Remold Jaka works to save people.

An image on the screen inside the car shows closed beds. No one is moving. "Mass murder?" Tovar asks as he is delivered inside the car. The others follow.

Remold, still watching the vitals, speaks. "Of the one-hundred-thousand people monitored only two have awakened from the Wholack. Attendants are speaking to them now."

"So the backups kicked in?" Tovar asks.

Remold shakes his head. "They are down. The B&F drug servers are down. The delivery tubes are corrupted with salt water. Even if I could get the servers up today every single drug tube would need to be washed clear. She was very thorough."

"They are dead?" Hope asks.

A man appears on the screen. "Our two customers, a Mr. Lipps and a Mr. Cavanaugh are upset at being awakened, but little else. When they demanded to reenter, we told them there is a problem with their account. The attendants offered them sedatives to sleep. They are thinking about it."

"Thank you, Lucien. The death toll?"

The man on the screen seems confused. "None. All seem fine, in some kind of stasis."

At that moment other smaller displays begin to fold from the limousine's ceiling. The Laughs Unlimited network is back up. The screens light with managers and corporate executives funneling information to Remold. One executive named Smetana speaks first. He manages a large facility outside of Denver. "All the Wholack servers are down. About five-thousand people worldwide have been ejected."

"And the state of those still on the beds?" Remold asks.

"Their vitals are fine. The systems supplying nutrients and actuators managing muscle tone are still functioning. We can't see inside the game. Rebooting the media servers is our next task once we stabilize the network. Then we can see what is going on."

Remold leans forward. "Meaning what?"

"There's still activity. There seems to be."

A skinny man named Lars speaks. "Whoever did this knows our systems inside out. We can boot individual server clusters, but we cannot establish interconnect. It's like the wires connecting the scenario systems are severed and of course they are not. We need to track this down. Remold. Some of my people think those in the beds might be in a coma, brain dead."

"Anyone else?"

"Dr. Jaka, our technicians are saying there is scenario activity inside the system," says the man in Sweden.

"What system?" Remold says angrily. "The servers are down."

"I don't know. But on the other hand, we are not seeing any more ejections and it has been almost ten minutes since the last people were dumped out of the system."

"So we think rather than suffer the ire of the ejected. Mina just decided to paralyze them?"

"It is possible. It's not what we believe," says the man from Denver.

"Keep me informed." He looks directly at Hope. "I have been patient with you, but I need to find Mina. Sooner or later those people will eject--or die."

Benson speaks. "Remold, you have almost two billion people in the beds. Only five-thousand or so have ejected with the system down. The vitals all look good. Low level body support is fine. They are not brain-dead. This is about Mina being right--not danger. The Wholack's Agg is self-sustaining."

He looks at Tovar. "And what do you have to say?"

Hope speaks. Her dark eyes declaring her venom before her words. "You were wrong. Your system was a crutch--or at best a launch pad. You had intuitive talents the same way Mr. Plow has intuitive talents. You have Species Focus, Remmy. Or to put it another way, you are our Wholack."

"She tried a dozen experiments to prove it. They never worked."

"Mina told you it was a critical mass issue. The test groups were too small. It is an ecosystem and it needs a minimum number of participants to sustain," Hope says. "I was there." Her words silence the others for a moment.

"Where is she?" Remold asks.

Hope shakes her head no. Remold looks at his former Chief of Security. "Well?"

"She should be at the diner now--I would guess--waiting for you."

Hope stares wide eyed.

"Get in." The car rolls. "Why there?" Remold asks.

"She knows you will want to disprove her. Her system is the only one up and running. And you cannot get inside Wholack without computational assist," Benson says.

The inference turns his face red. "Computational assist?"

Benson looks around. "Ask your wife."

Remold pauses at the comment. "Ex-wife."

During the ride over, they listen to Remold processing information from his technical people.

"...No success trying to reboot the servers..It will be months before the system is back on line."

The limo pulls up in front of the diner. Black vans guard all sides--leaving only the front entry of the diner open. A pair of heavily armed men approach the car. "She's inside."

Remold nods. "Doing what?"

"Eating cake."

"That's Mina," Benson says, smiling.

Remold swings wide the doorway to see a single person in the diner. Her skin is pale and her arms weakened by a lack of use, but otherwise Mina looks healthy. Remold unconsciously breaths a sigh of relief. Remold speaks, "Mina, are you mad?"

"Not as mad as you." She sees the others as they follow him inside and cross to the table. Smiling hello to Hope and Tovar, she stares at Gus Plow. "Holy Shit, John Doe." She avoids the gaze of Benson Fong.

Gus notes the woman at the table does not look like

the Mina he knew, or the Mina he saw at the Womb inside Wholack. She is old, thin and haggard though her spark is the same. He stares at her. "You don't look like the Mina I know."

She pauses, looking at him for a moment.

Remold steps in between them and leans over to her. "And I even brought your newest lover with me."

She finally looks at Benson. "I'm sorry." He closes his eyes and looks away.

A confused Remold speaks, "What the hell do you think you are doing, Mina?"

"First comment, Remmy: I have been ejected so I am in a bitchy mood. Second comment: Nobody has gotten hurt. Third, some get left behind."

"You shut down the servers. Give me the code to reboot them. People are dying by the thousands."

She picks up a cup of coffee. "You lie. There were five-thousand-six-hundred-and-eight people ejected. There has been no injury. Except perhaps to your ego, Jakainthebox. There are zero dead." She waits for his apology. She prays there will be one.

"I want the code," he replies.

"Pretty smart of me to liberate Wholack. You never suspected it."

Remold scowls at being technologically outfoxed.

"Remmy, you refuse to see you are more than a tool maker and less a master of reality. You breached an Agg inadvertently--making you the fool. But only because you refuse to acknowledge the truth." She glances at Hope, then back at Remold. "Wholack need not be tortured by your ego anymore." She looks back at Gus. "I could not let it continue."

Remold speaks, "I am going to need your help to get this right."

Gus stares at the face of a fool. "I don't take orders from a Jakainthebox."

Mina watches Gus. "Tough SOB aren't you?" She takes another bite of chocolate cake. "Remold, you created a crutch for transport, but you concluded that crutch was like the wheel--that the crutch was needed by all. You were wrong. Still, what a marvelous tool."

Tovar speaks: "The esteemed Doctor Jakainthebox does not understand that sometimes a great man is also a fool. Lucky for him, he is loved by his wife."

Remold looks at Mina, stunned. He cannot speak for a moment. "You love me?"

A tall thin man with wild hair and a lab coat enters the diner. It is Doctor Wolf. He looks down at Mina. "All good. Word is we are related somewhere. Did you drink your skim milk today, sweetie? I baked chocolate chip cookies."

She smiles.

A female researcher enters. "Doctor Jaka, they have gotten a link into the game. The feeds show activity. The systems report live scenarios and people going about their business inside their scenarios--no change." She looks at Mina. "She loves you, Doc. Why else would I work for you?"

Remold is almost in tears. He cannot cope. "The beds are on a local system back up?"

"Negative. They are independent of support."

Remold asks again: "Are you telling me the scenarios are self-perpetuating? A placebo effect?"

"A John Doe effect, Remold," says Doctor Wolf. He looks over to an anxious Gus Plow. "I am sure she is fine." He looks back at Remold. "Life support systems are functioning per spec. The servers are toast for the sub-scenarios. We are working to begin a reboot--but the corruption is so deep it looks like the code is hash. They are trying to load backups in Zurich and Denver, but it will take time."

"Dr. Wolf, I suggest you put some of the servers on hot standby. So you can quickly bring people into them."

Mina speaks, "The rest can be shut down. By my calculations I'd say any big server farm like Denver will handle the load. Talk to Gregor."

"Ten percent server usage?" Remold says. "That's impossible--and irresponsible."

She glares at him. "If you are self-perpetuating in this Agg then so is Wholack."

"Wholack needs software. It is the basis of his existence."

"The code was a crutch for us, not him. We know nothing about Wholack. Remmy, we have the transcendence you have been working towards. Kicking out the crutch allows us to stand." She watches him stare at her--wearing that same stupid grin he wore as a young man. "Remold, maybe you are a boy masquerading as a man?"

He reddens, but he smiles. "Dr. Wolf, arrange for the hot standby. Twenty-five percent capacity. How many newbies do we have this week?"

"That was the second item. Of the five-thousand people ejected, forty percent of them were newbies--less than twenty hours inside the system."

Mina sips her coffee, staring at Remold. "When is the next set due to enter, Doctor Wolf?"

"We finished a cycle this morning and we have no one going in for three days. I am monitoring the rest of the newbies. So far, they appear to be having a harder time than most. The entire group has recycled back to the beginning. There have not been any other ejections from stasis. Other than that, we are clear for three days. Then we have, forty-one-thousand going in--beginning at 1200 hours GMT."

"So where are the scenarios coming from?" Gus asks.

Remold points to his head. "Us, the universe, a box of popcorn, who knows?"

"It's all just a big question mark," Tovar says quietly. "We're becoming plants." He shakes his head. "Does the load reduction mean what I think?"

Remold speaks: "If Wholack only requires a training cycle and presumably some kind of safety net, I'd say resource consumption can be cut by almost eighty percent."

"Ninety percent," says Mina.

Surprisingly, Remold laughs. "I'd say we could add people as quickly as we can build the beds."

"So a four times increase in capacity?" Tovar says.

"Right," Remold says. He smiles at Mina. "Home Fires-- that whole scenario was a cover for this, sabotage of our Agg." He looks at Gus. "You paid dearly for our interference." He notes Gus shows neither anger, nor gratitude.

Gus looks over at Mina. "Where is Winston?"

She shakes her head and points to Dr. Wolf. "He will send you through. He knows where." Mina looks at Remold. "You also know the build version for his Agg, right?"

Remold nods, "Always did. I needed to keep it hidden just in case you failed. We could recycle."

She laughs. "I did the same. In case I was successful."

Remold looks over to Gus then looks away. "I had to know the truth."

"How could you love a man like that?" Gus asks.

Mina takes her last bite of cake and shrugs her shoulders. "Don't know."

Apologize, you ass. Hope wears a smile.

Remold speaks to Doctor Wolf. "Make sure the training servers are functioning, then tie the ejected group into my diagnostics." Remold faces Tovar. "She was right. I was wrong." He begins to stand. "I am sorry, Mina. I was a jerk."

She looks at him. "A manipulative jerk." Mina has never seen Remold so happy. She hides her delight, wondering about Benson. He is a man lost.

Remold continues completely unaware, his brain working on calculations. "We can use solar generators for the life support, and make the nutrients from waste and the algae farms. Tidal systems can used for backup along with the flywheels. I'd say calorie requirements for the population will average right around twelve-hundred calories per day."

Mina interrupts again. "Closer to eleven-hundred per day. I've made some improvements."

Remold looks at her trying to hide his caring. "If that is correct, our impact on the planet goes to zero. He shakes his head. "Hell, I bet I can turn it positive." He turns to leave. "I might as well go back work. I am good for nothing else. I am sorry, Mina. I truly am. You were right. We have turned the corner as a species thanks to you. I am an ass."

"Always. Remold, don't you want to see it?"

He stops at her odd question. "See it? What for? I created it. So you can gloat? I know I am the fool. You win."

Mina holds her face tight. "Remold, you have created the greatest invention known to humanity. You've breached dimension, time, and space. You've freed humanity to explore the universe. Don't you want to see that?"

"I just want you to be happy."

"What an ass." Her lips tighten she looks at Gus. "Could be worse I suppose." She stands. "Come on, Remmy." She walks through the kitchen into Hope's office. "I want you to meet a fully sentient human. A person who will perceive the future. That is your last task. Then, if you wish I will leave you alone."

"You, with me?" Remold asks, his mouth open.

"Funny what a woman will do for a man," says Tovar. "Forgive her, Remold. Forgive her for putting up with the biggest ego on the planet."

Remold Jaka looks around shaking his head. "Mina, is that what you have done?"

"So you could see you are the biggest ass on the planet--so I could have you all to myself. I was jealous of that damn game. This was the only way I could get you away from it."

He stares at her. "So I am supposed to believe you changed the entire course of our species just to be with me?"

"You saved Mr. Plow's world with Wholack. I just adjusted it to get what I want." She walks towards the kitchen knowing Benson will never forgive her.

Remold looks at Benson, then follows Mina through the kitchen.

She speaks. "Do you still eat those disgusting pizzas?"

"Most days," he responds.

Gus stares up at a blue sky. The moon, his moon, glows in the dusk. The grass around him is a dead green color. He jumps to his feet. Four ferries sit in the mud. Around them is a hubbub of activity. Hundreds of people going about their day. They are poorly dressed, but healthy. He looks up the hillside. There is smoke on the hillside, blinking white lights, and the stink of death. "Winston?"

No answer.

In a run he approaches the closest ferry, people wave to him, smiling. He hurries up the gang plank saying hello to people, smelling the cooked meat, rushing up the main stairs slapping open the doors and running into the main room. A thin woman with smooth skin and black hair smiles warmly at him. Her beautiful eyes call him like no others.

"Gus, you're so thin."

He kisses her, holding her in his arms. "Win, it's over. We did it. We can leave this place. But we must leave this place--now." He hugs her.

"I, I need to wait. We have to do this right."

He pulls her by the arm.

"Gus, are you sure? Wait." She rushes inside then returns, the others following her. Outside, when she looks up at the hillside her eyes widen. "And those lights are what? How come I never saw them before?"

"Doctor Biner was right. He saved us. He saved you." Gus looks down briefly. "He kept his promise to you."

She shakes her head. "I knew he would."

"There is a crossover into another reality. An Agg they call it. Do not cross through those lights or get closer than a few hundred meters at this point. It is also a human hunting preserve. I have some friends setting out a path for us."

"A hunting preserve?" She looks at her husband's gaunt features. "Oh dear." Winston touches his cheek. "And once we cross? What are we?"

"Safe. In fact at some point I'll take you to Hope's diner."

"She is alive." Winston stares at the line of lights. "Thank goodness." She reaches into her pocket removing a tattered rag.

Gus stares at it. He knows it intimately.

"As soon as you left, it changed." She points to the label. "It now says Mina Jaka Underwear, Inc." She hands it to him for inspection. Gus looks at the cloth. "Would it surprise you to know that to some, this is a computer representation of a piece of cloth?"

"I suppose. Are you okay?"

"Do you remember hearing anything about a place called the Boiler Room?" Gus asks her.

"Not a place, but an event," she replies, "The Boiler Room was Gregor's code name for apocalypse."

"And what does '*We are looking for this?*' Mean?"

Winston shakes her head. "No one knows the answer."

Gus laughs. "Roo did."

"Same way that he knew about the rubber band effect?" She says.

"I think so," Gus replies. "Winston, I left you here four years ago."

"You left me here about ten months ago."

"He said time was our curse." Gus takes her hand.

CHAPTER THIRTY

STOP

The image of the fool rides high above the clouds. Below, a man and a woman are in the tide pools picking clams and oysters. The fool comes to rest on the cliffs above them. A young boy, a teen, sits in front of him apparently unaware of Remold Jaka.

"Hi," he says.

The boy turns to Remold, then looks back at his parents on the shoreline--just as his father jumps into the water to retrieve a bucket of clams floating out to sea. "He can be so stupid..."

"My name is Remold."

"I am Russell, Russell Biner. My friends call me Roo. Those are my parents out there. What are you doing here?" He watches Remold watch him. "That's the Doc up on the porch--watching us. He is very protective, crazy in fact."

"I brought you a gift." He opens his hand showing the boy a rubber band. This is the answer to all your problems."

The boy stays clear of the odd man. The man on the porch is blind.

"You need not fear me."

"You'll have to ask the Doc to help you. He's a shrink. He's up at the house." Roo points to an old house, a Victorian on the hillside.

"Okay, can I ask you a favor?"

"Sure." Roo keeps his eyes on this odd man. He doesn't like it when someone new asks for something.

"When you look up and see all those people surfing the sky in all those crazy contraptions--what do you think?"

He shakes his head. "I don't know. I guess that I'd like to try it some time."

Remold looks around. "What about your dad and mom. What do they say?"

"They don't see it. Doc does, but he doesn't speak of it. He thinks he's seeing illusions."

"Because he is blind."

"How do you know about all those people up there?" Roo calms a bit.

Remold grins. "They are friends of mine. Would you like to know the code for playing with people in the sky?"

Roo smiles. "Sure."

"Try and get one of them to talk to you. Then you say Pilot Nothing. You will have whatever you need--but you will need to snap back here--like a rubber band--to get it."

"That doesn't make sense." Roo tilts his head. "I haven't got the time for games. Time is a curse."

"Did you know time doesn't matter?"

Roo nods. "Been there. Done that. I just don't want to leave my parents. My mom has trouble with change--she thinks that means there is something wrong with her. Trouble is she believes in death. That it is an end. You too I think. For me, I just get confused because there seems to be so many of me inside the carriage of my body. It's hard to understand all that's going on."

Remold Jaka nods. "So that's it." For another moment he believes in Mina's love. "Noting time is like eating death."

The young boy scratches his cheek. "I think that's why my Mom doesn't like it when things change too much. She is so brilliant. I think that is why my Dad loves her."

"Carlos?"

"You're pretty smart." Roo says watching a man ride the clouds on a surf board. "That looks like fun."

"You mom's name is Jenny."

"Right. She likes to make Dad crazy by calling herself Pilnouth sometimes. He has this thing about crutches. He hates them. That's why he walks funny.

"Is there something you want?" Remold asks. "I owe you, I think."

"A toe for him?" He points down the hill. "They say they are finding food down there but wouldn't you agree, they are looking for this?" Roo says pointing at the others.

"You're pretty smart to recognize source code."

"Source code, like computers?"

"That's why they can't see you down here. For them to see you, you need to be like them."

"Impossible."

"Dude, there are people flying bathtubs up there. Solve and you're a hero."

Roo nods. "Ego is bad. I don't need applause like you. You should watch out for that."

Remold shakes his head. "It is the way some cope. What about your parents?"

"They aren't so limited in the way they see the world."

"A simple matter of my coding." Remold says. His

hands move about working a hidden keyboard. "Done--one toe--gone but not forgotten."

"What are you some kind of God?"

"Just another fool."

"Like me?"

"Like all of us."

Roo watches Remold Jaka disappear. "So much for impossible. He looks up considering his own ignorance. At that moment, Roo Biner hears the song Flight for the first time in this life.